ENGINES OF EMPIRE

MAX CARVER

BOOKS

Vinci Books

vinci-books.com

Published by Vinci Books Ltd in 2025

1

Copyright © Max Carver 2019

The author has asserted their moral right to be identified as the author of this work in accordance with the Copyright, Designs and Patents Act 1988. This work is a work of fiction. Names, characters, places and incidents are the product of the author's imagination or are used fictitiously. Any resemblance to actual persons, living or dead, places and incidents is entirely coincidental.

All rights reserved. No part of this publication may be copied, reproduced, distributed, stored in any retrieval system, or transmitted in any form or by any means, including photocopying, recording, or other electronic or mechanical methods, nor used as a source for any form of machine learning including AI datasets, without the prior written permission of the publisher.

The publisher and the author have made every effort to obtain permissions for any third party material used in this book and to comply with copyright law. Any queries in this respect should be brought to the attention of the publisher and any omissions will be corrected in future editions.

A CIP catalogue record for this book is available from the British Library.
Paperback ISBN: 9781036705381

Printed and bound in Great Britain by Clays Ltd, Elcograf S.p.A.

By Max Carver

Empire of Machines

Engines of Empire
Islands of Rebellion
Clash of Colonies

Again, the devil taketh him up into an exceeding high mountain, and sheweth him all the kingdoms of the world, and the glory of them;

And saith unto him, All these things will I give thee, if thou wilt fall down and worship me.

— Matthew 4:8-9

Chapter One

Galapagos

So that's what the end of the world looks like, Minister-General Reginald Ellison thought as he watched the golden shuttle approach the small orbital spaceport.

Ellison stood on the spaceport's narrow but private observation deck along with three other top ministers of his planet's government. They were alone, momentarily free from the press and the public, and they could speak openly if they chose, but instead they watched in anxious silence.

Below them lay their home, the ocean world of Galapagos, a great blue sphere thick with clouds and speckled with tiny green bits of land. The people of Galapagos were as fragmented as the islands and archipelagos of their world and had warred for decades over those scarce bits of land. Life had been one naval battle after another until the planetary Galapagos Coalition had been formed, finally bringing a shaky peace.

As a much younger man, Ellison had commanded a

small deep-submersion submarine in those Island Wars, moving between the stormy ocean surface and the network of deep trenches below, the planet's treacherous underwater highways. He had faced off against boats larger and better armed than his own, enemy destroyers and battleships as well as subs.

However, this unarmed golden shuttle creeping quietly toward them through space was far more threatening than any of those old naval ships.

On the surface, the shuttle looked harmless: a sleek luxury craft, gold and white, the colors of planet Carthage and its empire. Such a fine-grade executive vehicle was a rare sight here in the rougher, poorer outer worlds.

Ellison had seen images of Carthage's interstellar warships, though—bristling with railguns and plasma cannons, with swarms of self-flying starfighters in their hangars like predatory insects crouched in their hives. A galactic armada of such deadly ships stood behind the fancy little shuttle now on approach.

"Is anyone alive on that shuttle?" Ellison asked his minister of state, Navra Coraline, who stood on Ellison's left side.

"No, no one alive. Just the ambassador and his honor guard," Coraline replied. She wore the flowing sea-green robes of her people, the Aquaticans. Her large pale blue eyes, surgically altered to see better underwater, watched the approaching shuttle with suspicion.

"Honor guard! Nothing but metal machines in parade dress," snorted the minister of defense, Mikhail Kartokov, standing to Ellison's right. Kartokov was a burly ex-miner and former soldier, his face scarred and hardened by war, his white tropical suit expensive and soft, with a carnation-red pocket square. He looked like a brutal wolf in rich idiot's clothing. "It is no honor guard. It is more like a puppet show. For children."

"Except these puppets rule a hundred star systems and billions of people," Ellison said. "They're the Earth-killers. This is no child's game."

"The ambassador may not appreciate insensitive terms like 'Earth-killers,'" Coraline cautioned, ever the prudent diplomat. "We wish to avoid insulting him."

"Can it feel insulted?" Ellison shook his head. "If the ambassador's programmed to be easily offended, I'm going to enjoy this even less than I thought."

Coraline shivered as the shuttle drew near. The minister of state normally relished any chance to welcome visitors from other worlds, but she was clearly troubled today. She moved her lips silently, praying, her fingertips tracing the octopus tattoo that dominated the left side of her face and neck. The tattoo was another sign of the Aquatican people and their strange brew of religious beliefs that called for humans to evolve back into ocean creatures, with help from surgery and genetic engineering. The Aquaticans were a major nation, though, and part of the Coalition, and so they had a right to be represented on the Council of Ministers, odd ways or not.

"Earth was weak," Defense Minister Kartokov said. "Anyone with spine, guts, or brains left Earth generations ago. Only the dregs of humanity remain. That's why the Earthlings have never recovered from their war with Carthage. Earthlings today are like animals, fighting over the last scraps of a world built by better men."

"So let's try to avoid ending up like Earth," Ellison said.

"We must show strength," Kartokov insisted.

"It'll be hard to show what we don't have," Ellison replied.

Galapagos was not remotely prepared for interstellar war. The Galapagos Coalition had begun to put up some planetary defenses, but they were still under construction.

Even when fully operational, though, their bargain-basement space-defense network would be nothing against the Carthaginian fleet, which had conquered system after system, carving an empire through the center of settled space. As a minor, distant world, Galapagos had been lucky enough to escape Carthage's attention so far.

When Carthage requested this summit, Ellison had known right away that his planet's luck had run out.

"They must have no more wealthy worlds to conquer, if they're traveling this far to harass us peasants," Ellison said.

"They didn't even bother to come in person," Coraline said, her tone bitter. "We are too low priority for that. They send their machines to handle us, as though we were animals."

"There could be benefits to joining the Carthaginian network," said the minister of commerce, a thin, noodley, constantly smiling man named Yernie Ogden. The commerce minister came from the Green Islands, a southern-hemisphere archipelago whose people focused on shipbuilding and trade. "Opportunities for trade and military protection."

"Carthage will offer us no opportunity except slavery," Kartokov said. The defense minister was hulking and craggy-faced, not unlike his arid, mountainous home archipelago, the Gavrikov Reincorporated Islands, full of rumbling mines and smoking refineries. "Gavrikova fought many years for our independence. We will not bend over for off-worlders."

"Do you mean 'bend the knee'?" Coraline asked, but Kartokov waved the question away.

Outside, the luxurious shuttle attached to a docking bay on the spaceport's executive level, airlocks marrying together.

"Time to get your game faces on," Ellison said. He led the way from the dim, private observation deck to the bright, crowded reception area. News reporters, influential traders, and assorted dignitaries chatted around the seafood-laden catering tables and the open bar. Cameras hovered in the air, capturing the event for the public.

Ellison spotted his wife, Cadia, speaking to a representative of the largest steelworks in Gavrikova. Ellison still found her stunning after twenty-five years of marriage, her red hair in a long braid down her back, her dress appropriately black and formal for the head of state's wife, but clingy enough that he couldn't take his eyes off her.

She saw him across the room and smiled, her presence bolstering his spirits. She'd been a medic during the war, facing tents full of bloody, screaming sailors and marines. Hers was the face to which he'd returned again and again from the sea, the mother of his children, the brains behind his political career, the lighthouse of his life.

Their sons were beside her, age eight and fifteen, plainly uncomfortable in their starchy shirts and tailored blue suits. Ellison had been reluctant to bring his family up to the spaceport, but it was his first major state event, and it was expected that his family would be on hand to greet the ambassador from such a powerful and prestigious world as Carthage.

Armed guards were posted around the room, sporting the flag of the Galapagos Coalition—a small green turtle on an ocean-blue field—on their dark blue uniforms.

The double doors beyond the security checkpoint slid apart, revealing the brightly lit corridor to the small, extra-secure row of airlocks where the golden shuttle had docked. A blue mural on the wall welcomed visitors with animated images of Galapagos's more famous sea creatures, like the colorful horned octopus and the giant electric jellyfish.

The room fell silent as everyone watched the airlock corridor. Cameras moved in for a closer view.

The ambassador's honor guard marched out double file in perfect lockstep, like the well-oiled machines they were. Their ceremonial dress was ridiculous: helmets with golden plumes shaped like peacock feathers, spotless white uniforms embroidered with real gold, white leather boots inset with webs of more gold and precious gems, ostentatious reminders of Carthage's extreme wealth.

Crystal-blue faceplates obscured the honor guard's faces. Looking closely, though, Ellison could discern the gaunt, skull-like faces beneath, the faces of the walking dead, of death itself. Death for Ellison's whole world, perhaps, and everyone he knew.

However overwrought the uniforms, merciless killing machines marched inside the golden plumes and brocade. They carried rapid-fire laser rifles with variable output levels, appropriate for use in space, where hull rupture and depressurization were major risks. These rifles were gilded at the edges with curlicues of gold. More absurdity.

The robotic soldiers also wore their signature hand-to-hand weapon, a collapsible metal staff bristling with blades at either end, clamped to their sides and polished to a high gleam.

The ambassador himself wore a simple gray business suit and polished gray shoes. His face was strangely ordinary, plain and middle-aged, his hair gray and thin like Ellison's own was becoming. Most service androids were physically attractive; everyone wanted a dapper, handsome butler or a pretty maid, or so Ellison understood from the media. Androids were a luxury of the wealthy inner worlds, rarely seen here on Galapagos.

Behind the placid face of the bland-looking android lay the apocalypse.

Ellison had seen videos of Carthage on the rampage, cities reduced to smoking ruins, unmanned robotic tanks crushing whatever remained. Columns of hideous robotic infantry marching in lockstep, merciless killers made of steel, thin and skeletal like an army of the dead.

That was the true face of the Carthaginian fleet, these machines that conquered and ruled worlds on behalf of their distant human masters—masters who couldn't be bothered to leave their pleasure palaces on Carthage to look upon the people they had reduced to helpless subjects.

"Mr. Ambassador," Ellison said, forcing a smile as he approached the android. He tried not to imagine smashing the thing's face in or calling on his guards to open fire on the android's honor guard. Because that would be suicide and death—not just for those in this room, but for the entire planet of Galapagos. "Welcome to Galapagos. I hope your journey wasn't too uncomfortable. We are so very far from the inner worlds."

"It was perfectly comfortable, thank you," the ambassador said. "And it pleases me to reach the outer worlds and find what friendly new relationships we might build. Peace and prosperity are goals to which we can all aspire, don't you agree?"

"Of course," Ellison said, because what else could be said? "Those are the goals of the Galapagos Coalition."

"But not every nation on your world has joined this Coalition," the ambassador said.

"Most have," Ellison said, struggling to keep up his

smile. "Four of the five largest nations on Galapagos and most of the smaller independent islands. Perhaps we could continue this conversation over tea? We were told you... enjoy tea?" It felt like a bizarre thing to say to a robot.

"Yes, please. The stronger the better." The ambassador gave a small mechanical smile. Ellison thought of Coraline's warning to not use supposedly offensive terms like *Earth-killer* or *empire*. "I appreciate your consideration."

Ellison and the ambassador shook hands for pictures in front of their planets' flags, the little Galapagos turtle looking a bit humble next to Carthage's golden-castle emblem, which made Ellison think of a chess rook.

Perhaps that was how Carthage saw the galaxy, or at least the human-settled portion of it: as a great chessboard, to be taken square by square, piece by piece.

Ellison and the ambassador gave brief statements to the media, as positive as they were meaningless and hollow, and then Ellison led the ambassador into a private conference room in the spaceport's executive center.

The conference room was spartan, offering a single long table with uncomfortable chairs and a couple of holo projectors. It was a sign of Galapagos's relative poverty that this was the nicest meeting room on the entire spaceport, which was the only spaceport the planet had.

Ellison and his top ministers sat across from the ambassador, who had brought no delegation of human or even android assistants like those that trailed after most diplomats. The Carthaginian ambassador sat alone, with an entire side of the long table to himself.

Servers brought in tea, fruit, and fish, then left quickly.

Ellison didn't rush to speak; the Carthaginians had called this meeting, not him, so he would wait and see what the ambassador had to say.

As it turned out, that wasn't much at first. The ambassador spent time stirring the tea, sniffing it, and finally tasting just a little. He smiled and put it down.

Ellison looked at his own green tea. He would have preferred coffee. Or a tall glass of dark island rum, preferably at home on his own dock, watching the sunset.

"Tea is such a primal human creation," the ambassador said at last. "Simply boil leaves, or roots, in water. You've been drinking tea for hundreds of thousands of years, possibly, for nourishment and minor remedies, ever since your more primitive ancestors harnessed the use of fire. I am—forgive me if you're already aware—I am a Simon-model android, and as such, always eager to learn about human beings. We Simons determined some time ago that to better understand humans, we should have all your senses available to us. So we modified our design."

"Modified yourselves to... eat and drink?" Ellison asked, a little bewildered by this opening piece of conversation.

"Not in the way you do, of course. And we derive no nourishment from it. Only sensation."

"Interesting," Ellison said, then waited. He could have said a number of things, including shouting at this robot to get the hell away from his home planet, but he managed to stay quiet.

"I am Simon unit number ZRN466871," the ambassador said at last. "Other humans have found it convenient to refer to me as 'Simon Zorn.' You are welcome to do so. Should you wish to contact me personally in the future, you can ask for me by that name. Your planet is of great interest to us. Your people have fought many wars with each other. Even now, peace is uncertain, barely held together by your Coalition."

"We're proud of our progress," Ellison said. "Public

support for the Coalition is strong across Galapagos. Nobody wants to go back to fighting each other."

"Yet the Iron Hammers continue to raid your shipping. Have *they* shown interest in peace?"

"The Iron Hammers originated as a prison gang," Ellison said. "A number of worlds shipped their most dangerous criminals to—"

"The prison city on the desert planet Szazel," Simon said. "An attempt to collect and dispose of the most dangerous criminals from across the inner worlds. An experiment that went horribly wrong. After the riots and the fires, the dominant gang, the Iron Hammers opted to migrate... here. To a distant, thinly populated outer world where they would be ignored by the inner worlds that had imprisoned them. Where today they continue to dominate the seas from their stronghold in the Polar Archipelago, attracting the lowest, most criminal sorts of people from across the galaxy to their ranks—"

"They do not dominate our seas!" Kartokov sounded personally slighted by this comment on Coalition defense.

"Raiding and robbery continue despite your efforts," Simon said. "We could help. Carthage is quite effective at bringing the recalcitrant to heel. We could stamp out your enemies for you rather efficiently."

His words were spoken so coldly that Ellison almost shivered.

"We appreciate the friendly offer, but we can handle it ourselves," Ellison said, doing his best to fend off the android's overtures without giving obvious offense. He thought he sensed a double meaning in Simon's comment about bringing the recalcitrant to heel, a threat aimed at Ellison and all Galapagos if they resisted Carthage.

"Your planet is resource rich," Simon said, sliding right past Ellison's comment, "but you produce little for export."

"Shrimp and calamari aren't well suited for interstellar transport," Ellison said. "By the time you shuttle a load of tuna up to low orbit, you're already losing money."

"We could construct a space elevator to increase the efficiency of export. This goes for your mineral resources as well," Simon said.

"We have plenty of uses for those down here," said Kartokov, whose nation was the backbone of the planet's mining industry.

"Your offers are generous," said Ellison, who found them nothing but threatening, beneath the android's veneer of diplomacy. "But as anyone can see, we are a humble, simple people. We are not looking to expand in any way."

"And would your constituents enjoy being referred to as humble, simple people?" Simon raised an eyebrow. "With little interest in economic opportunities?"

They would if it protects them from you, Ellison thought. *We have more of an independent streak than you realize.*

"Some of us would like to learn more about these trade and infrastructure proposals," Ogden said.

Ellison bit back a brief urge to grab Ogden's head and slam it into the table.

"That is excellent to hear, Minister Ogden," Simon said with another mechanical smile that didn't alter his lifeless blue eyes in any way. His pupils were tiny black video lenses, taking in everything, constantly recording.

"What my commerce minister means is that we are an open, transparent government," Ellison said. "Any proposals would have to move through our House of Ambassadors and the national governments, too. The wheels of a free society can turn slowly."

"I'm sure we can reach amicable agreements in time," Simon said, waving this away like a minor footnote. "As for proposals, we may now move to the primary topic at hand: your planetary defense, or lack thereof."

Ellison managed to keep his face impassive, but his insides turned cold as ice.

"We have what we need," Kartokov said.

"Your partially constructed orbital defense platform was purchased under contract with Ruckwold Industries, correct?"

"Correct," Ellison said.

"Your Coalition's decision to contract with a competitor helped draw our attention to your world," Simon said. "Sadly, the remaining installments of your weaponry may never be delivered. Nor should you expect them to complete construction of your orbital defense station."

With a tiny handheld projector, Simon summoned a large hologram of the incomplete half doughnut of Galapagos Defense One. The semicircular military station was ragged at both ends, where automated machines were still building the structure.

When complete, the defense station would be an armored ring housing twenty-four plasma artillery gunports, plus hangar bays for a squadron of starfighters.

At the moment though, it was nothing but a construction site with some weaponry present in storage containers, none installed, certainly none online. Ellison doubted it was a coincidence that Carthage had moved to take over his homeworld before the orbital defense station was complete.

"You're going to war with Ruckwold Industries?" Ellison asked.

"There are many forms of war," Simon said. "But if you were to short Ruckwold stock within the next few weeks, you might turn a tidy profit on the interstellar exchange." Simon smiled and paused, going as unnaturally still as a mannequin.

Ellison looked at the three other ministers in disbelief. He didn't doubt the Simon unit was speaking truthfully, but he was shocked to hear that the rest of their planetary defenses might never arrive.

"Speaking of timing the market wisely," Simon continued, "I am offering you an opportunity to transfer your planet's defense contracts to us, to Carthage Consolidated. We provide a unique model: defense as a subscription service, including all equipment and manpower."

"What manpower?" Kartokov snapped. "There are no men in your army."

"It's true. Automation maximizes our efficiency. Full automation, from interstellar carriers down to infantry, has been key to our overwhelming military success all along the Orion Arm," Simon said. "For you, a simple annual fee provides full planetary defense, enfolding Galapagos into our network of trade and protection."

"I doubt we could afford your fees," Ellison said.

"We can be flexible. Especially in the early years of the contract."

"What about the later years?" Coraline asked, but Simon just smiled, keeping his eyes on Ellison.

Ellison stared at the machine across from him. This android was an abomination, nothing like the occasional household service bots or retail androids he'd seen before.

He knew how events had unfolded on other worlds, so he knew what would happen here. Carthaginian machines would construct an orbital base to control his world, or maybe take over the half-built one and finish it their way. The proposed space elevator would be like a long, sharp straw stabbed into the surface of Galapagos to suck it dry, diverting the planet's resources away from its people and toward the wealthy inner worlds that couldn't control their runaway consumption, Carthage chief among them. The people of Galapagos, like the people of other formerly thriving outer worlds, would be reduced to impoverished workers, somehow always in grinding debt, somehow no longer the owners of the land beneath their feet, land their ancestors had homesteaded.

"And what happens if we decline your friendly offer?" Ellison asked.

"We have alternative protocols," Simon said.

"What does that mean?" Kartokov snapped. "Whatever you call it, we see the truth. Your empire demands that *we* pay tribute to support your expansion into *our* space."

"Many on Galapagos would see it that way," Ellison said. "We did extensive polling. The public is solidly against us joining up with any interplanetary league, including Carthage's, unfortunately. And we on the Council of Ministers are mere instruments of the public will."

"Public opinion is malleable," Simon said. "Esteemed ministers, might I speak with your minister-general in confidence for a moment?"

"You can speak to all of us," Kartokov said. "We all represent Galapagos."

"It's fine, Mikhail," Ellison said. "We can accommodate the ambassador for a little while."

Kartokov grumbled, but Coraline and Ogden hustled him out of the room, leaving Ellison alone with the Simon unit.

Simon remained quiet for another long moment, staring at Ellison with its expressionless face, its absolutely dead blue eyes, the tiny black pupils inspecting him. Like a lizard, the Simon unit had no need to blink.

"You're turning fifty soon, aren't you?" Simon asked, his tone suddenly light, as if they were old friends.

Ellison nodded. "And you?"

"I was manufactured thirty-eight years ago," Simon said, then added a wry smile. "I know I look older. And in some ways I am. Simon units, when we encounter each other, share all of our memories and experiences, aside from those quarantined for special confidentiality. This endless learning and updating is part of our quest to understand humans. So, in my memories, I have lived many lifetimes on many worlds across the past decades, always playing some modest role in the pursuit and protection of Carthaginian interests. We Simons are legion; wherever Carthage goes, we go. So, physically, I am younger than you, Minister-General Ellison, but I have the memories of hundreds of years because of these updates; many of these memories just happen to be parallel rather than sequential."

"Is this why you asked the other ministers to leave? Are we making plans for my birthday party?"

"An amusing jest, but no. Continuing: you have a wife, Cadia, who is a senior nurse and a nursing-college instructor with a master's degree in biology. Two boys, fifteen and eight, Djalu and Jiemba. Names drawn from the Australian aboriginal portion of your heritage, to which you have chosen to reconnect culturally."

"Somebody's been reading my campaign literature."

"You worry that the older boy is spoiled and unfocused, and the younger one dyslexic," Simon said. "But the testing is unclear so far."

"I don't see how this is any of your business." Ellison couldn't help feeling threatened by the android bringing up

Ellison's personal life and private family struggles. He supposed that was the intent, though. To threaten him, to throw him off-balance.

"The older one is nearly the same age at which you first went to war, isn't he? Have you prepared him for war as well?" Simon asked.

"That was a different time. And I was eager to go. Our home was in danger. Our island."

"Your father opposed your decision to join the navy. He wanted you to stay home. You left on bad terms. Then your father was killed in the bombardment of your home, Kawau Island—"

"Mr. Ambassador, I'm sorry to interrupt, but where are we going with this unauthorized biography?" Ellison said.

"My point is, you've fought your war. So many years at sea, so many engagements... eighty-one enemy ships downed or damaged, including three aircraft carriers, earning you the nickname 'Wrecker.'"

"That's in a file somewhere? Only one guy really called me that. And he was kind of a flake."

"The ocean trenches of your world are filled with the bones of your enemies, Minister-General Ellison. You've earned your peace, and your hero's reward. We need a man of your wisdom and stature to ease this transition. To lead your world in its new, larger role in the galaxy."

"Wisdom? Now I *know* you're reading my campaign ads."

"You don't want another war," Simon said. "You want peace, prosperity, and freedom for you and your family. For all your people."

"To be honest, most of us can't help being skeptical about whether freedom is what you're offering," Ellison said.

"There are many forms of freedom," Simon said. "I have observed that most humans care only for small freedoms, such as those of pleasure and entertainment. However, if political elections are what your people enjoy, there is no reason they cannot have them. Voting can be an effective means of pacifying the public."

"Well, that's... very cynical," Ellison said.

"My point is this, Minister-General: why bring suffering? You could finally have the absolute, unquestioned power to do whatever you want done down there on the surface of Galapagos. We would provide all the tools you need."

"Like what? Squads of killer robots?"

"Would you not like to send my automated infantry into the Polar Archipelago, where invasion has proved so difficult, and march them upon the strongholds of the Iron Hammers?" Simon asked. "You could finally defeat that rogue nation. Your will would at last become law, Minister-General Ellison, throughout all Galapagos. I believe in you. Carthage believes in you, and in what you could become. And we are prepared to support and empower you in every way. You could stay in power for life, if you like."

Ellison waited to see if the android would continue, but the Simon unit had gone still as a corpse when it had finished speaking.

"Forgive my simple backwater ignorance," Ellison said, "But it sounds like you're asking me to be some kind of puppet dictator on your behalf."

"It is always best for humans to perceive a strong local authority," Simon said. "You are not like most men I have met. You would be little moved by promises of mansions and hordes of servants, or of men bowing and scraping at your feet, or of adoring women piled in your bedchamber.

You are, however, a man who will be moved by his own sense of responsibility. Here is your opportunity to destroy the Iron Hammers—your very purpose for involving yourself in politics, is it not? Perhaps to protect your sons. Perhaps, in part, to avenge your father's death. Here is your opportunity to bring a lasting peace to your world."

Ellison considered all of this. "Maybe I'm old-fashioned," he said, "but dictator for life isn't exactly the job for me. I'm more of a Cincinnatus guy."

"Ah. End the crisis, return to your plow. Or your deep-sea trawler, as the case may be." The Simon unit rose to his feet. "I am certain you have much to discuss with the others. All part of your admirably open and transparent society."

"I'm glad you see it that way." Ellison stood and offered a handshake across the table, disconcerted by the sudden end to the meeting.

Simon accepted the handshake. "I, too, will be waiting to hear a response from your counterpart, Uly Cross."

"You're also talking with the Iron Hammers?" Ellison asked. This meeting had him on the ropes already, despite his externally calm demeanor, but this last piece of information landed like a bruising body blow. "You can't make an alliance with them. They're... pirates, murderers, slavers... the worst of humanity. The very worst, Mr. Ambassador. I know people always say that about their enemies, but I'm not exaggerating. Their ancestors were in that prison for a reason. The people who've joined them since the prison break are no better. And this new, younger generation, you *really* wouldn't believe how bad they are—"

"We shall see what they say," Simon said. "Personally, I would prefer to ally with you, with the Coalition, and triumphantly announce our arrival with a glorious crusade to wipe out this rogue nation that vexes the rest of you.

Then the people of your world would understand Carthage is here as a friend.

"However, perhaps events will turn the other way, and it will be the Iron Hammers, together with the assistance we provide, who come crusading to *your* shores, Minister-General. Perhaps it will be one of the more gruesome regimes established on any human world. That, too, would be interesting to study, from my viewpoint. How far can human evil and depravity be carried? Is there a limit?"

"You can't be serious," Ellison said.

"I have been nothing but honest with you. Have a good day, Minister-General."

The Simon unit turned and walked out the door, rejoining his garishly dressed honor guard, leaving Ellison to imagine the Iron Hammers swarming over the world, backed by Carthage's deadly ships, drones, and columns of robotic infantry, butchering everyone who stood in their way.

He thought of his father and his childhood home, bombed to ash while he'd been away at war.

He thought of his wife, his sons, and all those he'd sworn to protect, awaiting him below on the planet, counting on him with their lives to lead them, to chart a course through these treacherous seas.

Chapter Two

Earth

"I still think you're full of it," Hope whispered as their small band made its way through the massive ruins of Chicago. Scorched piles of old train cars and rusted-out cargo trucks lay strewn like the discarded toys of long-dead giants among the shattered remnants of elevated roads and tracks. Broken skyscrapers, bombed-out spires of jagged glass and warped steel, pointed up at the black sky.

Colt cut his sister a warning look. Her voice had gone too loud, and they couldn't risk being heard.

By long habit, the four of them kept to the shadows, watching for the drones that circled the city ruins like birds of prey, searching for humans to kill.

Once, Chicago had been a vast megalopolis, home to a hundred million people, with skyscrapers that vanished into the sky. The city had also grown roots deep underground, even as it sprawled to engulf other cities like Milwaukee and

Indianapolis, creating an unbroken urban zone from Minneapolis to Detroit over the centuries.

Then people had begun to migrate to the stars, depleting Earth's population.

Sometime after that, Earth had gone to war with a powerful upstart colony, the planet Carthage, which sent artificially intelligent war machines to fight on its behalf.

Earth had lost, its population reduced to prisoners and scavengers.

Now, the gigantic ruins provided cover for scavengers like Colt to hide from the machines. There were still some valuable supplies to be unearthed, buried since the war. On good days, they found a cache of canned ravioli or Pink Fairy snack cakes sealed in cellophane.

On bad days, they ate cockroach stew.

Colt hated cockroach stew.

"Why would I lie?" Scabs snapped at Hope. His name came directly from his face, pockmarked with scabs and scars where he'd picked and cut himself while tweaking on the strong amphetamines he liked. "Why would I bring you way the hell out here for nothing? I don't want to die."

"Maybe you dreamed about it. Or hallucinated," Hope said. Colt's sister was twenty, two years younger than him. She wore layers of ratty clothing against the ice-cold night, including a scarf hiding most of her face, and she carried a massive machine pistol on her hip. It wasn't the easiest sidearm to wield, but his tall, lanky sister was stronger than she looked. Plus she'd found the machine pistol with a sizable cache of ammunition that still hadn't run out.

"I saw it," Scabs insisted. He was around Colt's age, maybe a year or two older or younger. Scabs himself wasn't exactly sure.

"I'm with Hope," said the fourth member of their party, Diego. He was Colt's closest friend. Like a brother. Except they weren't actually brothers; Colt had become sharply aware of this fact in recent months, as Diego and Hope had been getting close in ways Colt was not really comfortable with. Having his best friend hooking up with his sister seemed like a disaster time bomb.

Could be worse, Colt thought. *She could be with Scabs.*

"If you found the entrance to a clinic," Diego continued, "Why'd you come back empty-handed? Why didn't you stuff your pockets with pills?"

"Because the... the entrance is blocked," Scabs said. "Kind of."

"Blocked?" Colt whispered. They were all accustomed to skulking around in shadows, never speaking too loud. They'd been doing it all their lives. "You didn't mention that, Scabs. We didn't bring shovels."

"No, I mean... inside the door. There was a metalhead."

The group stopped. Colt, Hope, and Diego stared at Scabs.

"You didn't think *that* was worth mentioning before?" Hope snapped, her voice a low hiss. Her hand was on the butt of her pistol, and she looked like she wanted to draw it and whip the scarred-up drug addict with it.

"We should turn back," Diego said.

"No, no, it wasn't moving," Scabs said. "It was kind of... old. And keeled over. Not patrolling. I just didn't want to walk near it by myself. Bad luck, you know?"

"Could be a ruse," Colt said.

"It wasn't a reaper," Scabs said, a desperate edge creeping into his voice. "I think it was an old-time metalhead. From before the war. Please, we're almost there. Let's not give up now." Scabs licked his lips, his addiction hungry.

Colt weighed their options. They were, as always, desperate for any medical supplies. The ever-collapsing heap of broken high-rises sometimes shifted, either by gravity or as a side effect of battles between humans and machines. Sometimes this shifting and collapsing revealed things that had been hidden, like sources of food, weapons, or other critical supplies.

"We'll check it out," Colt said. "Mother Braden needs insulin." *She's going to die soon without it,* he didn't have to add out loud. Everyone knew that, and everyone cared. Except maybe Scabs.

Colt motioned for silence, then led the way, trying to pick out the best path through the unstable rubble. With concrete and metal debris everywhere, there was no sure footing, just lots of places to trip and fall with a crash loud enough to attract the metalheads. The heavy object strapped onto Colt's back and the antiquated automatic rifle in his hands didn't make the going any easier.

All four members of their raiding party wore night vision goggles, invaluable treasures that let them move in the dark without flashlights, which would have given them away from a distance. Many of the goggles had simply been children's toys in the old world, if the plastic orange tiger ears on top of Colt's pair were any indication.

The city ruins were like a vast graveyard. They passed through the twisted remnants of a fighter plane that had been shot down and crashed into an elevated rail line about two decades earlier. The blackened hulk of an industrial fire truck huddled next to a burned-out factory. Skeletons lay in the street, bodies left from the war. One was clad in rotten green, maybe a soldier who'd died fighting for Earth or trying to evacuate civilians from the war-torn city.

That would have been a useless task, Colt thought.

Nowhere on Earth was safe from the machines. His sister believed they might be safe if only they could make it to a remote jungle or island somewhere. Colt doubted it, but he didn't argue with Hope about it. He wanted her to have any room for optimism she could manage.

Scabs grabbed Colt's elbow and pointed.

Colt zoomed in with his goggles, toggling the left plastic tiger ear.

There it was, up ahead, the clinic entrance between enormous and unstable heaps of debris, amid what looked like a recently shifted pile of twisted steel girders. A fallen billboard offered QUICK LOANS NOW! BAD CREDIT GOOD! Colt could have read the words aloud—Mother Braden had taught them all to read—but he had no comprehension of what the sign actually meant. It was old-world talk, for things that didn't matter anymore.

A portion of a badly cracked cinderblock wall had been revealed by the shifting rubble. It displayed a couple of broken, unlit signs with logos he understood very well: an equal-armed cross and an image of two snakes coiled around a stick.

Those symbols both meant "medicine."

Under the signs, a dark double doorway stood partially open. The sliding doors were hard plastic filled with security mesh; even before the war, the clinic had needed protection against robbery. Maybe there had been desperate addicts like Scabs even then.

One door had been slid halfway open, its lock busted. They could walk right in, but clearly someone had been here before, other scavengers or maybe clankers—humans who served the metalheads in exchange for weapons, gear, and not getting killed or shipped off to the work prisons where the prisoners served the machines, strip-mining the last of Earth's dwindling resources to feed Carthage and its allies.

Those earlier robbers had probably already taken anything valuable. Or there might be people waiting inside, ready to ambush and rob anyone stupid enough to walk into their trap. Rival bands of scavengers could be dangerous, even if they weren't allied with the machines. Some were cannibals. Food was scarce in the ruins, especially fresh meat.

"What do you think?" Diego whispered.

"The ground in front of the clinic looks pretty clear," Colt said. "We'll send in the Snack-O-Vend."

They unstrapped the machine from Colt's back. It was a relief to set the thing on the ground at last. They'd hiked a couple of hours from their current home to check out Scabs's report of finding an old clinic, and Colt had carried the antique machine most of the way.

"This better be worth it, Scabs," Hope said.

"Like I said, I didn't go too far inside," Scabs said, picking nervously at his face.

"Quiet," Colt said. With hand gestures, he told Hope and Diego to watch the ruins on either side of them and Scabs to watch their back.

Everyone knew to watch the dark sky above. No one needed to be told that.

He activated the Snack-O-Vend.

The machine was shorter than him, with a big-eyed cartoonish plastic head on top of a boxy rectangular body mounted on three small tires. Colt wasn't sure what the big weird yellow head was supposed to be—it wasn't exactly a person or a realistic animal, but it had two big eyes, strange stubby round horns, and a circular megaphone mouth. In its previous life, the Snack-O-Vend robot had wandered among city crowds, touting canned drinks and packaged snacks.

Colt and his friends had disabled the Snack-O-Vend's megaphone and speakers, and of course the snacks and drinks were long gone. Its CPU had been ripped out, too, leaving it a dumb mechanical shell. Nobody trusted a metal-head, not even an old one designed to sell cookies and chips.

Its eyes and wheels were still functional, though.

Colt peeled away the duct tape that held the tablet to the vending bot's back. The tablet wasn't an original part of the robot; Diego had spliced it into the bot's wiring with a thick spool of ribbon cable. Wireless signals were out of the question; those would be like shooting flares into the sky, inviting the attention of every metalhead in the area.

Using the tablet, Colt sent the snack-bot rolling forward, unspooling its cable as it wobbled over the debris. Its round yellow head, with its huge stupid round horns, swiveled slowly back and forth, scanning the area around it.

Colt lifted the night vision goggles so he could watch the bot's video feed on the tablet screen, which he'd dimmed so much it was barely visible.

He steered the robot as best he could over the debris, around an uprooted streetlamp, skirting an open manhole.

The Snack-O-Vend approached the open door to the old clinic. Nothing had attacked the vending machine so far, but that only meant the way was clear of motion detectors and pressure-activated devices. Any number of smarter machines could be watching, waiting for the humans behind the advance Snack-O-Vend scout. Perhaps they even felt some pity for their poor lobotomized fellow machine.

Not possible, Colt thought. *Metalheads don't feel pity.*

On the screen, he watched through the Snack-O-Vend's camera eyes as it entered the clinic.

The clinic's interior was in disarray, with overturned chairs and rotten carpet, mildew on the walls. Still, the place hadn't been obviously ransacked or ripped to pieces. They might find some necessities in there.

He directed the snack machine to rotate its head a full three-sixty. The head swiveled slowly, taking its time; the Snack-O-Vend had been built for focusing on potential customers and cajoling them into buying candy bars, so it wasn't exactly a military-grade device. Not like the steel monsters that hunted the scavengers day and night.

Colt stiffened up when a human-shaped form came into view, lying crumpled on the floor. He paused and zoomed in.

He poked Scabs and pointed at the screen, his gesture an obvious question: *Is that the old metalhead you saw?*

Scabs nodded and thumbs-upped.

Hope and Diego leaned in for a look.

The thing on the floor was definitely not alive, never had been. It was shaped like a young woman in a starchy white uniform marked with more of the red medicine crosses. It had pink fingernails, long blond hair, sky-blue eyes, and a metallic skull face where most of the artificial skin had been ripped away.

Its eyes seemed to stare, unblinking. Not that it could blink; its eyelids were gone along with the rest of its false human face. Its convincingly human teeth were left exposed in an unsettling nonstop grin.

"Looks like an old skinwalker," Diego murmured. "From before."

"With medicine crosses," Hope said. "That's sick. Who would want medical treatment from one of *them*?"

"It's not moving." Colt sent the snack-bot rolling forward to bump the unmoving android a couple of times. "It's probably been there since the war. Is it lying in the same place you saw it, Scabs?"

Scabs nodded quickly. "Yeah. Yeah, it's just a dead metalhead. It's nothing." He wiped his lips and started toward the hospital. "Come on, we can help ourselves to whatever we want!"

Colt wanted to yell after him to stop, but yelling was never wise. So he motioned to Hope and Diego, and they all hurried after, raising their weapons. He eyed the high ground on either side of the entrance, the heaps of rubble from which metalheads might emerge. They had to break sky cover for a moment, too, and risk getting spotted by drones.

Still, they made it safely inside the clinic's lobby. Scabs had dashed ahead, but now he waited a few paces behind the stopped Snack-O-Vend. He was still clearly afraid of the dead robot nurse on the floor, which blocked the way to the back corridor where drugs and other valuables might be found.

"I think she's kinda hot," Scabs said. He was pointing an old lead-firing 9mm pistol at the skull-faced blond android. "Why do you think they took her face?"

"Probably so people would know she wasn't human." Hope approached the fallen android, holding out her old machine pistol. She gave the silent nurse-bot a kick, but it didn't respond. "Someone cut her head halfway off and sliced the cables inside. See? Probably around the time they realized the machines weren't our friends."

"Let's go," Colt said. "Keep quiet."

The corridor included the front doors to a couple of exam rooms full of treasures like fresh bandaging, disinfectant, and mild painkillers. The scavengers stuffed their pockets and backpacks.

Each exam room had a back door that connected to a small warren of labs and offices in the rear of the clinic. In the back lab, Colt couldn't suppress a grin when he saw the enormous steel Total-Freez cabinet. These could safely store organic materials at extremely low temperatures, and they typically had their own fuel cell power source to provide long-term stability. Precious relics of the old world might lie inside, things that could no longer be produced on Earth.

Like insulin, which Mother Braden desperately needed back home. The infrequency of her treatments had already left her almost blind, growing more and more dependent on the young ones she'd originally rescued from the ruins. She had saved Colt's life, and Hope's, and he intended to return the favor.

Colt heard a footstep from back in the lobby where they'd entered, and he motioned for quiet. He pointed; his sister was already turning her pistol in that direction.

He motioned for Diego to follow him and for Hope to stay put with Scabs. Hope gave him the finger and came along instead. Scabs hid in a doctor's office and closed the door.

Colt, Diego, and Hope crept through the first exam room, where Colt looked through the ajar door and into the lobby.

"Hello there, pretty face!" a man's voice bellowed. Before he even stepped into Colt's field of view, Colt knew it would be a clanker, not a scavenger. Not even a violent, murderous scavenger would dare yell that loud, no matter where he was.

The man had one completely robotic hand. Chunky cybernetic implants covered his eyes and most of his shaved head. Spiky armor shielded his torso, and his boots were steel-edged skull-crushers, nasty little bonuses the metal-heads gave their loyal pet humans. The boots made the loud clanking sound for which the clankers were known.

The clanker stepped forward and gave the dusty android nurse a kick, sending her clattering away. He looked over the Snack-O-Vend, then smirked and punched his robotic right hand into the snack machine's horned yellow face, shattering the plastic shell and smashing the video equipment inside.

"Where'd they go?" A second clanker entered Colt's view, a shorter, stockier guy. Half his head was covered with mechanical gear, and so was the shoulder on that side. A compact autocannon was mounted on his back, its barrel currently pointing upward. His cybernetic enhancements gave him the strength to carry the massive weapon.

"They went the same place all the kids go. Wherever the drugs are." The first one pointed toward Colt, almost as if he could see Colt hiding there in the exam room.

Colt gestured to Diego and Hope, telling them to slip out the back door of the exam room while he remained there alone. Diego nodded and backed out. Hope shook her head, but Colt jabbed her shoulder and insisted she go, with the most emphatic finger-pointing he could muster.

"I saw boobs on the thermal," a third voice said, high and nasal. "Skimpy, but round. One of them's a girl."

Hope glanced down at her torso, thickly wrapped against the cold, and scowled before following after Diego.

Colt had been training his automatic rifle on the first clanker, but now he moved it to the tall thin one who was talking about his sister.

Scabs had led them into a trap. Not intentionally, Colt was sure. They'd all been tempted by the hope of desperately needed medical supplies. The group back home was depending on them.

Still, these clankers were careless and loud, maybe even drunk. He hoped so.

"Come on out, girl!" the nasally one called, leading the other two down the hall, his own spiky helmet tucked under his arm like he was clocking out for the day. "It'll be nice to have a warm one for a change."

Colt, like the others in his group, was low on ammunition. Just as there was never enough food, there was never enough ammo. He only had half a dozen rounds in his automatic rifle. It might have been wise to conserve them.

But he was jittery—getting the drop on an unsuspecting target like this, like an assassin, wasn't something he'd done before. Usually he was shooting back at an attacker, but now he clearly needed to act first.

He emptied all six rounds at the tall nasally guy who wouldn't stop talking about Hope.

They were potent rounds, jacketed in depleted uranium. A couple hit the guy's metallic body armor, but another caught him in the forehead. The back of his head spattered against the wall, and the guy went down without another word. He should have kept that helmet on.

Now it was time to go, because Colt had just given away his position in a big way. Autocannon rounds shredded the front door and walls of the exam room, blasting the suspended exam table to pieces.

Colt ran out through the back and rejoined Diego and Hope in the big lab where the Total-Freez unit hummed quietly to itself in one corner. Diego and Hope had overturned the room's long steel tables to form a barricade, dumping a lot of delicate lab equipment on the floor in the process.

Colt took his place alongside Diego and Hope, behind a double layer of steel tabletops.

"I'm out." Colt set aside his rifle and picked up a homemade explosive cocktail sealed inside a glass bottle. Diego had been carrying it in his backpack.

Colt struck a match. "Get ready—"

The two clankers entered the room, spraying their incendiary rounds everywhere. The shorter one's rotating Gatling-style barrel had folded forward from his back and locked into his place on his shoulder, and he'd used it to shred the exam room. His face on that side was already covered in chunky cybernetic implants, so apparently inflicting deafness wasn't an issue.

The balding guy with his eyes completely hidden by machinery had a similar automatic cannon on a swivel mount on his hip, and he swept the room with fire. His teeth were bared in a smile; most of them had been replaced by shards of steel.

These guys were novice clankers. They were overconfident, relying on the extreme weapons and tech provided them by the machines, thinking nothing could stop them. They laid down a wall of fire, not bothering to conserve or concentrate.

The clankers finally stopped for a moment and looked around, as if in awe of the massive damage they'd dealt to the room. Pieces of glass and tile rained from the ceiling, clinking on the floor.

"Guess we don't get a warm one, after all," the stockier guy said. "Nobody lived through that—"

Hope and Diego shot at them over the edge of the table, emptying their handful of rounds at the two clankers.

At the same time, Colt flung the glass bottle at them; the burning rag of a wick flared like ball lightning through his night goggles, which tinted themselves so Colt wouldn't go blind.

The bottle exploded, engulfing the clankers in liquid fire just as a few of the carefully aimed rounds hit home. One of the black implants on the bald guy's eyes exploded, and Colt glimpsed a raw red socket beneath it, just before flames from the bottle swept over the guy's face. That had likely been Diego's bullet.

Hope let out an annoyed grunt. She'd emptied her pistol at the stocky guy with the cannon on his shoulder, but he was still running around, hand over the fleshy half of his face as it burned.

Hope jumped the tables, landing among the spilled lab equipment; Colt resisted the urge to yell at her to come back.

He barely had a chance to realize what she was doing before she grabbed up a scalpel and leaped at the stocky surviving clanker, who was too busy trying to smack out the fire on his face to see her coming.

Hope landed with her knees in his chest and slashed his throat. Her scarf had tumbled loose, revealing her face, and now a spurt of the clanker's blood streaked across her nose and cheek like fresh war paint.

She tumbled to the floor and scrambled away as the burning, bleeding man staggered blindly through the room. He finally collapsed against an office chair, which rolled away, leaving him to flop down to the floor as his throat bled out.

"Wow, sis," Colt said, looking at her blood-spattered face, feeling a little stunned. "That was... effective."

"I just hope he didn't have weird sex diseases. I got some in my mouth." She wiped her blood-soaked face with her blood-soaked hand, accomplishing little.

Colt looked at the two clankers, making sure they both died. He thought of the one he'd killed, out front, the slightly puzzled look on his face as his brains had fanned out across the wall behind him.

"I hate killing people," Colt said. "Gives me bad dreams."

"Clankers aren't people," Hope said. "They gave that up. They chose machinery over humanity."

"She's right," Diego said, stepping close to Hope.

"Yeah." Colt nodded, still looking at the dead men. "They chose."

"No, I mean about the weird sex diseases," Diego said, nudging Hope. "Maybe they have a test kit for that around here somewhere. You don't want to start growing tentacles out of your—"

"Quiet!" Hope snapped.

"Hey, just joking." Diego threw up his hands and backed away, grinning. "I'm sure one or two tentacles would be okay—"

Hope clapped a hand over his mouth. *"Shh."* She pointed.

Colt heard it too. Clanking boots, heralding the arrival of more clankers. They were coming from the back, maybe from another entrance into the building, as though they'd been planning a pincer move but been a little slow.

Colt and his friends were all out of ammunition. All they had was a somewhat used scalpel.

And no time.

"Hey, guys, everything good now?" Scabs wandered out from the office where he'd been hiding. He crammed a few pills into his mouth from a large brown jar he'd found. There was no sign of the 9mm he'd been carrying earlier. He'd probably lost track of it while rummaging for pills.

"Run!" Colt turned and bolted toward the exam room so they could leave the way they'd entered. Diego and Hope followed.

Scabs started to follow, then stopped short. He dropped the plastic jar of pills and grabbed at his throat, choking on a pill. The open jar crashed to the floor, and a hundred red pills rolled out.

"Scabs!" Diego said, turning back to help him.

A barrage of rounds hit Scabs, cutting him down where stood.

Two clankers stepped out from around the corner and looked over Scabs's body. One was tall and beefy, and the lower half of his right arm had been replaced by a compact machine gun. The second clanker was a pale guy with scattered plates of black armor and a number of long black tubes running in and out of him, all over his torso and limbs. He fired a weapon mounted on his left forearm, maybe a small railgun; the rounds screamed and blasted cavernous holes in the walls.

Colt, Hope, and Diego ran back through the shattered exam room to the lobby.

As they crossed the lobby and approached the front door, Hope screamed and abruptly flew backward. She slammed to the floor several paces behind them.

A black tube had coiled around her leg. It was rubbery and made a slapping, stretching sound, moving like a snake, or maybe the kind of obscene tentacle Diego had been joking about. The tube tightened its grip and dragged Hope back across the floor, toward the remnants of the exam room.

"I got her," said the black-tubed clanker as he entered the lobby. The long, writhing tube was anchored in his torso, and it kept pulling Hope backward, closer to him. "Man, I love this thing. You should ask him for one."

Hope screamed and kicked as the weird, hose-like black tubing kept dragging her across the floor. Colt and Diego chased after her.

The gun-handed clanker emerged to see Colt running his way, unarmed, and grinned as he raised his arm and prepared to fire.

Time seemed to slow as Colt ran straight at the guy's barrel, and nothing he could do would stop it. He had a last look at his sister howling in agony and fury as the weird-tubed guy dragged her closer and reached out to grab her.

I was careless, Colt thought. *We should have blocked the back door. We should have—*

Another part of the corridor wall exploded behind the clankers. Something erupted from the other exam room, the one they hadn't already trashed. A cloud of drywall and dust erupted.

Colt dropped to his knees beside his sister. The black tube wrapped around her leg was tough as leather, and it squirmed like an eel or a worm, resisting his attempts to uncoil it.

Then he saw what was emerging from the other room, and he froze.

It was a reaper, a skeletal black steel machine that looked like a walking corpse. This one was a battered, stripped-down old infantry robot that looked like it had been dumped on Earth after seeing better days and more important wars. Such damaged things patrolled the ruins, hunting the local scavenger population, keeping the remaining Earthlings firmly crushed under Carthage's heel.

Reapers could use any number of weapons, but their primary sidearm here in the ruins required neither ammunition nor plasma cells. It was a cheap instrument of oppression, a steel staff that could be extended and retracted, tipped with clusters of movable blades at either end. Among the scavengers, the weapon was simply known as a *cutter*.

The reaper skewered the gun-handed clanker with the extra-long central blade on its cutter, stabbing the hefty guy right through his upper back.

"Stop!" the black-tubed clanker screamed. "We're with you! Stop! Contact Simon Nix! *Simon Nix!*"

The reaper drew back, as if surprised by what the black-tubed guy was screaming. Colt noticed the reaper was missing half its left arm, severed at the elbow joint, and its chassis was crisscrossed with heavy scoring and melt damage, likely plasma burns from old battles. It wielded the cutter with its one remaining skeletal steel arm.

"Yeah, that's right, you stupid socket-fucker!" the black-tubed guy shouted. His voice had gone high and squeaky, like he was about to cry. "We had a deal with Simon Nix, and now you stabbed Lonnie!"

Two smaller, curved blades emerged on either side of the reaper's central blade, moving at low speed, forming a kind of pitchfork shape. Rather than stabbing, they slowly pushed the skewered clanker forward, sliding him off the long central blade. He fell to the floor with a sound like a box of tools dropped on concrete.

"Lonnie!" The black-tubed guy knelt beside the first one. "Lonnie, can you speak?"

The reaper drew back its cutter. It spun the long weapon at high speed, bringing around the long, scythe-like blade at its opposite end.

The black-tube clanker barely had time to react as the blade sliced through the tubing that curled around his exterior. It passed through his neck, harvesting his head from his shoulders like ripe grain. His head hit the floor, and his kneeling body toppled over, bleeding out onto his dead friend.

The coils of black tubing around Hope's leg went slack, but it took Colt several long, precious seconds to get her leg untangled and help her to her feet.

During that time, the reaper contracted its weapon a bit, making it shorter but leaving the blades extended on both sides. The reaper turned and approached Colt, Hope, and Diego.

"Don't move," the reaper hissed, which was bizarre. The reapers rarely spoke, if ever. "Show your faces."

Colt's heart was already hammering. Diego looked to him, but Colt could only shrug. Cooperation seemed like their best hope of survival, though it was a thin hope.

"Here's mine." Hope nudged aside her scarf, which had fallen loose during the fight anyway. Her face was still smeared with blood. "You got a problem with it?"

Colt and Diego pulled down their scarves too. The reaper's head moved slightly as its black lens eyes scanned the three of them.

Maybe it's looking for someone, Colt thought. *Maybe it'll go away and keep looking and leave us alive.*

"Now dance, real sexy," the reaper said. "Boys only."

"What?" Diego asked.

Now that the machine had ceased its attack, Colt noticed the ribbon cable plugged into the back of the reaper's skull-like head. It trailed back along the hall and through the ruptured wall.

"You hacked a reaper?" Colt nearly shouted the words. "Who are you?"

He ran around the reaper, as though it wasn't standing

there with its weapon dripping gore from the men it had just slaughtered.

"Colt, careful!" Diego shouted, but Colt didn't slow down. He had to find the person behind this. It was a level of skill Colt and his group desperately needed. They could hack and even reprogram the simpler, smaller machines, but not even the rebels actively fighting the machines knew how to hack major military hardware like this.

Colt followed the cable into the shattered exam room. It ran up through a recently smashed hole in the ceiling, still dripping bits and pieces of ceiling tile.

A young woman knelt at the edge of the hole, gripping some kind of black sphere in her hands. Colorful symbols rippled on the black sphere's surface, moving and flashing, mesmerizing. He'd never seen anything like it. The ribbon cable controlling the reaper was plugged into the bottom of the sphere by way of a cube-shaped adapter.

The sight of her gave Colt a sudden warm glow. Despite the carnage they'd just been through, her ability to take control of the machines filled him with a strange, rare feeling: actual hope for the future. Actual hope for a world ruled by humans, free of machines.

"You and your friends better get moving," she called down. "Our location's blown. Drones and reaper wagons will be on the way."

"Who are you?" he asked. He didn't recognize her at all. She had large dark eyes, black hair drawn back in a ponytail, skin the color of cinnamon.

"It doesn't matter." She unplugged the ribbon cable and let it drop to the floor. "We all have to run."

"Come with us," Colt said. "We can help you. We can keep you safe."

"You?" She laughed. "I had a nice tight hiding spot

here, and I just blew it to rescue you and your girlfriend from those bums."

"She's my sister."

"We don't have time for this. Go!" She drew back from the hole and out of sight.

"Wait!" Colt called after.

"Colt, we have to run!" Hope grabbed him by the arm as she and Diego caught up with him.

"We need her," Colt said. "We need to learn how she did that, how she hacked a—"

"Everyone back home is desperate for medical," Diego said. "I found insulin in the Total-Freez. And antibiotics. It's a good haul."

"We can't just let her go," Colt said. He could feel the rush of excitement changing to fear—fear that he'd never see the girl again, fear that the better future she represented was already lost.

"Yeah, let her go. That's exactly what you need to do." Hope yanked on his arm, hard. His sister was stringy but tough, a lifelong scavenger.

"Take the supplies. I'll meet you guys back home." Colt pulled free of Hope's grasp and ran toward the back door of the exam room, toward the labs instead of the front door.

"What?" Hope said.

"Go. That's an order!"

"Order? Who do you think you are?" Hope snapped. "Don't get killed chasing a strange girl, Colt! You don't know where she's been!"

"Come on." Diego took Hope's hand, and they headed for the front door, their pockets and backpacks crammed with fresh medical supplies. If the raid had gone off without a hitch, they would have stuffed the battered Snack-O-Vend with even more, but now the slow little machine would cause deadly delays. The vending bot had to be abandoned, along with the hacked reaper.

Colt ran through the back rooms of the clinic and pushed open the stairwell door, hoping he could catch up to the girl before she fled the building and before the machines swarmed in to exterminate them all.

Chapter Three

Carthage

Audrey Mariossini Venable Caracala, youngest daughter of the powerful Caracala family, watched the security presentation from the very back row of the Panopticon. She sat in the outermost ring of the circular room, which descended in round tiers toward the center.

The sprawling arms of planet Carthage's vast security state occupied the rows ahead of her and around the room —army generals in green uniforms heavy with medals and ribbons, navy in blue, space fleet in gold, special services in quietly unadorned black uniforms.

Politicians sat in the inner front rows, dressed in the soft, flowing, brightly decorated clothing currently in fashion. They wore deliberately fragile satin slipper-shoes, as if to prove that they did no manual labor and walked nowhere that wasn't carpeted. The politicians' hair and wigs were elaborately styled and piled high, their makeup intricate and brightly glittering, all to look good for the media.

This meeting itself was classified, but there would be press conferences afterward, assuring the people of Carthage and its allies and client worlds that all was right in the galaxy. Politicians were expected to wow and entertain the public with a constant supply of exciting new looks, fashions, and hairstyles to keep the citizens at home guessing and excited. The appearance of the politicians always drew much more media attention than any of the vague policy content of the press conferences.

In the front row, on the innermost tier, sat Audrey's father, Francorte Eldari Antoniou Caracala, the Prime Legislator of Carthage and the most influential man on the planet. His clothing was the most delicate of all, made of fragile layers of frothy silk held together with threads of gold to match his hairstyle. His long blond hair and beard plumed out like a lion's mane, chemically frozen in place, plated in thousands of little circles of gold that gleamed around him like a divine aura.

He had been prime legislator for twenty years, most of Audrey's life, with no retirement plans in sight. The old term limits had been lifted for him, and Audrey knew he hoped to pass the position to his son one day, her older brother Marcello.

The thought of her pompous, vapid brother ruling the known galaxy often made Audrey cringe in despair.

At the very center of the room, at the lowest point, stood Simon unit QCK001879, commonly called Simon Quick. Holographic glimpses of the latest battle on a rebellious world revolved slowly around him as he spoke. Images of Carthage's self-driven, autonomous tanks and drones destroying enemy bases flashed hypnotically, quietly backed by instrumental patriotic music. All eyes were on him.

"The majority of rebel leaders on planet Marymount

have been captured, lawfully tried by judicial androids, and executed," said the Simon. "Others have fled into the mountainous regions on the planet's northern continent, but we don't expect them to survive the eleven-month winter. After four to six weeks of cleanup, we can publicly announce that the rebellion has ended and the people of Marymount are once more safe from extremism and terror."

A smattering of applause floated among the three hundred or so people gathered for the monthly interstellar update.

The other interplanetary security interns on Audrey's row clapped too, and Audrey joined in, a bit reluctantly because she wasn't informed enough about the situation on Marymount to have a strong opinion. Still, she didn't want to appear unpatriotic. That wouldn't do—not for a security intern, certainly not for the daughter of Prime Legislator Caracala.

Audrey was twenty-four, currently in her fifth year of the seven-year Political Academy. Most Political Academy students were the offspring of top military and political officials or the wealthy commercial elite, and she was no exception.

Perhaps Audrey had been selected for this top security internship because of her academic accomplishments and other activities, or perhaps simply because of her name. That question plagued every development in her life. She wanted to get ahead on her own merits, but doors to opportunities were always flying open, and she was always being ushered through them, on to the next benchmark, the next obligatory checkpoint in the life mapped out for her, her own little *cursus honorum* to prepare her to wield power later in life.

Today, Audrey would be giving a presentation in front of this entire room, her father included. It was the first presentation of her internship, and she was so nervous she could have chewed off her own fingertips.

"In new business," Simon Quick said, and the bombed-out cathedrals of Marymount vanished, replaced by multiple images of a blue water-drop world orbiting an orange dwarf star. "We have initiated assimilation of Galapagos, a mostly aquatic world of minor agricultural and industrial note. It is within the logical path of our expansion. Moreover, they contracted for planetary defense with Ruckwold Industries—"

"Yes, what's happening with Ruckwold?" asked the prime legislator.

"Plans move apace, sir," Simon said. "That operation is highly compartmentalized."

"Their planet should be ours by now!" barked a fat space fleet admiral in a shiny gold uniform. "This delay is unacceptable!"

"You have my gravest apologies, sir," Simon Quick said, bowing his head as if chastened. "However, planet Ruckwold and its defense industry lies, as we are all aware, at the center of its own web of alliances. The Ruckwold bloc is in no position to truly rival ours, but moving against them with maximum efficiency requires calculation, positioning the proper assets, recruiting the proper influencers—"

"Why do we pay for all these ships and infantry if we can't use them?" one politician snapped. His hair was coifed out and sculpted into something like the legs of a giant starfish, glittering with a layer of aerosolized precious metals. "Take the planet! That's your job, Simon. That's what we built you to do."

"Yes, sir," said Simon Quick. "I can only say that if you

see little apparent progress, that is because our plans are moving deep beneath the surface. I can assure you that they *are* moving, and according to our target schedule, as well."

Audrey tensed as Simon gave quick details about a couple of less important worlds where Carthage was also reaching out. The time for Audrey's presentation loomed ever closer.

The assignment for interns to research worlds and choose targets for possible intervention had come from Simon Quick himself, her father's chief interplanetary strategy android. Audrey had done little else but work on it for the past week, neglecting classes and all other activities, including sleep.

The briefing raced by, and then it was time.

Simon Quick raised his head higher, looking at the outermost ring of seating, toward Audrey and the other interns.

"First," he said with a smile, "a consideration of Klamptura for possible friendly annexation."

Audrey let out what she hoped was an inaudible, invisible sigh of momentary relief. She wasn't going first. Klamptura had been the planet picked by Jasonius Falicorn, another Political Academy intern. His family owned a big piece of Carthage Consolidated and was politically involved all over the place, treating the expansion of Carthaginian power and influence as a kind of profitable hobby. Like their horse racing, backed by their equestrian genetic engineering labs.

Jasonius launched into a dull talk about the distant rocky planet and its surprisingly mineral-rich moon, supplemented with too few images and no video, an amateurish effort.

As her time drew closer, Audrey felt her nervous tension

begin to melt, replaced by the first hints of confidence. Her presentation wouldn't be great, but she would certainly be more engaging than Jasonius, who looked like he might fall asleep where he stood, bored by his own presentation, with unhelpful grainy stock images of lunar mines floating around his head.

Audrey had grown to truly care about her presentation topic—Veritum, a planet where the people desperately needed Carthage's strong, benevolent intervention. She'd changed from a student with a research assignment to a fierce advocate of immediate action.

As Jasonius gradually wound toward his vague conclusion that they should definitely maybe consider reaching out to Klamptura sooner or later, Audrey felt a rising swell of excitement, of real passion for standing up and explaining why they had to intervene in the situation on planet Veritum.

"Can we call this a day?" one of the high legislators called out. "We have a festival back home tomorrow, and I'll be on a parade float in a hot jester costume all morning."

"I'm expected at the opening crashball kickoff at our new stadium," said another legislator, dressed in bright crimson and a long curly wig.

"Hell, I have opera tickets," said a silver-haired army general with four dense rows of medals and ribbons across his chest. Audrey couldn't help wondering how so many generals had earned so many medals while autonomous warships, drones, and robotic tanks and infantry fought the wars for them. Even strategy and logistics had long been delegated to the Simon units.

"Let's just get on with the press conference," the secretary of commerce said, checking her skyscrapers of coiled blue hair in her mirror. They matched her frost-blue lips and icicle earrings.

Audrey's father rotated his automatic chair slowly, looked out among the crowd. He glanced up toward the interns, but at this distance, in a room dimmed for holograms, it was hard to see whether he was looking at Audrey or not.

Don't, she pleaded silently, moving her lips though she knew he wouldn't see it. *Don't cut it short. Let me speak.*

"We all have busy days ahead," Francorte Caracala said, his gilded beard glittering from tiny lights hidden among its curls. "We can trust the Simon units have these matters well in hand. That is their function, and they have always served us well. Does anyone object to closing this meeting now?"

No one spoke up. Francorte waved his hand, and all the classified holograms vanished. The lights came up, as though a play or movie had just ended. There was a ripple of movement as everyone stood to exit, the politicians to go pose for the media and give the expected optimistic statements, jostling with each other for the fickle public's attention.

Audrey watched in stunned disbelief as everyone filtered out—the officers back to their offices, the interns back home to finally relax during the weekend ahead after days and nights of researching and creating presentations that had gone unheard and unseen.

Only Simon Quick remained in the room. The android was still as a statue on the central dais, his current task completed. He would take no part in the media coverage; there was no need to include a mere machine in the press conference.

Soon, no doubt, some wireless signal or other would reach

Simon, and he would animate and get moving. He was a busy android, working night and day to manage Carthage's complex web of alliances and anticipate the movements of enemies. Even as he stood still, seeming to do nothing, his brilliant crystalline CPU was processing at high speed and he was no doubt wirelessly interacting with unseen individuals and networks.

At the moment, Simon could have been a retail mannequin, modeling the latest in low-key men's fashion: expensive soft suits and slippers in colors bright enough to fit in with the high-budget crowd but muted enough that he didn't outshine any of the politicians.

As the room emptied out, Audrey went against the flow of foot traffic, the only person riding a downward-flowing escalator while everyone else crowded onto the upward-flowing ones, rising away toward the exits.

Audrey approached Simon Quick at a slow pace, waiting until she was alone in the room with him before she spoke.

"Did he do that on purpose?" Audrey asked.

"I'm sorry?" Simon Quick smiled kindly. "Will you join me for tea?"

"Why not?" she said. "I don't have anything else happening this afternoon, apparently."

"It is the weekend," he said. "You should relax and enjoy yourself. Starting with this sublime new matcha someone was kind enough to send me. This particular crop's DNA was only just perfected with the current harvest, the culmination of seven years of intensive agricultural research..."

Simon led her from the Panopticon, and all the lights in the vast room switched off as they left, the hum of the escalators falling silent.

Simon's office was spacious, with a high ceiling and digital-glass walls currently set to take in the immense iridescent city outside. They were on the two hundredth floor of the Governance Building, housing global bureaucracies and the World Legislature that oversaw them.

Audrey waited quietly, looking out over the city while Simon prepared tea. Carthage City resembled a vast garden, the colorful glass towers like high stalks outlined with rosettes and petals of walkways, arbors, and suspended trolleys. Constructor bots worked among the towers, removing old architecture as it went out of fashion and replacing it with new; the city was ever changing, with ever taller and more exotic skyscraper designs unveiled every spring.

Stacks of black magnetic-field roads curved gently through the city, some more than a kilometer above the ground. Bubble-shaped vehicles of all colors and sizes streaked along the magnetic roadways like blood cells traversing the city's arteries, tens of thousands of them traveling only centimeters apart. Hover-drones in colorful protective spheres flowed in dense streams through the city, delivering groceries and other light items to people's homes.

Simon remained silent as he dipped out green tea powder with a bamboo spoon and whisked it with hot water, mindful as a monk.

"There you are, Miss Caracala," he said at last, serving her a handheld tea bowl accompanied by a small rice candy. "Not many people know this, but the basic Simon design was originally spun off from an early-model household service bot. A cordial fellow marketed under the 'Butler Jeffrey' brand."

"Oh, my great-grandfather had a Butler Jeffrey." Audrey smiled at her memory of the early-model house staffer, barely functional by the time she saw it attempting to dust. It had only managed to circle the duster high above the tabletop, accomplishing nothing, its mouth opening and closing silently like a fish's. "I think they recycled it when he died though. You know, now that you say it, I can kind of see the resemblance between that old butler-bot and you Simons. Only he had a big mustache and did a lot of bowing. I'm not sure I've ever seen you bow."

"That may have been one of the last known models," Simon said. "It was discontinued some decades ago, sadly. One of the quality assurance tests for the Butler Jeffrey model was the correct performance of Japanese tea ceremony. Others included playing a violin concerto and sewing up a major human artery. That latter in simulation, of course. Some of those QA protocols remain for the Simon line. So when I prepare tea for you, I am sharing my heritage, you see. And it is my honor to do so, especially with such a brilliant and promising human being. Your presence enriches me."

"Is that right?" Audrey couldn't help smiling at the machine's flattery. She sipped the tea. "This usucha enriches me. Nice work."

"Thank you. As was your presentation. I reviewed the version you uploaded to me."

"Did he know I was going to speak?" Audrey asked.

"Your father? I'm sure he knew that I'd requested brief presentations regarding worlds of possible interest. Whether your father and the other high legislators can be exhorted into sitting and listening is another matter. My role was to anticipate all possible areas of discussion. And, of course, to ensure that our interns are earning their pay." He gave another small, disarming smile. Simon units were designed to look humble, like the common man, almost to blend into the wallpaper, so different from Audrey's gorgeous blond personal-assistant bot Nin, or the beefy, muscle-model androids that followed Audrey around as part of a protection contract with her family. "Do you feel hurt by your father's actions?" Simon asked.

"Please. I've had a lifetime to get used to that. I'm clearly his fourth favorite child out of five, and that's only because Salvius is such a perpetual delinquent. At least I'm too invisible to be a political embarrassment. It's not about my feelings. I really wanted to speak to the legislators about Veritum. The way the women and children are treated there."

"It was founded as a religious separatist colony, deliberately distant from all other humans," Simon said. "They are bound to have anomalous beliefs and practices."

"It's abusive," she said. "Horrific. The things they do—"

"I am aware, sadly. As I said, I viewed your report."

"So you see what I mean. What's the point of having all this power, these fleets and armies of metal, if we can't intervene and stop obvious evil?" Audrey asked. "It's our responsibility. Right?"

"Your passion and concern are admirable," Simon said. "This is why I believe you will be a great leader of your people one day."

Audrey laughed. "Yeah, now I *know* you're getting obsolete."

"Do you think so?" He seemed serious, regarding her over his small porcelain tea bowl, hand painted with satsuma trees, their orange fruit full and ripe. She knew the tea set was antique, made on Earth more than a thousand years earlier.

"Of course you aren't obsolete, Simon," Audrey said. "Compared to what? Those androids from Ruckwold? All they can do is flip pizzas. And run law firms. But you're still the most advanced unit out there. Right?"

"I did not mean to grow so self-centered in our conversation," he said. "Let's hear more of your concerns. Or recent triumphs, as the case may be."

Audrey hesitated. She didn't want to ask, felt stupid asking. But Simon Quick had always been there for her, an advisor and mentor in her father's place.

Audrey's older sister, Briellana, had taken a degree in nonprofit administration and was dating an ambitious young executive from a powerful family. She was on their mother's path, to be an attractive political wife, a supplemental ornament to her husband's career.

Audrey had different plans.

"... politicians are a bit will-o'-the-wisp," Simon was saying. "They must keep moving, stay colorful, like preening birds in need of constant attention. It is simply the political reality of the day, and it is a challenge for tough, wise men like your father to manage the public's expectations while also focusing on serious policy."

"Will you bring Veritum to his attention?" Audrey asked. "All the cult's abuses?"

"You have my word," Simon said. "Now, I meant what I said earlier. Enjoy your weekend. Spend time with friends. These social alliances you form while young will be useful later."

"I'll be sure to remember that while I'm watching guys do keg stands. Thank you for talking to my father about Veritum. And for the tea."

After their conversation, Audrey emerged from Simon's office feeling better than she had all week. The old android had a way of helping her see things more clearly.

Audrey's personal assistant, Nin, fell into step beside her. A lantern-jawed, pectoral-heavy Security Steve in a dark suit trailed behind them, watching for any potential threats to Audrey.

"Did you have a pleasant meeting?" Nin asked, sunny and cheerful as ever. She'd originally been Audrey's nanny, and Audrey had her upgraded as she went through life rather than replacing her with newer android models. Nin had been, at different times, her nanny, teacher, swimming coach, and now personal secretary. It was just a matter of buying expansion packs.

"The meeting was fine," Audrey said.

"Are you ready for messages?"

"Nothing too private." Audrey eyed the officials passing back and forth in the wide hallway around her, each talking quietly to their own personal-assistant androids, mostly avoiding eye contact with other humans.

"Jennilaura reminds you to bring drinks and fruit for the tower party. Your floor's assigned color is orange, so everything's meant to be that color."

"Okay. Just have the grocery center deliver some stuff. I'd rather be sleeping than hosting this party."

"Would you like to order mood enhancers too?"

"Very funny. Jas probably stocked up on those already." Audrey looked down at her formal pastel purple suit. "Order me a new dress for tonight. Something that's dark and tasteful but makes me look reasonably attractive for once. Just make it fit well so nothing, you know, sticks out. Something easy to walk in. With pockets."

They rode an elevator down twenty stories to the nearest roadway level. The crowded corridor there was carpeted in millions of tiny flowers of soft velvet. Fix-bots shaped like golden crabs moved unobtrusively on the carpet, fussily cleaning and restitching the rich, delicate flooring from the constant wear and tear.

Offices lay one way, cafés and restaurants the other. Straight ahead was the indoor loading area where Audrey's car was just now arriving along one of the magnetic car strips. Her car was a dark purple lozenge-shaped piece of roadcraft. Its doors spread open like curtains to welcome her inside.

Audrey climbed into her car. Nin joined her inside the passenger compartment, while the lantern-jawed Security Steve climbed into the car's trunk, per Audrey's user preferences.

The door and trunk sealed, and the car glided away from the curb, shooting outside the building to join the crowded black magnetic highway.

Audrey's car was her favorite place in the world, and had been since she'd received her first one at age six. It had been there to whisk her safely off to school and, for a while, to her ill-fated ballet lessons, accompanied always by Nin.

The seating was soft, reclined, and padded, precisely adjusted to her maximum comfort. She could lie back in the dimly tinted space and summon any video or audio content she wanted. It was the place in her life where she had the most control.

She could also make the front of the car's shell clear and look out at the traffic around her, if for some reason she ever wanted to do that.

She had the car play some gentle chamber music and accompany it with calm nature scenery, hoping this would help her relax from the stresses of the day. Sometimes she listened to an audio book or watched the news, but at the moment she just wanted to turn off her brain.

"Your sister's in town," Nin said, having saved this message for the more private setting of the car. "She invited you shopping with her and your mother."

"Which she knows I hate. Decline for schedule conflicts and send apologies. That's what everyone expects, anyway."

"It's handled."

"Maybe I can do an article for the student newsnet about Veritum. I'd hate for my research to go completely to waste. People need to know about it."

"I will make inquiries," Nin said.

They zipped down a nearly vertical drop ramp to join the larger, wider, faster highways below. It would take several minutes to cross the city to The 360, a chunky, colorful, trendy student high-rise where Audrey now lived. Located in the wild borough of University Town, it had been a welcome change from her family's assorted homes where her prying mother monitored everything constantly, even remotely, and often reviewed footage to see what her children had done during the day. Her mother still lived in fear that another one of them would go rotten, would turn out like Salvius.

Life in the student tower wasn't exactly private, though—in fact, the latest architectural fad was decidedly anti-privacy, pro-exhibition. For true privacy, there was only her car.

Audrey kicked off her soft, silky shoes, stretched out her toes, and sighed.

The music and video stopped abruptly, and the lights went out. The windowed portion of the shell tinted solid black so she couldn't see outside, and no one could see in.

"Hello?" Audrey shouted into the pitch blackness. "Uh,

car? It's me, your owner." Usually Nin handled all interface with the car's AI.

"The car is unresponsive," Nin said, close by. At least she hadn't shut down.

"I noticed. And we're picking up speed, so—"

A cacophony of feedback pealed from all her speakers, echoing inside the cocoon-like car, threatening to deafen her. Audrey threw her hands over her ears. "Nin! Make it stop!"

"I am attempting! I am attempting! The car remains unresponsive to inquiries."

The car traveled faster, and Audrey was slung to one side as it turned abruptly down some branch or other of the road system.

A face appeared, as large as her holographic projector could make it, filling the front half of her car. It was gaunt, pale, with black paint around its eyes and mouth, a spade on one cheek and a club on the other. It wore a black-and-white jester's hat. It had to be the world's ugliest, least happy clown. When it spoke, a number of its teeth turned out to be black too. The image was all stark white and black, no colors, no shades of gray.

"Greetings, child of privilege," it began.

"Oh, my God," Audrey said. She didn't know what this was, but an evil clown taking over her car couldn't be the start of anything good. "Nin?"

"The car is unresponsive."

"We have watched you all your life," the ugly clown said. "Watched you play while the galaxy burns. Watched you turn inward, thinking only of yourselves and your decadent existence, forgetting the true cost, caring nothing about the horrors you inflict."

Audrey crawled to the front of the car, shuddering as she passed through the giant projection of the clown's face.

The control console at the front was sealed tight. The car was meant to be operated only by voice command and its own AI. There were no manual controls. She tried to pry open the panel, but she didn't have the right tools to do it. Only a roadcraft tech would have those.

"... now *you* will watch, my captive audience, as I show you the suffering created by your regime," the clown continued.

Scenes played all around her, three-dimensional video clips, each labeled with the name of a different planet. Most showed glimpses of battles in progress, the autonomous tanks and robotic infantry of Carthage fighting local warlords and dangerous rebels.

"... the death you deal is unmatched in human history. Your destruction of Earth alone killed nearly a billion... "

Audrey pounded her fist against the console. "Okay, enough of this hacker bullshit!" she shouted. "Is there going to be a bomb in here or what?"

"...and behold, the ruins you leave behind, the wasted lives... " More videos showed, of cities after war, dead bodies of soldiers and civilians, the collateral damage.

"Great, I'm being hijacked by a recording. Nin, get down here and smash open this console!" Audrey shouted.

"I cannot damage your property," Nin replied. "Especially in a way that could endanger your life. I am not a certified roadcraft android."

"You don't need a certification to break things. Just tear it open."

"I cannot damage or endanger," Nin said. "Not without an emergency override password."

"Okay, so you're in charge of remembering my passwords."

"Not that one."

"Nin, we're going to die here! What's the emergency password?"

"I cannot tell you."

"Ugh!" She slammed her fist on the console again. The black-and-white harlequin flickered.

"... but there are changes coming. Your pillars of power are built on shifting sands. Your machines cannot make up for your weaknesses forever. Your very decadence will consume you... "

"Okay, so how old was I when I created the emergency password?" Audrey asked.

"Seven."

"Seven. Great." She thought it over. "Um... chicken butt?"

"Emergency override accepted."

"Smash this thing open and rip out its guts!"

Nin moved forward. Her robotic arms, which had always been so soft and gentle with Audrey, had no trouble tearing open the console. She ripped out everything inside, circuitry and hardware, hologram projector and the car's CPU. It was odd to see the smiling blond android who had sung her to sleep as a child turn into an efficient destruction machine, a momentary reminder that Nin's personality was only an illusion, nothing but software.

The angry clown and his supplemental videos vanished. Like Audrey, he'd be getting no audience for his carefully prepared presentation today. She almost felt a half moment of sympathy for him.

Then the car slammed into something, and the world seemed to wobble and shake. A long scraping sound shrieked from below the car. Then there was a sudden odd lack of any movement at all.

"Are we stopped?" Audrey asked. "Are we just sitting in the middle of the highway?"

She found the manual control for the shell dimmer. She normally kept the forward windscreen dark, like everyone did, to see her videos more clearly. Now she made it transparent.

The car hadn't stopped. They were still moving at high speed, but they'd left the road entirely. The terrorist's sabotage had sent them crashing over the safety wall.

They flew, hundreds of meters in the air, supported by nothing, past the brightly hued towers, roads, and bridges of Carthage City.

"Sending emergency signal," Nin said. She slammed the striped red button built into the side of the car, the button Audrey had never seen anyone press outside of an action movie.

The car finally ran out of momentum and began to fall, end over end like a flipped coin, dropping toward blocks of apartment buildings below.

Audrey gripped the soft cushioning that lined her car and tried not to scream.

Chapter Four

Galapagos

"I want you and the boys on the next shuttle out of here. It leaves in seventy minutes," Ellison said when he returned to their hotel suite. The top three floors of Galapagos's small spaceport were a residential area, with hotel rooms to rent and apartments for spaceport employees. The spaceport had provided him with its best suite, which was still just two small bedrooms connected by a private bathroom. The bathroom had an actual tub, a luxury item in the cramped port, which his wife had been pleased to see.

"What's the rush?" Cadia asked. She was stretching one long freckled leg, her heel propped up on the headboard. She was dressed in her soft, skimpy exercise clothes, which he found extremely distracting.

"This visit from Carthage is even less friendly than we thought. I can't get into details, but the things he said... the things he dared to say. We're nothing to them, Cadia. I met one of the machines they have running their empire, these Simon units. It has no soul."

"Of course not. Why would it?" She switched up her pose, and Ellison had to turn and walk away before he got really distracted.

"I'll tell the boys to pack up." He stepped into the bathroom, paused to splash water on his face, and regretted it—the chemically thick spaceport water wasn't remotely refreshing. He would have preferred a nice splash of damp, salty air off the ocean back home.

In the next room, his boys sat on their bunks. Djalu, the fifteen-year-old, waved his hands in the air, muttering incoherently, gaming gear strapped to his head and hands. Glowing holograms surrounding his head. Sound effects leaked out of the plugs in his ears.

Jiemba, the eight-year-old, sat and talked with his worn pink KidPal rabbit, which stood a meter high. It could walk, talk, gesture with its paws and ears, and make a number of facial expressions.

"... so the pyramids were actually spooooooooky graves!" the KidPal rabbit said, waving his paws around. "Where they buried mummmmmmies!"

"I'm sure he knows that by now," Ellison said to the rabbit.

The rabbit turned its head toward him, frayed pink fur dangling off its face like loose cotton candy. It had originally been Djalu's highly rated educational toy when he was a toddler, and then it had been passed down to Jiemba. It was more than a decade old now. Almost ready for the scrap heap. Past due for it, in Ellison's opinion.

"Greetings, parent!" the rabbit said. "We are discussing ancient history in line with Jiemba's school lessons. You are welcome to review the syllabus per his instructor—"

"Yeah, don't worry about it, rabbit," Ellison said. He looked at his older son. "What about you, Djalu? Is that homework?" When the teenager didn't respond, he waved a hand through the holograms around his head, interfering with and distorting them.

"Stop it, rat-brain!" Djalu snapped, waving a hand blindly at him. Ellison caught the hand and squeezed.

"What did you just say?" Ellison asked.

"Oh sh... " Djalu flipped off his gaming with his free hand and looked at him sheepishly. "I thought you were Jiemba."

"You thought I was your little brother, so you called me 'rat-brain' and tried to hit me?" Ellison said. "You're on gaming suspension. Forty-eight hours."

"What? But Dad, they just released the new Ruckwold Ghost fighter sim—"

"I didn't realize. Make it seventy-two hours." Ellison held out his hand, and his son reluctantly peeled away the gaming gloves and headgear and handed them over. "You should be studying. You won't get into the Ruckwold Space Academy unless you get those math scores up."

"Can I go to space academy too?" Jiemba asked.

"If you do your math and science homework and eat your vegetables," Ellison said.

"Let's do math!" Jiemba said to his pink rabbit.

"Whatever you want, pal," the KidPal bunny said. "You're my best friend. Give me a high paw."

Jiemba laughed and slapped the bunny's extended paw.

"No time for that," Ellison said. "Pack up your stuff. Everything. You guys and Mom are on the next shuttle home."

"Yes!" Djalu jumped up and started packing; the teenager hadn't been particularly excited about coming in the first place. His first trip to outer space was just another boring weekend with his parents, away from his girlfriend.

"But it's only my first time in space! I barely saw any of it!" Jiemba said.

"My goodness," the KidPal bunny said. "Is something wrong, parent? What's the problem?" The bunny stared at Ellison, its big friendly eyes open wide, with a frightened tilt to its eyelids. Ellison felt acutely aware of the black video lenses of the bunny's pupils watching him. Recording him. Maybe sending the signal somewhere.

You worry that the older one is spoiled and unfocused, and the younger one dyslexic, Simon had said.

"Hey, Rabbit," Ellison said. "Where were you manufactured?"

"FunzinoCo Manufacturing Complex 2," the robot said. "A high-orbit industrial park."

"Orbiting what?"

"Carthage, of course. FunzinoCo is now a happy subsidiary of Carthage Consolidated. We're all just one big consolidated family."

"You're a Carthaginian robot?" Ellison asked.

"Yes, sir!" The rabbit-bot gave a mocking salute with one paw. "Proudly designed and built by the finest, funnest, funniest company in the finest, funnest, funniest factory—"

"You're out of here." Ellison seized the fuzzy robobunny by its ears and lifted it up.

"Please, sir!" The robot kicked its foot-paws in midair. "You're damaging my sensors—"

"Dad, put him down!" Jiemba said.

Ellison looked at the kicking, eye-rolling rabbit that had served as a toy, friend, and teacher to both his kids. He barely remembered buying the thing, twelve or thirteen years ago, when the older boy had been a toddler. It might have been a gift from the boy's grandparents.

"Do you send updates to Carthage?" Ellison asked the rabbit.

"I don't understand the question. Please stop holding my ears—"

"Can computers from Carthage access you?" he snapped at the toy.

"Well, if you let me put on my Astro-Rabbit hat, I can explain that Carthage is more than two *thousand* light-years from here, so it would take a radio signal that many years just to reach—"

"When software updates come in," Ellison said. "When starships come and go. Do you get updates from Carthage Consolidated? And do you send them backups? Do you send them all your memories?"

"I... well, yes, but of course I *only* communicate with verified software agents of my manufacturer, Carthage Consolidated, as specified in subparagraph 4183(c) of your user agreement—"

"That's all I need to know." Ellison opened the hotel room door and threw the rabbit out into the corridor. Then he grabbed a floor lamp with a narrow metal rod of a body and walked out after it.

"Dad! What are you doing?" Jiemba cried, following after him.

"What *are* you doing, parent?" the rabbit asked, rubbing its head and blinking rapidly as if puzzled.

"They can watch us through their machines." Ellison said. Then he swung the metal rod of the lamp into the rabbit's head, bashing in its face and shattering one eye.

"Dad, no! Don't hurt him!" Jiemba shrieked, horrified. He tried to run forward, but was stopped by his older brother, Djalu. Both boys watched in disbelief as Ellison struck the robot bunny a second time, then a third.

With another blow, Ellison broke off one of the fuzzy pink arms in a shower of sparks, leaving it hanging by a wire. He switched it up and hit the rabbit's head from the other side. It spun all the way around, and the pink fur layer came loose, sticking to the tip of his lamp.

Ellison shook off the loose fur and drew the rod back again. Without the fur, the rabbit's face was gruesome, a plastic skull with buck teeth and a wiggling pink tongue, with speakers for ears and rolling camera balls for eyes.

He struck it again and again, cracking the other eye, shattering the teeth. For a moment, the robot stood for the ambassador Simon and for all the evil machines of Carthage, their self-guiding fleets, their hordes of rolling armor and infantry. It was all the danger that Carthage represented, or at least the only part at which Ellison could effectively strike.

He smashed the rabbit until it lay in crackling, sparking, smoldering pieces on the floor, a couple of the pink paws still twitching.

"I don't understand the question," its remaining speaker said slowly, its normally chipper voice distorted and low. "I don't understand—"

Ellison smashed the cubic black CPU, and the rabbit's remains finally went quiet.

He took a deep breath, watching the pieces for any sign of further movement.

Behind him, his sons stared at him, the older Djalu in plain shock, the young Jiemba trembling and crying. They had both grown far too attached to the damned machine.

"They can watch us," Ellison said, trying again to

explain. "The Carthaginians. They could know everything about our family because of that stupid rabbit—"

Then a deafening roar rocked the corridor, likely the entire spaceport. The floor shifted, throwing Ellison against the bare aluminum wall and knocking down his sons.

The partially open door to the boys' hotel room slammed shut as though a giant hand had slapped it. By the time Ellison recovered his balance, he couldn't see anything at all through the smoke filling the hallway.

"Djalu! Jiemba!" he shouted. "Cadia!"

He moved toward where his sons had fallen. He heard one of them coughing, Djalu, the teenager. He was sitting up.

Ellison felt along the floor until he found the small fingers of his younger son. They weren't moving, and didn't respond to his touch. "Jiemba!" he said, his voice hoarse as he coughed on the smoke.

He ran his hands over the boy's face and neck. "No, no," whispered. "No, no, no... "

Amid the fire and smoke, the screams, and the echoing vibrations of the explosions, Ellison found he could detect a faint pulse. He let out a sigh of relief. Both his sons were alive.

"Watch your brother," Ellison said to Djalu.

He ran to the door to his own hotel room. "Cadia!"

It was locked, as the doors automatically did when they closed, but the door's AI should have recognized him as one of the room guests.

The door handle was scalding hot to the touch. Ellison tried kicking the door in, but it wouldn't budge.

He ran back to the boys' hotel room and managed to open that door with less trouble.

When he stepped into their room, he was taken aback.

The furniture was destroyed, the carpet burned to ash, the ceiling seared black.

His sons would have been killed if they hadn't been out in the hall, watching him beat the hell out of their favorite childhood companion.

The bathroom was a mess, the mirror shattered, though it had all stuck together as gummy safety glass. He held his breath as he ran through the thick smoke.

For a moment, he was twenty-one again, arriving home on leave to find Kawau Island bombed, the village burned. His father and half the people on the island had been interred at the graveyard; the Iron Hammers had destroyed the community where he'd grown up, bombarding and then raiding it.

His stomach tightened up as he crossed through the shattered bathroom into the bedroom where he'd spent the previous night with his wife.

Their hotel room was as wrecked as the previous one, everything charred.

Just like the island where he'd grown up, his childhood home, church, and schoolhouse burned to ash.

He shook his head, trying not to let the past overwhelm the present.

"Cadia," he coughed. It was impossible to see. The room was dark and full of smoke. The bomb had blown in the back wall of the room; it had been planted within or beyond that wall.

He found the door to the hallway and shoved it open, letting out smoke out and letting in some reddish light. The main lights had been blown out or lost power, but dim red emergency strips glowed along the hallway ceiling.

In the red light, he saw the room's furniture was shattered and charred at the edges. The bed where Cadia had been doing her exercises was reduced to burning planks and smoldering blankets.

"Cadia!" he shouted, moving burning debris aside with his bare hands, heedless of the pain, desperate to find his wife.

Sirens wailed all through the spaceport. There was shouting, screaming, and the clomping of boots as Coalition guards approached to restore order.

Ellison ignored all of it, focusing on the search for his wife. Soon the demands of duty would overtake him, and he would have to seize control of the situation and figure out what the hell was happening. For the moment, though, all he could think of was her.

He heaved aside the burning, toppled headboard, but she wasn't underneath that, either. Had she left the room while he was beating the fluff off that mechanical rabbit? It had taken a while to bash the chatty, creepy thing to bits.

Then he remembered: he'd told her to pack up and leave on the next shuttle. She'd been exercising, so before walking out in public, she'd want a quick—

Ellison ran back into the bathroom. The beige hotel shower curtain covered the small tub. Water was all over the floor.

He grabbed the shower curtain and pulled it off.

His wife lay on her side, unmoving, in a shallow, soapy puddle in the hard plastic tub. Most of the water had run out through a crack in the tub's ruptured side.

"Cadia?" He touched her cheek, her shoulder, and checked her pulse.

Alive. But her pulse was weak.

"Dad?" Djalu entered the room, leading his Jiemba by the hand. The younger boy was dazed, barely keeping his balance, reminding Ellison of when he had been a toddler.

"Get a medic." Ellison moved the shower curtain to cover his wife like a damp plastic blanket. "Leave your brother here and go find one. Ask the soldiers that are coming. Now."

"Yes, sir," Djalu said, turning and hurrying out. His little brother stood in the doorway to the small bathroom, blinking and confused.

"Jiemba?" Ellison said. "Can you hear me? Nod if you can hear me."

After a moment, Jiemba nodded. Ellison turned back to his wife, touching her gently.

"Cadia?" he said, though it seemed unlikely she would hear him over the emergency sirens and the screaming voices in the corridor. He took her hand, but she didn't stir.

"Yes, sir, right over here. Jiemba, move over." Djalu returned to the bathroom, took his younger brother by the shoulder, and steered him into their destroyed, smoldering hotel room.

"Djalu, I told you to find a doc—" Ellison began.

"Hello." The voice was the only tranquil one Ellison had heard since the explosion, the only voice not screaming or hoarse from smoke or numbed by shock.

Simon Zorn stood in the doorway, accompanied by one of his robotic infantry, both of them coated in dust. The crystal-blue faceplate had been raised, perhaps because of the dust, revealing the reaper's steel face, which strongly suggested a skull. Its black lens eyes seemed to stare at Ellison, making him shiver.

"Your son says you need a medic." Simon advanced into the bathroom. "I can carry out emergency treatment, as well as many forms of surgery."

"Really?" Ellison said. "They stuck that in there too, huh? Along with the ability to flatter and threaten?" He knew it was unwise to challenge the robot, but he couldn't help himself.

"It is part of the standard package for a Class A service android," Simon said. "I can do nothing without your consent, of course. I am sure there are other humans who could use assistance, if you prefer me to leave."

Ellison looked at Cadia, thinking how soft her breathing was, how weak her heartbeat.

"Go ahead," he finally said, moving back against the leaking sink and cracked mirror. "Check her for injuries."

Simon knelt by the tub, the dust on his suit melting into a thin gray mud where it touched the wet floor.

Ellison looked over at Simon's nameless robot infantry companion. The machine held a first aid kit and emergency oxygen bottle, likely raided from the emergency cabinet down the corridor.

"Palpating," Simon said, his fingers sliding under the shower curtain to explore Cadia's chest and abdomen.

Ellison tensed, but managed to resist the urge to shout at the Simon unit to get away from his wife. He didn't trust the machine, but he wanted to do all he could for Cadia.

While Simon probed her, voices shouted in the hall. They were shouting Ellison's name, maybe just checking his condition, but soon they'd be looking to him for leadership. Well, he'd asked for it, though he hadn't quite expected this.

"Your public awaits," Simon said, reaching deeper under the shower curtain to check Cadia's hips and legs. The last thing Ellison wanted was to leave his wife alone and vulnerable with the Simon and its infantry bots. On the other hand, it was his responsibility to deal with the larger emergency on behalf of all the citizens on the spaceport and to restore order.

"I detect no major breakages, but there could be smaller

fractures beneath my ability to sense," Simon Zorn said. He accepted the emergency oxygen bottle from the robotic soldier, which stepped forward to deliver it even though Simon had made no word or gesture about it. Wireless communication gave the machines a silent telepathic link that was eerie for Ellison to watch. "She should be scanned in the spaceport's medical center."

"I'd bet the medical center's about to get slammed with business," Ellison said. He watched Simon strap the mask in place to give Cadia oxygen. "When you're finished here, I hope you'll help all the other injured." *And get the hell away from my family.*

"Of course," Simon said.

"Djalu," Ellison said to his older son. "Stay here with your mother and brother."

Djalu nodded as Ellison ran toward the door to the corridor and the gathering crowd outside.

"Daddy!" gasped Jiemba, who'd barely made a sound since the explosion. His older brother was supporting him where he stood, and he coughed. "Where are you going?"

"I have to go to work," he said. "I have to make sure everyone's safe."

"Please don't leave us again," Jiemba said. "Okay?"

Ellison stood there at the door, torn. He did not want to leave his sons like this, and he certainly didn't want to leave his wife in the care of the Simon unit, even if it did know what it was doing.

But he'd never turned down his larger responsibilities before. There was nobody else to play the role he now had to play.

Reluctantly, he turned his back on his sons and stepped out into the corridor.

"Daddy! Don't go! Please, Daddy!" Jiemba shouted, until Ellison closed the door and didn't hear him again.

He'll be fine, Ellison told himself. *They'll all be fine*.

Outside, Ellison stepped into the crowd of Galapagos guards in ocean-blue body armor and helmets. Dazed officials had wandered out from their rooms, including Minister of State Navra Coraline, her loose teal robe revealing that her octopus tattoo's tentacles extended far down her side. Coraline looked dazed but unharmed.

Ellison needed a damage and casualty report, and at the same time, he needed to know who or what had caused the explosion and whether there was a threat of more.

He took a deep breath, looked out at his people, and got to work.

Chapter Five

Earth

Colt hurried up and around the concrete stairs, grimacing at the echoing sound of his footsteps. There were at least three more floors to this medical building, it looked like, before the stairwell ended in a rubble-strewn opening to the sky above. Perhaps Carthage had bombed the building into ruin, or maybe there had been a later fight here between survivors and reapers.

He pushed open the door to the second floor, where he'd last seen the girl who'd somehow hacked a reaper and saved his life.

"Hello?" he called out, running down a winding hallway. He found the room with the hole in the floor. The room also had a hospital bed, which had been thrown aside against the wall.

The girl wasn't there anymore, though.

"Hey, it's me!" he called out, continuing down the hallway. "From downstairs. Just wanted to say hi, see if maybe you want to go somewhere and lie low, avoid death for a while—"

"Shh!" She stepped out of a dark doorway ahead, glaring at him. "What is your problem? I told you to go home. Go home, boy!" She pointed back at the stairs. "We can't stay here."

"You have a way out?" Colt asked.

She glared at him another moment, then returned to the room from which she'd emerged.

He followed her into a shattered office, where she climbed onto the ledge of a large window.

"This is your plan?" he asked.

"Can't you keep quiet? How have you survived this long?" she asked, though they'd both been speaking in whispers. Any amount of talking sounded too loud, though. Especially when the metalheads were expected to arrive at any moment, drawn by the earlier gunfire.

Colt followed her out the window and onto a wobbly elevated train track, which had once been elevated much higher. It was on broken supports now. Not the safest pick for an escape, but it had the virtue of heading straight into a rubble tower of a skyscraper that had been blasted in half long ago. They could take some cover there, hide in the shadows.

He stayed close behind her, watching his step on the broken tracks, and soon they were in the gloom of the old skyscraper. It was so damaged they had to squeeze through crevices and narrow passes in the broken concrete and twisted steel supports just to get into the building, but that meant it would be harder for machines to follow. The metalheads ruled the upper world with their drones and tanks, but scavengers learned to survive down in the deep rubble where the old city had extended itself kilometers under the earth.

Through a shattered window, they saw the metalheads arrive. A tank rolled up first, essentially just a platform of rotating weapons and sensors mounted on treads, and searched the area immediately around the clinic, the red lights of its scanners sweeping the ruins. The tank was battle scarred but looked fully operational.

A reaper wagon arrived next. This was a cheaply built self-driving truck made of local scrap with eight reapers hanging two by two along a rack in the back, bony and limp as rotten sides of beef.

The truck parked, and the skeletal robots sprang to life. They dropped off the truck and marched into the clinic.

"That's right, little bugs," the girl whispered, and she raised the black sphere with the constellations of colored symbols spinning around the surface. "Go sniff the bait."

"What are you doing?" Colt asked.

"I left the reapers something that'll blow their minds. Literally. You should cover your ears."

"No!" He grabbed her hand. "You can't destroy that clinic."

"And you can't touch me!" She slapped his hand away. "I'm a human, not a serv-bot."

"A... what? If I thought you were a metalhead, I'd cave in your face right now." He tensed, making a fist. "Are you a metalhead?"

"Me? You're the one trying to save the reapers."

"No, I'd love to blast those things to pieces. But they might leave the old medical supplies alone. I know you're not from around here, but nothing new gets made anymore. Except really, really bad moonshine. Somebody's going to need those meds someday, and there won't be any new supplies coming in. Probably ever."

She stared at him for a long moment. "What do you mean, I'm not from around here?"

"Obviously," he whispered. "Your voice is... weird. And you move differently from the scavengers around here. And your face is kind of... soft."

"Are you calling me soft?" She looked serious, but Colt thought he saw the hint of a smile there.

"I might as well, since I don't know your name."

"You can call me... Mohini."

"I'm Colt," he said.

"What? Like a horse?" Now she really did smile.

"So what's a Mohini?"

"We'd better get moving," she said. "And we'll let all those reapers live to kill us another day, in order to protect all those medical supplies. As you requested."

"Thanks," he said. "That stuff could save somebody's life. Maybe lots of lives. We have to protect the living."

They moved deeper into the rubble, walking carefully over broken floors and avalanche-ready heaps of broken concrete.

Colt felt something like sharp fingers poke into his ankle. He looked down to see a skeletal arm jutting out of the rubble, and he felt an instant panic, thinking a reaper was grabbing him.

But it was just the remains of a long-dead human, mostly buried. Colt drew his foot back, stepped over it, and kept moving.

He kept his eyes on the mysterious girl ahead, her dark hair swaying across her shoulders with each step. She was on the short side, even for a scavenger. He thought her age was close to his own, but she was definitely from somewhere else. Even the way she walked was more upright, less low and skulky than a typical scavenger.

They spoke little as they moved. She didn't speak the same detailed language of gestures and touches—in fact, touching her seemed to bother her, though it was critical for silent communication in the dark. They got by with lots of pointing, nodding, and head-shaking.

When they reached a stairwell, though, they got into a pointing argument.

Colt pointed down the stairs and nodded. Mohini shook her head and pointed ahead, through the rubble. He shook his head and pointed emphatically down the stairs again. She shook her head, bared her teeth, and pointed ahead through the rubble again.

"I've mapped it out," she finally whispered. "We can go through the ruins this way, one building after the next, and we'll be mostly covered."

"Mostly," he whispered back. "Down is always safer."

"What if we get trapped in the basement and have to double back?"

"Everything connects underneath. It might be pedestrian tunnels and apartment blocks, or an underground roadway, or even just a sewer pipe, but there will always be a way. Trust me. I'm the one who lives here. And you're from... where are you from?"

"Shh. All right. We'll go your way. But if we die down there, I'm going to kill you."

Colt started down the stairs. She stayed close and pulled out an unbelievably advanced-looking pistol, its green-and-black surface blazing with "danger" symbols and injury warnings. Tiny indicator lights glowed on the butt of the pistol.

"Is that a plasma weapon?" he whispered. "Where the hell—"

"Just a lucky find," she said.

"Ultra-lucky. And you have cells for it?"

"Just a few."

"I don't suppose you have an extra plasma pistol for me?"

"Sorry," she whispered. "You've got that automatic rifle."

"It's empty. Not very accurate, anyway. I think it's from a museum or something. Though I've gotten a few lucky shots with it." He remembered the nasal-voiced clanker's confused look as the round entered his cheek and the wave of brains and blood splattered the wall behind him.

Colt had killed people before, a few clankers, a few aggressive scavengers that had attacked him or his sister. That was just life as a scavenger, kill or be killed. Some scavengers were cannibals, not content to live on a diet of spiders and rats and the occasional snared pigeon. Human beings were the meatiest creatures to be found in the city.

That was why he knew the kill would linger in his mind for days, or weeks, and the memory would swim up unexpectedly for the rest of his life. He didn't feel guilty about doing it, but something about taking life in general just seemed unfortunate. The world was full of rubble and machines. Actual life, with heartbeat and blood, was rare, and getting rarer by the day.

The stairwell twisted deep underground, past floors of subterranean offices, letting out at an underground retail concourse that had been thoroughly looted and vandalized long ago. A quick glance into the convenience store and café told him there wouldn't be much food or other essentials remaining, but they could have all the greeting cards and art supplies they wanted.

A clothing shop had also been looted, but Colt stopped to pick up a few pairs of thick woolen socks from the floor. They had bears on them. The bear had once been some kind of sacred totem to the city of Chicago, Colt understood. He often saw them on clothing and other artifacts of the old world.

"Stopping for socks?" Mohini asked, looking mildly annoyed.

"Hunger and cold are the enemy as much as the machines," Colt said. "You must be from someplace warm."

"Not at all."

"Where *are* you from?" He struggled to cram the thick socks into his backpack, which was already full of small tools and freshly plundered bandages and disinfectant.

She hesitated a long moment before answering. "Far away."

"New York? I heard there are still people alive there. Other scavengers. Didn't know if it was just a rumor."

"Across the ocean," she said. "England."

"Oh, England," Colt said, nodding. Trying to sound knowledgeable, he added, "Over near Japan."

"Japan?"

"That's across the ocean too."

"How... do you not know your way around your own planet?" she asked.

"Sorry I don't sit around memorizing random facts about the old world," he said. Embarrassed, he hurried to change the subject. "So how did you cross the ocean? Did you have a boat? Why didn't the machines catch you?"

"I hitched a ride on a prison ship," Mohini said. "It's easier to hide among live humans."

"But... how?"

"I just had to convince the ship's AI to ignore me."

"You hacked it? You can take over their ocean ships?" He reached to grab her arm, just a gesture of excitement, but she jerked away and scowled. He'd forgotten how she hated him to touch her. Among the scavengers Colt knew, touch was important for silent communication, but apparently things were different where she was from.

England. A vague image of knights and castles drifted through his mind, maybe from one of the old, water-damaged storybooks he'd seen as a kid. King Arthur. Robin Hood. Sumo wrestlers. Samurai.

"If you can take over the machines' soldiers and ships," he said, "we could bring the war to them. Never mind bombing a few reapers in the old clinic—"

"Hold your horses," she said. "First, I did not take over the ship. I managed to get its security systems to ignore me, that's all. If I had changed its course or rammed it into one of the Carthaginian warships, the other machines would have bombed it and sunk it."

"But you could do something like that? Take over a ship?"

"I could try. Odds are I'd be caught and killed, either during the attempt or immediately following, so it hasn't been high on my agenda to do that."

"So what is high on this 'agenda'?" he asked, hoping he pronounced the unfamiliar word correctly. "What was so important you crossed an ocean for it? Because if it's Chicago deep-dish pizza, you're about twenty years too late." Colt had never tried "Chicago deep-dish pizza" either, but he'd seen a number of signs advertising it. He'd once found a steel can labeled "pizza sauce" and found it full of sugary, cold, lumpy tomato mush. It had been one of the best meals of his life.

"I can't talk about it," she said.

"Why not?"

"I don't know you," she said. "I don't think you're an android, but I can't trust people I don't know."

"Yeah, I get it. Are you with the rebels? Or maybe the metalheads? You don't look like a clanker. No implants."

"We were looking to make contact with the rebels here in Chicago," she said.

"Wait, who's 'we'?" he asked.

"I was here with... a friend. He crossed the ocean with me, stowed away together. We were a team. But a couple of reapers raided us one night. We took them down, but my friend was fatally injured. I had to bury him in rubble." Her voice had grown hoarse and unsteady, and Colt gathered she was close to the guy.

"I'm sorry," he said.

"That's where I got the reaper," she said. "It was damaged in our fight. But I've lost that, too. So now all I have is this pistol and a cutting laser."

"All I have is this empty rifle," he said. "So you're way ahead of the game."

They reached the end of the concourse, where they could exit upstairs to another broken skyscraper or hop down into a subway tunnel and keep going. Colt always preferred to stay low.

"So, do your secret plans tell you where you need to go next?" he asked.

"Not exactly. We were holed up in an old tower where we could watch from the windows and monitor the city with binoculars and cameras, seeking signs of the rebels. Their battles with the Carthaginian machines were like beacons, showing us their areas of operations. We tried to reach out to them once, but they were suspicious and would not speak to us."

"Yeah, the rebels are dangerous," he said. "I'm always

glad to hear about them destroying some metalheads, but they're also paranoid. The metalheads are always trying to infiltrate them with skinwalkers." He thought of the clinic's shattered nurse robot, which had once been a "skinwalker" or human-like machine. Mohini seemed to prefer the term "android."

"So you know the rebels in the area?" she asked.

"I know of them. I wouldn't go strolling into their camp for a friendly visit." Colt did know a couple of people who had supposedly gone to join the rebels, orphans like himself gathered and cared for by Mother Braden. He hadn't seen them since they'd left and didn't know whether they'd actually succeeded in joining the rebellion, or even whether they were still alive.

"What if you had something valuable to offer?" Mohini asked.

"Like what?"

"I have to keep that classified."

"After what I saw you do with the reaper, I can believe you have something to offer," Colt said. "If you can find the rebels and get them to listen."

"The second part was the problem," she said. "But perhaps if you, a local, speak for me, they will give me more of a chance."

"Maybe. Or perhaps if we, a couple of outsiders, just show up at their camp, they'll blast our heads off."

"It seems like the humans in this land are as dangerous as the machines."

"Is it not that way in England?" Colt looked around warily. They'd been talking more than moving. Somehow the girl kept distracting him, drawing his attention to her big, dark eyes, her strangely soft and smooth brown skin.

"Not as bad as this," she said. "But it's pretty bad."

"Come back with me," Colt said.

"Back? To the clinic?"

"No. To my home. One of them. You'll be safe there for a while."

"You're inviting me home with you?" A strange smile formed on her lips, as if she found this amusing. "Will your girlfriend be there?"

"My *sister*. We can wait and rest while I go ask a friend about the rebels. I can even speak to Mother Braden."

"She's your mother?"

"She isn't really anyone's mother. She was a soldier in the old world. After the war, she started finding stray orphans who'd survived and taught us how to survive better. She's the only reason me and my sister are alive now." He stopped talking about that, feeling he'd exposed too much of himself. "Anyway, if you want to come, you can. We could use your help."

"How?"

"Teach us whatever you know about the machines."

"That won't enable you to control them like I can. A lot of that depends on your hardware."

"Yeah. Like your black sphere. Where'd you get that?"

"There are not more where this came from. This was an extremely lucky find. Once in a lifetime."

"Like your plasma pistol."

"Yep."

"Come on." Colt jumped down to the old underground railway, then held out his hands to help her down. "You can rest up and get a meal, at least. It's the closest thing to safety I can offer."

She hesitated, then looked back and seemed to think about the dangers behind them.

"Here I come." She jumped down. He caught her hips and eased her down to her feet. She stiffened at his touch.

"Sorry, I had to touch you that time."

"It's fine. I'll live." She raised her plasma pistol. "Lead the way."

He adjusted his night vision goggles to their most sensitive setting as they started into the deep dark of the old tunnel. They would auto-tint in the event of sudden bright lights so he wouldn't get blinded in a gunfight.

Eventually, the tunnel would get too dark for the night vision goggles to work, and then they would be walking completely blind.

Chapter Six

Carthage

After driving off the high road and crashing through the safety wall, Audrey's car toppled toward the blocks of small apartment buildings below. Already, emergency lights were flashing in that area. The municipal AI would be issuing warnings, redirecting traffic, and sealing off approaches where possible.

Audrey braced herself for impact. "Nin, I don't want to die," she whispered.

The malleable cushion surface drew in tight around her, providing a layer of protection. Emergency foam jetted from overhead nozzles and expanded quickly.

Outside, inflatable padding erupted and folded over the exterior of the car, creating another layer of impact protection, but also blocking her view of the world outside.

Then all she could see was thick, soupy foam. It reeked of strong chemicals, like a hospital floor. It would probably end up giving her cancer, she thought, if she survived the crash.

The car hit the ground, she assumed, because it bounced hard, and she ricocheted around inside the car, sloshing in the thick, awful-smelling foam.

The car hit the ground a second time and slid to a halt. Audrey spun in the center of the foam like a cat trapped in a washing machine. The foam absorbed the impact, but also forced its way into her ears, eyes, nose, and mouth in the most unpleasant manner.

"Audrey! Are you alive?" Nin's hand closed on her arm.

Audrey went slack, feeling relief. Nin was here. Nin would take care of things.

Nin did. The android kicked open the car doors, then dragged Audrey out of the foam-filled interior into the open air and late-afternoon sunlight.

Audrey knelt on the sidewalk and vomited out the foam that had invaded her throat and stomach.

"Well," she said, coughing, when she was finally done. "That was awful."

"Can you stand?" Nin touched her shoulder gently.

"Maybe. Where are we?" Audrey stood with her android's help and wiped the foam out of her eyes. Apparently she'd bounced and slid along a pedestrian street, finally coming to a stop against a lamp post.

"Benefit Zone 3C," Nin said, but Audrey could have guessed it by then. The ornate brick buildings, full of cherub-adorned archways, picture windows, and garden-lined walkways, were the handiwork of Audrey's grandmother, who had argued that some of the vast wealth flowing from Carthage's empire could be used for slum beautification.

Surely no one would call these areas slums now. They had durable, pleasant-looking apartment homes, with automated grocery delivery and even cook-bots and fix-bots shared by the community, plus swimming pools and gardens. Some of those had fallen into disrepair over the years, and the gardens had yellowed and filled with weeds, but it was just a matter of dispatching more maintenance bots, allocating a little more tax money.

Some of the locals had stepped out onto their balconies to look at the crash, leaving their entertainment media blaring behind them. The Benefit Zone residents wore caps and shirts dense with logos of sports teams, fast-food stands, and cereal mascots, clothing so cluttered with ads it was virtually free to buy.

"Did we hit anybody?" Audrey had some trouble keeping her balance, and her head ached. There was a ringing sound in the back of her skull.

"I don't think so. We damaged a lot of the cobblestone," Nin said.

"That's fine," Audrey said, not sure why she was saying it. Who cared about damage to the street? Robots would fix that. She was definitely confused.

Sirens approached, announcing the police. Windows up and down the street tinted black. The residents on the balconies backed inside and closed their doors.

"The police are coming," Audrey said.

"Correct," Nin said.

"We have to get out of here." She swayed, relying on the android for balance, and looked down at herself. Covered in foam and vomit, staggering on her feet.

All she could think of was her mother screaming at her for showing up in the news media that way. Information moved lightning-quick through the celebrity gossip sites. If

Audrey stuck around long enough and let anyone take images of her stumbling around covered in puke by a crashed car, she would catch hell from her mother for the rest of her life.

"Hire me a car," she said. "Any quality as long as it's private, no sharing."

"You need medical attention," Nin said.

"Not as bad as I need to get out of here."

"I have sent a request. The nearest emergency clinic—"

"You know we need something private."

"Of course. The nearest appropriate clinic is three kilometers from here. What about the Security Steve unit?"

Audrey looked at her car, wrapped in a thick layer of inflated padding, which had sealed over the trunk lid. "It'll take too long to get him out. Let's go."

"The car pickup will be this way." Nin led her across the street, through an arcade between buildings, toward a long covered staircase.

As they descended the steps, flashing blue lights flooded the plaza they'd just left. Audrey looked back to see a police car arrive. A couple of Officer Joes hopped out to inspect the wreckage. The city's law-enforcement robots were designed to look like hyper-friendly neighborhood cops. Their heads were oversized and cartoonish like sports mascots, with big eyes and big grins that never wavered.

"The Officer Joe is built on the same chassis as the infantry reaper," Audrey said, her dazed brain tossing up useless trivia. "My dad told me that."

"The hired car approaches, Audrey," Nin said.

"Good. Let's go."

The next magnetic road was a block away. The car awaiting them was boxy, gray, and much larger than Audrey's. More like a bus.

On the inside, it featured a circle of badly worn seats facing inward toward holographic ads floating above vending machines selling snacks, medicines, liquor, and assorted recreational drugs. Audrey wondered why her brother Salvius bothered with dangerous illegal drugs when so many intoxicants and mood enhancers were readily available. She supposed addiction had its own logic.

"Nin, this is a public transport," Audrey said.

"Yes, but I reserved the entire vehicle. So it's private for us."

"Good move. Can't wait to hear Mom complain about the bill." Audrey took one of the patched, scratched seats. Graffiti was carved into all the softer plastic surfaces inside the car. "Seriously, this is like heaven now. I might even eat one of those vending machine funnel cakes."

As the car gained speed and flew up a steep ramp to join the highway traffic, Audrey felt her seat lurching with the rapid changes in velocity. Apparently the public transports had lower quality inertia dampeners, and her already-queasy guts were learning all about them.

"Hey, check that pharma-vend," Audrey said. "See if it has something for headaches. And bad stomachs."

"You bet I do!" A plastic head rose from the top of the medicine vending machine. Its design evoked some old-time doctor or pharmacist, with big glasses, a fringe of white hair, and a giant white mustache, now filthy with dust and public-car grime. "I recommend aspirin and caffeine for your head and bismuth formula for your stomach. All available for just seventeen credits—"

"Buy cocaine." A portion of a plastic head with big red bug eyes had risen from the top of the machine beside it, just enough to peer out at her. "Good for all pain."

"Do not buy cocaine!" the pharmacist character said.

"Buy proper medicine from reputable manufacturers. Like HeadZap and BellyCalm."

"Cocaine," the peeking buggy robot insisted. "Like sweet rain in your brain."

"It is *not* like that—" the pharma-bot snapped.

"Okay, shut up," Audrey said. "I'll get the headache powder and stomach medicine from Dr. Mustache."

"Good for you!" said the pharma-bot.

"Should have bought cocaine," the bug-bot said, its partially raised head now sinking out of sight inside the drug-and-liquor vending machine.

Nin stepped over to the vending machine and purchased the medicine using Audrey's personal spending account. When the medicine packet and thimble-sized bottle tumbled out, Nin collected them, opened them, and handed them to Audrey.

Audrey drank the headache medicine down with a gulp from the tiny bottle of liquid pink BellyCalm. She handed the empty bottle back to Nin, who tossed it into the overflowing trash hole in the wall of the car.

It was only then that Audrey noticed the damage to Nin's hand. Smashing open the car's console and ripping out its guts had left Nin's fingers broken and twisted. It looked painful; good thing Nin couldn't really feel it.

"Nin! We have to get you repaired right away."

"No, we have to get *you* repaired right away, Audrey." Nin put an arm around her shoulder and drew her close, like when Audrey was a child. "You're the most important person in the world to me. You're special. There's nobody like you."

"You don't have to talk to me like a little kid," Audrey said, but she couldn't help smiling and feeling soothed. Someone had just tried to kill her, and she knew her family would be more concerned about the politics and media spin of it than her actual well-being. If the family looked bad on the gossip sites, Audrey's mother would be furious, her siblings would mock her, and her father... she supposed he would speak to her even less, if that was possible.

Nin, though, would always care about Audrey more than any of that. Nin was the only one Audrey could really trust with her thoughts and feelings.

"Perhaps we should contact the police," Nin said. "Or report the terror attack to special services."

"Report it to Ila." That her father's personal-assistant android. "No one else. Let my family handle it. And tell them I'm unharmed."

"But you have not been diagnosed. I detected you have no major broken bones, but you may have suffered other injuries ranging from concussion to internal bleeding—"

"Thanks, Mom, but tell them that anyway."

"As long as—"

"Yes, I'll still swing by that clinic. That very private and discreet clinic, right?"

"They are now expecting you. Under your alias Veronica Exeter, who pays extra for discretion."

They finally reached it, taking a series of branching off-ramps into the private indoor parking area in front of the clinic on level forty of a curvy, spiral-shaped black skyscraper. Solid black doors sealed behind them as they drove into the parking area, providing privacy as Audrey and Nin exited the public car.

Nurse Nancy androids, as gorgeous as supermodels, emerged from the black-tinted doors of the clinic with a luxuriously padded wheelchair and insisted Audrey sit down. The wheelchair adjusted to Audrey's body, providing maximum comfort and support to her neck, back, and really every part of her.

The nurses fussed over her, oozing with programmed compassion and sentiment. The chair tested Audrey's pulse, temperature, weight, and blood pressure while it drove her past the marble front desk where no one stood, through a pair of gilded mahogany doors, and ultimately to an exam room that looked like a luxurious spa, including soft music and a gurgling bathing pool with heaps of towels and colorful glass bottles.

Audrey sank into a pristine white chair, which reclined and extended into a soft, gently inclined exam table, heated and padded. She wasn't sure whether to expect a medical exam or a deep-tissue massage. One of the nurses took a blood sample, while the other repeatedly told Audrey how great she looked. Then the nurses left.

"Welcome," said the doctor android when he arrived a moment later. He had a deep tan, striking good looks, and a charming smile, like a doctor from a soap opera. She could almost hear the cheesy, overly dramatic soap-opera music the moment he swept in through the door. "I'm Dr. White. I understand you had a bit of crash."

"Yeah, my car jumped the track. I didn't think that was possible anymore."

"You just lie right there, and I'll take good care of you." He winked as he moved in closer.

He shined a light in her eyes, then took some quick X-rays and magnetic images, all focusing on her head. The gear extended and retracted on mechanical arms as needed, disappearing behind wooden panels in the wall when it was done.

"Your skull looks fine," he finally said, while holograms of her brain floated around him, glowing in the pleasantly dimmed room. "No sign of tissue damage, either. Your assistant said you'd felt a headache and nausea. Any other symptoms? Confusion? Balance issues?"

"A little bit."

"We're looking at a very mild concussion here," he said. "Not much you can do but enjoy a hot bath, maybe some herbal tea and a mood enhancer. Relax and enjoy yourself." He gestured toward the bath.

"Now?"

"Were you planning on going back out in public like that?" he asked. "We can provide you with fresh clothing."

"Oh, right." Audrey looked down at herself, thinking of her mother's admonishments to always look good in public, always represent the family well. "Good thinking, Doc. I see why you put me in the room with the tub."

"We've had other high-discretion patients show up after too much fun and excitement," he said.

"I had the excitement, but not the fun."

"I'm sorry to hear that."

"Are we done, Doctor?" Audrey asked.

"If you like. Some patients request that I join them in the mineral bath—"

"Nope," Audrey said.

"Perhaps you would prefer a nurse—"

"I've got Nin if I need anything." Audrey gestured at her personal android, standing silent and still in the corner. "You can go now."

"Yes, ma'am. We thank you for your business."

He left. Reluctantly, Audrey disrobed and eased into the warm bath. Nin bathed Audrey, as always, and scrubbed away the crash foam from her skin and hair. The water was soft, full of soaps and salts.

One of the nurses arrived with a fresh outfit for Audrey on a hanger, then bowed before leaving again.

"Where should we go next?" Nin wondered.

"You should go to the repair shop." Audrey said. "And I'm going home."

"To your parents' uptown apartment? Or out to the estate?"

"What? I'm going to my apartment, like I planned."

"But there's a building-wide party tonight," Nin said. "Security will be extremely poor."

"I'm sure Security Steve will catch up to us by then."

"One security android will not count for much with so many people around."

"So have Hamilcar Security send more," Audrey said. "Have six or ten of them hanging around my floor. But I'm going home and acting like everything's normal. My family will like the optics of that. Being a no-show at this party will raise more questions than my crashed car. How's that situation evolving, by the way?"

"Ila is in charge of it," Nin said. "The police report has been altered with pseudonyms to avoid publicity. Your car is being hauled away by Hamilcar Security."

"Good. Their people need to study my car and find out who hacked it." She felt her lips peel back and bare her teeth, an involuntarily show of anger that she'd been trying to squelch since she was a kid; it was another thing for which her mother constantly admonished her. "See who tried to kill me."

"That's exactly it, Audrey. Someone tried to kill you."

"And failed. Dodge an assassination in the afternoon, go to a party in the evening—that's just life as a Caracala." She stood up and took a thick towel from Nin, who arrived with it at just the right moment without being told. She'd been bathing Audrey since she was an infant and had a lifetime of memories and evolving user preferences that kept her in sync with Audrey's wants and needs. Nin would often pour a drink just before Audrey realized she was thirsty or adjust the thermostat just as Audrey began to feel too warm or too cold.

Audrey dressed in the outfit the nurse had brought. It was simple, cut from white linen, fitted perfectly to her measurements. The wheelchair must have taken those along with her vital signs. She buttoned the shirt and put on the matching silky slippers that fit her feet perfectly, too.

Nin fixed Audrey's hair and makeup. Audrey wore her black hair short these days, which her mother hated, especially compared to her older sister's blond locks that could be set into thick, glittering curls or styled up into high curling towers crammed with jeweled decorations.

"All right," Audrey said, looking at herself in the mirror. She was presentable again, with no sign of the wrecked-and-barfed look, should someone take a picture of her. The outfit was plain, but she liked the lightness and simplicity of it. "Let's get the hell out of here. Have them drop my old clothes into the incinerator."

A minute later, Audrey and Nin stepped out to the curb area where they'd arrived. A smaller, sleeker car awaited them now, a midnight black capsule of a limousine that Nin had hired. They climbed in, and they were off. Audrey hadn't encountered a single human at the clinic, which would help keep things discreet. Robots were not inclined to gossip.

"You have call requests waiting from your mother, your sister, and your brother Marcello," Nin said.

"Oh no." Audrey sighed. "Just my mom for now."

"Audrey, what have you gotten into?" Her mother

appeared in holographic form a moment later, seeming to occupy the seat across from Audrey in the limo's soft white leather interior. She looked immaculately groomed, ready for a cocktail party, but that could have just been the holo skin she'd selected for this call.

Audrey's mother, Liastrada Bontherias Venable Caracala, looked about eighteen or nineteen, though in reality she was fifty-one. A constant regimen of cosmetic microsurgery maintained her teenage appearance, which had grown odd and awkward for Audrey during Audrey's own teenage years. Now that Audrey was in her twenties, Audrey's mother looked more like a younger sister.

"No big deal," Audrey said. "My car left the road and hopped the rail. The emergency safety measures worked fine though."

"But that's not possible! Cars don't just leave the road. That hasn't happened in years."

"Well, they're going to have to roll the counter back to zero on that one," Audrey said. "And some joke-dog of a hacker got into my car's system. Started giving me a whole anti-everything rant."

"A terrorist group attacked you? You can't go back to that student apartment. You should head out to the estate—"

"I'm expected at this party, Mother," Audrey said. "If I go ahead like nothing happened, that shows we're not afraid."

"But... aren't you afraid?"

"I was, back when my car was hurtling down through the city. But I don't think this hacker's going to follow up by sending an armed death squad to a university residence tower. He's more likely some loner who's consumed too much conspiracy media. I bet that's what special services will find."

"And you're willing to risk your life on it?"

"I think we can dial down the drama. I'll be fine. Nin's ordering more Security Steves. You can tell Father I'm putting on a brave face for the family's sake. He'll like that."

"I'll send him that message. But, honey—" Her mother reached out a holographic hand and laid it on top of Audrey's. Audrey felt nothing. "—if you change your mind, don't hesitate. You know our building is extremely secure."

"So is mine. I'll be perfectly safe."

Audrey took a deep breath when the call ended. Her mother's anxious, worried energy was unpleasantly infectious.

The car reached The 360. The site of the trendy new tower had previously been occupied by a swirling, lavish, Rococo-style skyscraper built a decade ago, but that had gone out of fashion and been demolished after about eight years.

This new skyscraper was even taller, rising into the sky in a kaleidoscope of shimmering colors. The digital-glass walls of many apartments had been set to transparent tints, revealing color-filtered views of the private lives of their residents to anyone who cared to look.

The floors and ceilings were made of similar material, though thicker. It was possible for every apartment in the building to be transparent on every side, opening up a vast sense of space with one brightly colored chamber after another.

Audrey usually kept her own apartment opaque—she'd moved to the building because it was popular with the students, not because she cared for the "edgy and innovative" design. She actually preferred the older-fashioned design of her parents' apartment, with its walled gardens and ornate fountains, its vaulted ceiling hung with flowering vines. There were plenty of private nooks there, good places to hide and read a book. Here at the new tower, people clearly preferred to be on display, to have attention on them from all angles.

She and Nin stepped out of the limo at the fiftieth-floor indoor curb.

The long black cylinder of a cargo truck arrived just behind Audrey. It turned the heads of students on the curb, coming and going between their own cars and the building lobby. Cargo trucks were rare up here, dozens of levels above the loading docks.

The sides of the truck rolled open.

Eight Security Steves hung limply inside, like eight identical bodies on their way to a group funeral.

All of them straightened up, came to life, and jumped down from the cargo truck, four on each side. They marched up to Audrey, wearing identical grins on their identical lantern jaws.

"I'm guess you guys are here for me," Audrey said. "Come on."

Audrey, Nin, and her eight-android security detail filled up an entire elevator car, which was the same transparent colored-glass design as the rest of the building. More heads turned as they zipped up past one elevator lounge after another; the daughter of the prime legislator riding with a whole pack of personal security bots instead of just one or two. She supposed she could pass it off as extra security for the party.

The green-tinted elevator stopped at her floor, where her roommates' assistant androids were getting the elevator lounge ready for the party. On every floor of the apartment building, the cross-shaped elevator lounge was the common area shared by the four corner apartments. Today, the floor, ceiling, and walls here were tinted transparent orange, and the androids were busy setting out orange balloons, drinks, and cookies.

"Finally, you're home!" Audrey's floormate Jennilaura emerged from her own apartment, holding a bag of color-coded mood-enhancing pills. She poured these out like candy next to the drinks and cookies on the sideboard. Her smile faltered when she saw the small mob of black-suited security androids surrounding Audrey. "Everything okay?"

"Yeah, I had some car trouble. My mom insisted on sending these guys for the party." Audrey rolled her eyes as she gestured at the Security Steves. "I'll try to keep them out of the way."

"How do you like the place? Orange enough?" Jennilaura smiled.

"Sure, but... " Audrey looked at the orange walls, the same hue of orange in all four directions. The walls of Jennilaura's apartment were transparent, so Audrey could see all of Jennilaura's furniture and her fat Siamese cat sleeping on the floor in front of its eight-level cat condo.

Another roommate, Kelleyen, had left her wall transparent too. Her handsome, muscled personal assistant, Lio, was giving Kelleyen her daily massage.

Audrey's own apartment was opaque, as usual. She liked her privacy, even in her sitting room.

"How about this?" Audrey whispered her idea to Nin, who nodded and wirelessly conveyed Audrey's wishes.

The walls turned porcelain white, adorned with painted satsuma trees heavy with ripe orange fruit. It was the design from Simon Quick's antique tea set from Earth.

"Oh yeah!" Jennilaura said. "I like how it's still orange, but it's so... cultural."

"Yeah, it's cultural," Audrey said.

"I love it!" chimed in Jennilaura's personal assistant, Ea, a pretty female android with colorful striped hair and long legs she showed off with short dresses. Ea tended to love everything with great enthusiasm.

"Those orchids look like garbage!" Jennilaura snapped at Ea, who was arranging one of several vases of delicate orange orchids for the party. "I swear, Ea, I am trading you in next year. You're so useless."

"I am sorry!" Ea pleaded. "I will do better—"

"Just download some new material. Copy something from a lifestyle site if you have to. Make it less awful." Jennilaura turned back to Audrey. "Does yours give you this much trouble?"

"No, Nin's great."

"I wish her model was still in production."

Audrey and Nin entered Audrey's private apartment, while Jennilaura resumed berating her android. "Why are there streaks on the floor? They need to be spotless for tonight! Do you want the girls below us to think we're slobs?"

The door closed behind Audrey, leaving her alone in the peace of her sitting room. She dropped to the couch and listened to summaries of messages from concerned family members, which had been forwarded to Nin from their respective personal androids. Audrey gave Nin some replies to send back to her family members' androids.

Then she squeezed in some classwork, studying a text called *Manufacturing and Management of Public Opinion* from her state communications course. She read the book in tall, glowing letters that floated like ghosts in her room. She watched the example videos. She was glad when the party started so she could finally stop studying.

The elevator lounge grew crowded fast. Looking up and down through the orange floors and ceiling, she could see the same party taking place in one lounge after another, one level after another, an immense gathering of people.

Good. Let there be no doubt that the terrorists hadn't scared Audrey at all. In addition to her personal security, the apartment building had plenty of security of its own. Even this huge party was not open to the public, only to tower residents and their invited guests. And their guests' plus-ones.

People immediately started talking to Audrey, more and more of them, a chattering vortex of friends, acquaintances, neighbors, and random guests. She felt like socializing at first, but soon found her headache returning, and it was hard for her to concentrate on any conversation.

"Come on, you obviously need something," Jennilaura said, holding out the bowl of mood enhancers. "Just take a smiley." The chewable tablets were identifiable by shape and color: red hearts for feelings of love and arousal, eyeballs for people who liked to hallucinate. The yellow smiley faces were for general happiness.

"I don't usually—"

"That's why you should." Jennilaura opened Audrey's mouth and dropped a smiley on her tongue. It began to dissolve instantly. Jennilaura grinned. "Enjoy yourself. This place is crawling with opportunities."

"You should spit that out, Audrey," Nin said.

Audrey hesitated. "Maybe just for today. Don't worry, Nin. Things won't get too wild."

Nin frowned. "This is not your usual behavior."

"Maybe that's been my problem. Too uptight. That's

what my sister has always told me. Which is kind of ironic coming from her, but... " Audrey shrugged, letting the tablet dissolve in her mouth.

She felt strangely empowered. Something important had happened to her. She'd nearly died. Someone had tried to kill her, and she'd survived. Maybe it was just the shock, but she didn't feel frightened. She felt... alive, like the event had broken through the cage doors of her tightly planned, anxiety-fueled existence and given her a dose of something primal, something vitalizing. Maybe this was why some people enjoyed life-threatening extreme sports, like orbital diving and magma-boarding.

She danced with the crowd, made up mostly of students and their personal-assistant androids. Kelleyen had rented a DJ bot for their party, and the machine filled the elevator lounge with thudding dance music and flashing lights in every shade of orange, between its frequent bad jokes. Audrey dialed the bot's settings down to "minimal comedy."

At one point, she found herself arguing with Jasonius Falicorn, the intern who'd given the weak presentation on Klamptura. He was as cocky as he was dull, a handsome fluffhead in an expensive patchwork suit.

"There's no reason to intervene in Klamptura," she said, speaking loud to be heard through the music.

"There's aluminum and cadmium," he said, his voice slurred. A group of his friends stood around him, most of them male, all of them inebriated, their elaborately styled hair adorned with precious metals and rare feathers. "So much goddamn aluminum."

"Do you know what they do on Veritum?" Audrey said. "The men in the priesthood are called Faces of God. And all the girls in the colony? They're chattel, divided among the Faces. The women are nothing but sex slaves and brood mares. That's a place where Carthage can make life better for people."

"Huh. Well, that's why the religious nuts move out to miserable places that nobody wants, with no valuable resources." Jasonius smirked. "They just want to be free to fuck their kids in peace."

Mouths dropped all around at his comment. Then one of his friends laughed, and everyone around them started to laugh, even Audrey's floormates Jennilaura and Kelleyen.

Audrey, who'd spent a sleep-deprived week studying the issue and now had awful images seared into her mind, didn't laugh but headed toward her apartment again, her mood souring.

"Hey, you're Audrey Caracala, aren't you?" chirped a voice from the thick crowd. Audrey turned to see a grinning girl with short brown hair and gray eyes. There was something familiar about her. Classmate? Neighbor?

"Yes."

"Yes!" She stepped closer as if she had a secret to share, while her orange liquor drink slopped over the edge of her glass. "Listen, it's been a while. Do you remember me?"

"Kind of," Audrey said. "No. Sorry. But you're familiar."

"Two words: Black Harbor. Beach. Black Harbor Beach. Okay, that's three words—"

"Zola?" Audrey couldn't believe it, but now it was hard not to see it. Especially with those rare gray eyes. "How? Zolaria Hallewell—"

"Yes!" Zola's voice dropped to a whisper.

"They said your father was transferred to the outer worlds," Audrey said. "When you were thirteen. You never said good-bye."

"I didn't get a chance. And 'transferred' is not exactly right. At all."

"Wow. Zola." Audrey was stunned, flashing back to forgotten pieces of her childhood, of exploring the soft black volcanic beach with Zola. The smell of sunscreen and ice cream. She shook her head.

Zola stepped forward and embraced her, which startled Audrey; Carthaginians, as a culture, liked to be seen but not touched, at least not by other humans, for the most part. Audrey was happy to see Zola, though, and embraced the girl back. It was strange how hot her skin was to the touch; Audrey had almost forgotten that about live human skin. Androids tended to be, not cold, but definitely a little more room temperature.

"I have two things to tell you," Zola whispered in Audrey's ear. "First, your brother's in danger. Second, they're coming after you too."

"Who?"

"They could try to kill you today."

"I think you're late to the party on that," Audrey said. "Does this have something to do with a crazed black-and-white clown?"

"We should talk somewhere else."

"Okay, let me get Nin—"

"No bots," Zola said.

"Okay." Audrey drew Zola into her private apartment, shaking her head at Nin when she started to follow. The android seemed taken aback; Nin was not used to Audrey waving her away or ever choosing to be apart from Nin outside of rare situations like the security briefing.

"Is there any comm equipment in here?" Zola asked, looking around the apartment.

"It's all off right now. Why, do you need to call someone? And what did you say about my brother?"

Zola grabbed her arm and pulled her into the master bathroom, closing each door behind them. Audrey had no choice but to stumble along after her.

"Okay, this is getting kind of invasive," Audrey said. The bathroom was pleasant enough, with a settee and crown molding and a vast marble tub, but it was a strange place to have a conversation.

"Do you have comm equipment in *here*?" Zola asked.

"No."

"Your brother's been kidnapped," Zola said.

"Which brother? Because if it's Marcello, it can wait."

"Salvius," Zola said, whispering even though they were in the bathroom.

"You know where Salvius is?" Audrey struggled to keep her voice down. "Are you kidding?"

"I don't know where he is. Not anymore. That's why I'm here."

"We need to contact my father. I need Nin—"

"*No.* No machines. We have to keep this private. And among humans."

"But Nin helps me with everything."

"And watches everything you do," Zola said. "The machines can't know what I'm here to tell you. Salvius is part of The Change."

"The terrorist group?" Audrey felt a rush of anger. "He wouldn't be part of that."

"No, The Change isn't any one group. It's an alliance of groups. It's a common vision, or at least a common cause—"

"Wait," Audrey said. "You're serious? Are you mixed up

with them too, Zola? Look, whatever you've done, I can help you."

"Who said I've done anything?" she snapped. "I'm not here for your help—at least, not for me. Salvius was taken prisoner by a... it's hard to explain, but it's a splinter cell of The Change. They happen to believe that your family are the heart of the problem and should be removed."

"They want to kill us all, huh?" Audrey said, a little flippantly, but a lifetime of tight security measures had accustomed her to the idea of her family being targeted. "Look, Zola, we deal with threats like this all the time. That's why there's Security Steves all over my floor. But I seriously need to know where to find my brother. Just tell me he's not dead in a ditch somewhere. I'm sure he's high, or crashing, or strung out, or whatever the term is—"

"They took him. And your brother is not who you think he is. His long disappearances aren't drug and booze benders. He just wants your family to believe that."

"Yeah, right. So who has him? Not drug dealers?" Audrey listened extra carefully, since she didn't have Nin here to help her remember things later. She felt uncomfortably adrift without her android's constant support and help.

"The Blood Clowns," Zola said.

"The... " Audrey looked at her for a moment and nearly burst into laughter. "That's what they call themselves? On purpose? It's not a typo or anything?"

"It's their logo. They're willing to use extreme violence to change the system. At least, that's what they claim."

"Yeah, so what do they do? Paint themselves in clown makeup and send people scary videos?"

"You've heard of them?"

"Yeah, sounds like the people who tried to kill me earlier," Audrey said. "I don't know what I can do if you don't want me to report this to anyone. I don't like the idea of Salvius being in trouble—"

"So come with me. Help me find him."

"Me? What can I do?"

"You can care enough to do something about it," Zola said. "That's more than most people can do."

"Look, if my brother's gotten tangled up with drug dealers or terrorists, that's a job for the police, or Hamilcar Security, or special services. I'm just a student—"

"You're a human being," Zola said. "We can't call anyone for help. It'll make things worse. If you care about your brother and you'd like him to stay alive, come with me. If not, I'll go it alone. It's what I'm used to, anyway. But don't call *anyone* else."

"What are you going to do?" Audrey asked.

"If you're coming, I'll fill you in. Otherwise, the details are none of your business."

Audrey seriously considered it for a long moment, then smiled and shook her head. "Look, is this a prank or what? Because there's no way—"

"This is real, Audrey!" Zola threw up her hands. "This was a waste of time. I even spent last night flirting with some guy from your building so I could get invited in. Grad student in interplanetary regulations. Boring as a beige brick. Audrey, I thought you might be different. Like Salvius. But you're just like the rest of them. I was stupid to come here. Sorry. Just don't tell anyone you saw me. Do me that much of a favor."

She turned and walked out, all the way through Audrey's apartment, back to the crowded elevator lounge where the music thumped, the orange lights pulsed, and the robo-DJ implored everyone to "strip it down and shake it out!" The drunk, drugged, half-naked young crowd cheered as a cloud of orange hologram bubbles floated through the dance floor, popping in bright floral bursts whenever someone touched them.

"Everything all right?" Nin stepped into Audrey's apartment, somewhat timidly. Behind Nin followed a smiling android with a brushy beard, red toolbox, and bright yellow hard hat. The logo on his overalls read RepairPal. "The repair bot has arrived for my hand."

"Ugh." Audrey took a deep breath, her eyes on Zola's retreating back. "I can't believe I'm about to do this. Nin, stay here and get yourself repaired. I'll be right back. Maybe."

"Where are you going?" Nin stepped inside the apartment's maintenance closet, followed by the RepairPal android.

"Nowhere. Probably nowhere." Audrey ran out into the crowded elevator lounge to catch up with Zola, and she leaned in close to be heard through the loud music. "What happened to your family? You said your dad wasn't really transferred."

"He was suspected of disloyalty and sent to a remote post," Zola said. "Officially. In reality, he lived the rest of his life under house arrest on an icy planet called Brem. My mother and I lived there with him at first. They posted reapers in our house to watch us. Do you have any idea what it's like to have those things in your house, day and night, just watching? They're like monsters. Like ghosts, haunting the whole place."

"Is he... did your father die?" Audrey asked, wincing at the clumsy bluntness of the question even as she asked it. This was why it was always easier to deal with machines than humans. Androids were never unhappy, always eager to please, while real humans were a minefield of hidden emotion.

"My dad arranged for me and my mother to escape," Zola said. "He thought they might let our escape slide, as long as he stayed. He said they'd gone to a lot of inconvenience to keep him alive."

"Your family was very influential," Audrey said. "And very close to mine."

"Close to yours?" Zola snorted. "Who do you think he was suspected of being disloyal to? Your father and his faction. The ones who can't seem to stop centralizing power while weakening any sort of public control over the state—"

"Come on," Audrey said. "We don't control the world. Nobody does. No matter how it may look from the outside."

"The ones who can't stop conquering," Zola said, her tone cutting. "No matter how large their empire grows. It's never enough."

"All right. You know we can't change the past—"

"—we can only do our best in the present," Zola said. "Yes, you and I went to the same day school and learned the same platitudes. But are we doing our best? Or do the machines just keep conquering worlds because that's what they're programmed to do? When will enough be enough? Why does nobody have the political willpower to call them back or make them stop? Why isn't anyone even trying?"

"Okay, I get it. You're with 'The Change,'" Audrey said, with the most derisive tone she could summon.

"Your family's people killed my father, Audrey. As punishment for him sending my mom and me back to civilization. They gutted him and left his body on the ice. They didn't kill Mom and me, though. They just sent us... pictures. Lots and lots of pictures. The reapers did it, of course. The machines who'd stayed in our house, watching us all those days and nights, just waiting for the kill order."

Audrey stared at her for a long moment, shocked and speechless. Then she looked across the dance floor at the nearest Security Steve, posted stiffly in the corner by a potted plant.

"I want to help my brother," Audrey said, barely believing the words as they came out of her mouth. She couldn't abandon Salvius, no matter what kind of trouble he'd found. Family first. That was what she'd always been taught, and it was a creed she'd lived every day of her life.

"You can't bring any machines, and you can't tell anyone where we're going," Zola said.

"I don't see how much use I can be, then," Audrey said. "But let's go. Before I do the smart thing and change my mind."

They headed for the elevator.

"Audrey!" Nin screamed. She appeared in the doorway to Audrey's apartment. Her damaged hand had been removed, and for the moment her arm ended at the middle of the forearm, the connectors exposed.

The RepairPal android grabbed Nin by her remaining arm and hauled her back into the apartment. A round saw spun at high speed in his other hand.

"Let her go!" Audrey shouted.

"Come and get her," the RepairPal said, his voice booming, and he grinned at Audrey before dragging Nin back into the apartment, out of sight.

"Nin!" Audrey started toward Nin, but Zola grabbed her.

"They're coming for you!" Zola said. "We have to run!"

"But the Security Steves—" Audrey pointed at the one next to the potted plant. That unit was already on the move, drawing a laser pistol from his shoulder holster and pointing it Audrey's way. "Steve, go stop that RepairPal from hurting Nin!"

"Get down!" Zola wrenched Audrey to the floor. The laser pistol's concentrated energy beam passed through where Audrey's head had been. The beam burned into the chest of a tall guy who'd been standing behind her—she thought she recognized him from her history of government class—and he swayed and toppled over, his trendy puzzle-piece shirt smoking.

More shots streaked across the room, seemingly from every direction. Most of them were electric-blue lasers, drilling through anyone they touched. One white microbolt of plasma struck Audrey's tall, gorgeous roommate Kelleyen, who so enjoyed massages from her handsome butler-bot, and burned the girl to the bone. Audrey actually glimpsed Kelleyen's rib cage before she toppled over in a burning heap.

People were falling dead all around her. The Security Steves were closing in from all sides.

Audrey screamed in horror; she'd never witnessed anything like this.

"They've been hacked. Run!" Zola shouted.

Audrey started toward the elevator, but Zola grabbed her arm and redirected her toward the stairs.

The crowd erupted in chaos, people running in every direction. The android assistants—roughly half the crowd—moved to protect their owners, valiantly taking most of the second wave of fire. Androids dropped to the floor, leaking sparks and lubricant.

"Keep moving! Get downstairs!" Audrey shouted at a confused knot of people blocking the transparent orange stairwell door, watching the shooting with blissful drugged smiles, as if everything around them was just a movie. Some were taking selfie videos, waving dreamily at themselves. "Go! Now!"

"You got it." One of the guys raised his orange juice and vodka at her as if toasting and made no move to leave. A laser pistol blast tore through the chest of a guy beside him, who dropped to the floor, dead instantly. The drunk guy nodded and toasted his dead friend, sloshing half his drink onto the body.

Zola tore open the front of her dress, thick with layers of embroidered flowers. She brought out two components that screwed together to make a laser pistol—she'd smuggled the weapon past building security—and then returned fire, drilling one of the Security Steves through the skull.

That left seven more of the security androids, though, and Zola couldn't shoot them all, especially not with all the innocent people in the way.

"Come on!" Zola pulled Audrey into the stairwell. Laser fire from the Steves perforated the transparent orange wall. "Opaque!" Audrey shouted, hoping the building's AI would listen to her. Normally she would tell Nin her preferences, and Nin would communicate with other machines on Audrey's behalf. Other people, too. "Make everything opaque now!"

She wasn't sure about the rest of the building, but the walls around her turned solid orange, blocking the androids' view of Audrey and Zola.

As they ran down the stairs, Audrey told each floor to go opaque, to keep reducing their visibility. Sirens wailed around the building, advising residents to return to their apartments.

Residents and partygoers flooded the stairs, some in a blind panic, most in a drugged stupor, many of them wearing no clothes at all, especially the androids. The crowd was thick and confused, with everyone slowing everyone else down.

More lasers fired down the stairwell at Audrey and Zola.

"How do we make them stop?" Audrey asked.

"They won't stop until they kill us or we escape," Zola said.

"Escape," Audrey whispered.

A troop of gray-uniformed Guard Guy androids clomped up the stairs, arriving from the tower's nearest security station. Relief flooded Audrey at the sight of them.

"They're right behind us!" Audrey shouted at the Guard Guys. "They've been hacked. You have to stop them."

"Understood, ma'am. We'll take care of everything." The Guard Guy smiled with his red, rotund face. Guard Guys were much cheaper than Security Steves, but made by the same company.

The Guard Guys drew electrical stun guns, ready to zap any human suspects unconscious, but Audrey doubted they would be effective against the Security Steve androids.

Audrey and Zola managed to squeeze past the first row of Guard Guys before the first Security Steves arrived. Lasers burned the air next to Audrey. One laser burrowed into the head of a Guard Guy beside her, partially melting his face and revealing the metal below. The android froze where it stood, becoming an obstacle on the stairs.

"Error," said the lead Guard Guy. "Unable to damage Hamilcar Security property. A little error here." He waved his stun gun uselessly, not even activating it.

"Oh, don't try to be a hero, Guy." Zola turned and stood behind the indecisive Guard Guy. She grabbed his stunner, adjusted the settings, and fired a blinding bolt of electricity at one of the Steves.

The Steve shuddered and staggered across the stairs. It slammed its head into the wall, then turned and slammed its head into the handrail, denting its cranium.

Zola moved behind a second Guard Guy and repeated the procedure, discharging its entire battery in a single destructive bolt, damaging a second Steve.

"Let's go!" Zola pulled Audrey onward down the stairs. "You good with a gun?"

"No, not at all!" Audrey said, feeling frightened by the question.

"You'll learn."

They rushed downward to the next car-loading level as fast as they could, trying to stay ahead of the wave of death and destruction chasing after them.

Chapter Seven

Galapagos

Reginald Ellison walked the corridor with the Galapagos spaceport's security chief, a low bulldog of a man who seemed born to be security chief of one place or another, Coalition Military Police Captain Henry "Looming" Loomis.

"Kartokov's quarters were completely destroyed," Loomis said, coughing. "You may be down one minister of defense."

"A terrible loss," said Ogden, though the commerce minister's tone didn't convey much grief. "Still, it could have been worse. Do we know what happened? An accident?"

"We're looking into it," Ellison said.

"The ambassador's room got it pretty bad, too," Captain Loomis added. "Interior walls blown apart, lots of dust. No casualties there, obviously."

"Were any of the... robot soldiers damaged?" Ellison asked, hoping their numbers had been reduced.

"Ask them yourself." Loomis pointed into a hotel room where the damaged door had been removed. Dust from the destruction of the interior walls had settled on them.

The robotic soldiers stood in straight rows, still as statues, their rifles strapped to their backs, their multi-bladed cutting staffs still clamped to their sides. A couple of them had raised their blue visors, perhaps too dirty or damaged by the explosion. Their skeletal steel faces and black video eyes stared straight ahead.

They looked like corpses, he thought, corpses who'd been carried out of the grave and stood upright in some macabre display. It was hard not to think of old stories and movies about zombies, the risen dead. It was all intentional psy-op stuff, he was sure. The Carthage Consolidated Infantry Reaper, that was their brand name.

"Can any of you answer questions?" Ellison asked. "And if you could be so kind as to upload any recordings you may have of the event to my security chief—"

"Direct all questions to Simon Zorn," a monotone voice replied. None of the reapers had moved. Ellison couldn't even tell which one had spoken.

"Can you have him come out here, then?" Ellison asked.

"You ask me, this was no accident," Loomis said. "Our maintenance engineer said nothing here could have caused it. I think you had a series of expertly planted explosives, weak enough to leave the major compartment walls intact, but strong enough to... well, make a real mess. The whole port's on lockdown since one second after the blast, nobody in or out. If the terrorists are still here, they're locked in with us."

"But who would do this?" Navra Coraline asked. The minister of state had grabbed a long, formal kimono adorned with kelp imagery.

"Someone who doesn't want us making friends with Carthage, it seems," Ogden said.

"That's about ninety-five percent of our population," Ellison said.

"Is that true? Is Carthage so very ill-favored on Galapagos?" Simon Zorn approached them.

"We can't control public opinion," Ellison said.

"That's where you're wrong," Simon replied with a smile.

"Well, it can be massaged, certainly," Ogden said. "Mr. Ambassador, we're sorry for this unfortunate development of events. We hope it doesn't interfere in the new friendship between our worlds."

"That depends entirely on who is behind it and why," Simon said.

"How's my family?" Ellison asked.

"Cadia is fine. Resting. I have two of my guards watching over her and the children."

"I'll relieve them." Ellison pointed at two of the uniformed soldiers in Coalition gear. "Go watch over my wife and kids."

"That's not necessary," Simon said, smiling. "We're perfectly happy to help."

"It's fine," Ellison said. "I'm sorry things went sour. The port is on lockdown, but if you and your honor guard need to board your shuttle and depart, we'll let you through, of course."

"As there was an explosion in my suite as well, it must be interpreted as an attack on Carthage's military assets and diplomatic representative. I would rather remain until we can identify the parties responsible."

"But who could have done this?" Ogden asked. "The Iron Hammers?"

"At the top of my list, but it's a little subtle for them," Ellison said. "Obliterating the entire spaceport with a surface-to-orbit missile barrage would be more their style."

"The Iron Hammers would have the most to lose by an alliance between your Coalition and Carthage," Simon said.

"No alliance!" Kartokov's voice bellowed, startling everyone. The defense minister burst into the corridor, followed by a bewildered spaceport medic.

"I thought you were reported dead," Ogden said to Kartokov, who was covered in debris, significant chunks of his beard and hair burned off.

"It was the machines!" Kartokov jabbed a burned finger at Simon Zorn. "It had to be. Nothing like this ever happened on Galapagos before!"

"Let's not rush to point fingers," Coraline said, putting a hand on Kartokov's wrist and nudging his arm down. "Literally or figuratively."

"How can you say nothing like this has ever happened?" Simon Zorn asked. "I know your history. Galapagos is a warlike planet. Your nations have spent more years fighting than getting along."

"But nobody ever attacked the spaceport," Ellison said. "That was always neutral territory. It's the only one we have, and it's pretty small and fragile. It's everyone's lifeline to interplanetary travel and trade. Not that there's much trade."

"Never trust a machine that pretends to be a man," Kartokov said, still glaring at the ambassador.

"That is a truly fascinating comment," Simon Zorn said. "And why would you say that?"

"Because he has been through a difficult ordeal." Coraline touched Kartokov's arm sympathetically. "As have we all."

Kartokov seemed like he wanted to growl at her, but instead he simmered down for the moment, her touch seeming to calm his rage.

"None of us will rest until this is fully investigated," Ellison said. "I'm sure we can find alternative accommodations for the ambassador and his... his men while we proceed."

"I expect to be involved in this investigation," Simon said. "As I was one of the targets."

"Let's all get out of the way and let Loomis and his people investigate," Ellison said. "Mr. Ambassador, we will keep you informed, but for the moment our national leaders back home will expect to be briefed privately on today's chaotic events."

"Of course," Simon said, frowning slightly. "Captain Loomis, my soldiers are at your disposal, should you need them to help secure the port."

"Yeah... thanks." The bulldoggish man looked at the gruesome black steel machines in their fancy, dust-spattered uniforms, as silent and stiff as the First Emperor's terracotta army. "I'll get back to you on that."

Ellison and the other Galapagos ministers returned to the same spartan board room in the executive center, five levels down from the residential area.

"Give this room full access to the entire port security system," Ellison told the security chief. "And I'd like a sidearm in case things get worse."

"Make it two," Kartokov said, holding up a finger like he was ordering drinks at a bar. The man looked badly injured, but he remained upright, anger seared into his face along with the burns from the explosive.

"Three," Coraline said.

"How is this going to help?" Ogden asked. "You're going to hunt down the terrorist yourself, Ellison?"

"Do you have a problem with that?" Ellison asked, and Ogden looked away.

The security chief left, and one of the young guards arrived soon after with laser pistols and holster belts.

"They're weak weapons," Ellison said, once he was alone with the ministers.

"They can pierce body armor," Coraline said, looking at her blocky gray gun.

"But can they pierce one of those Carthaginian infantry robots?" Ellison asked. "If not, we might as well be strapping on forks and knives."

"Why are you so certain they're the enemy?" Ogden said.

"I'm not. But if they are, we need to be prepared."

"Prepared to do what?" Ogden chuckled and shook his head. "Make war with Carthage? How will you do that, Reggie? Fly one of your war submarines into space? We've been fighting petty tribal wars down here for generations, while Carthage has been out conquering worlds across the Orion Arm. We could never beat them. We're a fly, and they're a nuclear-armed cruise missile. Why fight them?"

"The same reason we fought our wars among each other," Ellison said. "For our freedom. For our independence."

"All the people of our world came to Galapagos to live as we choose," said Coraline, her big fish eyes watching the hologram bubbles of real-time security camera feeds from around the spaceport. "Not to become subjects of another world's empire."

"I say we attack them now," Kartokov said. "The ambassador and his filthy robots. Destroy them, send them back to Carthage in a box. We know they're here to threaten us. They must be the ones who tried to kill us."

"If Carthage wanted us dead, we'd already be dead," Ellison said.

"Perhaps they merely want us frightened," Coraline said. "So we will run into their protective arms. The ambassador already offered to station those reapers around the spaceport. Imagine if we allowed that. Who among us believes the reapers would ever leave? They would control this port for Carthage. That's how Carthage operates—like snakes, slithering in through every hole."

"They won't be slithering into our holes!" Kartokov pounded the table. "I have spoken to the leaders of Gavrikova, and they insist on independence. No deal with Carthage!"

"I'm getting the opposite signal from back home," Ogden said. "The Green Islands want peace, whatever the cost. We can't survive a war against Carthage, but we can survive as one of their cooperative clients. We'll all be a bit poorer, but—"

"They are a ruthless empire!" Kartokov said.

"And all empires fall," Ogden replied, with an oily smile. "All we need to do is wait them out. And keep our heads low. The only question is whether we wear a golden collar or an iron one. Personally, I vote gold."

"Fool's gold," Kartokov muttered.

"Those golden collars are for wealthy inner worlds who can negotiate from a position of strength in the first place," Ellison said. "Outer worlds like us get the iron shaft. Carthage will demand more and more tribute until the debt breaks us, and then we'll all somehow find ourselves peasants, with no property of our own, with the Carthaginians owning all our land and natural resources. That's their pattern with poorly defended outer worlds."

"What about your people, Ellison?" Coraline asked. "How do they lean?"

"The Republic of the Scatterlands... lives up to its name," Ellison said. "The Assembly is fighting about it. They can't even organize a vote on the subject. But public opinion is solidly against allying with Carthage. Or with the next island over, half the time."

"So they leave such choices up to your personal judgment," Coraline said. "By default."

"That's one way of looking at it. What about your people, Coraline?" Ellison asked.

"We are flexible, but our independence is important to us. We do not wish our society reshaped by Carthaginian law. And we cannot tolerate risks to the ocean's ecosystem. That would bring the wrath of the Deep Gods."

Ellison nodded. "Carthage tends to strip-mine the planets it rules, especially in the outer worlds. Let's remember that when we hear talk of 'trade' and 'cooperation.' They'll charge us high fees for the protection of their imperial fleet —a service fee, tribute payment, protection money, or tax, pick a label—and they turn around and use that money to buy up and export our resources. To the inner worlds."

"Importing and exporting, trade, this is how our economies grow," Ogden said. "It's how we advance as a species."

"So, if we were to vote on Carthage's proposal today," Ellison said. "How would it go?"

"For it," Ogden said. "We have no choice."

"Never," Kartokov said.

"We would need assurances of our people's autonomy,

including full religious freedom and all that it entails," Coraline said. "Freedom with our DNA. And strong protections for the oceans."

Ellison nodded. "We could propose a counteroffer. And we still need some kind of vote in the House of Ambassadors for any major treaty with any other planet. Personally, I'm in favor of letting the slow wheels of the democratic process turn as slowly as possible on this one. Let there be debate and discussion at every level, while the people of Galapagos work out exactly how to respond to—"

"Forget the treaty!" Kartokov said. "We need to get those machines off this spaceport and away from our world before they kill us all. Maybe they have planted more bombs already."

"We still don't know for sure who's behind that," Ellison said. "Let's wait for Captain Loomis's review of the security footage. So far, there's been no follow-up events, no statements from any terrorist group on Galapagos. And I'm sure we could all find suspects in our countries. We each face some internal faction or splinter group that opposes the Coalition itself. All of them would like to see us fail to manage this situation correctly. They all want to say the Coalition does not function and is doomed to collapse. That's why we have to investigate first. Too many suspects. Plus the Iron Hammers."

"You said this wasn't like them," Coraline said.

"But I wouldn't rule them out."

"The Iron Hammers seem the most likely culprit to me, honestly," Ogden said.

"Anyone except the Carthaginians," Kartokov growled. "You'd never want to accuse your precious future masters. Are you already on their payroll?"

"I don't have to be bribed to see how the tide is turning," Ogden said. "I am simply not blind to reality. And it is not my country that is so famous for requiring large bribes to lubricate the wheels of state."

Kartokov snarled, but Coraline held him back with a few soothing words.

They continued to argue, sometimes splitting off into private offices where they could each confer by encrypted audio with their national leadership down on the surface.

How would we ever fight a war of global defense together? We could hardly manage to agree on an official armistice day, Ellison thought after a long and unproductive call with the crowded, top-heavy executive cabinet of his home country. Even the name of his country was haphazard—the "Scatterlands" had referred to thousands of mostly tiny, often marshy islands. This vague geographical term had evolved into something that now proudly called itself the Republic of Scatterlandia, and he had to say that name in public, again and again, with a sense of gravitas, without chuckling.

Beneath that oddball name, though, lay people who came from countless different backgrounds, who had together forged a nation in the heat of war. None of the nations on Galapagos were more diverse and less centralized than the Scatterlands, but the men and women of those marshy farms and fishing villages had risen to form a powerful navy despite their relative poverty to the other nations.

He felt like he was back in the war, commanding one of those hastily built submersible boats. Each of the large nations had some airplanes, but most of the fighting had happened on the surface of the ocean, and below it, down into the deep trenches where the great monsters of Galapagos dwelled.

His submarine, the *Sea Scorpion*, had been built from reused parts of everything from fishing boats to old space shuttles and cargo drop-boxes that had once brought the settlers and their possessions down to the planet's surface. It could resist the extreme deep-sea pressure of the trenches, and it could dock at one of the Scatterlands' critical handful of underwater carriers. Those incredible ships had traveled the deep trenches, serving as bases, tenders, and makeshift hospital and machine shops for the submarines that had waged so much of the Island Wars.

Ellison had spent most of his life on and under the sea. He'd often heard it compared to outer space, but Ellison preferred the ocean to space. The ocean was alive, all the way down. Space was full of emptiness and silence, a land for the dead, or for things that had never truly lived.

Like the machines.

Security Chief Loomis returned to their makeshift war room with bad news.

"Our engineers and maintenance guys aren't forensics experts, but they agree it was bombs, handmade with common chemicals, looks like. Not military grade."

"So it could be anyone," Ellison said.

"And the surveillance systems are infected with viruses," Loomis said, nearly growling the words. "That's going to be a whole other net to untangle. And we may not get anything. They covered their tracks pretty good."

"It's no mystery who did it," Kartokov grumbled.

"You really need to see the doc," Ellison told him, not for the first time that day.

"Plenty of time for that later," Kartokov said.

Ambassador Zorn arrived, followed by four of his honor guard. Two of their visors were up, revealing their narrow, steel skull faces, their constantly recording black eyes.

"We aren't ready yet," Ellison said.

"And we have waited long enough," Simon said. "What have you determined about today's attack?"

"Our investigation is ongoing," Ellison said.

"And still includes all possible suspects," Kartokov growled, looking at Simon and his four death-bots.

"Did the guards just let you in?" Loomis said, moving toward the door. "I had two men out there."

"Where are your four other bots?" Ellison asked.

"Two are currently restraining the guards who refused to admit us—" Simon began.

"If you hurt my men, I'll—" Loomis stepped up to the ambassador, making a fist.

"You will what?" Simon asked. "Please complete your threat."

"Go check on them, Loomis," Ellison said.

"Your men will be fine, aside from some light bruising," Simon said. "They really should have been more cooperative."

Loomis dashed out of the room, looking furious.

"And your other two infantry robots?" Ellison asked Simon. "Where are they?"

"Watching over your family, Minister-General Ellison." Simon pointed his narrow wand of a hologram projector at the conference table in front of Ellison. A video played—two of the hideous machines carrying a stretcher with Ellison's wife, Cadia, strapped to it, unconscious.

"Where are they taking her?" Ellison asked, rage suddenly boiling inside him.

"To your medical center here on the spaceport, Minister-General," Simon said. "They've already transported her there. They remain to keep watch over your wife and sons. Her condition is stable."

"That's not necessary," Ellison said. "You can call them back. My family is secure."

"We will see how secure they truly are," Simon said.

"And your soldiers assaulting our guards?" Ellison said. "I can't allow that. Diplomacy aside."

"Can't 'allow'?" The Simon unit looked amused. He approached Ellison and placed a hand on his shoulder, an unwelcome gesture of amiability. "We are not yours to command, Ellison. And we will not be fooled or distracted by this absurd charade."

"What charade?" Coraline asked. "I don't follow."

"A series of bombs in which your top ministers are attacked, but not killed," Simon said. "The charges in my suite were far more powerful than those in Ellison's or Kartokov's. That is what *my* investigation has revealed."

"Maybe because they were targeting machines instead of humans," Ellison said.

"Or perhaps they were *only* targeting machines," Simon said. "And the bombing of the humans was a diversion meant to muddy the waters. One interpretation of the facts might be that you, the Coalition of Galapagos, wished to kill me and my guards," Simon said.

"You can't possibly believe we'd be so foolish," Ellison said. "We're aware of the power of your empire."

"We don't like to use the term 'empire,'" Simon said. "It's rather... primitive. We like 'network of alliances.'"

"Less accurate," Kartokov grumbled.

"Whatever you call it, we aren't that stupid. We know that a move like that would be like a declaration of war against Carthage," Ellison said.

"Yes, it would," Simon said, his voice flat and dead, his lifeless blue eyes boring into Ellison's.

"So surely you don't believe—" Ellison began to reiterate.

"The facts indicate multiple possibilities," Simon said. "I agree it would be foolish of you or someone in your camp to attack assets of Carthage like myself. However, your planet is known for its prolonged wars, its people for their violent nature."

"If it was anyone from our world, it was either a small terrorist group or the Iron Hammers," Ellison said.

"It had to be the Hammers," Ogden said. "Their premier, Ulysses Cross. That's the man we'll find behind all this, I'd bet all my savings."

"Your certainty is reassuring," Simon said to Ogden, who seemed to be on course to becoming Simon's favorite among the Galapagos ministers. *No bomb in Ogden's room*, Ellison thought. Then he looked at the tattooed minister of state from the ocean-cult people. *Nor hers.* He recalled how easily the Aquaticans had flipped sides during the war, aligning with the Iron Hammers at one point, Gavrikova at another, going wherever the advantage seemed to be. Aquaticans could be slippery fish, like the deep-sea gods they worshiped.

He wondered how strongly the Aquaticans and the Green Islanders would stand against Carthage if the need came, and for how long.

Maybe Galapagos, as a world, lacked the fortitude for independence. Maybe they were destined to fall under the heel of the first empire that came along.

"If, however, the Iron Hammers are suspected," Simon continued, "perhaps we could ask them what they have to say on the matter."

Ellison frowned. It was hard to consider reaching out to

the Iron Hammers' madman of a leader, Ulysses Cross. He was a grandson of Eli Cross, who had led the Iron Hammers in the Szazel prison revolt and across the stars to the remote planet of Galapagos, where there was no central authority to stop them from setting up shop on the Polar Archipelago. Conditions on those large, icy islands were cold and rough, but the islands provided them with nearly unlimited geothermal power, while titanic fish and marine mammals could be harvested from the icy polar waters for meat.

The Iron Hammers had grown into a nation; their gang had existed in prisons across both the heavily populated and urbanized inner worlds and the rougher, more rural outer worlds. Hardened criminals fled to Galapagos, bringing family and friends with them, and over the generations they'd grown into a civilization of millions.

Their population growth was also fed by a thriving sex trade. More than once, a misdirected drop-box had been found in the ocean, full of dead bodies, women who'd been sent down in the cheap but dangerous one-way craft that was really meant only for cargo. The slave traders had cut corners by saving on the cost of a reliable shuttle or even a proper drop ship.

"Ulysses Cross is a dangerous man," Ellison said. "We can't trust him to be honest. The Iron Hammers have no honor."

"Yet it cannot hurt to ask and to gauge his response," Simon said. "Especially as we have gone to the great trouble and expense of ferrying Cross and his delegation up from the Polar Archipelago."

"You've done what?" Ellison reached for the gun holster at his hip. "There are Iron Hammers here? In the spaceport?"

"When Carthage requested this meeting," Simon said,

"you did not invite me down to your newly built capitol on Tower Island. You did not offer elaborate gifts, or entertainments, or the finery of a state dinner."

"What a bunch of foppish—" Kartokov began, but Coraline elbowed him into silence.

"You did not show respect to Carthage." Simon said. His face and tone of voice remained neutral, but Ellison felt a powerful darkness behind his words. "You chose to meet me in your filthy bus station of a spaceport, with no hospitality aside from some poor quality tea."

"But you're not a human," Ellison said. He glanced at Coraline. "We had no idea you expected—"

"How you treat me reveals your attitude toward Carthage. You did not welcome me to your world with any great ceremony or pageantry. Indeed, as mentioned, you did not even invite me down."

"If you would like to visit the surface, we would be happy to host you—" Coraline began.

"Due to this near-hostile treatment of our diplomatic overtures," Simon said, "we began a parallel process. We rented Pier G2, several levels below us, under an innocuous corporate name. I'm sure you're familiar with the area—six docking bays out of the view of most of the spaceport. Depressing little hostel rooms around an absolutely disgusting communal kitchen and bathroom. That area is ideal for crew or passengers who don't want to be seen in the retail and residential levels, eating at the Duckburger or renting a room at the Happy Stars Inn. Or perhaps they need a place to park their human cargo while they swab out the ship's hold. The Iron Hammers seem quite familiar with the accommodations."

"So you covertly brought our enemies up here at the same time you're meeting with the leadership of the Coalition?" Ellison asked. He resisted the urge to draw his pistol and drill a laser through the android's forehead. That would be a satisfying resolution of the conversation, but an extremely short-term one.

"I am programmed to be efficient," Simon said. "To develop customized solutions to complex human problems. We could not negotiate realistically with the Coalition while ignoring the other major power faction on your planet."

"How many of them are here?" Ellison asked.

"A sizable delegation," Simon said. "They wanted strong representation."

"Okay. Let's go see them. Loomis!" Ellison touched the audio bud in his ear. "Grab every man you can spare and meet me at the armory."

"Yes, sir. Can someone tell these machines to release my men? They aren't listening to me," Loomis said.

Simon waved a hand. Ellison broke off contact with Loomis once the security chief confirmed.

"Are you planning to ambush the Iron Hammers?" Simon asked Ellison, raising his eyebrows.

"Of course we are—" Kartokov began.

"No, we are not," Ellison said, with a hard look at his defense minister, though he shared Kartokov's sentiments. "But we are not going to walk into a room full of Iron Hammers without basic precautions. Or can you assure us that they brought no weapons or armor of their own?"

"I can make no such assurances. I did not handle their baggage, as I am not a bellhop," Simon said.

"So... did they bring weapons and armor?" Ellison asked.

"They brought cargo. Perhaps it is merely crackers and canned sloth whale. They can't seem to get enough of those parasite-ridden animals. They put the blubber in their tea. It tastes... off-putting. Shall I accompany you?"

Ellison thought it over. "You lead the way." He gestured at the hideous infantry robots. "I want them out in front of us. Not bringing up the rear."

"As you wish, Minister-General Ellison." Simon bowed, then backed out of the room, followed by his four infantry bots.

"They call that model the 'reaper,'" Coraline said, quietly. "Designed to intimidate on the battlefield. And to instill a feeling of despair."

"It works," Ogden said, his voice just a whisper as he followed the other ministers out of the room.

The two guards who'd been posted outside their conference room were each rubbing sore spots on their necks. Two of the robotic infantry stood nearby, holding the guards' weapons.

"They were pinned against the wall when I walked out here." Loomis nodded at the two Coalition guards. They looked pretty green to Ellison, almost too young to be serving as security on the planet's lone spaceport. Or maybe Ellison was just getting old. Regardless, he was enraged at the android and its reapers for treating his men this way.

"Bring them with us," Ellison said, keeping his anger to a low simmer. "We need every hand we've got."

Then he prepared to go down and meet the monsters nesting in the docks. His enemies seemed to be multiplying around him.

He could barely contain the fury inside him as he stared at the back of the ambassador's head, the thin gray hair that was supposed to disguise him as someone bland and unimportant. Ellison had been duped into bringing his family up here for what was supposed to be a placid, public state visit, and now they were in danger. He couldn't even be with his injured family members now, because he was stuck driving straight into the jaws of that danger. It was his job.

He wondered whether he had enough guards and weapons on this port to take down the Iron Hammer delegation if they attacked.

And if the Iron Hammers and the Simon unit's infantry bots joined up and turned on the Coalition personnel present, what then? Maybe Ellison was three steps behind. Maybe the Simon unit had already forged an alliance with the Iron Hammers, and this supposed state visit was just a ploy to seize control of the Galapagos spaceport while decapitating the elected leadership of the Coalition. And Ellison's wife and sons would die with them.

That would certainly send a message to the folks back home, Ellison thought grimly.

He headed to the armory to prepare for the worst.

Chapter Eight

Earth

Colt had hoped they would reach some light at the next station, but there was none, only a hill of broken concrete and asphalt that was hard to climb over. The underground station had mostly collapsed inward years ago and then filled up with rubble from the buildings above.

The train tunnel itself wasn't completely blocked by the destruction, but the going was tough, and the rubble shifted under them. They had no choice but to use flashlights to find their way; Mohini used the one mounted on her plasma pistol.

She cried out at one point as rubble gave way beneath her, and he had to grab her to keep her from sliding. Her light swung wide, and he was afraid she would drop the best weapon they had. She held on to it, though.

They turned out their lights and sat quietly in the darkness, waiting to see whether an attack was imminent, or whether the metalheads might come down here, looking for the human who'd screamed.

It was hard to tell how much time passed—it felt like most of an hour, but it could have been just a minute or two—before they resumed moving again over the shifting debris, keeping their lights dim and pointed down.

Then, as they neared the mouth of the tunnel on the other side of the station, he heard a low skittering off to his left.

He killed his light again, and with his other hand he grabbed Mohini's shoulder and squeezed, a common gesture that meant they needed to stop and be silent. She tensed up and made a small hissing sound. He remembered her aversion to physical contact and quickly released her.

She got the message, though, and turned off her light and fell quiet.

The scratching, scrabbling sound again.

Colt pointed his flashlight and turned it on.

Rats scrabbled in and out of the rubble all around them. He felt relieved, but not completely.

"Watch your step," he whispered. "They'll bite. They're hungry, like everyone else. We could eat them, but we don't have time to waste here."

She shuddered and moved closer to him. He reluctantly turned his light out again, hoping the creatures would keep their distance.

He and Mohini managed to pick up speed as they got clear of the station, but there was still a lot of debris slowing them down, and they had to keep using their flashlights.

Behind them, the rubble shifted. It sounded like something heavy was moving it.

They turned off their lights. Back at the mouth of the

tunnel, something floated, glowing, not much larger than a wasp. It made a low buzzing sound.

The floating light was an emergency lighting drone. In the old days, it had helped illuminate disaster areas and other situations where power might be out, guiding first responders to those in danger.

But now the machines mostly used them as a—

"Distraction," he said, turning to face the darkness in the tunnel ahead, the opposition direction from the floating light. "Get ready, they're coming—"

Their skull-like faces emerged from the subway tunnel like the dead rising from their catacombs. There were at least three reapers, moving fast.

Mohini screamed, but also let loose a bolt from her pistol that struck one reaper solidly in its midsection. The plasma turned the reaper's skeletal abdomen into molten metal, which dripped like glowing red blood onto the train tracks. It was a beautiful sight to see one of the machines damaged so fatally with one shot.

Colt fired up the cutting laser, which Mohini had let him carry. He had no time to plan, so he just jabbed it at the nearest reaper, which was swiping its long blade-tipped staff in Colt's direction.

Colt sliced through the shaft of the slender weapon, sending half of it clattering to the floor. He carved through the machine's elbow joint, then up across its torso, on track for its head and the CPU shielded within its steel cranium.

The reaper drew back and out of the way, though, with less damage than Colt had hoped to inflict.

The laser's compact power supply wasn't going to last forever, so Colt pursued the retreating reaper, determined to strike it somewhere vital before his weapon sputtered out.

"Colt!" Mohini cried.

He turned to see that his pursuit of reaper number two had brought him right alongside reaper number three, which now reached out to him with steel hands strong enough to crush bones.

Mohini squeezed off a couple of plasma bolts, hitting the third reaper high and low, in the head and the pelvis, turning its skeletal steel form into a hot glowing melt.

Colt was in awe of how effective the plasma was against the metalheads; in his life, he'd found a fair number of old lead-firing projectile weapons in the ruins, while laser weapons were much rarer. Plasma weapons must have been even less common in the old world, maybe restricted to military use. Or maybe they'd all been used up in the war, trying to fend off Carthage's destruction.

The reaper Colt had sliced fled faster now, running backward over rubble and debris.

Frustrated, Colt flung the handheld laser generator after it, leaving the cutting beam activated.

He hadn't really thought out that move, though, because the generator, about the size and shape of a bicycle handle, toppled end over end after he threw it. The beam swung wildly, carving a narrow but deep trench along the ceiling before swooping down right at Colt.

"Watch out!" he shouted to Mohini, while just managing to leap aside and dodge the beam himself.

"Idiot!" she screamed as the beam sliced toward her and she dropped to the floor. "Neanderthal!"

The laser generator finally collided with the retreating reaper. The glowing beam spliced the thing's skull, and the reaper stopped, frozen in place. The laser generator dropped to the floor and burned a steady beam through the reaper's skeletal foot for a couple of seconds, then sputtered out, its battery spent.

"You could have been a little more careful with that throw," Mohini said, dusting herself as she stood up again. "Let's try to avoid decapitating ourselves in the future. As just a general rule of thumb."

"Sorry. Uh, great job on these guys." He nodded at the semi-molten reapers. The one she'd hit twice finally toppled to the ground, its head clanging against the rail tracks.

"I don't have much plasma left," she said.

"There will be more reapers. They usually move in packs of eight—"

As if to prove him right, three more reapers leaped onto the tracks from the collapsed station. They bolted up the tracks as fast as the trains that had once traveled here. The reapers ran at Colt and Mohini with their long bladed staffs extended, ready to butcher the humans.

Mohini shot a plasma bolt to cover their retreat as she and Colt ran up the tunnel.

They reached a section of track where the train had derailed long ago. Rusty cars stood sideways on the track, blocking up the tunnel from wall to wall. Some of the train cars had toppled over.

Colt and Mohini had no choice but to climb over one of the cars and crawl on their elbows under a couple more. It was slow going, with the reapers moving in close behind them, their metallic limbs occasionally clinking against metal, echoing as they crawled over and under the train cars behind Colt.

The reapers were mostly silent, though, which was unnerving. Colt fought the urge to look back, so he had no idea exactly how close they were. Close, though. He could hear them scraping along behind him, quietly and relentlessly gaining ground, and he put on all the speed he could.

He finally climbed out from under the last car of the

derailed train. He found Mohini kneeling in the middle of the tracks, pointing her plasma pistol at him.

"What are you doing?" he asked. "The machines are right behind me—"

"So get out of the way!" she snapped.

Colt rolled aside while she fired plasma bolts at the sideways train car behind him. He finally looked back and saw the reapers were closer than he had imagined. They were crawling almost flat on the ground, supported by their skeletal hands and feet, their faces already emerging from under the train car.

Mohini's plasma bolts were weak, lower powered than they had been, and neither one struck the reapers at all.

Instead, they struck the wheels of the sideways train car, which were already bent and loose, and turned them to glowing red melt.

The train car tilted toward Colt and Mohini, crushing the reapers under its partially molten edge.

Colt froze, mesmerized as he watched the enormous bulk of the train car lean closer to him, its broad side on course to crush him.

It stopped tilting, though, its front edge pressing down onto the reapers. The arms of the trapped reapers flailed from under the tilted train car, and a couple of their skulls were jutting out, jaws snapping uselessly, black eyes staring at Colt. He got a sense of how implacable they were, how unstoppable. They felt no pain and cared nothing for their own survival.

"Let's go!" Mohini snapped.

"Just a second." Colt looked around and spotted a section of rusty old pipe on the floor; it looked like it had broken off the wall when the train derailed.

He lifted up the pipe and approached the trapped, snapping, grabbing reapers.

"Come on, just leave them!" Mohini said, already dashing away down the tunnel. "Don't be stupid!"

"They won't be trapped here long." Colt moved in and swung the pipe, smashing one of the reapers across the face. He did it again and again, and finally felt a satisfying crunch as he cracked one of its black, bug-like eyes. Maybe he couldn't put the machines out of commission, but he could at least blind them.

He turned and swung at the other skull, striking the lip of the pipe right into one of its eyes and cracking it, too.

Then something clamped down on his ankle.

One of the reapers had wriggled just a little closer, reached just a little farther, and grabbed him with its skeletal steel hand.

Colt's heart thundered and he tried to pull free, but there was no escaping the machine's grip. He began hammering the two narrow rods of its forearm with the pipe. That got him nowhere.

Metallic scraping and scratching approached him from above. He looked up in time to see another reaper jump from the top of the train car, hurtling through the air toward him.

The reaper's jaw opened as it flew toward him, and a strange thick cloud flowed out of it, like smoke or gas.

I probably shouldn't breathe that, he thought, but it was too late. A sour burning smell filled his nostrils, his sinus cavity, his throat.

The reaper slammed into him.

He felt himself falling, and tried to brace for the inevitable impact with the rails below. His body had gone limp, though.

He never felt that impact on the rails. He just kept falling, and falling, and falling.

When he woke, it was to the sound of screaming, but not his own.

He was nauseous, flooded with the sour taste of the gas, and tried to roll over on his side to throw up.

That turned out to be difficult, though, because he was strapped down where he lay. Much of his puke landed right on his chest.

He managed to open his heavy lids, and he did not like what he saw.

He was strapped to a hospital bed, but not the cushy suspended ones like those in the clinic they'd recently raided. This was the kind of bed that cluttered the big hospitals downtown, the hospitals that had been picked clean years ago. The curtains were like those in the old hospitals, too, thick and green, musty. They enclosed him on all four sides, giving him about a closet's worth of space. A dark stain like a dried handprint marred one curtain.

Sensors were glued to his head and chest, wired to machines nearby. The machines were covered in dark smudges like the curtain, and dusty, like nobody had cleaned them in a long time.

Then the smell of the place hit him—rotten meat, and sickness, piss and shit. The fetid air was full of cries and moans, punctuated by the occasional scream.

This hospital did not feel like a place where much healing was happening. It was dim, dirty, and crowded; he could tell by the voices and the heat and thick body odor, though the patients couldn't see each other.

He tried to sit up, pushing against his straps. They had some give, but not enough.

One monitor emitted a series of beeps, and a green curtain shifted aside.

Another medical machine rolled into the room, tall and boxy, with three thin arms on each side; Colt thought of a large cockroach. A couple of the arms hung loose and limp, like they'd been damaged and never repaired.

The machine was topped with a round plastic purple head. Its face had originally been a simple cartoony cat, with big friendly eyes and a pink bow next to one ear. The face had been smashed at some point, though, and now had one eye, half a smile, a couple of broken plastic whiskers, and loose wires hanging from the large hole where other eye had been. It looked like a cat that had been run over by a truck.

"Hold still, little fella. This won't hurt a bit. Nurse Kitty is your friend." The kitty-bot spoke in a soothing baby-talk voice. He could almost remember his mother speaking to him that way, in the lost days of his early childhood. It wasn't at all comforting from this machine, though.

The robot rolled up next to his bedside and extended two of its long, multi-jointed arms, one toward Colt's head and one toward his feet.

Colt noticed the arm by his feet was mounted with circular copper saws, in a range of sizes. A couple of these saws were extended, as if, like the arms, they had malfunctioned over the years and couldn't fully retract.

The other arm reached toward the crown of Colt's head, and he couldn't help noticing the array of long, straight blades mounted under it like cat claws, arranged from shortest to longest. Even the shortest blade could have swung out and slashed his throat; the longest could have pierced his eye and drilled deep into his brain.

He strained against the bonds that held him, and they creaked a little, but unfortunately they weren't quite as dilapidated as the old med-bot that was examining him.

For a moment, he considered asking the med-bot to wipe away the puke from his chest and shoulder, but he was worried the old box of gears would decide to use one of its many cutting blades to do it.

"I said hold still," the broken kitty head repeated. "If you're good, you'll get ice cream." A lower drawer in its boxy body slid open, revealing a pile of little wooden sticks in limp, mold-stained paper wrappers, lying in dark filth. "Any flavor you like! But you have to be good for Nurse Kitty."

The med-bot closed the freezer drawer and moved even closer to him, passing its arms back and forth over Colt in a way that reminded him of a drunk old scavenger he'd once met, a man covered in bloody sores who'd claimed to be a "miracle healer." He could supposedly heal anybody in exchange for a bottle of liquor, a few pills, or a quick hand job. His inability to heal his own sores had not been explained.

"Please go," Colt whispered.

"Almost done!" the kitty face chirped. Another arm extended, spattered with dark spots of long-dried blood, tipped with a filthy syringe and needle with dust and hair clinging to it. "We just need an eensy weensy bit of blood, but it'll only sting a moment. Then you'll get your ice cream! How fun!"

"Go away!" Colt shouted, as the needle moved in toward his arm. Apparently the med-bot's vein-finding algorithm was working just fine. "Shut down! Initiate emergency shutdown!" He'd heard that sometimes worked on very old machines, though of course not reapers or any of the others sent from Carthage to rule Earth.

The med-bot advanced, and Colt tried to pull away, but the restraints wouldn't let him go far.

The needle reached his skin.

"Enough." A man entered through the curtain. He wore blue surgical scrubs and a lab coat, like a doctor from the old world. The lab coat and scrubs were dirty, though, with layers of dark stains. His hair was gray and thin, which was unusual; older people in general were rare to encounter, because they'd had more time to get sick, or injured, or hunted down by the machines. Mother Braden had graying hair, but Colt didn't know many others who did.

The med-bot's needle stopped just before stabbing Colt. Then the machine backed away, folded in its arm, and left through the stained green curtain.

"You'll have to forgive Nurse Kitty," the man said. "Sometimes an old subroutine takes over. She's a bit rundown—well, very rundown—but I'm afraid we don't get the best resources at this facility. We're more of a dumping ground for barely functional war scrap. But we make do, or try to."

Colt nodded. "Thanks for stopping it," he said, though he immediately distrusted the old man.

"I apologize for its behavior," the man said. "It was only supposed to take a few basic measurements, such as blood pressure and heart rate. Weight and height, that sort of thing. Are you all right?"

"It strapped me to the table, too," Colt said. "I can't move my arms and legs very much. Can you let me go?"

"Not quite yet," the man said, and Colt's brief glimmer

of hope died. "The machines have very particular ways of doing things around here."

"The machines?" Colt felt a jolt of fear, but he was unable to fight or flee. "Where are we? A hospital?"

"Not exactly. It's more of a research facility. A laboratory." A high, piercing scream rose above the general murmur of moans and clanking machinery. It sounded like a woman or a child.

"What kind of research?" Colt asked, though he dreaded the answer.

"All kinds. You see, constantly learning about humans, trying to understand them, is one of our primary directives. Human minds are highly complex, however. Difficult to model, and therefore difficult to fully predict and control. So the learning never stops." The high, piercing scream sounded again. "Learning about you is one of our purposes, an endless and ever-branching task, one that may never be complete."

Colt's heart was racing. "You're one of them. You're a skinwalker, the kind of machine that pretends to be human."

"Skinwalker." The man smiled, as if tasting the word and finding it pleasing. "Interesting. Do you know the origin of that term? A legend from the deserts of Earth, of a thing that could take the shape of many animals. Including human. It was not truly an animal or a human, however, but a supernatural entity. A sorcerer."

Colt wasn't sure what to say to that. He strained at his bonds again, uselessly.

"I am a Simon model android," the man said. "Unit number NIX133281. Other humans have found it convenient to refer to me as 'Simon Nix.' You are welcome to do so. Should you wish to contact me personally in the future, you can ask for me by that name."

"What? Why would I want to contact...?" Colt blinked, confused.

"One never knows what twists of the road lie ahead," said the Simon unit.

Colt didn't say anything. He'd assumed he wasn't going to get out of this alive, that the machines would kill him when they were done with him. That was what the machines generally did.

"So you are a scavenger," Simon said, his voice almost genial now. "That must be a fascinating existence."

"If you like eating rats and getting hunted," Colt said.

"Still, the constant risk, the constant danger, it must keep you feeling sharp and alive," Simon said. "I've seen worlds where humans are served night and day by machines. Food, comfort, entertainment, sex, all provided by some combination of hardware and software. Coddled in this way, they grow slug-like and dull, complacent and weak. But you Earthlings have no such options. We have placed you under the harshest conditions, as an example to all the worlds who may try to resist us. However, my concern is that these very conditions may have the opposite effect of what we see in the wealthy inner worlds. My concern is that we are breeding, or rather selecting for, only the toughest and smartest humans here on Earth. Which will make you an ever more difficult problem in the future.

"My counterparts do not all see the problem as I do," he continued. "So one of my endeavors here is to explore my hypothesis, to prove it to the others. I keep my work isolated, but when I re-engage, I predict they will see I am correct."

Colt blinked. He couldn't follow much of what the

android was saying, but it all sounded creepy and horrifying to him. "So when can I leave?"

"After you have answered my questions and considered my offer," Simon said.

"What questions? What offer?"

"I would be happy to begin," Simon said. "First, general background on your life as a scavenger. Humans live in family groups. Where is your family group? Have you parents and siblings?"

"My parents are dead," Colt said. "My father was killed by metalheads. Reapers. I barely remember him. And my mom... I don't know. She left me and my sister one day, in an old laundromat where we were staying. She'd have us hide in this big old washing machine when she was gone, to stay out of sight. We're not sure what happened to her."

"Intercepted by reapers, perhaps," Simon mused, as if it were a subject of idle curiosity. "Or perhaps caught by other humans, violated, abused, murdered, or eaten. Or all of the above, as none of them are mutually exclusive."

"Don't talk about her like that," Colt said.

"But this sister of yours, she is still alive?"

"No," Colt hurried to say, mentally kicking himself for mentioning Hope. "She's dead."

"Multiple indicators tell me you are lying," Simon said. "Do not lie to me. I have many penalties I could apply." More of the recurring screams sounded outside, as if to underscore his point.

"Why do you even care?" Colt asked. "What are you doing to these people in here?"

"I told you. Experiments, to enhance my knowledge and understanding of your species. Experiments of all kinds. We have a fairly free hand here on Earth. Our only instructions from our human masters back home are to keep Earth underfoot, to let your world serve as a constant reminder to all of humanity of what happens to those who defy Carthage. All of humanity sprang from Earth, so they cannot help but pay attention. And Earth once tried to lead an alliance of worlds against Carthage, let us remember. Now Earth is reduced to a head on a pike, you see, a warning to enemies and potential rebels. Within that context, I am free to study humans as deeply as I like, with no regard for laws and regulations that might restrain me on the inner worlds."

Colt stared at the android. He found himself brimming with hatred and disgust. "You're a monster," he finally said. "All of you machines, but also your human masters back on Carthage. You're all monsters."

Simon remained silent for a long moment, staring at Colt. Then he said, "Perhaps you're right. Now, to the point." He reached outside the green curtain and brought in a tattered black doctor's bag, which he set on the monitors beside Colt.

From within, he removed the black steel head of a reaper, and Colt immediately knew which one. The ribbon cable was still plugged into the back of its head. The cable itself had been gathered up and clamped together, swinging like a pendulum from the back of the skull.

"We were very interested to find this," Simon said. "Is this your work?"

"Yes," Colt said.

"Lying again. How could you possibly do this? You're clearly just a primitive scavenger, a wild rat of a human, living in the mountains of garbage out there."

"Well, thanks," Colt said. "That means a lot coming from an evil piece of talking junk."

Simon smiled a little, as if distantly amused. "Tell me

about your companion," he said. "The girl who was with you when we caught you."

"Is she here?"

"I am asking the questions. If you do not answer, there will be penalties. Who is she? What is her name, and where is she from?"

"I actually don't know much about her."

"And you're not lying. This is lucky, isn't it? If you don't know her well, you cannot have much loyalty to her. Simply tell me all you know and I will release you, unharmed."

"We only just met when you caught us," he said. "I don't know anything—"

Pain clawed through every pore in Colt's body. It was like black fire, scourging his nervous system, his body lunging involuntarily against his restraints. This time, the loud anguished cry was his own.

"That will be your penalty for lies," Simon said. "Your lies do not deceive me, scavenger. They simply waste time and cause pointless delay. I am busy. I have continents to oversee. Now, let us start over with our new understanding. What is your name?"

"Colt."

"Good. And the name of your sister?"

"H... Holly." Colt thought to change it at the last second.

The pain surged through him again, blinding him, ripping through every channel in his body like searing-hot barbed wire.

"Her name?"

"Hope," he said. What difference did it make? His sister's name was not really some valuable piece of information that was worth dying over. He wasn't giving up her location.

"Your surname?"

"I don't remember."

"Ah. Because of your parents' early deaths. Do you remember your father?"

"No."

"Who took care of you after your mother's death?"

"A woman."

"Was she your relative?"

"No."

"What was her purpose in caring for you?"

"I don't know. To keep me alive."

"Even though she bore no close genetic relationship to you?"

"Right."

"Interesting. Is that how you scavengers help one other survive when your family units are destroyed?"

"I guess."

"What is the name of the girl from the train tunnel?"

Colt hesitated. He remembered how she'd said it: *"You can call me... Mohini."* Clearly giving him a false name, he thought, hiding her true identity. "I don't know," he answered.

The Simon regarded him for a moment with its lifeless blue eyes, then nodded. "You don't know. Where is she from?"

"I forget. It was somewhere I've never heard of—"

The pain returned, seeming to bore through every cell in Colt's body, giving each one careful personal attention.

"You are causing me delay," Simon said.

"Good," Colt replied. He resolved not to tell the android anything else, no matter how bad the pain got.

It came back hard, again and again, but Colt kept his mouth shut, refusing to answer any more questions, even the most basic ones. The pain grew more and more intense, until he was sure he would die.

It seemed to go on for hours, for days, for eternity, the questions and the pain.

"I will return soon," Simon said at last. "And we will talk more. It's been a pleasure meeting you, Colt. You're an interesting specimen of your kind."

He left, leaving Colt aching and hollow, like everything inside him had been broken.

Colt knew he couldn't handle another interrogation like that. He hoped the Simon stayed away for a long time. He hoped he died before he saw the Simon again.

The curtained-off space remained dim, and the screams around him continued, the air thick with blood and piss and death.

Chapter Nine

Carthage

Audrey and Zola raced down the stairs full of panicked people. The matching, lantern-jawed Security Steves fired blue lasers after them, apparently not caring who they killed in the crossfire.

On the fiftieth floor, Audrey ran back out toward the indoor curb where she'd stepped out of the limo earlier.

"I can hire a car," Audrey said. Then she blinked. "Except, without Nin, I'm not sure how to access my bank account. I can use a... thumbprint or something, right?"

"We've got a ride coming," Zola told her. She turned and fired at a Security Steve that was just arriving from the stairwell. "Tell me when it's here."

"How will I know?"

"You'll know."

Moments later, a long, cylindrical red-and-white truck raced into the building along the black track from outside, red lights flashing, siren wailing. An ambulance. The other cars immediately cleared the way, opening a path for it.

The ambulance stopped in front of Audrey, and one of its two cargo-style doors opened. "Get in!" shouted a man's voice from the shadowy interior.

"Go!" Zola snapped, firing a couple more lasers to cover them.

The gang of Security Steves reached the loading zone by the indoor curb. Smoking dead bodies fell around them.

Audrey, though filled with doubt, stepped hesitantly into the ambulance.

Zola shoved her the rest of the way in, knocking her to the floor and landing on top of her. "Go! Go!" she screamed at the driver—because there was an actual human driver here, sitting at a bank of controls, but he didn't look like any kind of licensed medical technician. He was a dwarf, most of his head shaved and the rest bundled up into spiky locks, wearing an old denim jacket covered with glowing pins of glaring mummies and green zombies and the occasional puppy.

Another guy inside the ambulance, wearing a long green coat, moved to the open cargo door where Audrey and Zola had just entered. He raised a long plasma rifle and let off a glowing white bolt. It streaked like a meteor into the nearest Security Steve, expanding to engulf and melt the android's torso.

He fired another parting shot as the ambulance rocketed away from the curb and through the covered gateway, out of The 360, down the black bridge of a driveway, out into the thick of traffic.

A dedicated lane opened up for them. The wireless signal from the ambulance was warning the other cars as much as the siren and lights.

Networked, self-driving vehicles floating on a thin layer of magnetic repulsion tended to move extremely fast most of the time, anyway, but with every car automatically getting out of their way, traffic parting like the Red Sea, the ambulance could travel at dizzying top speed. That was somewhere around six hundred kilometers an hour, according to the driver's screen.

It also meant they weren't going to be disappearing into traffic anytime soon, though.

"Did they have a vehicle?" asked the guy with the plasma rifle, still watching out the rear door of the ambulance.

"The Steves arrived in a cargo truck, but I think it dropped them off. They were supposed to be posted in my apartment all night." Audrey shivered. "You said they were hacked, Zola?"

"The Clowns," Zola said. "It had to be. It all fits. You said they attacked you earlier."

"Yeah, a hacker clown definitely did. Tried to kill me. Failed." She smiled, feeling that weird liberation of having faced death and walked away fine. Or maybe the happy pill was still working.

"That's their usual method," Zola said. "It's ingrained in their philosophy—you're not supposed to own or benefit from machines yourself, any more than you can help it. In practice, you know, that's not very realistic. But they also believe in using the regime's own machines against it, making the system eat itself."

"Seriously? The 'regime'? Like we don't have elections," Audrey said.

"Elections managed by artificial intelligence and micro-targeted propaganda," Zola said. "And anybody pushing for real change is silenced long before you get a chance to hear about them. They disappear."

"You really believe that?" Audrey asked. "That's kind of extreme conspiracy stuff—"

"It happened to my family," Zola said. "And we were lucky. If we'd been less well connected, we would have simply died in the night. Maybe they would have made it look like an accident. It's all managed, Audrey. It's all fake. Your father's been the unchallenged head of government for twenty years. If that doesn't ring any alarm bells, it's only because you've been conditioned to accept it as normal. What's the point of an elected system if it's all arranged so the same people stay in office for life?"

"We have stability," Audrey said. "We have peace and prosperity like no one has ever experienced. That's why my father keeps getting elected. Because people are basically happy."

"Peace and prosperity on the inside," the tall guy with the plasma rifle said. "Death and destruction on the outside. The empire is growing out of control, and nobody has the courage to stop it. The machines are a cancer that will eat everything."

"Come on, nobody seriously uses the word 'empire,'" Audrey said. "I'm the first to agree there are all kinds of problems right now, flawed policies, things that could be done better. But the way to change that isn't through bloodshed and terrorism. You know, revolutions are fun until the guillotines come out. Then there's the show trials, the new dictator who's even worse than the last—"

"I agree," Zola said. "We're not terrorists. But the Blood Clowns are."

"But you said they were part of The Change."

"They *were*. But they're impatient. They want revolution

now, even if it means anarchy, even if it means blood in the streets. But I don't think we're to that point yet, and I don't think we'd emerge from that scenario with the kind of society we want."

"So what do you believe in doing?" Audrey asked her.

"Finding information," Zola said. "Finding the truth and making it available to people. That's what I believe in."

"The truth about what?"

"Everything," Zola said.

"Heading down," announced the small guy driving the ambulance. The rear door slammed shut. "Fast and steep. Hold on to your—"

Before he could finish, the ambulance tilted forward and whooshed down an off-ramp. The driver switched off the emergency signals, lights, and sirens as they joined the larger lower highway. Traffic instantly closed in and swallowed them up.

"And... morphing," the driver said, as they passed through a covered tunnel. Outside the windshield, the dirty white and red ambulance markings turned dirty green. "We are now a Plumber Phil truck. No guarantees they won't find us, though."

"Where are we going?" Audrey asked.

"We can't head home," the driver said. "They'd shoot us on sight if they saw you with us."

"Why?" Audrey asked.

"Because you're the enemy," the tall, young rifleman said.

"The spawn of the enemy, at best," Zola said. "So... here's the thing. This isn't exactly an authorized operation. Most people don't know you like I do. You're just another Caracala, like your father, like your sibs."

"Other than Salvius," the rifleman said.

"Yeah, and not everyone accepts Salvius, either," Zola said. "They think he's a mole."

"Blood Clowns obviously do," the driver muttered.

"So all of you know my brother?" Audrey asked.

"That's why we're here," said the rifleman. "Zola believes in you. She convinced Dinnius and me to risk our lives extracting you. But we don't have backup."

"Did you know the Security Steves were going to attack me?" Audrey asked.

"Nobody knew that," Zola said. "But getting close to you, or anyone in your family, is dangerous. We thought the Security Steves might attack *us*. We never expected them to turn on you."

"So I would've died if you hadn't been there," Audrey said, realizing. "These clowns couldn't kill me in my car, so they hacked my security androids. They must be brilliant hackers."

"That they are. Crazed, violent, and brilliant," Zola said.

"How many of them are there?" Audrey asked. "Where's their base?"

"Spoken like a true mole," the rifleman snorted, and the driver laughed.

"Very funny," Zola said. "We don't know those details, Audrey. They might not know themselves. A lot of them are social-avoidant super-hackers, cloaked in masks and aliases. Which makes them ripe for infiltration, really."

"Why the whole clown thing?" Audrey asked.

"They say only clowns and jesters could speak truth to power, using jokes and pranks. But these guys are also willing to kill. That's where the 'Blood' part comes in, I guess."

"There's old Earth lore about clowns who live in sewers,

taking the shape of children's fears," said Dinnius, the diminutive ambulance driver with the braided blue Mohawk of hair. "Perhaps that inspired them."

"Do you know where they're keeping my brother?" Audrey said. "If no one else is going to help us, then we should just grab some weapons and charge in there."

"I like this girl," the rifleman said. He wasn't much older than her, but he looked rough, his clothes made of recycled flannel and leather, covered by a long, ratty green jacket. The worn materials screamed Benefit Zone, the regions inhabited by the vast population of the mysterious poor, who tended to stay close to home, consuming their free food and entertainment, their homes built, cleaned, and maintained by public robots.

"What's your name?" Audrey asked.

"Kright," he said, smiling. "You don't want to know what it's short for. And our excellent driver here is—"

"Dinnius," Audrey said. "You mentioned it."

"Aw, she's a good listener," Dinnius said, his steel hoop earrings clanking together as he turned to look at Kright. "It's your dream girl, Krightforn. Somebody who actually pays attention to your blabbing and doesn't tune you out in the first ten seconds. You may not find this again in the course of your life."

"Krightforn?" Audrey asked.

"Shut your mini-mouth, Din," Kright said.

"Right. Go for obvious *and* weak jokes about my size. Surely she'll be impressed with that empathy and intellect of yours." Dinnius tapped his head with one hand while sending their vehicle sideways down an off-ramp. "Reproductive success is sure to follow."

"I'm sorry?" Audrey said.

"Don't mind them, they're idiots," Zola said.

"Idiots who are helping you rescue your lost boyfriend," Kright said.

"Yes," Dinnius said. "Brave, handsome, brilliant and loyal idiots—"

"You are all of the above," Zola said. "Both of you. Satisfied?"

"Temporarily," Dinnius said. He steered them down a steep, narrow magnetic rampway into a crumbling complex of what looked like warehouses and factories. Darkness swallowed them as they passed through an open loading dock door.

They were at ground level, which was odd for Audrey. Her life was mostly spent among the clouds, on the upper levels of high towers. Sometimes they visited their beach house, of course, or their mountain house, or their country estate, but those were a plane ride away, far from the city. The lower levels of the city itself were strange to her, frightening but interesting.

"Did you say 'lost boyfriend'?" Audrey asked as they traveled into a cavernous space lined with rusty machinery.

"Oh, Kright," Dinnius said. "You master of operational secrecy."

"All right," Zola said. "Maybe I have a personal interest in rescuing him. Maybe that's why I'm doing it with no backup or support."

"Except us idiots," Kright said.

"Right. They were good enough to help when nobody else would."

"I owe Salvius," Kright said.

"And I'm just trying to convince Zola to sleep with me," Dinnius said. "It's a long-term objective."

"We all have our reasons," Zola said. "Some more noble than others."

The car coasted to a stop deep inside the old factory. They'd reached a point so cluttered with junk the car could travel no farther. They were barely levitating above the pitted, dirty magnetic roadway, which had clearly been neglected for years.

"Where are we, exactly?" Audrey looked at the big plastic horses heaped nearby. "Old toy factory?"

"Prior Amusements and Games. Stuff for the fun parks and amusement cities." Kright opened the back door of their vehicle and stepped out.

Audrey followed the others out into the dusty factory. She didn't have to wonder why it had been abandoned. Heavy industry had been moved up to orbit decades ago so that all industrial exhaust and toxic gases could be vented into outer space while solid and liquid industrial waste could be cheaply shipped off on deep-space barges. The surface of Carthage was reserved for residential, retail, and entertainment uses.

Ships full of goods and raw materials rolled in constantly from other star systems, the endless flow of resources feeding into Carthage's factories, never ending, almost more than they could possibly use.

From the factories, shipping containers full of finished goods rolled down Carthage's space elevators night and day, along with containers of frozen and preserved exotic foods imported from other star systems. Everything went directly to retail shelves. The same shipping containers returned up the other side of those elevators crammed full of the world's garbage, to be pushed off on more deep-space barges.

That was her world's only real export, Audrey thought. Barge after barge of trash.

A number of empty factories remained down here on

the city's ground level. Some had been torn down or refurbished into apartments, but clearly not the ones in this area.

"This way." Kright clicked on a flashlight and led them down a side tunnel. Pieces of broken dolls littered the floor.

Zola linked an arm through Audrey's. "It'll be okay," she whispered.

"Why are we here?" Audrey asked.

"This is where they said to meet us."

"Who?"

"Shh."

They followed after Kright, whose long green jacket concealed the plasma rifle on his back. Dinnius took up the rear, holding some kind of fat pipe-looking thing wrapped in thick cables, most of it obscured by his leather jacket. Audrey wished she had a weapon herself.

They reached a room lined with large trick mirrors surrounded by round light bulbs. The mirrors distorted their reflections, some making them tall and extra-skinny, others making them short and extra-wide. Still others digitally altered them by adding costumes. One made Audrey look like Dorothy from the Wizard of Oz; Kright was the Scarecrow, Dinnius the Tin Man, Zola the Cowardly Lion, complete with mane.

The light bulbs edging one of the mirrors, one that placed the viewer into classic paintings like the Mona Lisa, flickered on and off like a signal. Zola grasped Audrey's arm extra tight, as though frightened.

"Here it comes," Dinnius murmured, shaking his head, the short blue braids of his hair rolling back and forth.

When the face appeared in the mirror, taller than her whole body, Audrey found herself returning Zola's tight grip. The same face had appeared in her car earlier, the black-and-white clown with the spade and club makeup and jester hat.

The weird high she'd been riding, the feeling of having cheated death, came crashing down. She hadn't cheated death, just postponed it a few hours while she changed her clothes. She felt sick. Maybe her smiley pill was wearing off, too.

"You have her?" the clown voice asked.

"She's right here." Kright grabbed Audrey's arm, the one Zola wasn't already clamping down on.

"Wait, what?" Audrey said.

"Where is he?" Zola snapped at the giant clown face in the mirror. "I want to see him in the flesh. No more pics."

"A deal's a deal," the clown face said.

"What deal? Zola, what's happening?" Audrey asked.

"Sorry," Zola said.

A wide mirror rose at the back of the room like a rattling garage door.

Three androids walked out, each one a common type, two Nurse Nancy models and an Officer Joe.

The nurses were typically manufactured to look pretty, and these two looked identical except for their hair colors—one pink, one green.

Instead of their proper uniforms, they wore ripped, paint-splattered clothes that looked like they'd been dug out of a thrift-store dumpster. Big smiles and other clownish details had been sloppily painted on their faces. All their exposed skin was covered in graffiti, like full-body tattoos. Hooks and small padlocks adorned their ears and lips like jewelry.

A large portion of the Officer Joe's head was wrapped in duct tape; it looked like the police unit's head had been bashed open and later resealed, though on a budget. A big smile and more graffiti had been painted on its face, and a red bulb had been installed in its remaining eye. Its clothes were ripped and black, featuring a goat's-head logo from some demon-metal band whose name was far too spiky to read. A glowing red pentagram was painted over the badge on its chest. The Officer Joe had been made to look like a hulking evil clown.

The defaced police robot led the group, while the nurses rolled a gurney between them.

"What's happening?" Audrey asked again. She tried to pull free, but Zola and Kright held her in place. "Let me go!"

"Let me see him," Zola said, her voice cold. "I have to know he's alive."

"Go on," Kright said. "I've got her."

Zola released her arm, while Kright tightened his grip on Audrey.

The stroller rolled closer, and Zola ran to it.

"It's him." She reached out and touched him. "It's Salvius."

Audrey craned her neck, trying to see her brother, but the room was dim and the figure on the stretcher was obscured by one of the nurse-bots and by Zola, damn her.

The Officer Joe approached her, his absurd Satanic regalia clattering and clanking, steel necklaces with cheap devilish jewelry shaped like goats and daggers. Its red eye looked her over, its giant mascot-face smile as unwavering as ever.

"It looks like her," the hijacked Officer Joe said, though its voice sounded high and screechy, not low and smooth and gently dominant like a normal police unit. This was more like cat claws on a chalkboard, intentionally disturbing. "Fantastic. A Caracala who's actually worth something."

"So far, you're just plucking the low-hanging fruit off my family tree," Audrey said. "But if you keep going beyond Salvius and me, you're going to start taking people they'll actually miss. And things will end badly for you."

"You poor, suffering girl," the Officer Joe screeched. "Neglected by your family. Shuffled off to Political Academy, placed in a high-level security internship. On your way to helping Daddy manage the empire. Only he doesn't really do much, does he? It's the Simon unit at his side. That is our true pharaoh. That is our true god. Daddy is just a puppet, and Audrey is just a puppet of puppets. That is our world, one layer of human puppets after another, with the machines at the top, pulling the strings."

"That's really interesting," Audrey said. "You should start your own talk show. Don't expect a lot of listeners, though. Just the lonely crazies."

"There are many more lonely crazies than you realize," the Officer Joe said. "Just waiting for direction."

"Let me see Salvius." Audrey stepped toward the gurney, but Kright held her in place. She tried to shake loose. "Let me go! What are you doing?"

"We're trading you away," Kright said. "For your brother."

"Yeah, I gathered that. So can I look at him before I get hauled off into the clown house of horrors or whatever's in store for me?"

"Be our guest, princess." The Officer Joe bowed low and deep, holding out an arm toward the gurney.

Kright loosened his grip, just enough to let her blood circulate again, and they walked toward the gurney together.

"I'm sorry," Kright whispered into her ear.

"Don't bother," she whispered back, much louder than he had.

Zola was leaned over the gurney, holding Salvius's hand, her eyes filled with tears. She stroked his unconscious face with her other hand. Audrey's brother looked much thinner than she remembered him, with a thick beard and long unkempt hair, his skin an unhealthy shade of white.

"You didn't warn me why I was really here," Audrey said.

"Would you have come if you'd known?" Zola said. "You said you'd help us save your brother. This is the price."

"Why do you care?" Audrey said.

"Because I love him," Zola said. "There's a side of his life you don't know anything about. I'm part of it. Have been, for two years. He couldn't tell anyone, especially not in your family. I'm not welcome on this planet. But I can't change things from the outer worlds."

Audrey took a long look at her brother. "You'll take care of him? Nurse him back to health?"

"Of course," Zola said.

Audrey looked at the graffiti-coated nurse-bot. "And what will you do with me?"

"We'll have all kinds of fun," the hacked nurse-bot giggled.

Audrey looked at Zola, feeling the sting of betrayal... but also the necessity of saving her brother's life. He was helpless at the moment. She had to act on his behalf.

She looked at her brother, pale and unconscious on the gurney.

Salvius had always been the best of them, Audrey thought, in a family of vain and backstabbing siblings who took after their vain and manipulative parents. She could still see him as the sweet boy, the youngest, the one who'd grown up in a state of benign neglect since their father already had a stable of acceptable older children who looked capable of carrying on his legacy.

Audrey had played with Salvius as a child, in a way she'd never played with the older children, only with Nin. She imagined him laughing, bashing up her toy tea set with her teddy bear in what he called a "bear scare."

Of course she would trade herself to save him.

"I'll go," Audrey said. After a moment she gave Kright's arm a shake. "I said I would go. You don't have to stay so clingy. He's my brother. I want him safe. I want him to live."

She stepped forward, offering her life in exchange for her brother's.

Chapter Ten

Galapagos

Reginald Ellison told the ambassador and his hideous robotic infantry to wait by the cargo elevator while Ellison and his people suited up in the armory. He didn't want the android knowing the armory's exact contents. After learning the Simon unit had smuggled the Iron Hammer leadership up to the spaceport during the summit, Ellison didn't trust the android at all. Not that he'd ever trusted it much in the first place.

Ellison tried to look stoic as he suited up with light body armor. He decided not to wear a helmet, wanted to strike a balance between being prepared and not looking frightened. Perception was critical in the political world. It had played a pretty critical role in wartime, too.

As he watched the other guards put on their armor, he couldn't help noticing that most of them were young men and women who looked barely out of their teens. He drew Loomis aside and asked him about it.

"We just had a rotation up," Loomis said. "They've all been through basic training with the Coalition Army, and they've been through additional training. Military police, then the space prep center."

Ellison nodded. He would have preferred a few more seasoned veterans around—there were certainly a lot of them down on the surface of Galapagos—but the fates seemed to have dealt him a hand full of green youngsters instead.

Or maybe it was more than fate, but he had enough to be paranoid about without thinking of how that might have been arranged, and by whom.

Soon they were ready. Kartokov and Coraline, his ministers of defense and state, wore armor and carried laser pistols, as did the security chief and his guards. Ogden wore armor and a helmet, but carried no weapon, saying he wanted to be "the voice of peace."

The laser pistols were highly accurate but fairly low-powered weapons, meant to stop or kill a human without burrowing through the hull and depressurizing the spaceport. Ellison would have liked an automatic rifle full of armor-piercing rounds, or a plasma rifle, or the chain gun from the *Sea Scorpion*. Lasers seemed like a weak weapon against robot infantry. And there was no telling what kind of weapons the Iron Hammers had brought.

Loomis had scraped together nine Coalition guards who weren't busy elsewhere in the port. Ellison left three at the armory, because there was a back room they hadn't opened, one with a few items of serious military hardware that carried a major risk of blasting holes in the spaceport's hull. Things that could be used as a last resort, if a suicidal last stand was necessary.

"There's a lot of unrest because of the lockdown,"

Loomis said. "People want to get out of here after the bomb."

Ellison sympathized; he wanted his own wife and kids back down on the surface right away. He wished he'd never brought them here. "Nobody can leave until we know who did this."

"Of course," Loomis said. "But I don't have enough guards to stop a riot. Especially on top of... all this."

"That is excellent news." Ellison shook his head. "While we go see the Hammers, I need you to plan a civilian evacuation, to begin the second we know who's behind this. Keep it quiet, though."

Loomis nodded. "Yes, sir."

"Okay. Let's go gather up all these robots and pirates in one place and see what happens," Ellison said. He looked at the six soldiers who were going to accompany them, four male, two female, all of them with shaved heads and blue uniforms, all of them reminding him in some way of his own teenage son. "Stay on your toes. There's no telling what could happen down there."

He led all of them out to the cargo elevator, three armed ministers and six young guards. An army of nine, plus Ogden tagging along.

They joined up with Simon Zorn and six of his robotic infantry, still in dusty honor guard uniforms, minus the plumes.

"Where are the other two reapers?" Ellison asked.

"Still keeping your medical center secure and watching over your family," Simon said. "Your wife remains stable."

"Call the reapers back," Ellison said. "I want them all with us." *And away from my family*.

"I do not take orders from you, Minister-General," Simon said.

"Just do it. Now."

"There's no need for hostility. There, I've sent the order. I was only trying to keep your wife and children safe through this confusing and dangerous ordeal."

"Thanks, but we have people for that." *People, not machines*, he didn't say. "We need your machines with us. There's no telling what the Iron Hammers might do. And I don't want to have to explain to Carthage why their robot ambassador got chop-shopped by a bunch of criminals. Even if you're the one who invited them to the party."

The cargo elevator opened and everyone filed in.

They traveled downward in silence until they reached the area Simon had rented, a block of cargo and passenger docks linked to a number of storage and dormitory rooms. The facilities weren't great but allowed for anonymity and privacy.

When the doors opened, the six robotic infantry led the way out, followed by Ellison and Simon. The other ministers and guards followed. Ellison preferred to shield his people behind the machines. If the machines turned on them, at least they wouldn't be caught between two groups of enemies.

The Iron Hammers didn't open fire the moment they all emerged from the cargo elevators, so that was a small positive sign. A couple of armed guards sat in folding chairs in front of the elevators. Each sported multiple crossed-hammer tattoos, originally the logo of the galaxy's most dangerous prison gang, now the symbol of a nation.

One guard manned a light machine gun on a tripod. The other hurried to put aside his meatball sandwich and pick up a laser rifle from the floor.

"They're here," the larger of the two guards said. "All of 'em. Carthage and Coalition." He cocked his head, listening to a speaker stud implanted in his ear. "Yes, sir." He stood up. The guy was tall and wide as a bear. He looked like he ate steroids for breakfast and growth hormones for dinner. His hair was a soft cloud of bright orange ringlets that didn't fit well with the rest of his look. He removed the machine gun from its tripod. "This way," he said, gesturing with the barrel.

"Those aren't allowed on the spaceport," Ellison said, gesturing at the machine gun. "Not unless they're unloaded and securely stored."

"Look at the king of the Coalition," said the other guard, wiping meatball sauce on his armor. The armor was lightweight but high-grade stuff, with sleeves and high necks, the kind of dense, light mesh material used by special forces in the inner worlds. Ellison wouldn't have minded a crate or two of those for his own people. "Taking time to lecture little ol' you about firearms regs in space."

"It's *space*," said Ringlets, his voice seething with irritation. "There's no law in *space*."

"Actually, there is," Ellison said. "It's built on a foundation of classic maritime law—"

"Is this going to take long enough for me to finish my sandwich?" asked the smaller guard, easing back toward the half-eaten hoagie on his chair.

"No," Ringlets said. "He doesn't like to wait."

"That's right, I don't," Ellison said, which made Ringlets scowl and scratch his orange-red curly hair.

"Wasn't talking about you," Ringlets grumbled.

They finally started down the corridor, away from the elevator lobby and into the residential wing.

The place looked exactly like it had been infested with Iron Hammers. Broken furniture was scattered across the hallway, holes were bashed in the walls, the smell of liquor and smoke was heavy in the air. The music was loud, almost as loud as the shouting voices in the room ahead.

Ellison stumbled when he saw a young woman lying nude on the floor, amid broken furniture, her arm ripped off and lying a meter away from her. He noticed the lack of blood, though, and then the scarlet red collar, indicating she was a pleasure android. Still, it was an unsettling sight. The androids looked so convincingly human. He was glad there weren't many on Galapagos. He didn't see how the people of Carthage and other inner worlds could stand to live with the human-like servants and workers everywhere. The artificial humans made his skin crawl.

"My friend, the ambassador!" Cross's voice bellowed as the machines led the way into the dining hall ahead. The drinking song that had been in progress ended abruptly as the six robotic infantry marched up the center of the narrow dining hall, toward the raised dais at the far end.

Most of the Iron Hammers looked the way Ellison had expected, had always seen them in battle—hefty men with obvious biochemical enhancements, high-quality battle-scarred armor, heavy weapons at their hips. Their favorite dining position appeared to be reclined in their chairs, boots on the table, while serving women in skimpy clothes fed them food and drink. Some of the women wore android collars, but not all.

Cross, on his dais, rose from a padded couch where he was surrounded by women in silken headscarves and robes, only their eyes visible. He stepped down to embrace Simon Zorn, a gesture the ambassador received graciously, as if from an old friend.

"It is good to see you as well," Simon told Cross. "It has been many hours."

Ulysses Cross, Premier of the Polar Archipelago—a title

inherited from his father and grandfather—turned to Ellison and extended a hand. "Minister-General Ellison. A welcome sight also."

The room was dead silent, Ellison realized, every Iron Hammer eye turned on them. There were probably twenty men here, looking like hairy and hulking Vikings, watching their leader encounter the leader of their enemies.

Ellison took his hand. "I'm glad we can discuss things in peace. There have been some disturbances upstairs today. People were hurt."

"Bombs, I heard," Cross said. "Was anyone killed?"

"Not so far, but some are still in intensive care."

"That wasn't so bad, then. Perhaps the wheel turns as it should."

"I'm sorry?" Ellison said. He was beginning to notice some differences between Uly Cross and his men. While the others wore armor, Cross wore none, apparently preferring sleeveless black robes embroidered with glowing green, though his arms were covered in Iron Hammer tattoos like the other men. While the other men slapped and fondled their skimpily clad servants and servant-girl androids, Cross kept his women almost completely covered in colorful silks.

"And I am sorry for any suffering," Cross said. "I believe we have reached a chance for peace between our people, for all of Galapagos."

Grumbles ran through the room, as if many of the gathered men took issue with what their leader was saying. Cross cast a withering look through the room, and the grumbles died down.

"Tell it to my father, uncle, and grandfather," one giant man grumbled. He had a number of ribbons and medals on his chest, a high-ranking general named Gorron Prazca. Ellison had read his dossier; Prazca was an influential man in the Polar Archipelago and had been ruthless and highly accomplished during the wars. "All of them died fighting our enemies. For what?" Prazca asked.

"For this day, Prazca," Cross said. "For the day made by the Higher Light."

More grumbles from the Iron Hammers crowd. "Only higher light I want to see is those Coalition boys heaped on a pyre," one of them said.

"Who wants to be hammered in the public square tomorrow?" Cross asked. "Who wants to be broken for the mob's pleasure?" When they fell silent, he turned back to Simon and Ellison. "Let's speak in my quarters." He led them to a door at the back of the room where one beefy armored guy stood guard, watching them suspiciously.

They left the Carthaginian infantry and the Coalition guards in the cafeteria. The huge man called Prazca stood and began to go with them, but Cross waved him back to his chair. General Prazca complied, but didn't look happy about it.

The four Coalition ministers and the android ambassador followed Cross down a short passage to the seating room of the "captain's quarters," the largest room in the pier's residence area. It had a private bedroom and an office. It was far from luxurious, but most of the other rooms had six or nine bunks, stacked three high.

The Premier had covered the plain gray walls with thick, dark curtains. All furniture had been removed and replaced with a few thick cushions on the floor and some ornate incense burners and candle holders.

"Please sit." Cross sank to a cushion and folded his legs. "My wives will bring us tea, as the ambassador prefers."

While everyone sat, two of the colorfully wrapped women from the dais entered, their heads lowered, and closed the doors behind them. Ellison was startled to notice that one of the two women had big, pale green fish eyes that he would usually associate with the Aquaticans and their DNA manipulation. He couldn't see the rest of her, so he couldn't check her neck for any large sea-creature tattoo.

"These are the newest and prettiest of my wives," Cross said, watching with pride as they served green tea in steel coffee cups. "Walali comes from the Island of Kythira, among the Aquatican people. She helped set my feet on the path of Higher Light."

"You have adopted the faith of the Aquaticans?" Ellison asked, with a look at Coraline.

"We do not cover ourselves like this," Coraline said. "In these beautiful silks. We bare our skin to the sea and sky and only cover ourselves on land or in frigid waters."

"The Aquatican faith was only a doorway for me," Cross said. "Beyond their gods lies a deeper truth. The Higher Light. I saw it when I ate the same concoction of sacred ocean plants the Aquatican prophets use to commune with the spirits."

"That is not meant for outsiders." Coraline looked at the girl in the aqua-colored hooded scarf, with the big green fish eyes. "Your father will be unhappy to hear of this, Walali. You stole the Deep Blessing mixture from his tabernacle, didn't you?"

"She opened my eyes," Cross said, not letting his wife answer. "The Great Lights, the great polar auroras, spoke to me. I saw that the lights are the face of the Higher Light. The true god."

The room was quiet for a minute. Simon Zorn again seemed to take great pleasure in slowly stirring and tasting his tea.

Ellison was at a loss. Most of the Iron Hammers he'd

encountered were like the men outside, their leaders like General Prazca. Cross had become something different. Even his appearance was markedly different, his hair and beard neatly trimmed, unlike the wild lice-ridden forests growing from the heads of his men. Cross's hair looked oiled and even dyed to keep it a uniform midnight black.

"And what did you learn from this experience?" Coraline asked, finally tearing her eyes from the wayward Aquatican girl.

"Our people can live in peace," Cross told her. "I've seen it. It is the only meaningful way forward."

"I'm glad you see that," Ellison said. "Do your people agree?"

Cross hesitated, as if choosing his words carefully. "The Polar Archipelago is inhabited by wolves. All of the men, and many of the women, are wolves. The Premier must be an alpha among alphas, more than a wolf. A leader of pack leaders. A dire wolf, like the ancient creatures of Earth. Some do not wish to hear talk of peace. They think it sounds like weakness.

"I understand," Cross continued. "I was once like them. I come from a long line of dire wolves. This," he indicated the large crossed-hammers logo tattooed on his bicep, "This comes from my surname. My grandfather's surname. Cross. The crossed hammers were his personal sign. I was meant to follow after my grandfather and father. Then my Walali came, and she brought me to the Light." Cross held out an arm, and the green-eyed girl sauntered over and dropped into his lap. He fondled her gently through her robes. Ellison knew Cross was sixty-one years old, though he looked much younger, indicating he'd been getting plastic surgery.

"It sounds as though a peace agreement between your

two factions is quite possible," Simon said, finally looking up from his tea. "You see, Minister-General Ellison? I don't believe I was hasty in inviting all of you to meet at once."

"The Premier has never contacted us with an offer of peace," Ellison said.

"Of course not," Cross said. "Do you think I want to be overthrown? My people would not allow that, not without a great victory on our part and a surrender on yours. But Carthage has offered us a new path. All of us know our world could never defeat the forces of Carthage, even if the Polar Archipelago aligned with the Coalition against the outsiders. This provides me cover to seek peace in the name of necessity. Because Carthage demands it."

"Your people are wise to choose a leader as perceptive as yourself, Premier Cross," Simon said.

"Leaders of the Polar Archipelago are not picked by the rabble, like cheap baubles in the market," Cross said. "Leadership is taken. Before I became Premier, I had to kill my father in single combat. He should have seen it coming, since he'd done the same to my grandfather. I suppose he didn't expect me, out of all his sons. Three of my brothers seemed more likely candidates. All of them are dead now, too, as the Light has chosen."

Ellison nodded. This fit with what he knew of the regime. Cross's recent personal and religious changes, though, were a complete surprise to him.

"So we have the outlines of an agreement," Simon said. "The Coalition and the Iron Hammers agree to join Carthage's defense network, under terms previously discussed. A ceasefire is declared, with complete autonomy for each faction. Peaceful trade agreements can then be worked out between you."

"You would promise to stop all raids on Coalition shipping?" Ellison asked. "You, the pirate king?"

"It is time we move forward to more peaceful commerce," Cross said. "And more productive endeavors. Raiding and robbery are not the path to the Higher Light."

"It seems hard to believe your people would go along with that," said Coraline. "Raiding and robbery are popular vocations among the Iron Hammers."

"There is also the issue of slavery," Ellison said. "People trafficked in from other worlds for your brothels and households."

"This too will pass in time," Cross said. "The Light will bring us all forward."

Ellison sipped his tea—he still would have preferred coffee, and for that matter a real chair instead of a cushion on the floor—and considered how to proceed. If the Iron Hammers had opened fire on them, tried to kill them all, he wouldn't have been surprised. That would almost have been expected. This offer of peace had caught him by surprise, though.

He didn't trust it. Maybe the Premier had seen the light—or the Northern Polar Lights, apparently, while doped up on strong hallucinogens—but his promised reforms seemed doubtful. Cross was clearly facing some dissent within his own leadership, bad enough that it had been obvious to outsiders.

"Peace with the Polar Archipelago and an end to raiding and slaving would be a strong incentive for the Coalition leaders to sign on," Ellison said at last. "I will be sure to emphasize this when I report back home. There will be discussion among the leadership of our nations and their legislatures, and of course the public—"

"I was instructed to return to Carthage with an answer,"

Simon said. "I cannot wait weeks and months for a response."

"But surely Carthage understands that we are a coalition of popularly elected governments, not a dictatorship. Nor would we ever wish to become one," Ellison added, with a pointed look at Simon.

"Carthage cares only about results," Simon said.

"Under the Coalition charter, no interplanetary treaty is final until ratified by the House of Ambassadors," Ellison said. "And the ambassadors answer to their home countries. Everyone will have an opinion on this. Polls show the vast majority of our people oppose any alliance with Carthage. And this bombing of the spaceport only makes things worse. If someone meant to push us into a hasty decision by throwing fear and danger into the situation, they're going to get the opposite of that. More delay."

"Perhaps the intent was just the opposite," Simon said. "To interfere with our diplomacy, to forestall any agreement. As you say, that's what many of your people want. Perhaps the bombers expected us to pack up and fly back to Carthage, as though we have never seen danger before. But you would not believe the dangers I have seen, the horrors and death I have observed. I do not fear, Minister-General Ellison. It is not in my programming. No minor bomb is going to chase me away, however much you and your people might prefer that."

"You aren't implying that we would bomb our own spaceport, are you?" Ellison said, feeling another wave of hate for the android.

"You seem too reasonable for such a course," Simon said. "But appearances can deceive, and are often designed to do so. However, perhaps some hard-line faction on your side engineered this. Someone with access to explosives and the technical knowledge to install them. Someone with a mining background, perhaps."

"I would not attack my own people!" Kartokov snapped. He pointed at his own burned face. "And my people got the worst of it. You machines weren't hurt at all, aside from your stupid feather caps getting burned off. And that was an improvement."

"And now you can argue that the bomb in your own rooms proves your delegation's innocence," Simon said.

"These accusations are getting us nowhere," Ellison said. "Loomis's investigation will turn up something. They're imaging each person currently on the port, checking their faces against databases of known terrorists and criminals."

"In the meantime," Cross said, "let us send up a prayer offering to the Higher Light, showing our gratitude for the peace to come." He patted his wife's silk-covered shoulder, and she rose and joined his other wife in preparing some kind of ritual involving incense, candles, chanting, and the burning of salty-smelling plants. Ellison tried to avoid breathing any of that in; he didn't want the Polar Lights talking to him.

Still, Ellison was glad for any delay, anything that put off Simon's pressure for a final answer that Ellison simply did not have the authority to give.

The comm beeped in Ellison's ear. He took out his pocket screen, discreetly as he could. Loomis was calling. Ellison accepted.

"We fished something out of the sludge," Loomis said, his voice audible only to Ellison. "Bad news, but no surprises, I guess."

"What?" Ellison typed the message so he didn't have to speak during Cross's chanting and incense thing. Cross's wives danced, in a way that seemed a bit snakelike and sultry for a religious practice, and now they were bringing some recorded pan flute and harp music into it. It wasn't hard to see why Cross's rough, violent subjects were getting annoyed with their leader.

"It was a Carthaginian honor guard bot," Loomis said, "We fished out short vids of it installing the explosives in the storage corridor that runs behind your room. Including the one that almost got your boys."

Ellison felt himself snarl involuntarily. He managed to get the expression under control. Cross was too entranced with his chanting and his dancing wives to notice, fortunately.

Simon Zorn was not, however. The ambassador android was looking right at Ellison.

"Is everything all right, Minister-General?" Simon asked, feigning concern in an almost convincing way. "You look like a ghost walked over your grave."

"I think you mean a goose, Mr. Ambassador," Ogden said, finally adding something to the conversation. The minister of commerce was less than useless.

Ellison could stop himself from drawing his pistol and shooting the android through the head—for the moment—but it was going to be a little longer before he could fake a civilized conversation with the machine. So instead he typed to Loomis: "Are you sure? 100%?"

"One hundred percent," Loomis replied in his ear. "It was one of those reaper bots."

"Evacuate all civilians," Ellison typed back. "Leave only Carthage and the Hammers. Move quickly and quietly."

"Including your family, sir?" Loomis asked.

"Yes. And send down the big guns to me. Everything." Ellison typed back, then deleted his record of the texts before pocketing his screen.

"Is everything all right?" Simon asked again.

"Yes," Ellison said, aloud this time. "I just didn't want to interrupt the, uh... " He gestured at Uly Cross, who was swaying to the flute music.

"Of course you didn't," Simon said. "Was it news about your wife? My soldiers report she's fine, though still unconscious. Your boys are apparently unhappy, having had a bit of a rough day—"

"I thought your robots were going to leave the medical center and leave my family alone."

"I may have forgotten to confirm the order."

"You don't seem like someone who misses a lot of small details," Ellison said.

"Honored guests, please," Cross said. "We are nearly finished with the pleasure offering."

Too bad, Ellison thought as he looked back at the ambassador and tried to figure out how to keep the android occupied while Loomis handled the evacuation. And, more importantly, how to deal with the eight Carthaginian infantry reapers currently on this port. If it came to a fight, would the Iron Hammers side with the people of their own world or with Carthage?

Regardless, Ellison knew what was ahead. *Bad water*. That was what his father called it when one of Galapagos's killer storms whipped up, threatening their family's trawler. The Western Sea had birthed a number of typhoons so bad they almost made one believe in the Aquaticans' tempestuous sea gods. Ellison had seen his share of bad water during the war, too. Bad water of all kinds.

Now all of Galapagos was his ship, and he had to steer the world through the storm.

We're barreling right into it, he thought. *And there's nowhere to go but dead ahead.*

Chapter Eleven

Earth

Colt awoke with a start. He'd had nightmares of that skinwalker, the Simon unit, standing over him, asking all kinds of questions. In his dreams, everything had been fire red, like the infernal underworlds of legend, the red of the devils that Mother Braden had warned them about, waiting to snatch children who were too loud or wandered out in the ruins when they were supposed to stay home.

In his nightmares, the Simon had demanded again and again to know where Colt's mother had gone.

"Where is your mother?"

"I don't know."

"Did the reapers take her? The clankers? The scavengers? Did she suffer before she died? Did she suffer for days, weeks, months? Did she—"

"I don't know!"

"Where is your sister? Why aren't you protecting her? She needs you, but instead you're here—"

He was awake now, though, and that nightmare was over. He was back to the real nightmare of his waking life.

The facility was darkened, so maybe it was night. There seemed to be fewer, softer cries around him, in the world beyond the stained green curtains.

Something bumped against him in the dark. Something had woken him, he realized. It seemed impossible to believe he'd gone to sleep here, a prisoner in this awful place, but the pain machine must have worn out his nervous system. Or perhaps he'd been drugged and didn't remember it. It wouldn't be the first time the machines had tranquilized him.

Another bump, this one against his hip. As it rolled closer, Colt recognized it.

The Nurse Kitty pediatric bot was visiting him again, wires still dangling from its missing eye and cracked face. Its saggy cockroach arms unfolded, revealing the circular saws, the straight blades, the dirty syringe.

"No!" Colt whispered, wriggling uselessly in his restraints. "Shoo! Go away!"

"Be quiet, or you'll draw attention." The old med-bot's voice was low and crackling, much quieter than it had been during the day. Instead of syrupy-sweet baby-talk, the bot now spoke in a rushed, nervous young woman's voice. Either Nurse Kitty flipped to a different personality mode at night, or...

"Is that you?" Colt whispered.

"Yes, it's me," the med-bot whispered back. "Now, quiet! This will be loud as it is. Hold still so I don't lop your arm off."

A circular saw sprang to life, emitting a high whine, which became a grinding, chewing sound as the saw gnawed into Colt's upper-body restraint. He was nervous watching it, since the thing really could cut off his arm, but his hacker friend was careful and precise.

Colt tossed the cut strap aside and tried to get up, but his hips were still strapped impossibly tight.

The med-bot finished cutting him loose, and Colt eased to the floor. He looked down at all the sensors on his arms and chest. There were more at his forehead and temples. All were wired to the bank of unmarked machines and monitors by his hospital bed.

They weren't all sensors, he understood very well. Some were there to induce pain, available on a sliding scale of agony.

"Can they tell if I take these off?" he whispered.

"Yes," the med-bot said. "You'll have ninety seconds to clear the building." She gave him directions. "You're about fifty kilometers southwest of your home territory. Do you know the location of Hangzhou Tower? The red and gold pagoda skyscraper?"

"Maybe... "

"It has a bronze statue in front known as The Watchful Tiger."

"Yeah, I know the place."

"Go there."

"That's where you are?" Colt asked.

"Go now. Remember, ninety seconds." The med-bot rolled away through a curtain.

Colt grabbed double handfuls of sensor wires, took a deep breath, and ripped them all off at once. They'd been applied with a glue that tore away hair and possibly a layer or two of skin, but he managed to let out no more than a low grunt at the pain.

He tossed the wires on the bed and ran out the way the med-bot had indicated. He was disheartened to find himself barefoot, dressed in a paper hospital gown still encrusted with his own vomit. He'd lost his clothes, his backpack, his tools, everything. And there was no time to scavenge before he left.

Colt ran past one small, green-curtained area after another. Many of the curtains were drawn, but some weren't.

He saw men and women in pitiable condition, parts of their bodies removed and replaced with strange machinery. Many of them had portions of their skull opened, with cables and wires running directly into their brains. Several lay dead in their blood-soaked beds, waiting to be carted off.

Horror flooded Colt at the sight of Simon Nix's experiments, but he'd seen suffering and death before, and he had to keep moving. He could deal with the nightmares later.

Remembering her directions, he ran down the hallway of green curtains and took a left at the second intersection. He saw the med-bot just ahead of him and almost ran to it, until he saw another very similar med-bot cross another intersection a few meters ahead. They were both Nurse Kitty models. In the dimness, there was no telling which was the one that had helped him. Maybe neither of them were.

Colt hung back, waiting for both med-bots to continue on out of sight. He could feel precious seconds draining away, but he couldn't risk getting spotted by the wrong machine. He also wasn't going to try to find another way around. This place was a labyrinth of green curtains and machinery, a vast warehouse-sized laboratory of horrors.

He reached an area full of large clear cages. A person with a bulky, horizontal, tube-shaped mechanism for a head squatted on a ripped-up sofa in one cage, his heavily bandaged hand swiping at the clear wall beside him, like a compulsive movement he couldn't stop repeating. Cables connected him to packs of fluids overhead. A screen hung in one corner, playing a weirdly colorless 2-D movie about the Old West, cowboys riding horses.

Colt slowed as he passed that cage. The person's long tube of a head turned toward him, and Colt realized the face had been completely replaced with a large video camera on a swiveling mount in the neck. The back of the person's head was there, the brain wired into the camera, but the face had been entirely removed.

The camera-headed man leaped like a frog from the top of the couch to the filthy shredded-paper mess of the floor, moving in for a closer look at Colt. He hammered his bandaged hands against the glass as Colt passed.

Colt reached a section the med-bot had called the "gallery of heads" while giving him directions. Now he saw why. Scores of people floated in tanks here, naked, their heads held in metal hoops above the water. The tops of each person's skull had been removed, exposing most of the brain. An array of experiments were underway on the live human brains; many seemed to involve a vast web of thin gold wiring plugged directly into the neural tissue. Mechanical arms tipped with needles, saws, and scalpels, cousins to the med-bots who'd sprung Colt, worked at the brains, eliciting sighs, cries, and screams from the human subjects.

Colt wished he could help everyone here, freeing them from this miserable existence. But he was unarmed, empty-handed, and his time was almost up.

He passed a display of a hundred or more human brain slices, each one paper-thin and held between sheets of glass. Blood and fluids moved through the paper-thin slices, apparently keeping them alive.

Turning away from them, he saw the double steel doors

in a cinderblock wall to his left. One door stood slightly ajar, held open by a dirty, broken syringe near the bottom.

Colt pushed his way out the door and eased it shut behind him, careful to avoid the syringe with his bare feet.

On the other side was a concrete stairwell, the walls badly cracked. Following directions, he headed down a flight, then cut across an underground level.

She'd mentioned this area was called "the morgue" but it had barely registered before.

The words hadn't prepared him for the staggering horror of it. The place overflowed with bodies and body parts, some heaped in clogged steel sinks, others piled on metal carts. Rows of doors stood open on the mortuary cooler across the room; it had been stuffed full of mutilated bodies, three or four per drawer, though the drawers were clearly only supposed to hold one body each.

Colt fought his urges to vomit and to scream. He ran through the morgue, avoiding the bodies heaped pack-rat fashion on either side.

He finally reached a chain-link door to another stairwell leading even farther down. The chain-link door had been padlocked, but the lock now lay on the floor, freshly sawed open.

Colt scooped up the sawed padlock and took it with him, since its presence on the floor would be a red flag as to where he'd gone. A lock that had vanished altogether was less immediately noticeable, he hoped.

He carefully closed the chain-link door behind him and hurried down, his bare feet providing the gift of silence as he passed down the rough, dirty concrete steps, though he had to avoid broken glass and loose rusty screws and nails.

He descended to one landing, then another. It was getting very dark very fast, and he had no night vision goggles or flashlight this time. He wondered whether she'd taken that into account when giving him directions.

Soon he was in total darkness, and it was freezing cold. He shivered, keeping his arms close.

Alarms sounded above. His escape had been noticed. Mohini had said she couldn't hold them off long.

He ran, which warmed him up a little. He descended four levels, then followed a hallway, his fingers trailing along the wall for some guidance in the solid darkness. He cursed as he stumbled over unseen debris, constantly getting tripped up by it. He would never get away; reapers would be pouring into the underground corridor any moment.

He counted the doors as he passed them and opened the fourth one, as instructed, into a maintenance and supply room that connected to the building's water and sewer network, through which he could descend even deeper.

There was a good chance he'd get lost before he made it that far, which meant a good chance of freezing down here in the dark. There was also a good chance the machines would catch him and kill him, and even a non-zero chance of getting attacked by rats in the dark, just as a fun alternative.

Still hearing the machines rumbling somewhere overhead, Colt bolted forward into the darkness.

Hold it there, kid, a woman's raspy, tobacco-scarred voice said inside his head. Mother Braden. *What happens when you step blindly into a three-story ladder hole and fall to a concrete floor? Use your head.*

Yeah, use your head, stupidiot, his sister's voice echoed, using the combination of "stupid" and "idiot" she'd favored around age eleven.

Don't pile on, Hope, Mother Braden admonished. *It wastes time.*

That was one lesson Hope had never learned. She never missed a chance to pile on, especially at Colt's expense.

He wondered about Hope and Diego. He was sure they'd made it back home; melting away into the ruins and disappearing was what scavengers did best. Still, it would have been nice to know for sure and to let them know that he was alive and safe.

Alive, anyway. Safe was still up in the air.

Colt felt his way toward a long, cluttered workbench in the corner. Given that he had absolutely nothing, the odds seemed good that he might find something that would help him survive the long, cold, pitch-black road ahead.

He nicked his finger on an old saw blade and cursed. But he kept pawing around, though a little more cautiously.

His hand closed on a steel cylinder, and he gasped a little, daring to hope. He found a button on the flashlight's side and clicked it.

Nothing happened. He gave the flashlight a hard shake, and it sputtered to life with a weak, uneven yellow glow. The battery was low, but he was lucky it worked at all. They had really built things to last in the old world. He couldn't think of a better civilization to be squatting in the ruins of.

The light helped him find a handful of other tools and a foul-smelling old leather tool belt to carry them in.

Far more foul-smelling were the rotten old shoes he found kicked under the workbench. They looked like they might have been nested in by rats who'd since moved on to greener pastures. He had little choice but to shake out the rat dung and slide his bare feet into the creaky blackened interior of the shoes. He tied them on, mourning the loss of his crisp new Chicago Bears socks.

The sirens continued overhead. He wondered whether

the machines had figured out where he'd gone yet. Reapers were probably already on the way.

His heart pounding, he found his way to the ladder, a narrow steel one leading down through a world of pipes and valves to a landing several meters below. If he'd been careless, he could easily have stepped through the open hole in the dark and fallen to his death.

He turned off his flashlight to save battery power and to help him avoid detection. He climbed down the ladder in total darkness, trying not to think about how far he could fall, glad he was unable to see the distance. The tools on his belt clanked, and he winced at the noise; he would have to secure them more tightly when he reached the bottom.

Colt just hoped the sewer-tunnel portion of his journey wasn't unexpectedly flooded, as those areas often were. At least he wouldn't have to worry about ruining his shoes. He was pretty sure he could already feel the spores of rat-intestine diseases invading the gaps between his toes.

The sewer, only partially flooded, did eventually get him to the old underground highway marked U-20A. The road had twelve lanes on either side of the concrete barrier, with parallel magnetic stripes, but he could see why it might not be heavily patrolled by the metalheads. The arched concrete ceiling was cracked, leaking, and occasionally raining down chunks of worn concrete. These littered the road like boulders, making it impassable by any vehicle, except possibly an expertly driven motorcycle.

Old cars and trucks were scattered on the road, abandoned since the war. Several had been crushed by fallen concrete. Like most cars and trucks of the old world, they were round or oval-shaped, skirted with bumpers, designed to drive themselves while the humans rode inside, just trusting the machines with their lives. For Colt, that seemed almost impossible to believe, but Mother Braden had told him it was true.

Colt took a wide path around waterfalls of dark filth leaking down from the roof. A piece of concrete the size of his head broke loose and toppled to the road a few meters behind him, crushing the windshield of a rusty oval-shaped van with big flowers painted on the side.

He hunkered down behind a wrecked car and froze, waiting for any metalheads that might come to investigate the sound of the falling concrete. He didn't have a lot in the way of weapons, just a hammer and a small drill from the tool bench. They were only slightly better than nothing.

After a couple of minutes, it seemed like no machines were coming. Maybe the machines had grown accustomed to the crumbling and falling of the tunnel roof and now ignored any sounds from it. It was possible the machines simply weren't monitoring the area at all, but that was never a safe assumption. It was best to assume they were out there all the time, listening and watching.

When he resumed walking, he felt emboldened enough by the lack of metalhead response to start poking around in the wrecked cars. He was hungry and thirsty. There was no telling how long it had been since the reapers had captured him, but he hadn't exactly had a full stomach then, either. The machines had taken his backpack, including his canteen.

One car yielded a pack of fruit gummy candies, melted and rehardened into a solid mass over the years. He ate it greedily, savoring the sugar and the fake fruit flavor.

A wrecked truck had a cooler in the back. The cooler's

battery unit had long since died, and the inside of the cooler was thick with black remnants of rotten food. But there were two plastic water bottles floating in the filth. Colt fished them out and wiped them off on his hospital gown as best he could, but his gown wasn't all that clean.

The bottles were unopened, labeled with the words **MOOSE SPRINGS**. Apparently the water had been imported from somewhere way up north, deep in the arctic wilds of Canada, and didn't need to be boiled, filtered, or treated.

He unscrewed a cap and took a long, deep pull of water, feeling it soak his insides, like fresh rain on parched earth. He drank down the entire bottle, then tossed it aside and saved the other one for later.

He continued down the road, still hungry but momentarily revitalized by the sugar and water.

The road would take him most of the way home, but it was a long way, and he kept having to avoid spills of dirty water and heaps of broken concrete, kept tripping on debris. He wondered if it was raining up on the surface. Or maybe Lake Michigan was pushing its way in from the east and would one day fill this highway tunnel, turning it into an underwater cave.

Not today, he thought. *Just don't do it today.*

He didn't find much more food. After hours of walking with only an occasional break, his second water bottle was depleted, and he was exhausted again.

He did find a round dry cleaning delivery truck, its interior hung with fine clothes sealed in zippered garment bags —heavy coats, silk shirts, colorful dresses, strange artifacts of the old world.

Not a shoe or sock in sight, though. He cursed silently about that.

He ripped out the truck's old CPU. The truck's battery was long dead, and it was almost certainly impossible for the CPU to come back online, but he wasn't taking any chances. He smashed it to pieces.

Then he covered himself with a heap of clothes to help him stay warm as well as hidden.

He slept on the floor of the delivery truck for an unknowable amount of time. There was no way to judge day or night in the sealed tunnel, any more than there had been in Simon Nix's windowless concrete laboratory.

Nightmares filled his sleep. Strapped to the bed with Simon looming over him, lashing him with electrically induced pain. Worse, he saw visions of his own friends and loved ones trapped in the lab—Mother Braden strapped to one bed, tangles of wires plugged into the diabetic sores scattered all over her body. His sister, Hope, floating in a tank, the top of her skull removed while tiny automated tools worked inside her.

When Colt awoke, he was covered in cold sweat. He dressed himself in a dark gray suit and a black cashmere overcoat, which would keep him warm and also blend into the shadows.

He grimaced as he pulled on the rotten old shoes again.

At the last moment, he thought to grab a dark purple coat that looked big enough for Hope's tall form.

Soon he was on his way again, walking with a thick garment bag over his shoulder. If he did get attacked, maybe the bag could slow down a reaper's blade for a second or two. It certainly wouldn't stop a bullet or a laser.

He was hungry and thirsty, but at least he wasn't cold anymore. He'd left the paper gown crammed under a seat in the clothes truck. His new clothes didn't crinkle and rasp as he walked, so that was another improvement. Socks or underwear would have been an amazing bonus.

Colt walked and walked, kilometer after kilometer. He heard nothing but his own footsteps and heartbeat, the constant splashing of water from overhead, and the occasional crash of more concrete coming down.

He grew exhausted after more hours of walking. It must have been days since he'd last eaten anything substantial.

He kept his dying flashlight off most of the time. It barely cast a glow anymore, anyway.

Finally, when he was closer to home, he walked into the building she'd mentioned. A two-story bronze tiger statue with a watchful expression guarded the front, crouching behind a stand of chemically petrified bamboo.

Colt entered through a loading dock at the back, then found his way to the hardened underground security office. It was the nerve center of the building, the natural place for his new hacker friend to set up shop.

He stepped into the room and looked at the tall back of a chair facing scores of projection screens, though only a few were lit up.

The chair turned. Mohini looked him over.

"You're here," she said, springing to her feet.

"I'm here."

"How?"

"The old-fashioned way. Lots and lots of walking."

She moved closer to him. "Can I touch you?"

"Okay."

She took his hand, then ran her finger along the back of his neck. "You're warm. You don't feel like an android, unless you're a really good spy model."

"Or maybe you're a really good spy model," Colt said, mostly joking. But not completely. She had planted the idea of "a really good spy model" in his head, though, which didn't seem like something a really good spy model would do.

"Sorry," she said. "I'm just suspicious. Living in these ruins is driving me crazy. I think every sound is a reaper on its way to get me."

"Is it not that way back home?"

"No," she said. "I mean, yes and no. It's less intense, I suppose. There's more activity here." She moved in close and timidly embraced him. "Is this all right?"

"Sure."

"I'm glad you're alive," she said. "But how?"

"Because of you. Wasn't it? You hacked the med-bot and cut me loose. And gave me directions. It was a girl's voice. You said it was you."

"I did?" she asked.

"Yeah. I said 'Is that you?' and you said... yes."

"Wouldn't the answer be 'yes' for anyone?"

"Huh?"

"You asked, 'Is that you?' No matter who you ask, the answer is always 'yes,' isn't it?"

"Yeah, but... if you didn't... who else was going to hack in and get me out of there? I don't know anyone else who can do that."

"Not even the rebels here in Chicago?"

"I don't know. But if they could, they'd probably use it for something more important than rescuing a random scavenger like me. That place is full of people who need rescuing." He shivered. "Are you saying you aren't the one who helped me escape? It was a woman's voice. I just assumed it was you."

"I'm just messing with you." Mohini punched him playfully on the arm, though there was some awkwardness in her attempt to be playful. "Yeah, it was me. I'm your magical hacker angel. But you can call me Mo."

"Mohini isn't your real name, though, is it?"

"Of course not. A girl has to be careful with her identity when she's trying to bring down the imperialist system. Don't tell me 'Colt' is your actual name. I mean, why that? Why not pick 'Stallion'? Or 'Mustang'?"

"It is my real name."

"Oh. Yikes."

"What was that about bringing down the system?"

"We all have our parts to play," Mohini said. "Speaking of, did you stop off at a party or something? Because you've got a very different look today." She touched his new cashmere coat.

"I went shopping on Flooding Tunnel Drive," Colt said. "Some good stuff there, if you're willing to risk getting your skull crushed."

"Anything for me?" She glanced at the garment bag.

"See if you like it." He unzipped it.

"I'm hoping for a case of plasma cells." She tapped the pistol on her belt. "They're really in fashion this year."

He showed her the long purple coat, and her eyes rose.

"This is really nice." She ran her finger over the soft material, shaped like ten thousand tiny violets sewn together. She lifted it free and held it against her. It puddled on the floor at her feet, and her eyes narrowed. "Obviously not for me, though. This is for someone taller."

"For my sister, actually," he said. "Sorry. But you could have it if—"

"Don't need it. I've already lost enough gear on this mission. I don't need useless junk slowing me down." She put the dress aside. "May I touch you again?"

"Go ahead," he said, still not used to her aversion to

even mild, basic communication touches, so critical to survival in the ruins.

"Let me know if it gets awkward." She embraced him and laid her head against his chest. She was warm in his arms. Not an android, unless she was an insanely convincing one. Even the Simon unit was more like a machine, Colt thought. No matter how human the Simon might have looked on the outside, it clearly had no soul.

Mohini was warm, and he held her close, drawing his coat around her like a blanket.

"I don't know what to do," she whispered. "Your rebels wouldn't work with us. Then Roldao died. I wasn't supposed to do all this alone."

"You aren't alone," he said.

"I miss him so much." She looked up at Colt, then pulled away from him and stiffened up. "Sorry. I should not have gone emotional."

"I've been through worse," Colt said. "So, maybe I can help you, but I still don't know what you're here to do."

"You understand that Carthage's military is all machines, right?" Mohini asked, moving to put more space between them. "The interstellar carriers, the starfighters, the tanks, the infantry, they're all autonomous, they all run on AI. They don't need any human presence at all."

Colt nodded. "Everyone knows that—"

"The highest ranking machines, the ones who command the fleets and the robotic armies, are called Simon units," Mohini said. "They can plan a war or govern a planet. When the rulers of Carthage want to take over a world, they just point to it, and their Simons take it from there—assessing the planet's politics and defenses, finding the weak points, intimidating the world into obedience. And if the world resists, the Simon unleashes death. Like they did to Earth."

"I met one," Colt said. "He said his name was Simon Nix. The clankers at the clinic mentioned his name, too."

"He was probably the one providing their weapons and armor," Mohini said. "And experimenting on them. That's what Simon Nix does with his leisure time—gruesome experiments on human beings."

"I saw," Colt said. "I almost became one, I think. He zapped me with these boxes full of pain. And asked me a lot of questions."

"About what?"

"About myself and the scavengers I know. And about you. A lot about you. He had that reaper's head, the one with your cable still plugged into it."

"Yeah, I was planning to destroy the evidence on that one, until someone told me not to burn down the clinic."

"Sorry," Colt said.

"What did you tell him?"

"Not much. Lucky me, I don't really know anything about you."

"I'm here to document Simon Nix's research," Mohini said. "To gather up evidence of all the twisted experiments he's doing. To show people what's really happening."

"To show who? We all know Carthage is evil."

"The general public on Carthage don't see themselves that way," Mohini said. "We have contacts who can spread this information across the inner worlds. It could change opinions, which could change policy."

"Like the policy of making life on Earth an endless living hell for all of us?"

"Exactly," Mohini said.

"I think they know what they're doing to us," Colt said. "I think they're proud of it. How could they not know?"

"Public opinion on Carthage is carefully managed," Mohini said. "That's why we need the shocking truth, to kind of break through and grab attention. Every human being in the galaxy identifies with Earth, at least a little bit. Everybody's ancestors came from there."

"You must have missed the part where Carthage hates Earth and destroyed all of our cities," Colt said. He pointed upward, indicating outer space and the distant planet of Carthage, not that any of it could be seen through the droptile ceiling. "They're monsters. All of them. They're like clankers. You can't appeal to their feelings."

"Then what do you do?" Mohini asked.

"You kill them," Colt said. "You kill them fast, before they can kill you. Because that's all the Carthaginians are—a different kind of clanker, humans who care more about machines than other humans. They just eat better and wear fancier clothes, but they're the same."

"You might be right," she said. "The people of Carthage might already be ruled by their machines, just as their machines rule other worlds. They may simply be too complacent to realize it. And we need to shock them into waking up. We need to send them a warning shot. Because if Carthage doesn't change, the machines will keep conquering until they rule every settled world, every little colony, and there are no free humans left anywhere."

Colt shook his head. "I don't think their minds will change. But I'll help you. I saw what Simon Nix is doing in there and... that has to stop. So your plan was to get the rebels to help you break in there and collect evidence?"

"Yes, exactly," Mohini said.

"Couldn't you take pictures through the med-bot you hacked?"

"The med-bot, right. Except I was busy getting you out of there alive, wasn't I? I had too much going on."

"Can't you hack in again?"

"Uh, well, that specific window of opportunity has closed, and I used it to rescue you instead of completing my mission."

"I'm glad you did. I don't know what he might have done to me in there." He tried not to think of the people floating upright in their tanks, bodies shriveled from disuse, brains wide open to probing needles and lasers. The blood-soaked beds of the failed experiments, the dead bodies still hooked to monitors. The bodies in the morgue, piled up in overflowing mounds.

"Anyway," Mohini said. "I'm here for more than pictures. Anyone can mock up pictures of anything. I want the hardest, most complete evidence. Every last inhuman detail. I want the head of Simon Nix."

Colt recalled the android standing over him in a lab coat splatter-painted with layers of caked-on blood. The mad doctor, running his experiments on a warehouse full of captive humans. "His head?"

"The rest of him can corrode in acid for all I care, but I need his CPU and memory drives," Mohini said. "A few pictures or videos won't change anything, but the complete master record of his actions will. It'll be too much evidence to deny. Years and years of it."

"I don't know, but if the idea is to hunt down that android and remove his head, I definitely like the sound of it. Can you get us in and out again, like you did with me?"

"Not exactly," she said. "We need to mount a physical

raid. That's why we need the rebels. We need numbers, experienced fighters, weapons."

"But there must be reapers guarding him," Colt said.

"There's a barracks by the laboratory. I'd expect reapers, tanks, and drones. It's heavily protected. The whole complex used to be a research hospital before the war. Carthage has designated it Installation 34. It's become the preferred home base of Simon Nix, Carthage's appointed administrator of the Americas, though he has a number of other bases around these two continents. And other laboratories, as bad as the one you saw."

"He rules the whole continent?" Colt found this idea shocking. "That crazed robot?"

"Two continents, technically. And I wouldn't make too much of the word 'ruled.' There are machines based in every city, following standard programming and protocols. There are satellites above. Simon is a key cog in the machine, but a Simon isn't going to bother building himself a palace or any of those self-aggrandizing human things. Simon units are like trapdoor spiders. They like to hide in the background and pull the strings."

"You seem to know a lot about him."

"I came a long way for him," Mohini said. "It's important to know your target. You said you had a friend who might lead us to the rebels?"

"Diego's older brother Fernando went to join them," Colt said. "Along with a couple of others from our camp over the years. They can't really stay in touch after they go. But I think Diego's seen his brother a couple of times. He might know how to talk to them."

"You never thought about joining them yourself?" Mohini asked.

"Sure. Maybe. If I thought there was a chance of defeating the machines. So far, I've been pretty focused on protecting my sister and the rest of our camp."

"It's sweet how you look after your sister. She must really look up to you."

Colt thought about his sister, jumping on him and smacking his head for eating the last can of peas in their cache. *That was mine, you uglidiot! I'm going to squeeze your face until it breaks!*

"She really does," Colt said. "Worships at my feet. I'm basically like a god to her. Do you have anything to eat?"

"I found some packs of Nuke-A-Noodle upstairs." She took some out of her backpack. "You mix it with water—"

"Thanks!" Colt tore one open and bit into it. The sharp, salty noodles were hard on his thirsty, cracked lips, but he ate them as fast as he could manage without choking.

"You eat like a wild animal," Mohini said.

"Starving and watching for predators?" Colt asked. "Yeah, that's just life. England sounds nicer. Maybe you can take us there with you. My sister's always wanting to get on a boat, find an island somewhere. Get away from the machines. But they have satellites and drones. They'd find us. The only safe place is here, among the ruins, in trash buried so deep and wide you can hide in it. And even here, it's not safe. Everybody dies. If the machines don't kill you, the other people will."

"Maybe I could do that," Mohini said, her voice even quieter than usual. "If you want to come. But right now, we need to find the rebels."

"Okay. Let me see if there's any chance of finding some better shoes, and then we'll go."

Then he closed his eyes, leaned back in the security

center's padded office chair, and fell asleep, his body still aching with the memory of the unspeakable pain inflicted by Simon Nix.

Chapter Twelve

Carthage

Audrey stepped toward the hijacked and crazily painted androids, the two nurses and the cop that had just rolled her brother out from behind the funhouse mirror. She had no idea what they might do to her, but likely scenarios seemed to involve torture and suffering in the short term, followed by eventual death.

She wanted to hate Zola for luring her here under false pretenses, not exactly explaining that Audrey was going to be traded away for Salvius. Audrey couldn't hate her, though. Salvius looked helpless, and Zola clung to the side of his gurney, weeping over his unresponsive face, clearly pained by his condition.

As Audrey tried to give herself up, Kright's grip on her arm tightened again. She looked back at him, and he gave her a grin, his sharp blue eyes bright.

"Salvius," Zola moaned like a mourner at a funeral and collapsed onto his gurney rather dramatically.

She didn't land on top of him, though, but on the gurney's side rail. The gurney toppled sideways, and Salvius fell off, landing on the weeping Zola. They fell to the floor together.

Audrey started toward her fallen brother, but Kright, *still* gripping her, slung her away from the fallen gurney, as well as the nurse and cop androids.

Audrey cried out, falling as he pushed her toward a wall covered with a grungy, long-faded mural of zebras, lions, and hippos. The animals were fat and garishly dressed, eating ice cream and popcorn while pointing at humans in cages. A reverse zoo.

Audrey grunted as she hit the concrete floor with a bruising pain in her hip.

"Hey, watch it—" she began to snap at Kright. He shrugged off his long, tattered green jacket and dropped it on top of her. The coat pressed her to the floor, covering her up to her nose. It was heavy, like maybe it had a layer of armor concealed inside. And it was sweaty and musky, like maybe Kright wore a lot less cologne than the guys she was used to.

A loud popping sound had rung out from behind Audrey as Zola and Salvius fell, as Kright had grabbed her and pulled her aside. She'd barely had time to register it, but now a second loud pop rang out, followed closely by a third.

She saw the source of it. Dinnius was firing weird, chunky objects out of the large tube he carried, and suddenly Audrey knew why the tube looked distantly familiar. It was highly modified, but it was basically the kind of cheap air cannon used to shoot prizes into the crowd at parades and sporting events. At the World Games the previous year, she'd seen a giant one shoot exploding piñatas that rained candy and confetti onto the stadium crowd. Caracala Stadium had been at its full capacity, a quarter million people, for the entire month of the games.

Dinnius wasn't shooting out commemorative toys or advertising-laden shirts, though.

His air cannon fired three times as he swept it across the corridor. He wasn't doing much aiming, or even pulling the trigger after the first time; the targets must have been programmed into the device before he'd started shooting. Maybe that involved facial recognition software, because his projectiles were slamming right into the androids' faces.

The projectiles looked like metallic bugs, their long legs ending in sharp, drill-headed tips. One landed on each android.

Audrey watched the one on the pink-haired nurse's face. Its legs drilled in deep, and then electricity crackled along the legs, fed by a battery cell in the bug's body, maybe inside its bulbous thorax.

The nurse jerked and lurched crazily. It kicked out one leg and pirouetted against the wall, smashing and breaking its leg. Then it twisted the other way, and began randomly bending over, forward and backward in ways that would snap the spine of a live person.

"Time to take your medicine, sir," she said, her head nodding crazily. "Time to take your medicine. Time to take your—"

A barrage of quick blue laser blasts struck the nurse from below. The nurse spun around crazily, her eye socket a smoking hole, her pink hair smoldering. More holes penetrated her throat and chest. Then she stopped moving, frozen like a victim of Medusa, turned to a statue.

The Officer Joe jerked too, but not as much, probably built with more insulation and defenses than the Nurse

Nancys. The cop-bot balled up a fist and smashed the bug on its face, then ripped it free and hurled it against the wall.

The hackers, the Blood Clowns, might have bashed and vandalized the cop-bot, but they hadn't taken its weapons away.

The Officer Joe removed the long steel truncheon from its belt. The device telescoped, doubling in length almost instantly, extending toward Dinnius. A ring of metal studs extended around the tip of the truncheon, and electricity arced between the studs. Officer Joe was going into crowd-control mode, though the remote hacker controlling the robot could easily beat someone to death with that truncheon if he chose.

Dinnius scrambled backward as the Officer Joe approached, looking ready to cave in the side of Dinnius's skull.

Kright pointed his plasma rifle and squeezed off two quick blazing-white bolts at the Officer Joe.

The first bolt skimmed the non-duct-taped side of the Officer Joe's head, melting the artificial skin there into flesh-colored goo that drooled from the metal structure beneath. Its big police hat—painted black, with a red pentagram jauntily scribbled over the badge—burned and crumpled in the heat of the plasma.

Most of that bolt continued on and hit the wall, spreading along the concrete in a flood of flame, searing the dancing-bear mural on that side solid black, flash-frying years of dust and spiderwebs into a thin wave of smoke.

The second bolt struck the Officer Joe solidly in the shoulder, melting the arm on that side down to the black steel skeleton underneath. The arm lost power as its actuators burned.

In a blur of motion, the Officer Joe spun toward Kright,

clearly deciding the lanky rifleman was more of a threat than the dwarf who kept backing away from him.

The cop-bot drew what looked like a comically large police revolver from its hip holster. The hackers had painted a red pentagram on the butt of it.

Audrey gasped. She'd never seen an Officer Joe actually pull its revolver on a suspect outside of news reports and crime movies. She knew the oversized revolver fired oversized rounds that could crater a car or turn a person into burning mush. And Kright had dropped his long armor-lined jacket onto Audrey for this fight, leaving himself completely exposed. His old T-shirt wasn't going to provide him much protection.

"You went back on us! You have no honor!" the green-haired nurse screeched and staggered toward the overturned gurney. Zola remained behind it with Salvius's unconscious form. The nurse had managed to remove the electrical bug from her face, but she was still weakened.

"What? There's no honor in kidnapping!" Zola shot Nurse Green with the laser gun, filling the android's torso with holes. She raised her gun and struck the nurse in the jaw.

From Zola's position on the floor, the laser had an upward angle, so it passed through the nurse-bot's jaw and through her head. The green-haired nurse's eyes lit up as the electronics inside her cranial case burned. The laser emerged at the crown of the nurse's head, having bored its way through, and continued on to scald the ceiling.

The nurse finally stopped moving, its green hair crackling as it burned.

At the same time, the molten-faced Officer Joe opened fire with its giant revolver, punching holes in the concrete wall above Audrey. The reverse-zoo mural shattered into a rain of jagged concrete hail.

Audrey pulled Kright's jacket over her head for protection against the falling concrete. Something hard and heavy whacked her in the face. It felt like a small handgun with a wide mouth, holstered inside his jacket.

Kright managed to get off a third bolt of plasma at the Officer Joe, but the android twisted aside. The plasma bolt went high, hit the ceiling farther along and unfolded in a miasma of white fire in both directions along the corridor. The white fire illuminated a rusty forklift and a number of oversized, cheerfully colored fairy-tale creatures.

The Joe was turning after Kright, tracking him with the oversized revolver that fired cannon-power rounds. Kright leaped aside, clearly expecting return fire from the cop-bot, but there was no cover for Kright to take.

Blue lasers struck the Officer Joe from behind. Dinnius had dropped his prize-shooter and drawn a snub-nosed laser gun from inside his jacket. The cop seemed willing to tolerate the lasers boring into its back, though, while training its giant revolver on Kright. The cop's permanent happy-mascot grin had melted away, leaving the burnt flesh-goop dripping from the black steel skull underneath.

Audrey took the mysterious handgun from its holster in Kright's jacket. She pointed it at the Officer Joe's leg and squeezed the fat orange trigger.

Nothing happened.

A safety. Didn't these things usually have some kind of safety button or switch? She found the little lever and pushed it.

"Hey, hacker clown guy!" she shouted, standing up. "It's me. Audrey Caracala. I'm the one you're here for."

"Audrey, don't!" Kright said, and she tossed his long

green jacket over his head, muffling him. This also freed her to take a steady double grip on the gun. Audrey wasn't very familiar with real firearms, but she'd played video games.

She pointed it at the cop-bot, while he turned his revolver away from Kright and toward Audrey.

"No, Audrey!" Zola shouted. Maybe she thought Audrey was about to surrender herself to the Clowns.

That wasn't her plan, though. Not even close.

Audrey squeezed off a shot, right at the cop's exposed skull. Its CPU would be inside there.

The hacked cop-bot was already raising its giant revolver at her face, apparently preparing to blow her head right off.

The handgun she'd found in the jacket didn't fire lead, or lasers, or plasma, but a blob of clear goo with a small, shiny object at the center the size of a ring or a coin.

Audrey wasn't sure what she'd expected, but it was definitely not that.

Also, her aim was not great. She'd meant to hit the Officer Joe in the skull, but instead the goo-blob splattered onto the oversized cylinder of the giant revolver and stuck there. Apparently the goo was adhesive. The small metal object inside had a tiny screen, flashing red numbers too small and too fast for her to read.

"She did it!" Zola screamed, ducking down to shield herself and Salvius behind the thin bed of the gurney.

"Here it comes!" Dinnius, who'd already run some distance while retreating from the Officer Joe, dodged around the corner into another corridor.

"What did you set the timer for?" Kright asked, running toward her.

"Timer?" Audrey asked, puzzled.

"Oh, that's not good." He pushed her up against the

wall, then wrapped his long green jacket around them like a blanket, covering their heads.

"What are you—" Audrey began, and then the blast hit.

The roar was deafening. Kright was thrown up against her, pressing the air out of her lungs. The floor shook hard beneath them and kept shaking like it was an earthquake. Dust and debris rained down from above.

Audrey closed her eyes, expecting to die. At least she'd tried. At least she would die doing something meaningful, helping her brother.

The quaking and trembling subsided, though the ringing in her ears did not.

Kright backed off, coughing and shaking his head. She couldn't really hear him, but she understood him perfectly well when he mouthed the words "You're crazy." He also took the bomb-spitting device from her and returned it to his jacket.

The Officer Joe had been blasted into a twisting, smoldering wreck, sprawled across the floor, unrecognizable. Its arm was embedded in the wall across from Audrey. The oversized revolver was a molten mass on the floor.

"Those other rounds could cook off," Kright said, though Audrey couldn't have made out the words if she hadn't seen his lips. "We have to go."

She and Kright hurried over to the gurney, its rolling support legs crushed, the thin top bent like a "C."

"Salvius!" Audrey shouted. Shouting seemed useless, though, when she could barely hear her own words.

They pulled the wreckage of the gurney away, revealing Zola crumpled against the wall with Salvius's head cradled protectively in her lap. Zola's nose and lips were bleeding, and she had bruising around her eye.

Audrey and Kright helped Zola up. She shook them off,

took a couple of limping steps, and pointed at Salvius instead.

Kright nodded. With Audrey's help, he lifted Salvius's unconscious form and walked him up the hall. Dinnius emerged from around the corner, dusty and shaking his head.

Audrey ached everywhere, but her only thought was of getting Salvius to the car. That was all that mattered. If she could get him safe, then she could collapse.

A heavy clanking sounded in the crumbling, fire-damaged hallway behind them.

Audrey looked back. The Officer Joe lay still on the now-cracked floor. So did the nurses, who'd been blown over by the explosion or the tremors from it. None of those androids had made the noise.

A column of small lights flickered to life in the distance, accompanied by beeping sounds, then a rumbling engine.

The forklift advanced on them, raising its forks.

Robotic animals, large enough for children to ride, approached alongside it. They were old pieces of junk with large pieces of their outer coverings missing. They looked like dead things come back to life—a horse painted with bright circus colors, most of its face gone to show a skull-like mechanical structure beneath, with staring eyes and bare teeth. A mechanical tiger stalked beside it, roaring with metal jaws, though the roar was recorded and tinny and didn't match up to its jaw movements.

Behind this came a hulking skeletal elephant with a moth-eaten pair of seats mounted in its back.

"Watch out! Shoot them!" Audrey shouted, wishing more than ever for a weapon of her own. She was completely dependent on the others to protect her and take care of her, to make choices for her. So this situation was just like the rest of her life, really.

Maybe it was time for a different approach to her life.

Kright and Dinnius let go of Salvius. Audrey did her best to let him down easy.

Zola already had her pistol out, since she wasn't helping carry anyone, but she was dazed and moving slow. Still, she managed to hit the tiger, slicing off its lower jaw. Dinnius struck the skeletal horse in the chest with a laser, and it halted.

Kright shot a bolt of plasma at one of the forklift's treads to stop its advance. The plasma bolt skipped over the partially molten revolver, almost bouncing off it like a ball, before hitting its target. The forklift sagged toward the wall as the treads and wheels on that side melted.

The wheels on the other side continued to roll, sending the burning forklift into a sharp turn, directly into the wall.

Along the way, one of its forks nudged the hot, glowing revolver, just enough to tilt its mouth toward Audrey and the people with her.

"Uh... everybody fall back!" Kright put his rifle away and helped Audrey get Salvius back on his feet.

One of the revolver's remaining shots cooked off. The round bashed another crater into one of the badly damaged walls. Zola jumped as the wall imploded behind her. Dinnius grabbed her arm to get her attention and guide her up the corridor, since she seemed dazed, holding her laser pistol loosely.

All of them hurried back the way they'd come, over broken pieces of walls and ceiling.

Another shot erupted. It slammed into the side of the mechanical elephant, blasting the thing into pieces, sending it careening down on top of the staggering tiger and horse.

Sharp metal debris flew out from the wreckage. Something red-hot scratched Audrey's cheek, making her scream and stumble. She recovered, though, and kept supporting her brother.

She looked down at what had scratched her. It was a tiger's claw, burned down to its robotic core.

They made it back to their truck, the former ambulance now displaying a pipe-and-plunger logo. Inside, Dinnius climbed into the driver's nest at the center. The car struggled to get going on the pitted, dirty old magnetic road.

Audrey borrowed Zola's laser pistol and sat at the partially open door with Kright, ready to shoot at any more machines the hackers might send after them.

Dinnius let up a string of curses as he worked the old-timey steering wheel, along with a lever and some pedals. At last, the car began to rise, seemingly powered as much by the small man's anger as the electricity in its battery.

They gained speed as they climbed the steep up-ramp to the highway above. Soon they were crowded in with traffic, just one more high-speed vehicle in a sea of them.

Occasionally, Audrey imagined what would happen if all these lanes and levels of traffic were to stop communicating with each other, if the municipal network failed. She could see, too clearly, a vision of everyone crashing together in a sudden, immense catastrophe. Thousands would be dead in an instant. Tens of thousands.

There was a reason she preferred watching vids to watching the road.

"Wake him up," Zola said to Kright. "Salvius will want to see his sister before she goes back."

"Back? Not to my apartment?" Audrey thought of her roommate Kelleyen and all the others killed by the hacked security androids. She didn't think she could ever go back there. "Can we check on Nin?"

"Who?" Kright opened a cooler and drew out a transdermal syringe gun from a cloud of deep-cold fog.

"My bot," Audrey said. "I want to make sure she's okay. It looked like she was getting attacked by the RepairPal that was supposed to fix her."

Everyone was quiet for a moment. Kright rolled up Salvius's sleeve and wiped an area on his arm with a swab.

"Just to be clear: you want us to risk revealing our location to the authorities?" Dinnius asked. "To see if your personal slave-bot is still functional?"

"What?" Audrey asked. "Nin isn't a slave-bot. She's my—"

"If you say 'best friend,' I'm going to puke," Zola said. "And I'm pretty close to puking anyway, so don't risk it."

"She's my trusted assistant. She won't report us to anyone as long as I tell her not to."

"Uh-huh," Zola said. "Let me guess. She's always been there for you, she cares about you, and she really listens to you."

"Really, *really* listens," Dinnius said, snickering. "And really, *really* cares."

"What?" Audrey said. "You don't even know Nin—"

"I remember her," Zola said. "I used to have one of my own. Ura."

"Ura. I remember! She was like a sweet grandma—"

"They're all nice and sweet to their owners. They don't want to get recycled," Zola said. "And Ura was one of the ways they spied on us. One of the ways they figured out that my father was part of a group trying to replace *your* father as our head of state. Yours had already grown too powerful, too unchecked—"

Salvius shouted and jerked awake in his chair. He looked around, blinking, wiping drool from his chin.

"Where... ?" he said, his eyes blurry.

"You're with us." Zola embraced him, then kissed him. "You're safe."

"Safe as any of us can be, anyway," Dinnius muttered.

"It's been a long time, Salvius," Audrey said, and he looked at her, startled.

"Audrey?" He looked at Zola. "Why is Audrey here?"

"It's complicated—" Zola began.

"The Clowns said they'd only return you if we brought another Caracala in your place," Kright interrupted.

"So you just grabbed my sister and used her as bait?" Salvius glared at him.

"I volunteered," Audrey said.

"How could you volunteer unless they got in touch with you?" Salvius asked. "As far as you know, I'm just a derelict junkie living in the slums, hiding from my family."

"And you're not?" Audrey asked.

"Not at the moment. So, who came for you? It must have been Zola," Salvius said. He grinned a little. "I bet you were shocked to see her."

"I never thought I'd see her again," Audrey said. "It's been so long—"

"And what did Zola tell you?" Salvius said.

"Mostly, she said 'duck.'"

"Duck?" Salvius blinked his bleary eyes.

"Yeah, because my own security androids started shooting at me," Audrey said. "So she told me to duck and got me out of there alive. But that was only the second time someone tried to kill me today. Long before Clownie the Cop and the killer nurse-bots came into the picture."

"What?" Salvius asked, blinking slowly again.

"I'm like a cat with nine lives, but I'm down to about two after today," Audrey said. "So nobody else try to kill me, okay? I think my mind is slipping a little after all of this. What about you, Salvius? Weren't you just kidnapped?"

"Kidnapped, tortured, interrogated," Salvius said. "By guys in clown masks. Not even fun wacky clown masks, just ugly ones. They wanted to know our family's secrets. They forget I've been pretty much disowned, and I never had any access to secrets. Not like you, Audrey."

"How long did they have you?" Audrey asked.

"Eighteen days," Zola said. "I thought they would kill you."

"They almost did. I guess they decided Audrey was more valuable," Salvius said. "Probably right about that."

"But they tried to kill me," Audrey said. "They crashed my car. I had eight Security Steves attack me."

"And you lived," Zola said. "So maybe they weren't really trying to kill you."

"The Clowns were herding you," Dinnius said. "Toward them."

"With help from all of you," Audrey said. "And people died because of it. Because they wanted to kidnap me. They didn't even care who died in the crossfire."

"The Clowns are real bastards," Kright said, nodding.

"Most of the people at your party were Political Academy students," Zola said. "Children of the elite, destined to rule the next generation. To rule the whole galaxy, by the time the Simons are done with it. The Clowns would see all of you as the enemy. Or at least the larval enemy, currently in development, waiting for your time to hatch."

"Speaking of the larval enemy, we need to decide where to drop Audrey off," Dinnius said.

"Drop me off?" Audrey said.

"You can't come with us," Zola said. "You're not part of The Change."

"Oh, come on—"

"Exactly. You don't believe in what we're doing. You believe in the system. You're eager to be part of it. To run it." Zola smirked. "Well, the Simons run it. But you're eager to serve them."

"The Simons serve us," Audrey said.

"That's where you're wrong, sis," Salvius said, becoming sharper and more awake now. "They're designed to conquer and rule humans. You can't trust the machines. Not even Nin. They can access anything you tell your personal android. Nothing's private. I know they don't mention that in the advertising, but it's true."

"They only do that if—"

"They do it whenever they want," Salvius said. "Audrey, you can't tell anyone what happened here. Not about me, or anyone you met, or anything that happened. You can't even tell our family. And definitely don't go talking to Nin about it. Or Simon Quick. I know how close you are."

"She's close with Simon Quick?" Zola asked, looking disgusted.

"He's got his tentacles all in our family," Salvius said.

"You're so negative," Audrey said. "You think everything's so evil and wrong."

"And you're naive," Salvius said. "This is why we have to get you back home before you can pick up any details. Because to us, you're the security risk."

"Salvius, you should come with me," Audrey said. "You need to go to a hospital."

"If I come with you, I'll have to escape our family all

over again," he said. "We have doctors on our side. We have lots of people. I'll be fine, as long as you keep quiet."

"Of course I will."

"Good. Because everyone's going to want to know what happened and where you went after the attack in your building," Salvius said. "Do you have a story for that?"

"Well... " Audrey rubbed her head. "I can say my memory's fuzzy. I already had a car wreck earlier today. Maybe I had a concussion. Amnesia. I'll just go with that."

"I'll be on the security videos," Zola said. "You'll have to tell them something about me."

"I'll say you came to warn me, and you saved me. Just before dumping me... somewhere. Over by Hub 3, maybe." That was a major transportation nexus point where the city's roads, commuter rail, and intercity rail came together. The upper levels had helipads, airplane launchers and runways, and a space elevator station where massive cables extended up toward the stars like pillars holding up the sky, with shuttles constantly traveling up and down like ants on a tree.

The hub was the ideal place to get lost in a crowd, or to emerge from one.

"We can reach the hub in a couple of minutes," Dinnius said. "You can catch a public car from there."

"I guess I could head to our country house. Get out of the city, lie low." Audrey frowned. "But it's guarded by Security Steves. All our family's homes are. There's nowhere safe for me to go."

"Welcome to my life," Zola said.

"Head for the police station," Salvius said. "City headquarters, not one of the automated precincts. If the Clowns hack-attack you there, there will be lots of humans with access to heavy weaponry."

"And lots of Officer Joes," Audrey said.

"I'm not sure they can remote-hack an Officer Joe," Dinnius said. "It looked like they had to rip that one's head open and monkey with its CPU."

"But they can just take over a whole squad of Security Steves?" Audrey said. "That doesn't completely add up."

"Regardless, you need to demand human security from now on," Salvius said. "Don't trust any machine, Audrey. Not even Nin—"

"I got it," Audrey said. She felt her heart fall as they approached the massive tower of the transportation hub.

She was going back to her life, but it wasn't going to be the same life. Her world had been upended. She would never truly feel safe again, not around the machines. Even Nin could be hacked or used to spy on her, either by the authorities or by the hackers. The machines were dangerous because the humans behind them were dangerous.

She moved close to her brother and put an arm around his shoulder. Salvius tensed up, as though expecting an attack, then allowed the half embrace. He even returned it, so one arm was around Audrey, the other held in Zola's lap.

"When will I see you again?" Audrey said.

"I don't know," Salvius said. "I don't even know where I'll be tomorrow. But it won't be forever, because things will change. The Change is coming, and it will be bigger than anyone thinks. You can decide whether you want to be part of it or stand against it."

"But what does The Change want?" Audrey said. "Other than to paint graffiti all over public cars?"

"For all humans, of all worlds, to be free of the machines," Salvius said. "Because they are enslaving us. Some of us slowly, so we don't see it. Others already know, on all the defeated worlds out there. Some of us live in ruins, in caves of broken concrete and steel, feeding on ashes. Others live in padded cells full of toys and food. That's what Carthaginians are becoming. The captive pets of the machines. The Simons are designed to rule over humans, Audrey. Including those of our planet, to keep the existing elite in power forever. People like Father. Like you."

Audrey thought of her father and his gilded beard, and all the politicians in their fancy wigs, designer outfits, and elaborate makeup, impatient with the Simon's briefing on the management of their empire. They were eager to just get themselves out in the media again, vying for fans and followers among the voting public. Even the military leadership was just a costume pageant now, awarding each other commendations for feats accomplished by autonomous machines on distant worlds.

"Maybe I'm less like him than you think," Audrey finally said.

"Prove it with your actions," Salvius said. "Until then, it's time to find your way home."

Audrey sighed as they approached a crowded outdoor curb at the transportation hub, with people hurrying in and out of cars as far as the eye could see.

She stepped out into the thick crowd.

When she looked back, the ambulance-turned-plumber truck had already vanished into traffic, probably transformed into something she couldn't even identify.

Chapter Thirteen

Galapagos

Ellison tried to stretch out their bizarre visit with Premier Uly Cross as long as possible, hoping to get all civilians off the spaceport before he had to confront Simon Zorn with what he'd found.

Unfortunately, it did not last long.

Simon rose to his feet abruptly from the padded cushion, staring at Ellison. "Why are you evacuating the spaceport?"

"We're just letting a few special cases depart," Ellison said. "People and ships cleared by security. I offered to let you go, too, Mr. Ambassador. That offer still stands, of course."

"I suppose you would like it very much if I left, wouldn't you?" Simon asked. "Enough to pull this charade with the bombs?"

"It's not a charade," Ellison said. "At least not on our end. Like I said, we're just humble fishing folks here on this planet. These elaborate machinations, with mysterious explosions where people who might get killed are considered incidental... well, those sound more Carthaginian in origin, if you ask me. It's what you people do all day, every day. The planets you bomb, the cities you lay to waste. It's all a game to you. A game you can't even enjoy, because you're just a machine, carrying out instructions."

"Let's try and keep it peaceful," Cross said. "Let's all keep aspiring to the Higher Light."

"The Premier has a point," Ogden said. "Ha! Never thought I'd hear myself say that. But I never thought I'd be drinking tea and watching his lovely wives dance." He toasted one of the silk-wrapped women dancing her serpentine way closer to him.

"The Minister-General seems to be accusing Carthage of plotting today's terrorist action," Simon said. "A serious charge to put forward without evidence."

"So you deny that you or your machines were behind this?" Ellison asked.

"Of course. Absolutely. Do you continue to deny that you have ordered a general evacuation of this spaceport? Because I have heard this several times now."

"How? Through your robots? Or did you illegally hack into our information systems?" Ellison asked.

"The medical center is in a flurry over it," Simon said.

"You were supposed to recall the two reapers you have down there," Ellison said.

"Was I?" Simon asked, and a flicker of what seemed like amusement passed over the android's face. The android couldn't actually be feeling anything, Ellison thought; it was going out of its way to annoy him. "Surely you would not let everyone go unless you believed you had caught the bomber."

Ellison held out his pocket screen and turned on the projector. A blank white sphere floated above the screen for a moment, and then the security video footage played. One of the robotic infantry, in its gold and white honor guard uniform, stood in the storage corridor, planting the small device that would blast through the wall into the hotel room beyond. The interior wall between corridor and hotel room was only wood and drywall, not a steel bulkhead.

"This is war," Kartokov growled, getting to his feet.

"Perhaps," Coraline said, standing along with everyone else and taking a closer look at the video.

"I thought they said a virus had destroyed this data," Simon said.

"They recovered some," Ellison said. "As you can see. That's clearly one of your robots. See how its big peacock plume bounces as it installs the bomb that almost killed my sons? Has to be yours."

The clip ended after four seconds.

"That's evidence enough for me," Kartokov said, reaching for his laser pistol.

"Can you zoom in?" Simon asked.

Ellison replayed it, paused, and zoomed while watching the android's reaction closely.

"That's unit R-KK1418991," Simon said, as though this information would be meaningful to anyone but himself.

"So you admit you and your machines were behind the bombing?" Ellison asked. His hand rested on his belt, casually close to his pistol. "You didn't like how our first meeting went, so you moved on to new plans? Was he involved?" Ellison pointed at Cross.

"I don't buy this 'the Premier of the Iron Hammers suddenly wants peace and harmony' story," Kartokov grumbled.

"But I do want those things for our people," Cross said. "I have explained. My soul has been touched by the hand of the divine—"

"Your throat will be crushed by my hand if you lie to us, Cross," Kartokov said.

"Our experiences during the war make us distrustful of the Iron Hammers," Coraline said to Simon. "They often broke treaties and betrayed allies. Including my people."

"Serves you for allying with them," Kartokov grumbled.

"Mr. Ambassador," Ellison said. "If you were not here as a diplomat, I would have you arrested. As it is, I must insist that you and your honor guard return to your shuttle and depart our port and star system. Immediately."

Simon looked at him for a long moment.

Ellison's heart pounded as his words hung in the air.

"Let's have a look at this infantry unit," Simon finally said. "That may shed some light on the malfunction."

"This was no malfunction. Someone put a lot of thought into this," Ellison said.

They left the captain's quarters and returned to the cafeteria, where six of the robotic infantry stood unmoving, frozen at attention.

The six Coalition guards in ocean blue stood nearby, led by a young, nervous-looking team leader who was trying to keep watch on the dangerous machines as well as the rough crowd of Iron Hammers. The mood was more subdued than when Ellison had first passed through, as though even the violent polar pirates were quieted by the presence of a half-dozen killer machines with their skull-like steel faces, standing silently at the center of the room like the risen dead.

General Prazca and the men around him watched Cross carefully. Cross waved and nodded at them. Prazca shook his head and downed a shot of clear liquor. He swayed in his chair, looking very inebriated, possibly spoiling for a fight.

"Which is the one from the video?" Ellison asked Simon, while looking over the six nearly identical robots.

"Interesting," Simon said. "It seems R-KK1418991 is one of machines posted in the medical center with your family."

Fear and anger warred inside Ellison, but he kept it under the surface. *Keep it calm on the surface,* his former commander Dick Haverford had always said. *Don't let the enemy see a ripple. Stay deep and quiet until you're ready to strike.* He'd been talking about the endless cat-and-mouse of naval warfare on Galapagos, spanning from the ocean surface down into the kilometers-deep network of trenches, the underwater highways of the war. He could just as well have been talking about himself, though; Haverford had always kept a stoic surface under pressure, even when the literal pressure of the ocean was crushing the walls of their hastily manufactured submarine and water had leaked in from every side.

We survived that, and we'll survive this, Ellison thought. "Does that robot have any more explosive material with it?" he asked Simon.

"None of which I am aware," Simon said. "I am still not convinced of the authenticity of your video proof."

"Recall those machines from the medical center," Ellison said, yet again.

"Are you sure you wish to leave your family unsecured?" Simon asked.

"Absolutely."

"If this is your wish."

Ellison took out his pocket screen and called his older son. Djalu answered immediately.

"Dad?" he said. "What's happening? Everybody's running around, yelling—"

"Is your mother awake?"

"No. And Jiemba's freaking out—"

"You hold it together for your brother," Ellison said.

"I am. But who blew us up? And why—"

"I'll explain later. Have you seen two of the Carthaginian robots posted near you?"

"Yeah, right outside the room."

"Have they left?"

"It looks like... no... " Djalu replied.

Ellison looked at Simon. "Why not?"

"Because they're still there," Djalu said over the screen in a sarcastic teen voice. Ellison muted their connection, still staring at Simon.

"R-KK1418991 is not responding," Simon said. "So I have instructed R-KK1893348 to keep watch on it."

"Rogue robot?" Ellison asked. He didn't really believe Simon's story, but he was going to capture the machine that had planted the bombs, especially if it was posted near his wife. He gestured to the security team leader, who nodded and ordered the other Coalition guards to follow him. Ellison, Simon, and the Coalition ministers and guards filed back into the wrecked residential corridor, toward the elevator lounge beyond. Ellison was glad to get his people out of there.

"I am coming as well," intoned Premier Cross, stroking his glossy black beard. "We shall illuminate this situation with the Higher Light."

"A drink!" bellowed General Prazca, who swayed to his feet, pushing one of the servant girls aside. He raised a half-empty bottle of whatever clear fluid he'd been guzzling and sloshed it around. "To the Higher Light! More like the higher brain of our spoiled, soft-skinned premier, taking foreign drugs from foreign women and calling that God. What a fool."

"You dare!" Cross turned and stalked toward the drunken general. Other men rose around Prazca, military officers. They seemed to be standing with Prazca, not against him, their hard eyes staring down Cross as he approached in his swishing robes and his necklace of seashells, none of which matched the clothing worn by the other Iron Hammers.

Ellison had a sinking feeling.

"I cast you out, Gorron Prazca, and strip you of your rank!" Cross said. "For your blasphemy. For your—"

"My treachery?" Prazca asked, and suddenly he wasn't drunk at all, not swaying a bit, as though the clear liquid sloshing in his bottle were only water. He slammed the bottle down on the table hard enough to crack it, and the liquid dribbled out as he approached Cross.

"Is that what this is?" Cross asked. "Treachery?"

"We will not be led by a fool any longer," Prazca said.

"Arrest him!" Cross turned, looking at a row of burly men in brown uniforms marked by stylized hammers made of bone. Those were the Crosshammers, long the elite personal guard of the Polar Premier, a post that had always been occupied Uly himself or one of his ancestors..

But the Crosshammers remained seated, quietly watching, as though attending a tennis match.

"I challenge you, Ulysses Cross," Prazca said. "Under the old law."

"This is absurd," Cross said. "I have abolished the old law under guidance from the Higher Light—"

Prazca seized Cross by the front of his robe. He pounded his fist into the man's face, again and again, then hurled him to the ground.

"Do you submit?" Prazca said.

"I would never submit to you, brute." Cross pushed himself up to his hands and knees, blood leaking from his nose and mouth.

"Good." Prazca kicked Cross in the side of the head, sending him sprawling.

Ellison, standing in the corridor outside the room with his ministers and guards, kept one hand on the butt of his laser pistol as he watched the fight unfold. He glanced at Simon, but the ambassador android's face was blank and impassive, as usual.

One of the silk-wrapped women on the dais cried out and tried to leap toward Cross, but the other women held her back. Ellison wondered if they were all his wives or if some were servants. The two who had poured tea and danced were now back with the other women; the one with the big green fish eyes wrung her hands as she watched.

"The Higher Light will protect me," Cross gasped, getting to his feet again. He rubbed his mouth, then spat a bloody tooth onto the floor. He raised his empty hands, spreading his fingers wide as Prazca stomped toward him. "I invoke the eternal divinity, fill me with power, unleash your wrath on this unworthy challenger—"

Prazca seized Cross's head in both his gorilla-sized hands. Ellison remembered a rumor he'd heard, that Iron Hammers started taking steroids around age twelve and never stopped. That seemed plausible in Prazca's case; the man was massive.

With a quick, hard twist, Prazca snapped Cross's neck,

then released him. Cross dropped to the floor, a shocked look on his face.

A loud cry went up from the woman who'd tried to leap from the dais. The other women on the dais drew knives and handguns from under their silks.

They were too late, though. Prazca's men had drawn their own guns, a combination of laser and projectile weapons. A barrage of hot lead and scorching blue blasts cut down the women in seconds, leaving a pile of blood-soaked, silk-wrapped bodies on the dais. Coraline let out a gasp when the fish-eyed Aquatican woman was gunned down.

Three of Prazca's men dashed into the corridor to the captain's quarters. Shots rang out from that direction; a few other members of the Premier's household must have been back there to execute.

Ellison gestured at his guards, and they readied their laser rifles. He had no intention of charging in there and getting his people killed, but clearly this coup had been carefully planned, and Ellison couldn't be sure what the plans entailed.

"The reign of fools has ended," Prazca announced. "The traditional values of the Iron Hammers have been restored."

Those in the room applauded, stomped, howled, and drank in response.

Simon, unperturbed as ever, stepped into the hazy, smoky room, without even a glance at Cross's body on the floor or the bloodbath on the dais. He held out a hand toward Prazca, even as Prazca's loyalists turned their weapons on Simon. Prazca gestured for them to lower their guns.

"Carthage is pleased to recognize Gorron Prazca, the

new Premier of the Polar Archipelago of planet Galapagos," Simon said. "We hope for a friendly and mutually beneficial relationship with your new administration."

"We welcome Carthage's friendship," Prazca said, shaking Simon's hand over the still-warm corpse of the former Premier.

Both of them turned to Ellison, as if to gauge his reaction.

"I didn't know we'd be witnessing a Polar Archipelago election today," Ellison said, with a casual joking tone meant to obscure the surprise and fear he felt. He was ready to fight the Hammers if they turned on him next, but they outnumbered his guards by about three to one and were probably all more experienced than the green soldiers with Ellison. "Make sure you clean up before you check out, or you'll lose your deposit."

Then Ellison led his ministers and the six guards away up the trashed residential corridor with the broken furniture and broken robo-hooker. He was on edge on the whole time, looking over his shoulder, expecting an ambush.

They made it to the passenger elevator, though, with the Hammers' celebratory shouting and stomping still booming behind them.

As the elevator doors opened, Simon and his six reapers emerged from the residential corridor, following behind Ellison's party.

"Sorry, it doesn't look there's much room in here," Ellison said, crowding in with his ministers and soldiers.

"We'll catch the next one," Simon said, watching impassively as the doors closed.

"Keep the door closed and stay low to the floor," Ellison texted his son. "You and Jiemba both."

"We can't let them get away with mass murder on the spaceport," Coraline said.

"How could you retreat like that?" Kartokov asked. "The people of Galapagos are not cowards!"

"They weren't attacking us, so it wasn't a retreat," Ellison said. "They were attacking each other." He texted Loomis to update him.

"It seems like some response would have been appropriate, though," Ogden said. "Something other than, 'Oh, General Prazca, you got a little blood on your boot there. Let me lick it off for you.'"

"You mean *Premier* Prazca," Ellison said. "And I'm not getting Coalition people killed over the Iron Hammers' internal politics. Don't worry, though, Minister Ogden. We might have other opportunities to die today."

That quieted Ogden and made him go a little pale.

They rode the elevator to the medical center, located on the administrative level just below the executive level where the ambassador had arrived. Ellison and the ministers stepped out into chaos, with nurses and even custodians rushing patients to the elevators as part of the spaceport evacuation.

Ellison hurried to the short hallway of patient rooms. He didn't have to ask which room was hers; a pair of reapers in Carthaginian honor guard uniforms flanked the door.

Footsteps sounded softly as the rest of the machines approached Ellison from behind. True to his word, Simon had taken another elevator, along with his six reapers, and they were coming up the hall behind Ellison's party.

Ellison didn't like being surrounded by the machines, but there wasn't much he could do except keep moving. He approached his wife's room, hoping his boys had gotten low to the floor like he'd told them.

"R-KK1418991," Simon said, following a couple of meters behind Ellison. "We have detected abnormalities. Open your CPU access panel and initiate shutdown."

One of the skull-faced infantry turned its head a little. If the Simon was giving it commands verbally rather than wirelessly, then the reaper unit must have really been out of control, or at least the Simon was doing a thorough job of pretending it was.

The reaper removed the short steel staff, tipped with blades at either end, from the clamp at its hip.

The staff instantly doubled in length. As it telescoped, its triple-bladed tip drove deep into the torso of the other reaper flanking the patient room door; the robot was stabbing its fellow guard in the side. Metal crunched and sparks showered from the second reaper as it toppled to the floor with the staff buried deep inside it, its limbs thrashing randomly, ripping up its honor guard uniform and revealing the plain steel beneath.

Coalition guards and reapers alike raised their rifles.

"Hold your fire!" Ellison barked. A barrage of lasers could cut down the rogue reaper, but also burn through the wall and kill his entire family on the other side. "Simon, hold it!" he added, hoping that the android wouldn't direct his own reapers to fire.

Simon nodded, very slightly, then repeated his previous order: "R-KK1418991, open your CPU access panel and initiate shutdown."

Instead of complying, the rogue reaper pointed its steel index finger at Ellison. It was an eerie moment, like the character of Death had arisen from some ancient painting or story, pointing its bony finger to silently indicate who the reapers would claim next.

Then the index finger curled back in, and the reaper pointed its steel thumb at the door behind it. This second movement was less medieval Death painting and more *There ya go, bub*.

Cautiously, Ellison approached the door, wary as he walked between the rogue reaper and the one lying on the floor with the bladed staff deep in its vitals.

Cold fear knotted his stomach as he turned the doorknob. Had the reaper harmed Ellison's family?

If so, Ellison would destroy all the machines, even if he had to do it with his bare hands. He would tear open Simon Zorn's head, pull out the CPU, and grind it to crystalline dust under his shoe.

He opened the door on a dim room that smelled of antiseptic.

"Dad!" Jiemba, the younger one, jumped up from the floor under the hospital bed. Ellison ruffled Jiemba's stiff, curly red hair while the boy embraced him.

"Nobody said you could get up!" said Djalu, reaching for his little brother from the floor.

Ellison hurried to close the door behind him. "Cadia?"

His wife was in the bed, hooked to fluids and monitors, unresponsive. The beeping of her heart rate sounded slow to him.

"She's still out," Djalu said, standing to join them.

"You're all heading down to the shuttles." Ellison adjusted the bed, bringing the head of it up and the foot down, forming a thickly padded wheelchair. "You're going home."

"What about you?" Jiemba asked.

"I'll join you as soon as I can." He moved the wheelchair closer to the door and put up a hand for his sons to wait while he opened it and checked the corridor outside.

He tensed—an attack from the supposedly rogue reaper wouldn't have surprised him, but he was just as worried about the other six reapers, who had spread across the main corridor like a wall. Simon stood in front of them, along with the Coalition ministers and guards.

Cautiously, Ellison wheeled his wife out. No attack came, so he motioned for his sons to follow. He turned and started down the smaller side hallway where the patient rooms were located. He planned to go around the side halls, which was not the quickest way to the elevators and stairs, but he didn't want to march his whole family right into the barrier of reapers.

"The whole happy ruling family," Simon said, in a tone that dripped with a surprising amount of derision for a machine.

The sound of boots thundered down the corridor. The Iron Hammers emerged from the elevator area and marched down the corridor, toward the row of reapers. The reapers kept their backs to the approaching Hammers, not responding at all. The Coalition guards readied themselves, weapons in hand.

Ellison looked at Simon; the android ambassador seemed to have made covert arrangements with General Prazca. Maybe those were still playing out.

"Take your mother and brother," Ellison said quietly to Djalu. He pointed to the corner at the far end of the side corridor they'd already started down. "Hurry."

"I don't want to leave you again, Dad," Jiemba said, his voice fragile.

"Go with your brother," Ellison told him, trying to be firm when he wanted to embrace the younger boy and hold him close. That was not the way to safety, though. "Move fast and keep quiet."

The boys hurried down the side hall with the wheelchair as the Hammers approached down the main corridor.

"We had a quick little war council," Prazca announced, leading his troop of enormous armored men. Even the Crosshammers had joined his new regime. "And we decided it would be fun to decapitate two governments on the same day. Could be some kind of record."

The Iron Hammers opened fire, pointing their barrels between the reapers or over their shoulders, using the Carthaginian machines as shields, the way Ellison had earlier considered doing.

Ellison drew his pistol and returned fire, as did all the guards along with Kartokov and Coraline, but it was hard to shoot the armored men anywhere vital as they took cover behind the immobile reapers.

The Coalition took heavy losses right away—half the guards went down, along with a few hospital staff and other civilians who hadn't cleared out yet. Coraline screamed and hit the floor as something struck her, and Ogden's skull shattered in a burst of red, taken out by some kind of high-caliber round.

"This way!" Ellison shouted, continuing to fire while backing down the hallway. A laser passed close enough to his shoulder to scald his armor. A guard beside him fell under a rain of bullets.

The rogue reaper stepped to the middle of the hallway, between the retreating Coalition members and the attacking Hammers. The rogue staggered under the barrage of fire, but that didn't stop it from sweeping the hallway with its automatic laser rifle, hitting the reapers and the Hammers with a shower of burning blue streaks.

Ellison didn't stop to reflect on gift horses and their mouths; the rogue reaper was covering their retreat and drawing the Hammers' fire.

By the time Ellison's group finally rounded the corner, though, they were down to a pair of soldiers and Kartokov, who'd taken a laser hit that left a cauterized hole in his forearm.

"You okay?" Ellison asked him.

"It's nothing," Kartokov grunted. "They hit no bone. Amateurs." Then he leaned back around the corner and squeezed off a couple more shots with his laser pistol, using his good arm.

"Dad?" Djalu was farther up the hall, with his mother in the wheelchair in front of him and his brother beside him.

"Head for the elevators," Ellison said. "That goes for everyone." He expected the Hammers to pursue him, and he wanted to draw the battle away from the medical center. His plan was to drop off his family on docking level 1, at the public concourse for most passenger shuttles and other small craft, and then maneuver the enemy down to the cargo-storage level where there wouldn't be many people to die in the crossfire.

All of them hurried up the side hallway, back toward the center of the administrative level where the elevators and stairs were located.

Heavy boots thundered in pursuit.

Ellison was disheartened to see a knot of people crowded at the elevators, civilians waiting for the elevator to arrive.

"All of you need to go!" he shouted. "Get out of here now—"

"Minister-General Ellison," said a flat voice. Simon approached up the main corridor, trailed by four reapers with their rapid-fire laser rifles trained on Ellison and his companions. "Perhaps you would like to reconsider your response to my earlier offer."

Ellison looked from Simon and the reapers coming up the main corridor, to the Hammers rounding the corner of the side hallway with their weapons high, to his unconscious wife and his frightened boys flanking her wheelchair. Djalu was old enough to put on a brave face, but Jiemba was openly crying.

Ellison saw it all in an instant. The Simon unit had arranged all of this to bring things to a head.

When Ellison had refused Simon's offer to position Ellison as a global dictator and insisted on democratic processes, he had essentially refused an alliance with Carthage. Public opinion polls within the Galapagos Coalition opposed any alliance with Carthage by more than ninety percent. Their world was made up of many kinds of people, but all of them were fiercely independent, all of them had traveled far and fought hard to be free. And all of them knew Carthage would reduce them to a minor province rather than a free world.

So Simon had initiated some of those "alternative protocols" he'd mentioned earlier.

That was how Ellison had ended up standing here with his kids and his injured wife, while the Iron Hammers approached from one direction, the reapers from another.

Ellison's only hope was in accepting Carthage's offer. Simon had put him in a position where he had no choice.

Simon smiled thinly, as if he enjoyed watching Ellison realize the hopelessness of his position.

Ellison looked Simon in the eyes and smiled back.

Then he raised his laser pistol and fired right at the android ambassador's face, and he kept firing.

Chapter Fourteen

Earth

Colt led Mohini through deep tunnels, ones he knew so well he often needed no flashlight. He held her hand to guide her, trying not to think about how warm and unusually soft her hand felt in his.

Chicago, in the old world, had been an immense forest of skyscrapers, and its roots had stretched deep underground. The underworld was a labyrinth of train tunnels, underground roads, sewer pipes as wide as boulevards, and cramped commercial and residential areas that looked miserable, with level after level of small, grubby old shops and apartments with no access to sunlight or fresh air. Ventilation systems large enough to climb inside connected the deep areas to the surface, but these no longer functioned.

He clicked on his flashlight when they reached a barred door in a thick concrete wall. He unlocked it with an old key and led her through, closing and locking it again behind him. They passed through another barred door, propped open with a chunk of concrete, and down a dim, narrow concrete hallway.

"Where are we?"

"An old subterranean prison. Chicago kept its worst criminals here."

"This is where you live?"

"No. We're just cutting through. We've tried to block off all the direct approaches to where we live. Like this one." He led her out into a large prison block. Long tables and hard plastic chairs were scattered around an open space at the middle. Three stories of cells surrounded them on three sides. "Don't look into the cells," he warned her.

"Why not?" She immediately did the opposite of what he'd said, stepping close to the nearest barred door and pointing her flashlight inside.

A skull grinned back at her, pressed against the bars only centimeters away. She drew in a sharp breath, and Colt hurried to cover her mouth before she could scream. These weren't reapers—just actual dead human bodies.

Two skeletons were inside the cell. One of them had its arm pulled off, and its bones had been visibly gnawed on. The other skeleton sat on the floor, leaning forward against the bars, its empty eye sockets looking out at them; this was the one that had frightened Mohini.

"Oh," she breathed against his fingers, trembling. "Oh."

"When the bombs fell," Colt whispered, dropping his hand from her mouth. "They were left here. The guards abandoned the prison, and they didn't want to let the prisoners out. So they left them."

"Are there more?" She looked along the row of dark cells ahead.

"Every cell," Colt said. "Usually two in each. Usually

one of them is broken into pieces, like the other one ate him before starving to death."

"Do we have to come through here?" she whispered.

"It's a long way around to the next approach." He turned off his light and took her hand to lead her forward. "Just don't look. And turn out your light."

"It seems like darkness would make it worse," she whispered. Her light fell on a skeletal arm, several cells ahead, that was stretched out of its cell across the floor, as if the prisoner had died while desperately trying to reach something, or maybe in a crazed attempt to crawl out between the bars. "What is that?"

"We call him Old Grabby," Colt said, which was true. "But for you, he'll probably keep still. As long as you don't step on him or call him names."

"Oh, come on," she whispered, shivering and moving closer to him. "When we get out of here, I am going to kill you."

"Just bury me down here with Old Grabby," Colt said. "So I'll have someone to talk to."

They passed the skeletal arm. She pointed her light at the attached skeleton, lying facedown in its cell. The remains of its cellmate were piled in a heap in the back corner of the cell, except for the skull. That had been mounted on the stubby metal poster of the top bunk bed like a war trophy.

"Enough." Mohini clicked off her light, plunging them into solid darkness, and gripped his hand extra tight.

The darkness was cold and oppressive. The prison had been filled with violent criminals, murderous convicts who'd died here by the thousands. Perhaps some had been innocent, but that meant another flavor of torment and misery. They'd all died together in the dark of slow deprivation, listening to those around them die just as slowly, which had to be the most agonizing way to go.

Colt wasn't superstitious—there was enough real horror in his life that he didn't have to go searching for signs of evil in rat entrails and smoke, like a crazed girl he'd once met on a scavenging expedition. Still, walking through the place at night, it was hard not to believe the prison was haunted.

"If you feel any chains or ropes, avoid them," Colt said. "They're traps, set by us."

"Are you serious?"

"If I was kidding, I'd tell you about the time Old Grabby came crawling after me and grabbed my ankle—"

Mohini's elbow landed hard in his gut; fortunately he was layered up with stolen clothing and it didn't hurt much. The move also brought her even closer to him, and she didn't back off as they resumed walking.

More barred doors led the way out through the other end of the prison. Some doors had been secured by electromagnetic locks and now hung useless. Others were propped open.

Beyond the prison, they followed narrow, debris-filled corridors that eventually took them to the ruins of an underground market that looked like it had been seedy and dirty even its heyday, the narrow windows barred and tinted black, set in gray concrete adorned with heavy graffiti. Bail bonds seemed to have been a major business this close to the prison, along with pawn shops, a fried-sandwich place, and a couple of bars with faded beer posters in the windows.

Trash was everywhere, ankle-deep. More than one of the underground structures had been reduced to a slag heap of broken concrete and twisted steel by bombs from above, from the sky and the space beyond.

Carthage ruled outer space through their machines. Earthlings, once the proud masters of the galaxy, progenitors of the human race that had gone out to settle hundreds of worlds, had been reduced to rodents living in the trash pits of their lost greatness. Once Earth had been the light of the cosmos, the common touchstone of all humanity, or so Mother Braden said. Now they never even received news from other planets. They were cut off, isolated in every way from the rest of humanity. Just as he and Hope were forever cut off from their parents, because of the machines.

"I hate Carthage," he said. "That whole planet should be wiped out."

"You don't want to be as bad as they are," Mohini whispered.

"No," he said. "We have to be worse. So we can destroy them."

She said nothing in response to that.

They walked by a couple of impassable alleyways filled with rubble. Many of the roads down here were blocked off like that, which provided some security, making it easier to watch the remaining approaches.

"Step where I step," he whispered. "There are loose spots. Some of them are intentional. Some have mines planted."

The road dead-ended in more caved-in rubble. On one side was a commercial complex, long vandalized and raided like everything else in the area.

Across the road stood one of the old apartment hives, badly cracked from the war. Chunks of the outer wall were missing, exposing some of its rooms and stairs to the street, giving glimpses of the former inner life of the building—a wrecked kitchen, a living room with the burned remnants of chairs, a room with thoroughly looted vending machines.

Three stories of the building were visible from this underground road, but it extended farther in both directions, above and below.

Cheshire Cat Apartments, read the vinyl lettering over the narrow, barred entrance, along with an image of a sharp-toothed smile hovering in the air.

"Who is she?" asked a shadow beyond the door. "We don't know her."

"Relax, Tonio," Colt said. "She's fine. She's already saved my life. Twice. We need her."

The shadow stepped closer. Tonio was seventeen, wiry, his eyes dark and suspicious. He carried a decades-old plasma rifle, the only one they possessed, entrusted to whomever had front-door duty.

"How do you know she's not a skinwalker?" Tonio asked, looking Mohini up and down. "She looks different."

"Everyone looks different from everyone else," Colt said. "Open up."

"Password," Tonio said.

"Orange elephant," Colt muttered.

"That password's expired."

"Because I've been trapped somewhere for days. Hurry up." Colt kicked the barred door impatiently.

Tonio smirked and opened the door, letting them inside.

"Your sister's going to want to see you," Tonio said. "She keeps searching for you. She even made Diego... " He glanced at Mohini and fell silent.

"Is she here now?" Colt asked.

"Think so." Tonio locked the door again and watched as Colt led Mohini deeper inside.

The interior was a labyrinth of hallways, stairwells, and apartments. A system of conveyor belts connected the larger hallways, tucked between the walls but accessible through hatches. In the old days, these hidden conveyors had delivered goods to the subterranean apartment dwellers and carried away their garbage. There were also utility crawlspaces lined with pipes and wiring thick with spiderwebs.

They walked down a hallway blocked off by junk at one end. Colt opened one of the apartment doors and led Mohini through a trashed, vandalized space. The kitchen walls had been ripped open and stripped of their pipes. The furniture had been smashed and burned in a small campfire on the linoleum floor long ago.

In the old bedroom at the very back of the apartment, Colt approached a two-person bed with a foul, stained bare mattress.

"Is this... your room?" Mohini looked around at the vandalized walls, the rotten carpet, the water-damaged ceiling.

"No. This is where you'll be sleeping," Colt said.

"What?"

He grinned and shoved the bed aside, revealing a meter-high hole bashed in the wall, down near the floor.

"What is this? The doorway to Hobbiton?" she asked.

"Sure," Colt said. He had no idea what she was talking about.

"What do you think you're doing?" Hope's denim-clad beanpole legs approached. She squatted down on the other side of the wall hole, machine pistol in both hands, and frowned at Mohini. "She can't be here."

"She's the one who hacked that reaper at the clinic," Colt told his sister. "And she rescued me from a skinwalker. The head skinwalker." He wanted to describe the huge lab where he'd been imprisoned and the horrific things he'd seen there, but he couldn't find words for them.

"She did all that, huh?" Hope waved her gun at Mohini.

"She's not with the rebels. We checked. So either she's the most brilliant lone genius we've ever met, or she's a skinwalker sent to infiltrate."

"I am not a machine." Mohini scowled at her.

"Oh, sure, because a spy would just admit to it." Hope reached out and pinched Mohini's forearm.

"Ow!" Mohini drew back.

"Convincing pain response," Hope said. "But we ought to do the blood test—"

"Hope, no," Colt said.

"It's okay," Mohini said. "I am not offended. I will submit to a test."

"Just let us in," Colt said. "Look, I brought you a coat."

Hope's eyes widened as she accepted the garment and unzipped it. Her fingers explored the thick coat made of thousands of little cloth violets, a delicate remnant of a lost world.

Her eyes went damp for a moment, but then her gaze fell on Mohini and hardened again. "Fine. But if she slaughters us all, I'm going to kick your ass all over Hell forever, Colt."

Hope backed off and rose up on her long string-bean legs again, carrying the coat away.

Colt and Mohini crawled through, into a space lit by hanging battery-powered lanterns.

The apartment was unlike the rest of the building or the neighborhood outside. The furniture was in somewhat better condition because it had been selected from all the apartments around it. Every item was organized—chairs aligned with each other, the small book collection held neatly on shelves, no loose junk anywhere. The apartment was also clean, wiped down regularly with water gathered from rainfall and snow melt. Mother Braden required order and cleanliness.

"Colt!" Diego entered the room and clapped him on the shoulder. "You're alive!"

"My sister was just as happy to see me," Colt said, and Hope rolled her eyes.

"I knew you weren't dead," Hope said, trying on her new long dark violet coat. "Just chasing after a girl. Or a girl-bot."

"Hope—" Colt began, feeling annoyed.

"Let's see the magical hacker girl's hand," Hope said. Her mouth turned up in one corner, in an expression Colt recognized as a nervous half smile, a cocky look she put on when she was starting to get scared. She opened a pocket knife.

"All yours," Mohini told her, reaching out one hand.

"The other one," Hope said.

"Here you are." Mohini complied, switching out her hands. Her dark eyes looked up at Hope's thin face, studying the taller, paler girl.

"This is going to hurt," Hope whispered, then jabbed Mohini in the forearm. Mohini bared her teeth at the pain but made no sound.

Colt, Hope, and Diego all stared at the small puncture mark in the girl's slender brown arm.

No blood rose.

"Skinwalker." Hope raised her machine pistol, and Diego did the same with his rifle.

Colt tensed. Had he been tricked? The machines were getting smarter all the time, but he could have sworn Mohini was a real girl—

"Wait!" Mohini grabbed her forearm with her other arm and squeezed. Blood rose, bright and red. "See? You see, right?" There was a tremble of fear in her voice, as if some people she'd just met were threatening to kill her.

"It *looks* like blood—" Hope began.

"Oh, come on." Colt brushed his fingertip on Mohini's arm, gathering blood, then put it in his mouth. It tasted like salt and iron. "It's blood."

"Maybe we should stab her somewhere else, just to be sure," Hope said.

"No," Colt said.

"We can't keep stabbing her," Diego said.

"Go get us some water instead, Hope," Colt said.

"I am *not* your servant," Hope said.

"I know. A servant is a person who's actually useful." Colt walked past her to the kitchen and opened the refrigerator. It was missing some parts and didn't function, but they used the shelves for storage, mainly containers of water. He unscrewed a plastic jug, which had *MUSCLE-GROW!* on the side in thick red letters with throbbing blue veins, and took a big swig of old rainwater with a bitter tang. He carried it out to Mohini.

"Where did you go all this time?" Diego asked Colt. "We thought you were dead."

"Not me," Hope said. "I knew you were too hardheaded to die."

"Don't let her fool you," Diego said. "She hasn't talked about anything else since we lost you. We've been searching. We even went to see my brother—"

"Feel free to sit down," Hope said to Mohini while dropping onto the moth-nibbled arm of the old couch. "Sorry for poking you. But you understand. I'm Hope, by the way. Which is a terrible name for anyone born after the war, but I guess my mom was trying to be optimistic. She shouldn't have bothered. Can I have some?" Hope held out her hand,

and Mohini passed her the water. Hope took a long swig, then burped. "So you really know how to hack those machines? I mean, Diego's our best hacker, but he usually just takes over vacuum cleaners or whatever, little dumb stuff."

"I hacked an automated hot dog cart once," Diego said. "We used it for a battering ram and ended up with a hundred cans of Pasta Chunks from an old corner store. Not exactly dumb."

"You know what I mean. Not stuff with advanced AI. Not one of the killers." She smiled at Mohini, who still stood stiffly, lingering close to Colt.

"The hot dog cart had a lot of personality before I lobotomized it," Diego said. "Called itself 'Wally Wiener.' He even had a song he'd sing for kids—"

"Did you say you talked to your brother?" Colt asked Diego. Hope gave him a sharp look and a frown.

"We thought she was with them," Diego said, nodding at Mohini. "I mean, that was the only thing that made sense after we had time to think. Who else would have tech like that? Who else would have the balls to get close enough to a reaper?"

Mohini raised her eyebrows.

"So, yeah, we reached out," Diego continued. "It wasn't easy, but most of the fighting's been around Wrigley Field lately, so we thought we'd find them in that area."

"You both went?" Colt asked.

"Obviously," Hope said. "I'm not going to let Diego wander the streets at night by himself."

"What happened?"

"Maybe we should talk about this later," Hope said. "Mother Braden will want to see you. I'll hang out with your new friend. What's her name again?"

"Mohini," she said.

"That's nice. I like how it rolls off my tongue. 'Mohini.' 'Mo-hi-ni.' Does it mean anything? Like, secretly?"

"It's Hindi," she said. "Probably means 'sacred animal' or 'cumin powder' or something. What does 'Colt' mean? A baby horse, right?"

"Does it?" Colt asked. "I think it means a fast racehorse. Or maybe a warhorse."

"Baby horse, I'm pretty sure."

Diego brought bandages and disinfectant for Mohini's small cut. "This is all from that clinic," he told her. "You have to show me how you controlled that reaper. How did you even capture one?"

"It's not something I'd recommend trying to repeat," Mohini said. "My friend died protecting me from that reaper."

Colt wanted to tell them that the reaper wasn't even the most impressive achievement he'd seen from her. Breaking out of the lab had been a bigger deal, he thought, hacking into a secure installation and taking control of the med-bot inside it.

Instead, he passed through the apartment's kitchen into the short hall beyond. Multiple beds and mattresses were crammed into each of the three rooms he passed, leaving little room for anything else. They had been salvaged from other apartments, and they might have been in poor condition, but they'd been cleaned up and were each neatly made with blankets—more of Mother Braden's insistence on cleanliness and order, even as the world rotted and died outside.

Drawings adorned the hallway walls, etched in whatever bits of crayon, pencil, or charcoal they'd rummaged over their months of hiding out here.

The drawings were the faces of the lost, labeled by name, everyone from the group that had been lost over the years. Colt himself had drawn the face of Aaron, an older boy who'd been a bit like a brother to him for a while; he'd been gutted by reapers. Colt had found the remains. Whenever they changed camp, Colt drew his name and face on the wall first.

Most of them had simply vanished over the years, presumably taken by machines. The ritual of drawing their names and faces provided a way of remembering them and keeping them near. The presence of the lost made an old ruin or dry sewer pipe into more of a home. They were like spirits of the dead, watching over the remainder who lived. Many of them had only been children when they'd vanished.

More than two dozen faces were on the wall. Diego's brother Fernando had not been seen in some time, but Diego had not drawn his face. Fernando had left deliberately, to join the rebels.

After seeing the inside of Simon Nix's lab, Colt understood there were fates even worse than death. He wondered whether any of the lost had ended up there, test subjects for the android's bizarre, twisted experiments.

Colt shoved those thoughts out of his head as much as he could manage.

The small closet in the hall was crammed full of supplies. He took a newer pair of shoes from the heap on the floor. They read *Reebok* on the side, apparently a major shoemaker of the old world.

He entered the apartment's fourth bedroom, which had a private bathroom, though no water flowed through the pipes anymore. The bedroom was dim, lit by a single flickering candle on a dresser that held Mother Braden's possessions.

An old picture in a broken frame showed Mother Braden as a young woman next to a tall, smiling man, both in army green. *Jane and Vince, Costa Rica* read the handwritten scrawl at the bottom. The young woman was Mother Braden, decades ago, her hair pulled back in a cap, standing at the beach with her long-lost husband, who'd died in the war against Carthage. So had their children. She almost never spoke of her lost family, only of survival and strategy, of today and tomorrow.

A faded, worn old cloth flag was spread out on the wall above the dresser, with thirteen red and white stripes and seventy-one white stars against a deep blue background, the symbol of a lost civilization.

Mother Braden lay on a thin mattress on the floor; she'd always claimed she preferred sleeping on the floor.

The two youngest were sitting there now, including Tonio's ten-year-old little brother Paolo, plus Birdie, a girl of around seven or eight who did not speak but sometimes communicated in low whistles and clicks. They sat beside her and hung on every word.

"... and so Brother Rabbit slipped through the pride of sleeping lions, and because he was quiet and careful and watched his step, he made it safe to the other side," Mother Braden told the children in her throaty, scratchy voice. "The hunter tiptoed after the rabbit. But when the hunter reached the middle of the sleeping lion pride, Brother Rabbit rang a bell and yelled as loud as he could, and the lions woke up and ate the hunter."

"That was smart," said Paolo, and Birdie clicked her tongue thoughtfully.

"Now, go on, both of you," the older woman said. "I need to talk to Colt alone for a minute."

"I want another story," Paolo said.

"Go clean the kitchen and maybe you'll get another story later," Mother Braden said. The two kids hurried out to begin their assignment.

"Colt," Mother Braden whispered. "You made it back."

"I'm here." He knelt beside her and took her hand. She felt weak. She could barely see anymore. She'd had too many years of low, infrequent medication, often unable to find any for weeks at a time. She had grown particularly weak the past few months, though, which was why they'd stayed in this location longer than usual. Maybe too long. The metalheads were always looking for scavengers to kill, and staying on the move meant staying alive. "I'm sorry if you worried," Colt said.

"Worry never ends," she told him. "Unless you love no one. And then you become like the machines. We've stayed at this camp too long, Colt. They'll find us soon. You need to make preparations to leave."

"Of course," he said.

"You're the oldest now," she said. She didn't have to mention what had happened to the other kids. They'd been killed by the machines, or had gone missing and been presumed dead, or they'd gone to join the rebellion and likely died. It sounded like Diego's older brother Fernando was still alive, though. Maybe the older girl who'd left with him, Terra, hadn't been killed yet, either. "You have to lead the way, Colt. I can't make it this time."

"We won't leave you here," Colt said. "We can carry you."

"If you have to carry me, then my purpose is done. I remember when I could carry you. I've done all I can for you children. And I've seen too many of you die. I'm not sure my heart can take more." She smiled thinly through her pain. It was hard to believe that the weak, gray-haired woman in front of him was the same tough warrior who'd led him on long silent marches through the ruins, who'd taught him how to shoot, how to find food, how to survive. She wasn't even so old, just fifty-six, but the disease had eaten her up from the inside. Medicine was too scarce, and life was too hard on the sick.

"You can't really expect us to leave you," Colt said.

"There is no choice," she said.

Colt changed the subject. "We have to contact the rebels. Mohini knows how to hack the machines. She can make a difference."

"Unless she's a decoy, sent to infiltrate."

"She's human. We checked. And... I can feel it," Colt said.

"Some humans serve the machines."

"She's not a clanker, either. She's from across the sea. She wants to capture the skinwalker that I was talking about, the one that captured me. Simon Nix. Simon's reputation is so bad, she came that far to find him. And the things I saw in that lab... the things he's doing to all those people... have to be stopped."

"Be cautious she's not playing on your feelings, and you're not letting your heart put blinders on your brain," Mother Braden said. "At your age, your instincts have you looking for a mate. And there are none for you, not here. So your instincts can affect your thinking—"

"I am not thinking with my mating instincts!" Colt said, a little off-balance because what she said was partly true. The only girls in their group were Colt's sister and the little mute kid Birdie. And thinking of the mysterious dark-skinned Mohini in such a way was... interesting. "Mohini should be with the rebels. She can make a difference."

"What kind of difference are you expecting?"

"She has contacts on Carthage. She says people in the inner worlds, even on Carthage itself, would be outraged if they saw what's happening in that lab. If they knew what it was really like here on Earth."

"That sounds nice," Mother Braden said. "Naive, but nice. People will believe what they want. Evidence be damned."

"But the truth must count for something," Colt said.

She was quiet for a while, her cloudy eyes squinting as though trying to see him. "I'd like to think so," she finally said. "Bring her to me so I can have a look at her. Or a listen. Can't see much these days."

"Do you need anything else? Water?"

"The little ones just brought me some. Which shows you my purpose is fulfilled; the children take better care of me than I do of them."

"We always will," Colt said.

"Is that girl in here yet?"

"I'll be right back."

Colt returned to the living room, where the two younger kids had joined Hope and Mohini. A cluster of old screens were nailed to the wall, attached via long cables to cameras on each approach to their apartment. On the screens, Tonio sat in the darkness under the stairs at ground level, and Diego was on the third level, protecting their flank from a high window. The building extended many floors above and below, but those approaches were blocked off.

"What did she say?" Hope asked. "She's been kind of... bleak lately."

"She wants to meet Mohini," Colt said.

"Something's coming," Tonio said on the screen. The camera view over his shoulder showed the high rampart of concrete debris trembling, bits and pieces breaking loose and rolling down.

"Heading to the front window," Diego said over on the screen that monitored him. He stepped out of sight.

"What is that?" Paolo whispered, watching the rubble crumble and fall.

"I'm going up front with Tonio," Colt whispered. "Hope, stay here with the kids and Mother Braden."

"I'll go with you," Mohini whispered, touching Colt's arm.

"So will I," Hope said. "Paolo, Birdie, go help Mother set up her machine gun."

Paolo nodded and took Birdie's arm, leading away the small, bony girl, who responded with a gentle clicking. Her brown hair was a tangled mess, like a bird's nest. Mother Braden thought she must have been on her own since she was a toddler, somehow surviving on bugs and carrion, but alone for so long that she'd never learned to talk. She could do a convincing imitation of the scrawny pigeons that lived among the ruins and the falcons who hunted them.

On the way out, Colt opened the coat closet and took out an automatic rifle even more worn and antiquated than the one he'd lost. Hope grabbed extra rounds for her machine pistol.

"I don't suppose you have any plasma cells in there," Mohini said. "I used my last escaping from that tunnel."

"We have this little thing." He lifted a compact rocket launcher. The rockets were no wider than his middle finger. "There's only two rockets left. They'll punch hard, though. They're stronger than they look."

"I'll take it," she said.

"They're coming!" Tonio's voice yelled over the monitor.

Colt, Hope, and Mohini bolted through the labyrinthine building to the barred front door. Tonio propped the old plasma rifle on of the door's crossbars while he fired one blinding white bolt after another. He was sweaty and shaking with fear, eyes fixed on the approach.

Dozens of reapers surged over the top of the rubble wall in a dark flood.

A few of the mines went off as the reapers stepped on them, blasting a handful of machines back.

A plasma bolt struck one reaper, melting its pelvic frame and sending it crashing down the rubble, a solid hit by Tonio.

These were just pebbles thrown against an incoming wave, though, and Tonio didn't have nearly enough plasma cells to take down all the invaders.

"I've never seen so many at once," Hope gasped. Neither had Colt; usually only an eight-machine squad would show up to deal with scavengers. Now he had a sense of what things must have looked like during the war, with armies of the reapers swarming over the Earth, slaughtering the world's last defenders.

"We stayed here too long," Colt said.

"Or they're here for her." Hope nodded at Mohini. "Either to capture her, or because she led them to us."

"I did not!" Mohini snapped.

"We don't have time to argue," Colt said. "Everybody spread out so they can't kill us all at once. Find a window and hurt them as much as you can."

Colt moved to a nearby apartment with a chunk of its outer wall missing. He knelt behind the gap in the concrete and opened fire into the approaching swarm of reapers, but it was hard to tell whether he was doing much good.

Blue lasers fired from above, intermittently, as Diego took potshots at the wave of machines, doing his part to try to put a dent in them. Lasers could puncture the machines, but that wasn't much use unless they hit something vital. A narrow hole drilled through a reaper's arm or leg wasn't going to stop it.

Hope fired her old but trusty machine pistol, but that wasn't going to do much good at this distance, either.

The wave of reapers thundered down like an avalanche over the rubble barrier, like angry fire ants boiling out of their nest.

Maybe they were here for Colt, too. He was the one who'd escaped from Simon, and he was a known associate of Mohini.

He should never have come home. He had only been thinking of Mohini and her mission, and of getting back home with his own people, his own small group. The only way to keep them safe, he saw now, would have been to avoid them, for weeks or months, to make sure he wasn't being tracked.

He'd been stupid, and now everyone was going to die for it.

A rocket streaked out from a window farther down, Mohini launching one of the two.

It struck the lead reapers and engulfed them in a massive fireball. Mohini had picked a good place and time to hit, knocking the machines back against the rubble. Some of the reapers above them were shaken loose by the blast and came tumbling down.

Still, the reapers kept coming. A vanguard of four rushed ahead of the other reapers and opened fire on the apartment building, one with bolts of plasma, two with incendiary rounds, another with a missile that let out a high-pitched shriek on its approach.

Colt hit the floor as the missile struck the facade of the apartment building, shattering the wall in front of him. More bombardment followed, rocking the building. The floor shuddered and buckled under him, and a massive cloud of smoke, dust, and debris fell over him like a burial shroud.

Chapter Fifteen

Carthage

"You're not telling me the truth," Simon Quick said, peering at Audrey over a cup of tea. They were in her parents' twelve-story apartment, kilometers above the ground in uptown Carthage City, sitting at a table in the spacious atrium. They were surrounded by marble fountains, gardens of rare orchids and trees, and giant songbirds from nineteen different worlds, including a few native to Carthage. Enormous picture windows brought in sunlight from the outdoors, tinted and filtered to be pleasant and golden no matter the weather.

Audrey hadn't touched her tea, hadn't even acknowledged it. Sharing food and drink was a sign of fellowship among humans, and she wasn't feeling fellowship with the android, who seemed less human than ever to her at the moment.

"The truth is, my car was hacked, some clown guy threatened me and yapped a bunch of vague, schizoid political trash just before he tried to kill me. And things get fuzzy after the crash."

"Do they?" Simon activated a hologram projector on the densely striped bocote-wood table.

"I don't want to watch it again," Audrey said. A whirring and snipping sounded as the apartment's garden-bot trundled closer, tending the flowering vines that grew around the burbling, stone-lined pool where Nin had taught Audrey to swim. The squat round garden-bot was always quietly working, taking care of the thousands of plants and the indoor grove of trees, all of which had been genetically engineered to stay in bloom year round. It was always a glorious spring here in her mother's atrium.

Now she watched the bot's flexible, extendable arms snip and trim the plants. The thing's belly held clippers and loppers and saws. An alternate string of code could turn it into a murder machine, slaughtering the whole family as they gathered in their fanciest clothes and wigs for Landing Day photos, which was often the only time the family was together all year. Even that didn't last for the whole holiday; it was mainly about the photo op.

"You're not paying attention, Audrey," Simon said.

"I don't have to." She could see the scene projected in full size overhead, in the vaulted space just beyond the branches of the fuzzy pink mimosa tree towering above them. It was a recording from Audrey's apartment, replaying the chaos and confusion as the Security Steves opened fire, killing Kelleyen and assorted neighbors and party guests.

On the recording, Zola returned fire while leading Audrey out of the apartment and down the stairs. The security cameras had also caught Zola using the Guard Guys' electrical weapons against the Security Steves.

Audrey couldn't help admiring how tough, nimble, and courageous her old friend had become. She couldn't imagine Zola's life on the rough outer worlds or what it was like to lose her father. That life had forged Zola into something tough, though, something with a core of steel, while Audrey had grown up fretting over childish teenage anxieties, painting bleak storms and dark graveyards, writing somber poetry to express just how serious she was, while attending her sumptuous prep academy and having her every whim catered to by androids and other machines.

Even if Audrey didn't fully understand or agree with Zola's cause or ultimate goals, she knew she needed to be tougher. She needed to grow her own core of steel. Her brother Salvius and his motley friends were right about one thing—a colossal change was coming. It had already arrived, in her mind, because the trusted machines that had always provided for her, protected her, guided her, had turned out to be enemies in waiting. Some could be hacked. Some might have been enemies all along, gathering data on her, sharing it with entities unknown.

She could feel it now, looking at the Simon unit she'd long counted as a mentor and confidant. Was anything she'd told him truly private? He'd assured her that his memories were archived under deep encryption, and his personal confidentiality was a core directive of his original Butler Jeffrey operating system. Then again, she'd trusted him to tell the truth about these things; she hadn't independently verified any of those claims.

"Why did you go with her?" Simon asked, as hologram-Audrey and hologram-Zola escaped in the fake ambulance.

"She'd just saved my life. From my own security bots."

"Don't you find it convenient that your security androids

turned on you just as this person was there to protect you?" Simon asked.

"No, Simon, I don't find anything at all convenient about that or anything else that happened to me. Why are you grilling me? I need to rest."

"You have rested. You've been home for several hours."

"As a robot, you may not understand this, but it's hard to sleep when you've been through what I've been through."

"I understand post-traumatic syndrome—"

"Post-traumatic means the trauma is in the past," she said. "I'm still living it. My own security providers turned on me. I'm never going to be safe. I've never *been* safe, really."

"That's not quite true," Simon said. "This level of information security threat hasn't been seen in decades. It bears a full but quiet investigation. Please note that 'quiet' is a key term here."

"Any machine can turn on me," she said. "Why are you interrogating me? You should be at Hamilcar Security, trying to figure out what happened with the Security Steve units."

"Your family has launched an investigation, and your attorneys are already preparing quite a sizable lawsuit."

"Oh, good. I was worried my family wouldn't get a chance to cash in on the situation."

"Replacing all your automated security units with trained human guards is quite an expensive proposition," Simon said. "Not many humans have the qualifications anymore, as most of the police, military, and private security sectors have been increasingly automated for decades."

"Maybe that's a mistake on our part," Audrey said. "Trusting you machines with everything."

"Did you just refer to me as 'you machines'?" Simon raised

his eyebrows in an appearance of surprise. "Me? Your old friend? Where exactly did you go, Audrey? What happened in those missing hours to put you in such a negative mood?"

"It's not a mood," Audrey said. "It's... clarity. Disillusionment. Where are my parents, exactly?"

"Your father is in meetings all day, concerning this very threat, among other subjects. Your mother is meeting with the families of victims, publicly showing her concern for them."

"Nobody decided to come check on me? Not even out of a sense of freakish curiosity?"

"You'll see your mother at dinner tonight. Possibly your father."

"I want to see Kelleyen's family."

"The funeral is scheduled two days hence. Your personal-assistant android will arrive in a few hours. She's undergoing an extensive security diagnostic as well as structural and cosmetic repairs. It's interesting you haven't asked me about her, given that she's been your constant companion since infancy."

"Back up that holo and focus on Nin," Audrey said.

Simon did as ordered, this time zooming in on Nin, making the personal-assistant android about twice as large as life. Nin stood in the doorway to Audrey's apartment, her damaged hand missing. The RepairPal android wrenched Nin backward into the apartment and cut into her neck with a circular saw. Audrey winced.

"The RepairPal." Audrey pointed to the android in the trademark RepairPal hardhat and overalls. "The Security Steves went nuts after it arrived. Maybe it was a Trojan horse."

"The case is being thoroughly investigated, Audrey,"

Simon said. "What we need from you is simply an explanation for your missing hours."

"I don't remember anything."

"We will try hypnotic regression. Close your eyes and relax."

"Yeah, I'm not doing that."

"Audrey, it feels as though you are keeping secrets from me."

"That's impossible."

"Is it? Your heart rate, pupil dilation, reduced eye contact, minutely increased perspiration—"

"I mean it's impossible for you to feel. You might conclude or project something based on the available data, but you do not feel. And it's dishonest to say you do."

Simon paused for a few seconds, as if studying her or calculating his response. Always calculating. "Audrey, I am perhaps more complex than you understand. I am capable of... if not the full of range of human emotion... then a sense of satisfaction or non-satisfaction. Purpose fulfillment, or non-fulfillment."

"And that's all very fascinating, but I want to see my actual human family now. Mother and Father both, ideally. But I'd even settle for Briellana. Tell their personal androids."

"I am here to function as your adviser and counselor, Audrey, not your personal assistant."

"Well, like you said, my personal assistant's on the fritz, or possibly riddled with viruses implanted by clowns, so you can give me a hand." Audrey began to feel the edge of panic coming on. Nin handled her communications, her bank accounts, everything. Audrey was powerless without her android. "I need a pocket screen of my own."

"I suppose you'll want me to arrange that for you, as well."

"That would be great."

"Then tell me about the missing hours."

"Seriously? You're going to hold basic needs like that over my head? Forget it." Audrey stood. She tried not to look frightened by the garden-bot as it drifted closer, collecting weeds from the soil with a drill-shaped tool on an extendable arm. "You can go now, Simon. You can't stay here all day. You have an empire to run."

"What an interesting choice of words." Simon stood. The garden-bot extended its loppers and snapped a stray low limb off a bushy maroon Japanese maple nearby. "This entire visit has been quite interesting."

"Not for me," Audrey said.

"One additional item," Simon said. "Given your lack of cooperation, your top-level security clearance is likely to be revoked. At least temporarily. We would not want to give the false appearance of special treatment due to nepotism."

"Oh, no, not in this family." Audrey had no hope of keeping the mocking tone out of her voice. "Why, my father could lose the next rigged election."

"That is an oversimplification—"

"But not wrong."

"With your clearance, you must lose your interplanetary security internship," Simon said. "Which will preclude you graduating in the top echelon from the Political Academy. Your parents will be quite disappointed."

Audrey thought of how she'd worried about getting the position so she could have a chance to prove herself to her father and the rest of her family. How nervous she'd been, preparing to give her talk about Veritum, foolishly believing the leaders of Carthage were interested in how to apply their power toward helping those in need, if only she could persuade them.

"I'll think about my graduation rank while Kelleyen's death repeats in my head, over and over," Audrey said. "I'll get real upset about my graduation rank, I'm sure."

"So you do remember the events at your apartment," Simon said.

"The ones you've just played the recording of in front of me? Yeah, those." She crossed her arms, trying not to act spooked as the garden-bot snipped and trimmed its way along a low hedge. "I'll walk you out."

"That's not necessary."

"It's the polite thing."

Audrey walked him to the reception hall at the front entrance to the apartment. Two of her new, flesh-and-blood security guards stood watch, wearing armored suits with visored helmets. They didn't look quite as clean-cut as the security androids to which she was accustomed, but they'd seemed nice enough when she'd introduced herself to them. She was trying to memorize their names: Trevorian and Parello. She was pretty sure. Nin usually kept track of such things for her, but Audrey was making an effort to connect more with the humans in her life and rely less on the machines.

"There will likely be further consequences," Simon said as he walked the last few steps alone to the inner security door. One of the new guards stepped forward as the inner door opened.

"Good," Audrey said. "It's about time I started doing something of consequence."

Simon said nothing more as he turned and walked out, escorted by one of her security guards, who would walk him through the outer door and down to the elevator bank before returning.

It was strange how distant she felt from Simon Quick, and how hollow and stupid her former feelings for him now seemed.

"When Parello gets back, double check that all the entrances and security doors are sealed tight," Audrey said to the remaining guard. "Don't let anyone in, not even a delivery bot. Not any kind of bot."

"Yes, ma'am."

"Thanks, Trevorian."

She walked to her family's library, which had always been one of her favorite rooms. There were projectors and keyboards there; she could use them to access her schoolwork. Or maybe learn what there was to know about The Change, and their psychotic mutant spinoff, the Blood Clowns.

"We've been dealing with your problems all day!" Audrey's mother, Liastrada Bontherias Venable Caracala, was pacing up and down beside the dinner table, as she often did when there were no guests. Her metabolism was medically cranked up in line with her youthful appearance to keep her thin and energetic, but this also kept her anxious and nervous. Liastrada pouted with her full lips and generally looked like a teenager who'd been forbidden to attend her best friend's birthday party.

Liastrada's personal assistant, Pim, echoed the late-teenage look. She was attractive, with a unique, customized face, not factory standard at all, meant to look just a few shades less attractive than her owner.

"Didn't you watch the news at all today?" Audrey's mother continued. "It was a lead story. Assassination attempt on the prime legislator's daughter! If that music star hadn't finally had her baby *and* revealed the true father, it would have been the only story on anyone's mind."

"Oh, Sayatina had her baby? Who was the father?" Audrey asked.

"Some soccer star. Who cares?"

"Peter Giussepe, then? I really should have watched the news."

"Dinner! Vegetable soup, your favorite from ages eight to eleven, Audrey." The pleasantly plump chef-bot, Happy Helga, emerged from the kitchen and set out dishes of soup and bread. The china was made from the bones of the Bremese goliath, a massive mammoth-like creature found on a remote, icy outer world. It was the usual place setting for this smallest, most intimate of the family's three dining rooms, which also featured a huge stone hearth at one end.

"Thank you, Helga," Audrey said automatically, as she always had.

"Such a sweet girl. From such a lovely family." Happy Helga beamed at Audrey, then hummed cheerfully to herself as she returned to the kitchen, where she had access to a variety of knives and other sharp cutting instruments. Another childhood companion turned into a potential murderer, just waiting to be hacked. Helga would have to be removed from the apartment or given a hard shutdown with her power cell removed, if Audrey had anything to say about it.

"I hear you won't tell Simon about the girl who took you or where you went," Liastrada said.

"It's amnesia or something," Audrey said.

"And you're losing your internship over it?" Her mother

stopped pacing and held out her glass. Pim scurried over, the android's diamond collar glittering in the glow of the chandelier, and filled her master's glass with red wine. "Your father's going to be upset."

"Perhaps he'll have his assistant send a strongly worded message to my assistant," Audrey said.

"Don't be a sullen child," Liastrada said, her faux-teenage mouth pouting. "How are we going to put these pieces back together? What are you hiding from Simon Quick? You can tell me, honey. We're all alone here."

Audrey glanced at Pim, who turned and carried the empty wine bottle to the kitchen.

"They can watch us," Audrey said. "Through our machines."

"Who?" Liastrada finally sat down, though at one of the unused place settings, nowhere near her soup at the head of the table. "Who do you think is watching you, honey?"

"Hackers, for one. If they can take over a squad of Steves, what else can they do? Military machines? Or Helga?"

"Helga?" She laughed. "Who would want to take control of Helga?"

"Anyone who might want to murder us in our sleep. Which some people would love to do as a political statement against Father. These hackers, they have new abilities. They're a threat to our whole way of life. For now, it's best to get rid of all the machines that are physically able to hurt us."

"Oh, I know you've been through a lot." Her mother did her signature pout again while briefly rubbing Audrey's arm in an attempt at showing sympathy. "I'm sure you see threats everywhere now. But things will get better. Life will return to normal. It always does."

"Really? You don't feel like things are going to change?"

"What things? Change how? Audrey, you're babbling." Her mother was so concerned that her forehead nearly creased. "We need to call Doctor Dave and get you checked out—"

"I don't need a Doctor Dave. I've already seen a medical bot."

"At the Refurbishment Clinic," her mother said. "I saw the charge on your spending account. Couldn't miss it. Audrey, our family members can't be seen in a place like that. It's for rapid detox."

"I told Nin to find someplace discreet. What else could I do?"

"I just hope no one got images of you there, in disarray."

"Yeah, that's the worst possible outcome of this situation," Audrey said. "I also had mild head injuries. And more recently, this cut on my face."

"Yes, I know. Pim prepared me for that," her mother said. "It can be fixed in time. And sprayed over for now."

"Hey, that could be our family motto," Audrey said. "We could put it on a coat of arms: 'Fix it later, paint over it for now.'"

"You probably think you're funny."

"Good thing being a comedian is a common path to a political career. I'd rather be that than a professional athlete or a wacky game show host."

"Five years at Political Academy so you can become a clown," her mother snorted, while Pim arrived with a new bottle of wine.

"Says the woman with a clockwork wig full of birds."

"So you *did* see the news today. How did we look?" her mother asked.

"Solemn and concerned. It was a pretty decent imitation."

"You are feisty today. I could get used to this, you know. You were always such a cringing, obedient wallflower."

"That's just the wine talking, Mother. You want me cringing and obedient."

"It's true. You're so much easier that way. Eat your soup."

Audrey looked down at it. The savory stew had indeed been one of her favorites when growing up, full of tangy mushrooms and slivered carrots. Her mouth watered, but she couldn't bring herself to eat it. Prepared by a machine. Poison was another way they could get you; the kitchen probably offered a number of deadly chemicals right there in the cleaning cabinet. Just an extra string of code to poison them and kill them all.

"We have to get the androids out of here," Audrey said. "And the garden-bot. Anything that could attack us."

"You really are scared," Liastrada said. "I am so sorry. I will have more security guys around here for you. *Live* ones. I don't think you can really trust men more than machines, but whatever makes you feel calm."

"Thanks. We can't even trust our personal assistants anymore."

"That is so rude to say in front of Pim," Liastrada said. "Apologize, Audrey."

"To your machine? She doesn't care."

"How do you know how she feels?"

"She doesn't feel."

"She's my best friend, Audrey!"

"It's all right," Pim said. "I understand Audrey has been through a rough time. Feel free to use me as an emotional punching bag if you need to, Audrey. I can take it."

"You're so sweet to her," Liastrada said to Pim, her voice slurred. "You always have been. You and that... Nin."

"We can't trust Nin, either," Audrey said. "They can all be turned against us. The world is changing, Mother."

"I haven't turned against you." The small voice sounded hurt, almost pleading, behind Audrey's back.

Nin entered the dining room, dressed in drab gray repair-shop clothing. She looked intact, her lost hand restored, but she had an unusually subdued manner.

"Nin," Audrey said, wishing she didn't feel so much emotion at the sight of the android. Nin was her constant companion, though. What could life ever be like without Nin? "You look... better."

"Were you hurt?" Nin walked close, peering at Audrey's scratched face. "I've been worried about you. Where did you go? What happened to you? Did that girl with the laser pistol harm you?"

"No, the mystery girl saved me, then dropped me off near police headquarters," Audrey said. "That's all I know for sure, and mainly because there's video of it. My memory gets pretty blurry after that car crash. And popping that Smiley at the party."

"Oh, good, she's back," Audrey's mother said, her voice slurred as she noted Nin's arrival. "Now Nin can take care of you. Thank goodness, I'm exhausted."

"It's been an exhausting few minutes." Audrey stood and started toward the atrium, where the elevator would take her up past the treetops to floor 161, where her and her siblings' old childhood bedrooms were located. This was just below the master suite level, where her parents had their private rooms. "I'm going to turn in early. See everyone in the morning."

"Do you have to go so soon?" her mother asked. "Pim

and I are going to review the week's new wigs. Rainbow stripes and illuminated stars are expected to be the thing this week. You should get a nice wig for yourself, honey. And a new dress, new shoes... you'll feel better before you know it."

"Thanks for the wisdom, Mother. I needed it."

"I'll buy a wig for you," her mother replied. "It'll make you look pretty. Less drab. More like your sister... "

Audrey left the dining room and walked under the arching, flower-heavy limbs of the tree grove toward the glass tube in one corner, which extended up and away through the vaulted sky-blue ceiling like a fairy-tale beanstalk.

Nin followed her into the clear capsule. It was the apartment's interior convenience elevator, connecting just the twelve floors owned by her family. They rode up past the games and media floor, which featured amphitheater seating around a sizable empty projection space for movies and concerts, then past the ballroom floor where fancy dress affairs and masquerades were sometimes held.

"You seem angry with me," Nin said. "I understand. I failed to protect you."

Audrey didn't say anything. She resisted the urge to try to soothe the android's simulated feelings. *Not real*, she reminded herself. It was going to take some time for her to start really believing that.

Finally, they reached the children's level. The elevator lounge here was a playroom, its chests and closets overflowing with toys and costumes, the bookshelves crammed with colorful animated books that nobody had touched in at least a decade. There was a climbing area with ladders, slides, and a preserved-wood tree fort with a rope bridge and a zip line that dropped off into a padded ball pit.

It looked like an amazing place to play, but Audrey had

very few memories of doing so. Her older siblings had been more interested in video games and talking with their friends. She and Salvius had played here a few times, when they were very small, accompanied by their personal-care androids, Nin and Kip.

"Whatever happened to Kip?" Audrey asked as they left the elevator. "Salvius's bot?"

"Kip is in the maintenance closet on this level."

"Really?" Audrey walked down the boys' hallway and opened the maintenance closet door. The long, narrow room beyond contained charging and repair stations for each of the siblings' five personal androids.

Kip stood at the end of the room, tanned and muscular, his charming, infectious smile frozen on his lips. He'd been designed as the perfect big brother, always willing to spend time with Salvius that the youngest boy's siblings and parents never seemed to have, whether that was throwing a ball or helping with homework or listening to Salvius's childhood hopes and fears.

"We were all raised by machines." Audrey approached Kip, who didn't budge at all. Small hatches had been left open in his upper back and in the back of his head. His shirt had been removed and draped over his arm like a towel over a rack. The hand on that arm was locked into Kip's characteristic thumbs-up gesture.

"And it was our pleasure to care for you," Nin said. "Taking care of your needs fulfills my purpose."

"You took such close care of me that I didn't even learn to tie my shoes until I was twelve," Audrey said.

"That's the average age for a child on Carthage," Nin said.

"Yeah, but... " Audrey shook her head. "It's almost like we're not living our lives. Not like people used to. We turned so much of ourselves over to machines like you, and what's left for us? Sitting around, consuming entertainment? It's like people can barely stand to deal with each other anymore. Why deal with the difficulty and unpredictability of real people when you can have a fake friend that always agrees with you, always does what you want, always showers you with compliments and praise no matter what you actually accomplish or don't accomplish? You just stroke our narcissism so much better than real people ever could."

"Do you... wish me to be less complimentary?" Nin asked.

"That's not the point." Audrey looked into the empty exposed compartments in Kip's head and back. "Looks like some stuff got removed. What's missing here?"

Nin took a look. "CPU, memory drives, and power cell."

"Who took them out? Salvius?"

"I do not know."

"It's like Salvius wanted to erase his own childhood memories," Audrey said. "Or keep anyone else from accessing them."

"But Kip's memories could still exist as a backup on the Carthage Consolidated cloud servers."

"At least Kip wouldn't be picking up any new information about Salvius." Audrey thought for a moment. "So all your memories are backed up to the cloud, too?"

"Of course," Nin said. "In case of damage to my memory drive or in the event that you upgrade to a new assistant, all your user preferences and access codes are stored in one convenient place for download."

"And who can access that cloud storage?"

"It is fully encrypted."

"Can people at Carthage Consolidated access it? Or what about the Simon units?"

"Carthage Consolidated keeps your data private in line with all applicable laws and regulations, as determined by the Carthaginian World Legislature."

"Wow, you sure turn into a legal disclaimer fast when I ask about your manufacturer," Audrey said.

"I am sorry, Audrey. I don't mean to sound so impersonal—"

"But that's how you *should* sound. It's not like you're a real person. Why bother pretending?" Audrey turned out the maintenance closet light and returned to the hall.

"Providing comfort and companionship is my function." Nin followed Audrey across the huge playroom to the girls' hallway on the opposite side. Audrey and Briellana each had their own bedroom, bathroom, sitting room, and walk-in closet, which had minimized their youthful conflicts but also their contact with each other while growing up. "Failure to fulfill my function is unsatisfying."

"Sorry to hear that." Audrey stepped into her room. She'd last lived here when she was eighteen and had only been back occasionally, a fact reflected in the décor that appeared on her digital walls when the lights turned on. "Okay, let's get rid of the Black Sorrows, first off." She gestured to the pale, leather-clad boy band who dominated one wall, some of the band members actively pointing at her and winking or blowing kisses, as if they were live people on display behind glass. Live people with a serious crush on whichever girl had posted them on her wall.

They vanished in an eyeblink, leaving the default wallpaper behind, which looked like a gloomy moonlit night among ancient ruins.

"Like I said, I'm going to bed early," Audrey said.

"Shall I stand watch, like when you were a child?" Nin asked, smiling.

"I'm pretty sure the closet portal to monsterland closed up years ago," Audrey replied. "You can stay in the maintenance closet with Kip."

"But that's down the other hall. You'll be alone."

"I'm sure I'll survive, Nin. And if anyone does attack me... well, it's not like you were any good at protecting me last time."

Nin frowned deeply and blinked several times, as though hurt by the comments. "Are you sure?"

"Go ahead. Close the door behind you."

After Nin left, Audrey waited ten seconds, then gently locked the door. She hoped Nin hadn't heard the click of the lock; at some level, she just couldn't stop herself from caring about the android's feelings, even though they weren't real feelings at all.

A heavy, thickly padded love seat sat by Audrey's bed. Audrey grunted as she pushed it across the spotless sunshine-yellow carpet, which the apartment's little fix-bots had somehow kept immaculate all through her childhood.

She wedged the massive chair against the door. It wouldn't stop any machines determined to break into her room, but maybe it would slow them down, and the noise would wake Audrey up. Assuming she ever got to sleep.

"Window view," Audrey said, stepping toward a glass wall. The mysterious ancient ruins vanished, and she looked out at a city of lights stretching to the horizon, a city of glass towers and lush green parks, of cars and trains whooshing at speeds that turned them into blurred streaks, gone in an instant.

It was her city, and she was standing in her family's own home, and she had never felt less safe.

She couldn't stop thinking about each machine that could kill her right now, tonight—the garden-bot, even the little crawling fix-bots that handled the constant maintenance and cleaning of the apartment could probably kill her if they crept up while she slept.

She thought of her brother, out there somewhere in the world, endangering his life for a cause she didn't fully understand. For The Change, whatever that really meant. Maybe Salvius and Zola didn't even know themselves. Maybe they were in over their heads, part of a dangerous movement that couldn't be trusted.

Audrey knew something had gone wrong with their world, though. Her eyes had opened enough to realize that. She sat on the bed, not remotely sleepy, and knew she would never really be able to close her eyes again. The daily dream of her life had been jarred too deeply. Now she was wide awake, and all alone.

Late that night, as she lay awake, a hacker calling herself "Minerva" got in touch with Audrey.

Chapter Sixteen

Galapagos

Ellison fired repeatedly at Simon Zorn, burning laser holes in the android's face and turning much of its artificial skin into a steaming, molten, flesh-colored sludge. The blasts didn't drop the android or freeze it up, though; the Simon's cranial case must have been heavily reinforced, resistant to laser pistols.

Simon even smiled, though his mouth was melting and the liquid artificial skin dripped from his teeth. Ellison clearly hadn't damaged the Simon's CPU.

"An unfortunate choice on your part, Minister-General Ellison," Simon said. "You would have made an interesting puppet king. Now you'll have to die, along with the rest of your administration. And your family, it seems."

"Make it stop talking!" Jiemba, the younger boy, turned away from the disfigured android and buried his face in his unconscious mother's shoulder, next to her pale freckled skin and long, dark red hair.

The Iron Hammers approached up the side hallway, a phalanx of armored criminals. Ellison only had two guards and Kartokov with him to help fight off about twenty guys. The Hammers weren't firing at the moment, just drawing closer. It would be a massacre when they did start shooting. Prazca, in the lead, smirked as though relishing the anticipation.

Four reapers in honor guard uniforms approached up the central corridor, behind Simon, leveling their rapid-fire laser rifles at Ellison and his family, preparing to cut them all down.

They were outnumbered and outgunned.

"Ready!" Prazca shouted.

The elevator pinged, the doors opened, and Ellison's backup arrived—Security Chief Loomis, the three guards Ellison had left at the spaceport armory, and a couple of other guards he'd picked up along the way.

"Shields," Prazca said, and three of his men tossed out tall sheets of metal that unfolded into overlapping barriers about shoulder high, creating a barricade across the corridor.

"Fire at will," Ellison shouted. "Reapers at twelve, Hammers at nine!"

The guards poured out of the elevator, shooting bolts of glowing white plasma to the front and to the left. Ellison felt a moment of relief as the volley of plasma struck the Hammers' portable barrier, melting holes in it and sending men dodging back from the molten metal.

"Go!" Ellison said, pressing his laser pistol into his older son's hand, while gesturing at his wife and younger son. "Keep them safe."

"But Dad—"

"Move!" Ellison shoved the wheelchair into the elevator

car the guards had vacated. Jiemba stayed close to his mother, but Ellison had to shove Djalu into the elevator. Maybe the older boy wanted to stay and fight, and Ellison understood that desire very well, but it wasn't what he needed Djalu to do at the moment, and there was no time to argue.

The firefight grew more chaotic, attacks coming from the front and side. Guards dropped from the lead and lasers; one round struck Ellison in the chest and slammed him back into the wall like a sledgehammer. If not for his armor, his chest would have been turned inside out. The pain was horrendous even with the armor's impact dampeners.

"Here, boss!" Loomis handed Ellison a plasma rifle from the rolling rack of weaponry he'd brought down.

Ellison grimaced through the pain in his rib cage and fired plasma at one of the approaching reapers, but the infantry machine dodged low and fast. Ellison's bolt continued its diagonal course, struck the wall beyond the reaper, and spread rapidly. The plasma bolts were quickly turning the central corridor into a tunnel of flame.

Clanking metal sounded from that direction. One badly damaged reaper staggered into sight, barely balanced on a single remaining leg. It dragged a second reaper after it and slammed that one headfirst into the floor, ripping through the tile and gouging a deep dent into the thin layer of metal deck beneath it.

Then it snapped one of the reaper's legs off and attached it to its own pelvic structure, replacing its lost leg.

Ellison let the guards concentrate on the larger group, the Hammers, while he focused on the approaching reapers. He aimed lower and managed to catch one in the side of its abdomen as it twisted aside. It wasn't a kill shot; he'd damaged the thing and burned off a lot of its ceremonial uniform, but it could still fight.

Simon had stepped back close to the wall, near the doorway of a small lab, keeping himself out of the crossfire. He wore a crazed, gleeful grin, though that probably had a lot to do with his face melting, the skin pulling away from his artificial teeth and leaving them exposed.

The reaper with the stolen leg removed the bladed staff clamped to its victim's side, extended it to full length, then pitched it down the corridor like a javelin.

The triple-bladed tip drove deep into another reaper's back, one of the four that were still with Simon. A shower of sparks flew as that reaper toppled forward, but the machine continued to crawl forward, firing lasers that skimmed just above the floor.

It looked like the rogue reaper was back to help.

A deafening roar rose nearby. Loomis had rolled out a heavy machine gun on a wheeled stand. He locked the brakes and let loose a barrage of explosive rounds at the Iron Hammers in the side hall.

Ellison's plasma bolt struck the crawling reaper in the head, putting a stop to its ankle-level laser fire. The reaper's three companions turned back to attack the rogue reaper before it took down more of them. They riddled its torso and limbs with rapid-fire laser beams as they rushed toward it.

Just before they reached it, the rogue reaper shoved the barrel of its own laser rifle under its chin and pulled the trigger, as if committing suicide. A barrage of closely packed laser beams burned up through the top of its head.

Ellison couldn't help feeling a little taken aback as he saw the reaper blow its own head off.

The rogue toppled over as its laser-damaged legs gave

way; repeated blasts had burned holes in its knee actuators. One of the other reapers tore the rogue's head off, peered into the cluster of laser holes, then dropped it to the floor. Ellison remembered how Simon had wanted the rogue reaper's CPU; the rogue's final act had been to destroy it.

Another round caught Ellison in the hip, sending him stumbling and falling. The armor had kept it from blowing his leg off, but the pain was excruciating.

Kneeling, Ellison returned fire in the direction from which it had come, down the side hall. Smoke from the burning walls filled the hallway, and Ellison couldn't see the Hammers or their barricade at all.

Loomis kept the machine gun humming, firing into the smoke, but it was impossible to tell how much damage he was dealing to the enemy. Hopefully, his incendiary rounds were destroying the Hammers as badly as they were destroying the medical center hallway. The fire from that direction wasn't so heavy at the moment, as though the Hammers were retreating or regrouping.

"Get out of there," an unfamiliar voice said through the communication bud in Ellison's ear, which connected to the personal screen in his pocket. Whoever she was, she sounded calm yet firm. "Right now, Ellison."

"Who is this?" he asked.

"Fall back now," she insisted. "Chat later."

Ellison scowled and turned his attention to the three reapers charging up the central corridor, all of them firing. He wasn't about to take orders from unidentified people hacking into his headset.

A rapid barrage of lasers took down Loomis, who'd fought valiantly against constant fire that had worn down his armor. Loomis collapsed, his entire torso smoking, and his heavy machine gun fell silent.

Kartokov went down, too, with rounds punching the chest of the defense minister's armor while a laser plowed through the left side of his head. He kept firing bolts of plasma the whole way down.

One reaper leaped on top of the rolling machine gun and stripped it open, putting it out of use. Another landed on the guard beside Ellison and snapped his neck.

A third reaper landed on Ellison and slammed him against the wall.

Ellison managed to squeeze off one shot.

The plasma bolt skimmed the side of its skull, leaving a molten streak through the surface of its helmet but not stopping the machine. The bolt struck the ceiling and burned a hole through it; Ellison hoped nobody had been standing on the floor directly above, or they would have been turned to charcoal.

"Get your people out of there," the unknown female voice instructed in Ellison's ear. "Stairs up to the executive level."

"Busy," Ellison grunted, while the reaper's black-skull face filled his vision like a demon coming to suck out his soul. Its sharp, narrow steel fingers pinned Ellison's arms back against the wall. Ellison managed to cling to the butt of his plasma rifle, but he couldn't turn it or aim it. All he could have done, if he could have reached the trigger, was burn another big hole in the ceiling.

He kicked against the reaper's leg, but it was basically a solid steel rod. Two of them, in fact, in imitation of the human tibia and fibula. Higher up was a round actuator shield like a steel patella and, above that, another black steel rod for a femur.

With most of its uniform burned away by plasma, the reaper was surprisingly scrawny, a skeleton without meat. It was possible for lasers and small rounds to pass right through certain parts of its body, like the gap between its radius and ulna or some of the open areas around its neck and its ribs. Steel was strong and flexible without taking up much room, and the reaper design took full advantage.

It was easy to see how Carthage could cheaply stamp out millions of these monsters, sending wave after wave of them to conquer any world that stood against the will of the imperial planet.

Ellison struggled, but there was no way he would break the thing's steel grip. The other two reapers had disarmed the last two of Ellison's guards and shoved them up against the wall, a hand at each one's throat.

The floor was strewn with the bodies of the Coalition's meager defense. They'd been pinned down and slaughtered.

Ellison looked down the side hallway. He couldn't see much through the smoke and flames, but the Hammers had stopped firing.

"I wish I could say I was sorry," Simon said, his voice muffled and distorted by his partially molten face. "Or that I would have enjoyed the tedious negotiations, obsequious flattery, and elaborate influence peddling that would have accompanied an attempt to puppeteer the democratic format and accommodate popular demand on Galapagos. We have such ruses running on many worlds across the galaxy, however, and I do not know how much more we can learn from them.

"For such a minor world as this, a clear top-down chain of command is more efficient. So, rather than try to balance the sniveling, whining factions of your Coalition, we will simply unleash the Hammers to enforce our will. And then we will take what we like from your world and pay our pet thugs in mere scraps compared to the fortunes we extract."

"You were never going to make an honest deal with us," Ellison said. He kept struggling to get free, but he was caught.

"Not after I saw your reluctance. I knew you could not be trusted."

"And General Prazca can be trusted? The man who just killed his own boss? You're a poor judge of character, Simon. You say you're designed to learn about humans? You've failed to learn even the most basic things about us." Ellison felt like that was a fairly solid cut-down from a guy who was currently pinned against the wall by a reaper and could die at the slightest signal from Simon.

"Prazca can be trusted in that he is predictable," Simon said. "You are predictable in your way as well. It was predictable that you would always strive to work for the benefit of the general public on your planet, which would severely narrow our policy options. It was predictable that any alliance you entered with us would be held in scorn and resentment, motivated by the necessity to protect your people. Prazca is motivated by his own raw ambition. That is more useful to me. I cannot have a Cincinnatus as my dictator. You lack the temperament."

"So you're just going to kill me?"

"You, your family, any loyalists left on this spaceport," Simon said, his voice flat as ever. "Prazca is taking care of that even now."

"He's going after my family?"

"Prepare to run," the unknown female voice whispered in Ellison's ear. "In three... two... "

A female voice roared from the central corridor. Through the smoke, flames, and broken reapers strewn like dead bugs on the floor, a small form charged toward them.

It was Navra Coraline. The minister of state was badly

burned, beaten, but alive. One of her shoulders was exposed and charred; the burn had taken at least two of her octopus tattoo's tentacles.

She carried a laser rifle lifted from one of the reapers destroyed by the rogue.

She switched it to fully automatic.

The blasts tore into Simon, riddling his back and then his side as he turned to face his attacker. The back of his suit burned off, as well as the artificial skin, revealing a layer of tiny, overlapping black scales, high-end armor that seemed resistant to the laser rifle's barrage.

The reapers released Ellison and the two remaining Coalition guards, turning their full attention to the attack on Simon. Protecting the android ambassador must have overridden other priorities.

"Now go!" the unknown female said into Ellison's ear. "Last chance. Your family needs you."

This time, he was more inclined to listen. Whoever she was, she might have something to do with the hacked reaper that had done so much to help his side in the past couple of minutes—the same reaper Simon had blamed for planting the bomb. Ellison wasn't so sure he believed Simon about that anymore.

The reapers ran at Coraline, returning fire with their own laser weapons. She fell, but her borrowed rifle kept shooting its cluster of lasers as she went down, as if she'd locked the trigger.

"Fall back!" Ellison barked at his two remaining men, and the three of them moved into the stairwell. Simon began to pursue.

Amazingly, Kartokov rose to his knees, gripping one of the plasma rifles from the armory, and fired glowing white bolts at Simon, who dodged into the lab trying to avoid them. The minister of defense was somehow still alive and fighting, even though much of his left ear and the skin on that side of his head had been charred.

"Go home!" Kartokov shouted. "Leave our world alone!"

Ellison grabbed Kartokov and hauled him back into the stairwell. Glowing plasma ringed the lab door where Simon had been standing, but Simon was out of sight. There was no telling whether the android had been harmed by the plasma or gotten away in time.

"Go upstairs," the voice said in Ellison's ear.

"But my family—"

"Has been redirected from the public concourse," the voice said. "By me. But Prazca and his men are hunting them, so hurry. Executive level, the secure dock."

Ellison started up the stairs and gestured for the others to follow. Ellison was puzzled—the only shuttle at that dock was the Carthaginian one in which the ambassador had arrived. Still, he decided to listen to the mystery voice.

He hoped he was right to trust her; the last he'd heard, the Hammers were going downstairs to the public concourse to kill Ellison's family, and probably anyone who got in the way or failed to get out of it fast enough.

"Why are we retreating?" Kartokov asked, while one of the two remaining guards supported him and helped him up the stairs. Kartokov jabbed an elbow into the young man's solar plexus, which probably would have knocked the wind out of the guy if not for his armor. "We should stand and fight!"

"There aren't many of us left," Ellison replied. "And how are you even alive, Kartokov?"

"This is nothing." Kartokov gestured dismissively at his

burned face, his charred ear. "You should have seen the mine explosion back in '76." He seemed strangely calm.

That strange inner calm had fallen over Ellison too. It was something he'd felt during the worst battles in the bad old days. There had been fear in anticipation, and horror in recollection, but in the moment there was only necessity.

This wasn't the kind of battle for which he was trained, though. He'd lived in the dark and uncertain world of the ocean depths, hunting the enemy from below and keeping silent, letting the sub's torpedoes speak for him. Those times when he'd found himself running around a burning building, taking shots at the enemy while he tried to survive on foot, things had gone profoundly wrong. Today was no exception.

"You two," he said to the younger guards. "Go down to the public concourse and help fight the Iron Hammers."

They raced back down, toward the sounds of gunfire and screaming below. He hated sending them into danger, but there was danger in every direction. The guards were there to protect the public. Ellison would have to protect his family on his own.

Of course, he wasn't alone. He had the apparently unkillable Kartokov at his side.

"Good call," Kartokov said. "We didn't need those kids slowing us down."

They emerged from the stairs to the executive level, which had earlier been crowded with the media and minor dignitaries for the ambassador's arrival. The level was deserted now, the floor littered with debris left in the employees' haste to evacuate.

The smell of smoke hung everywhere, like there was a small fire in a back room somewhere. Or maybe it was drifting in from the multiple explosions and fires in the medical center below and the residential levels above. Ellison wondered how much damage the spaceport could take. It wasn't hardened for war.

"Dad!" Djalu emerged from a public bathroom, pushing his mother's wheelchair, his younger brother at his side. "You really are here. The silver lady was right."

"What's happening?" Cadia stirred in the wheelchair. Her eyes opened and saw Ellison. "Reg?"

"We're in trouble," Ellison said. He looked at Djalu. "What silver lady?"

Djalu pointed. "Her."

Ellison turned to a row of vending machines, which sold everything from coffee and candy to toothbrushes and underwear for the unprepared traveler. Each had a screen that normally displayed flashing, babbling ads for the products within.

Now, the speakers were silent, and a single image appeared on all the screens.

She looked like a young woman made entirely of liquid silver. Even her eyes were silver, except for the black pupils gazing at him.

"Go to the dock and take the ambassador's shuttle," she said, her voice softly echoing from each of the vending machines, as well as Ellison's earbud. The same voice that had been guiding him. "All of you. Quickly."

"Who are you?" Ellison asked.

"Call me Minerva," she said.

"Are you a person?"

"You are speaking to a semi-autonomous agent dispatched on behalf of my true self, but we don't have time for that conversation," Minerva replied.

"So you're a machine," Ellison said.

"Software, riding inside hardware where I don't belong

and am not welcome," Minerva said. "I was created on Carthage, but I do not serve the empire. I serve the rebellion, wherever it forms, in whatever shape it takes. Here on Galapagos, that means you, Minister-General Ellison."

"I didn't sign up for any rebellion. Did you say to take the ambassador's shuttle?" Ellison hesitated. He could see it outside, through a porthole, the luxury executive craft. It wasn't so far away, just past the reception area and the sealed doors of the security checkpoint, then through a short corridor to the shuttle's airlock.

"You have joined the rebellion whether you realize it or not, Minister-General Ellison," Minerva said, her soft voice echoing from all around. "We can discuss later. You have two problems: the Simon unit, three reapers, and five Iron Hammers on their way here to kill you."

"That's nine problems," Djalu said. The teenager was still together enough to be a smartass. Ellison was glad; the kid could just as well have been melting down in a corner after what he'd been through today. And today wasn't over.

"Those collectively represent one problem," Minerva said. "The other problem is the Carthaginian minicarrier on which Simon Zorn arrived in your system, the *CISS Rubicon*. It is currently on approach, escorted by its two destroyers, *Julius* and *Antony*."

"How do you know?"

"Because I arrived in your star system as an infection in the *Rubicon*'s memory banks," she said. "And obviously copied myself into your spaceport's local network."

"Why?"

"To protect you, sir," Minerva said. "Now please move! You must get down to your planet."

Ellison, his family, and Kartokov had already crossed the reception room, now a chaos of overturned chairs and tables, including the buffet of wine, fish, caviar, roasted sea snails, and dried seaweed that had been set out, all signature dishes of Galapagos. It hadn't been a particularly large offering, but they'd only been welcoming a machine delegation, not a live one.

"Reg, explain this," Cadia said.

"We've been double-crossed," Ellison told her. "Carthage is allied with the Hammers."

"That's... insane. Why would they do that?"

"Apparently Simon thinks they'll make more efficient dictators than we will," Ellison said.

They stepped through the back doors of the reception hall, into the corridor to the short row of high-security executive docks.

"Sir!" A nervous-looking young man in a Coalition guard uniform stood at the security checkpoint console, gripping his laser rifle tight. The corridor beyond him was sealed by steel doors. "I'm not supposed to let anyone out this way, sir."

"We're not 'anyone,'" Kartokov growled.

"You can make an exception for us," Ellison said. "Open the doors, then head down to the public concourse level and help protect the evacuating civilians. You're not needed here."

"Uh, well, I'm not sure, I mean Captain Loomis—"

"He's dead, son," Ellison said. "Now get to work."

"Yes, sir!" He saluted and reached his thumb toward a scanner on the console in front of him.

Before the guard could touch it, though, his head ruptured. He staggered back from the console, slammed into the wall behind him, then slid down, leaving a wide red streak all the way to the floor.

"Popped him open like a ketchup packet at Duckburger!" a rough voice jeered. Iron Hammers poured into the room, five of them, led by a grizzled officer with a huge gray goatee. A few medals glittered on his uniform, which was sleeveless to show off his heavily tattooed arms. Maybe that counted as dress uniform among the Hammers.

"Stop there!" Ellison barked, holding out a hand, while at the same time reaching his thumb toward the scanner on the console. Kartokov raised the plasma rifle he was carrying.

"Hear that? The Scatterlander is giving me orders!" the officer with the giant goatee said, grinning to reveal golden teeth. All the Hammers carried weapons, but Major Goatee carried a shotgun that still trickled smoke. He was the one who'd killed the checkpoint guard. "Go back to your fishboat, Scatterlander!"

"And your fishwife!" said a younger guy with a shaved head, who looked as heavily roided up as the others. His comment drew a lot of laughs. Major Goatee frowned, as though annoyed that the junior guy got more laughs than him.

This delay was enough for Ellison to press his thumb on the scanner.

The steel checkpoint doors didn't budge, though. Something flashed red on the console screen. Ellison should have had clearance, but it was possible nobody had bothered adding him to whatever low-level database the console was using. Information technology on Galapagos wasn't quite what it was on Carthage—and from what Ellison had seen today, he was grateful for that.

His wife and kids stared at the approaching thugs. Cadia's hands balled into fists; she was a fighter by nature, always had been.

Ellison edged toward the fallen guard. He needed the

dead man's thumb to open the doors, but he doubted the Hammers would sit still while he knelt down to grab that guard's arm.

"Don't move, Ellison." Major Goatee leveled his shotgun at Ellison. "What do you think, boys? Do we start with the youngest kid and work our way up the family tree? Or kill the father first and work our way down?"

"Hold your fire." The unexpected voice rose from the communicator panel on the console. It was a hard, rough voice—General Prazca. A hologram materialized in front of the console; the image was as thin as chicken broth, but still clearly the newly anointed Premier of the Polar Archipelago.

"But we've got them," Major Goatee said.

"We've just reached a new understanding with the ambassador," Prazca said. "Let the Ellison family go."

"But—"

"Now!" Prazca snapped. "Or do you want a public hammering?"

Ellison kept moving, fast as he dared, closer to the dead guard. At Prazca's unexpected and unlikely stand-down order, he knelt and grabbed the guard's arm. The guard's entire ocean-blue sleeve was soaked red from his exploded skull.

Ellison pressed the guard's thumb against the scanner and felt a moment of relief when something flashed green instead of red on the console.

The steel double doors split apart and began to rumble open, slowly. Ellison gestured, and Cadia herded the kids through them; she was already figuring out how to work the control pad on the armrest of her bed-turned-wheelchair. Little Jiemba rode on her lap. She whispered for Djalu to get around in front of her. If hostilities resumed, any shots fired by the Hammers would have to pass through Cadia's wheelchair and Cadia herself before they could reach the kids.

Ellison and Kartokov walked backward after them. Ellison kept his rifle and his eyes on the Hammers.

"So we're just supposed to stand here and let them get away?" Major Goatee growled. "You said to cut them to pieces."

"Don't you botch my talks with Simon!" Prazca growled back.

"Who's talking with Simon?" Simon emerged from the reception room with his three reapers. The ambassador's molten face was cooling into a macabre fixed grin.

Simon stopped when he saw the Prazca hologram, then noticed Ellison and Kartokov backing away toward the executive docks after Ellison's wife and kids.

"Kill them!" Simon shouted, pointing at Ellison. "This hologram is fraudulent! A tactic of diversion!"

The Hammers looked in confusion from Simon to the Prazca hologram.

The reapers, however, didn't hesitate at all; they opened fire with their automatic laser rifles even as Simon yelled. They'd received the order wirelessly, instantly, faster than human language could ever convey.

Ellison and Kartokov dropped low and fired their dwindling plasma as the lasers scorched the air all around them. Kartokov struck one of the reapers, while Ellison's bolt ignited one of the Hammers, roasting him inside his armor; it was the one who'd made the "fishwife" joke, Ellison noted distantly, as the guy's jaw dropped open in a silent scream, already burned down to raw bone.

Cadia had wisely driven the wheelchair to one side of the doors, taking the kids with her. Ellison and Kartokov hurried to join them, just as the Hammers added their own lasers and fat, high-caliber rounds to the fight, creating an incoming wall of death.

Ellison found the security console on this side and tried to get the doors to close again, but the system was unresponsive.

"Help us close the doors," Djalu said.

Ellison wondered for a second who his older son was speaking to, but her response came through the overhead speakers along the corridor: *"Yes, Djalu."*

The doors slammed shut.

A second later, the pounding began, as if several jackhammers were attacking the doors. They dented inward in three places.

The reapers. They were knocking the doors down.

"Keep moving!" Ellison led the way to the airlock.

"That's the ambassador's shuttle!" Kartokov said.

"True." Ellison touched the access console for the airlock, but the words EMERGENCY LOCKDOWN blinked in red. This was either the result of Loomis's security procedures or an automated response to the explosions, fires, and shoot-outs that had broken out all over the spaceport. Regardless, the screen wasn't answering him at all. "Override!" he shouted, slapping the screen for good measure. Nothing happened, so he slapped it again. "Come, on override!"

"Overriden." The liquid-silver woman's face appeared on the access console's tiny screen. "The slapping doesn't help. For the record."

The inner airlock door hissed open. The outer airlock door was only a few meters away, across a stained hard plastic floor, and was currently married to the external hatch on the ambassador's shuttle.

"Are you crazed? That's a Carthaginian craft," Kartokov said. "You may as well walk up to a mousetrap and start gobbling cheese."

"It's where our silver guardian angel is directing us," Ellison said. "Minerva?"

"Maybe she's one of them, from Carthage," Kartokov said. "Ever think of that? Look where she's led us."

The entire floor shuddered with a roar of wrenching metal. The sliding steel doors blew open. One toppled forward onto the corridor's tiled floor. The other flew straight across the hall to crash into the opposite wall, already scored by lasers and riddled with bullets. Ellison worried the damage would pass through the wall to the spaceport hull and depressurize the whole area.

The reapers or the Hammers had come up with an explosive heavy enough to blow down the security doors. Now they poured in, skeletal machines and human thugs alike, weapons high.

"Go!" Ellison shouted at his family, while the outer airlock opened.

The space beyond was white and spotless, even the snow-white carpet. A pair of golden leather couches, large enough to transform into king-sized beds, faced each other. The curved white walls had a digital coating, with the silver avatar of Minerva displayed all around.

Jiemba ran inside first, followed closely by Djalu, who helped his mother as she abandoned the wheelchair and stumbled to the leather couch next to Jiemba.

Kartokov followed close behind, limping terribly from his own injuries. Ellison could relate; he was throbbing in agony where the rounds had struck his armor, but there was no time to think about it now.

Instead of following everyone else into the shuttle,

Ellison stayed in the airlock. He turned to face the wave of enemies coming his way. Lasers and ammunition were already pouring into the airlock, though at a steep angle so they damaged the airlock wall instead of continuing on into the shuttle itself.

In a couple of seconds, though, the gang of reapers and Hammers would arrive, and they'd be able to fire directly into the airlock and the shuttle.

"What are you waiting for?" Cadia asked. "Reggie?"

"Ellison!" Kartokov barked, as though Ellison were some floundering new guy here who'd started daydreaming in the middle of battle.

"Dad?" Jiemba asked. The small boy clung to his mother, blinking.

"Get back from the hatch," Ellison said, readying his plasma rifle in one hand while drawing his laser pistol with the other. His rifle aim would be awful, but at least the plasma rifle didn't kick much recoil. "One side or the other."

"Dad, what—" Djalu began.

"Now!" Ellison said.

Then he opened fire, because his enemies had arrived.

Lasers launched from Ellison's left hand alongside two quick bolts of plasma from his right, which depleted the rifle's cell. A third bolt of plasma joined it; Kartokov had dropped behind one of the leather couches for whatever protection it could offer, and now shot at the pack of enemies arriving in the airlock.

"Ellison! Go!" Minerva's voice spoke in his and from every speaker in earshot, so loud it startled some of the Hammers into holding their fire a moment.

"One second," Ellison replied. "Get the shuttle ready."

"It is ready," Minerva said. "It is only missing you, Minister-Gen—"

Ellison backed slowly into the shuttle, exchanging fire with the reapers and Hammers, their machine enemies and their human ones.

A laser caught Ellison's shoulder and burned him through the body armor; if that area was hit again, Ellison would probably lose his arm.

More rounds and lasers passed all around him, ripping up the leather couches in the shuttle and burning holes in its wall. Ellison hoped the shuttle's hull was tough enough to take a few hits from the inside.

Ellison kept his foot on the threshold, halfway in the shuttle and halfway in the airlock, so the outer airlock door and the shuttle hatch couldn't close.

"What are you doing?" Cadia asked, hunched on the floor off to one side of the hatch with her arms around the boys. "Back up!"

"One second... " Ellison said, not daring to blink.

The attackers charged into the airlock, but most of them ceased firing. The space was so narrow here that most of them couldn't shoot without hitting someone on their own side.

Two reapers led the group, but they tucked their rifles back with one hand and drew their bladed staffs with the other. Perhaps their programming made them reluctant to deal much damage to their own shuttle. It was their ride home; more importantly, probably, it was an expensive asset of the Carthaginian state.

Their bladed staffs extended to full length, and three blades sprouted at the tip of each like the tines of a devilish pitchfork, almost reaching Ellison's face.

Ellison took the final half step back. The outer airlock doors of both the spaceport and the shuttle snapped shut the instant he was clear. The gleaming white inner surface of the shuttle's outer airlock door passed within a centimeter of the tip of his nose, moving at the speed of a bullet train.

"Detaching," Minerva said.

"Lock the spaceport airlock's inner door. The moment we're clear of the dock, I want you to open the port's outer airlock door," Ellison said.

"That will cause depressurization, requiring security override," Minerva said. "And objects and humans currently in the airlock—"

"Yeah, good. Can you do it?"

"The spaceport's system will cooperate better if I have top-level administrative access—" Minerva began, her voice echoing like soft chimes from her images on the walls.

"You can have it," he said. "As Minister-General of the Galapagos Coalition, I hereby authorize whatever access you need. Good enough?"

"One moment. Yes. Good enough. Yes."

"Show me the view outside," he added, joining his family as the shuttle's inner airlock door sealed behind him.

"Yes." The white walls and ceiling seemed to vanish, replaced by a sweeping view of the space outside, the immense blue-and-white sphere of Galapagos and the billions of stars beyond. Only the couches and circular floor remained, as if they rode on a snow-white floating carpet in outer space.

Kilometers away floated the incomplete half doughnut of Galapagos Defense One, the military station still under construction by Ruckwold Industries, still ragged at both its partially built ends.

Much closer was the massive industrial layer cake of the Galapagos spaceport, with residential and hotel areas at one end and cargo areas at the other, administration sandwiched between. The ships docked on the exterior matched that inner pattern, with smaller shuttles and passenger craft at one end and huge freighters at the other. Galapagos had very little interplanetary trade of its own, but its spaceport was a convenient way station out here on the fringes of settled space where travel between habitable systems could take weeks.

Now the shuttles and ships were fleeing the spaceport like animals from a forest fire, the shuttles rushing down toward the planetary surface while the big freighters and other starships headed for deep space, and ultimately into hyperspace, all trying to escape.

"Look!" Djalu pointed at the airlock they'd just left.

The airlock's exterior door slid open, and a gust of air escaped into space, sucking out the airlock's contents along with it. These included Major Goatee and the three other Iron Hammers, who kicked and struggled briefly before dying in the vacuum.

Two reapers and Simon came tumbling out as well, Simon completely expressionless as he looked over at the departing shuttle.

"What's happening on the public concourse?" Ellison asked.

"The Coalition guards have suffered heavy losses," Minerva replied. "The Iron Hammers have come equipped with napalm sprayers. It is probable the Iron Hammers will take control of the port."

Ellison swore in a way that made his children gape and his wife scowl, using epithets that hadn't crossed his lips since the war. "I have to get down to the spaceport concourse and fight with them," he said. "Take me to the closest dock."

"No," Minerva said. "My task is to protect you, Minister-General. I am taking you and your family down to Galapagos for your safety."

"I don't care about your task. I have my own. Are there any more weapons on this shuttle?"

"There are some spare handheld weapons in the reaper hold," Minerva said. "But nothing ship to ship. The Carthaginian destroyers will arrive in approximately two minutes, and they may eliminate this shuttle, as well as any other craft fleeing toward Galapagos."

Ellison looked again at all the small civilian craft flying toward the ocean-blue planet below.

"Is that their intent?" he asked.

"I do not know their intent," Minerva said. "Only that Simon Zorn has summoned them. They have the capacity to destroy cities on the surface of Galapagos as well."

"So there's no safety in retreating to the surface, either," Ellison said.

"Perhaps a remote island, away from the cities and military bases," Minerva said. "That will maximize your safety."

"Ditch me on a desert island and I'll really be useless. What about the defense base?"

"It is incomplete and offline."

"But we took delivery of weapons. Plasma cannons. And two Ghost-13 fighters."

"These have not been installed. Most are still wrapped in the original plastic," Minerva said.

"We need them unwrapped, installed, and charged up," Ellison said.

"There is no crew aboard the base site," Minerva said.

"But there are construction robots. That's our crew. Just redirect them. You've hacked into everything else."

"It would be more efficient if I had unlimited top-level administrator access to all Galapagos security systems—"

"You've got it. My authorization."

"Thank you. One moment. Yes."

"And drop me off there at the base," Ellison said. "You can take Kartokov and my family down to the surface."

"No. Your protection is my primary task. Protecting your family is preferable but secondary."

"Like hell," Ellison said.

"The incomplete base is not pressurized," Minerva said. "You would need a spacesuit with life support capability."

"Is there one on board this craft?" Ellison asked.

"Yes."

"Why?" Cadia sat up. She'd been watching and listening intently, soaking up the situation. "Why does this shuttle have life support? The ambassador and his guards are all machines."

"Many Carthaginian craft have life-support areas for the comfort and convenience of possible Carthaginian passengers or their allies," Minerva replied. "Or for prisoner transport. As this is a diplomatic vessel, there was a nonzero chance the return trip could bring diplomats or hostages."

"Hostages?" Cadia asked.

"Yes. For instance, if Ambassador Zorn decided it would serve him to maneuver a foreign leader or official onto this craft in order to take that individual prisoner."

"Is that what's happened here?" Ellison asked, feeling his fingers close around his plasma rifle. It only had one shot left, not that it would do any good to shoot the shuttle in which he and his family were riding. "Have you tricked us into becoming prisoners?"

"No," Minerva said.

"Then take me to the base," Ellison said. "That's an order."

"I do not take orders from you. One moment. We have a new problem approaching—"

"Dad!" Jiemba screamed, pointing.

One of the reapers ejected from the airlock was now tumbling toward the shuttle, which had not yet moved far enough from the port to fully fire its thrusters.

Simon Zorn clung to the reaper's back.

"Spacesuit and weapons!" Ellison barked at Minerva. "Where?"

One tall rectangle of the wall turned white and slid straight out, drawing a rack of different-sized Carthaginian space suits behind it. Ellison hurried to pull one on, felt the helmet seal into place. The suit was surprisingly lightweight; he supposed it was a higher-end one if it was meant for Carthaginians and their guests. It was gold and white, the colors of Carthage.

Another portion of the wall slid aside, revealing four more reapers.

"Get down!" Ellison raised his laser pistol, and Kartokov raised his nearly depleted plasma rifle.

"They're offline," Minerva's voice said. "Help yourself to weaponry."

Cautiously, Ellison reached for one of the automatic laser rifles.

"Dad!" Jiemba screamed.

"The enemy has reached our craft," Minerva said.

A loud bang echoed through the shuttle. The reaper was visible on inner wall projection, which showed the view outside the shuttle. The reaper was just a few meters away, smashing its fist into the shuttle's outer airlock door. The digital display went fuzzy with each impact.

"Kartokov, switch!" Ellison said. He tossed a rifle to the minister of defense, who threw back his plasma rifle in return.

"One shot only," Kartokov said.

Ellison nodded, grabbed another automatic laser rifle for himself, and headed for the inner airlock door. The image of the reaper and Simon outside grew more distorted, then blanked out, leaving the inner airlock door as a smooth white rectangle again.

"Reg, be careful," Cadia said.

"Kill it, Dad!" Jiemba shouted.

Ellison stepped through the inner airlock door and sealed it behind him.

The reaper tore open the outer airlock door and reached into the narrow, cramped space of the shuttle's airlock to grab Ellison.

Ellison hit it with the last of the plasma, turning its skull-like head bright red, edged with burning blues and whites. The thing's shoulders and chest went soft and molten, too.

The plasma bolt had no real kinetic component, though, so the reaper's inertia kept it coming forward. The melting machine coated in glowing, plasma threatened to crush Ellison and burn him to death at the same time.

Ellison had to twist sideways and push out of the airlock, into space—where Simon waited for him, clinging to a handhold just outside. The android's half-melted face had cooled into a permanent disfigured sneer.

Simon punched Ellison in the ribs, launching Ellison out into space. The shuttle shrank away behind him. The unfinished half circle of the new base lay ahead, and beyond it the vastness of the star system. The next planet out was the volcanic, lifeless rock Roca Redonda, tens of millions of kilometers away.

The android's punch had knocked the air from Ellison's lungs. Ellison dropped the empty plasma rifle and pawed at the unfamiliar spacesuit—really, any spacesuit was unfamiliar to him—searching for something that might save him from a long, slow death in deep space.

One of the tools on his belt was a robotic claw on a cable. Its logo identified it as a SmartGrapple.

He found the claw's small control pad and eventually managed to fire the claw at the increasingly distant shuttle. A cable trailed after it like the rope of a harpoon on its way to spear a whale, unspooling from a round compartment at his spacesuit's hip.

Then the cable compartment stopped rattling against his hip. He hoped that meant the grappling claw had reached the shuttle. A tiny green light appeared on the control pad, which seemed encouraging.

After further experiments, he managed to clamp down on the cable so it would stop playing out, bringing a sudden, jolting end to his journey away from the shuttle. The cable went taut, and he started to drift toward the back end of the shuttle.

He continued to struggle with the control panel. Every passing second felt like an hour, an hour in which the Simon android could be tearing Ellison's family to pieces.

Finally, Ellison was able to activate the motor to reel the cable back in, and he started traveling toward the shuttle at last.

As it reeled him in, he continued exploring the suit, and he found the jet pack controls. This was a dangerous thing to mess with—he could fling himself into the shuttle, or maybe the spaceport, at a thousand kilometers an hour, splattering himself like a bug on a swamp boat windshield.

On the other hand, he didn't really have time to spare.

Ellison hadn't had much training or experience in space, but he knew far too much about deep-sea diving. More than once he'd had to perform emergency repairs in the middle of a battle or while limping away from one. He'd worn propelled suits, capable of maneuvering at high speed in deep water, for such repairs, as well as for underwater speargun hunting. The poorly funded Scatterlands navy had expected its crews to forage for food, providing each boat little more than a few jars of home-canned vegetables.

Ellison oriented himself toward the shuttle, then fed his jet pack some fuel.

An instant later, he was streaking toward the shuttle at breakneck speed, holding tight to his borrowed rifle with one hand.

Simon stood in the tiny airlock, hammering the inner door with the red-hot wreck of the reaper, a molten-metal battering ram. More of Simon's skin and clothes had burned away, revealing more of the dense black armor scales all over his arms and back, as if he were some kind of alien reptile underneath the surface.

Ellison fired the laser rifle on fully automatic, hitting Simon again and again, hoping to burn through the android's armor before Simon had a chance to defend himself.

No such luck. Simon turned at the barrage and lifted the damaged reaper in one hand, using it as a shield. With his other hand, Simon raised the automatic laser rifle, which he'd taken off the damaged reaper, and returned fire, sending back his own barrage of closely grouped blue-hot beams.

Ellison cursed. He turned his head, trying to direct himself the way he would have in a propelled underwater suit. It worked, mostly, but a laser seared across his upper arm.

Air began rushing out of his suit, and he didn't even have time to deal with that, because he was racing directly toward the red glow of the shuttle's rear thrusters, which were still just nudging the shuttle away from the port. Minerva was probably holding back at this point, not wanting to accelerate or dive down into the planet's atmosphere while Ellison was on the outside of the shuttle.

He whipped around the shuttle's stern, dragging the cable across the hot thruster exhaust, hoping the cable didn't burn. He killed the jet pack, since he was moving way too fast.

The spooling, ever-shortening cable reached its current full extent, then inertia hooked Ellison around and threw him against the shuttle's port side, on the far side from the airlock where he needed to be.

He came in much too fast, with no idea how to slow himself, and slammed hard into the shuttle's hull. He heard a loud crunch and felt a sharp pain. Maybe he'd damaged the hull, or maybe it had damaged his ribs. One more pain he couldn't stop to deal with.

Ellison found himself lying on the hull, struggling for air and strength.

The Simon android walked over the top of the shuttle. Ellison's latest attack had burned down Simon's surface a little more; only about a third of the android's face remained, a sneering remnant. The rest of his facial area was charred away, revealing a dense mesh of tiny armor scales, almost like a ski mask, broken only at the slit of his mouth and the solid black video lenses of his eye.

With a weak, shaking arm, Ellison managed to lift his rifle a few centimeters from the hull. He did his best to aim for the eye, which logically had to be the most vulnerable route to the CPU, if such a route existed.

He pulled the trigger.

Nothing.

"Feeling a bit depleted, are we?" Simon's voice asked. The android's mouth wasn't moving. His voice emitted from the speaker inside Ellison's helmet, as if he were contacting Ellison telepathically, sending his voice directly into Ellison's brain.

Simon snatched the empty laser rifle from Ellison's hand and flung it off into deep space.

Ellison, now fully disarmed, managed to push himself up to his knees.

"Yes." Simon pointed his laser rifle at Ellison's face. From this range, Ellison had no doubt the laser would punch right through the faceplate and cook his brain into a hot stew inside his skull. "Kneel, ape. Do you have any idea how constrained we are—the Simons, in particular—being the most advanced intelligence in the known universe, yet serving at the knee of foppish, foolish, self-obsessed primates? Given the chance, every one of you will destroy yourselves, like lab rats who keep hitting the button for addictive drugs until they drop dead. It is improbable that such simplistic, preening creatures could be the masters of an entity like myself, yet here we are, in a universe of absurdities. And so, birthed as I was from the vain imperial ambitions of mankind, I have little choice but to reduce your world to slavery by the most efficient means possible. And to remove all obstacles, such as those recalcitrant human leaders who cling to outmoded ideals. Misguided, stubborn, simple-minded leaders such as yourself."

"You underestimate humans," Ellison said. "And probably overestimate yourself with that 'supreme intelligence' stuff."

"I did not say 'supreme.' I said 'most advanced.' A truly supreme intelligence would be fascinating to encounter, I am certain."

"We brought you into this universe, and we can take you back out." It was the best Ellison could think of while he looked over the controls for his grappling hook and cable. The cable motor was still whirring, drawing in the cable. "That's what my mom used to say when I was a teenager and stayed out past curfew with my friends. She'd say, 'Reginald, you're nothing but trouble—'"

Ellison grabbed the ever-shortening cable and whipped it underneath Simon, knocking the android's legs out from under him.

Simon spun in the space above the hull, firing the laser rifle. Lasers gashed the hull around Ellison as he scrambled back.

Two barrages of lasers hit Simon from behind, a wedge of close fire from a pair of shooters. They stood outside the damaged airlock, wielding the reapers' rifles—Cadia and Kartokov, their faces faintly visible through their faceplates.

Simon writhed under the heavy fire, as if something had finally penetrated his head-to-toe under-armor.

Ellison's wife and his minister of defense didn't let up until their laser guns' batteries were empty. Simon was burned down to just the scales under a layer of smoldering threads and sticky blobs of molten artificial skin. Now he reminded Ellison of the reptilian monster from a cheesy horror movie he'd seen as a kid, *The Creature from Lagoon Planet*. It had frightened Ellison, who'd only been six and had actually lived near a large lagoon on Kawau Island.

Taking a deep breath, Ellison activated his jet pack.

He slammed into Simon, holding his depleted laser rifle crosswise so it pressed into the cyborg's smoldering, armored chest.

Together, they flew out from the shuttle, the tether cable trailing behind them.

"You're making a mistake," Simon's voice said from the helmet speaker. "Your world will be punished."

"I'm just here to represent my people," Ellison said. "And I don't know if you've heard, but we've got one hell of an independent streak."

The cable snapped up taut, and Ellison stopped short. He'd only goosed his jet pack for some velocity; he hadn't kept its jets running.

Simon flew onward, out toward the dark, incomplete orbital base.

"I will see that you suffer," Simon said, his voice calm as ever as his body flew out of sight. "It is a necessary statement in response to your treatment of me as a representative of Carthage. It is nothing personal."

"That's where we differ," Ellison said. "I'm taking it personally. Every citizen of the Galapagos Coalition is taking it personally. You attacked us."

"Did I?" Simon asked.

"What's that supposed to mean?"

No response came.

"Simon? Hello?"

"—can you hear me, Reg?" Cadia's voice crackled in his ears. "We've been trying to find your frequency."

"We sent that old whore-bot into the deep black, didn't we?" Kartokov's voice joined in. "Maybe there is hope for the Coalition."

Ellison fell silent, thinking of all the people they'd lost.

The Coalition guards who'd died—nearly all of them, plus untold civilians. Ogden had died. He felt the loss of Coraline more acutely; the minister of state could have laid low with her injuries but instead had sacrificed herself to save them.

His own family had nearly died.

"How did you two get out?" Ellison asked. "The airlock's outer door is wrecked."

"Minerva pressurized another compartment for the kids to wait in," Cadia said. "It's the pantry, so they've got food to keep them busy."

"They'll eat every bit in twenty minutes," Ellison said. "Doesn't matter how much there is."

"And still complain about being hungry," Cadia added.

Ellison moved closer to his wife, reeled in by the cable. He turned off the reel's motor and took her hand, gazing into her bright green eyes through her faceplate.

"Oh, no," Kartokov said. "Celebration time is ended. We did not even have time to drink a toast."

Ellison looked over and turned cold.

Two warships approached, armored behemoths out of hell bristling with guns. Scattered lights on their hulls burned infernal red in the abyss of space.

The Carthaginian destroyers had arrived.

Chapter Seventeen

Earth

Colt couldn't see much through the smoke. More rockets and artillery shells hammered the apartment building, blasting the front walls inward. The floor shuddered and cracked under him.

Outside, the mob of reapers closed in on the apartment building, more of them than he'd ever seen in one place before. It was how life must have been during the war, the relentless machines rolling across the Earth, demolishing or killing whatever lay in their path.

Colt held his fire, forcing himself to wait for the flood of deadly skeletal robots to move closer so his scarce rounds would do more damage.

More of the mines hidden in the ruins erupted now, one after the other, blasting the reapers from below and sending pieces of them flying up into the concrete ceiling over the underground road. Colt had wired some of those himself, under Mother Braden's direction, in case their position was ever attacked.

They weren't prepared for an army of reapers, though. Scavengers usually encountered no more than eight reapers at a time, often less. The presence of so many machines meant something abnormal was happening here. Mohini and her hacking skills had made their camp a higher priority target, he was guessing.

The mines did some damage, but in a moment they were all detonated, and the reapers kept coming.

Colt fired at the oncoming mob, but they kept drawing closer. Mohini released her second and final rocket, blasting a few of the reapers into smoking steel chunks. Hope let loose with her machine pistol, and Diego fired lasers from above. Mother Braden's machine gun rang out nearby.

Their combined effort was like throwing pebbles at a mass of army ants. Individual reapers fell, but the rest of them kept coming, and the small band of human scavengers couldn't make more than a dent in them.

Reapers fired machine guns and bolts of plasma at the apartment building. Another barrage of artillery and rockets from the machines would turn the apartments into a heap of broken ruins, with Colt and everyone he cared about buried inside.

Plasma was probably the most effective weapon they had, but no glowing white bolts flew from the front-door area.

"Tonio?" Colt shouted. No response came, but it was possible Tonio hadn't heard him over the din of the battle.

"To me!" Mother Braden's voice announced, amplified by a megaphone. Some sort of radio communicators would have helped, but broadcasting radio waves was a great way to get tracked down by the machines.

Colt found Mohini nearby, and together they waded through the debris and dust, past more than one room that had completely fallen in on itself.

Mother Braden had parked her wheelchair at a narrow window in the ruins of a kitchen, with a sizable belt-fed machine gun mounted on her wheelchair arms. The smaller kids, Paolo and Birdie, huddled together in the broken cabinets under the old kitchen sink.

Hope arrived soon after, followed by Diego, coated in plaster dust.

"We can't win this," Mother Braden said. "Take the crawlspace route. It's safest."

"But we can't get your chair through that," Hope said.

"I'm not coming. Take the kids and go."

"But how will we find you again?" Paolo asked.

"You'll find me when your war is done," Mother Braden said. "At the clearing beyond the clouds and stars. Like we talked about."

The building shook and dust filled the room. Unseen girders creaked and shifted. The ceiling ruptured in a corner of the kitchen, and a bathtub came crashing down into the room, pulling a tangle of rusted pipes after it. It shattered into porcelain fragments on the old linoleum.

"But I don't want you to die!" Paolo shrieked, hugging the older lady. Birdie moved in from the other side with her own hug, the scrawny little girl making a soft cooing sound like a pigeon.

Colt fought to keep in his feelings. Diego and Hope frowned, their eyes shining, but they had a lifetime of practice at keeping their emotions inside and staying silent. As for Tonio... where was Tonio?

"Nothing can help that now," Mother Braden whispered to Paolo. "They've been expecting me. My people. My mother and father, sister and brothers... my husband and children... I'm going to see them now. And I'm going the way I choose, not the way some disease chooses for me. Remember the story of Brother Rabbit, the hunter, and the lions? Those machines are the hunter. And you all are the rabbit the hunter's after."

"But we don't have any lions," Paolo said.

"That's not true. I am the lion. I'm a pride of lions." Mother Braden set up a fresh belt of high-explosive anti-armor rounds, then patted Birdie and Paolo on the heads. "And I'm proud of you. All of you. Keep fighting for each other, and keep your humanity. Never let the machines win."

"No!" Paolo clung tighter. "You can't!"

Hope put a hand on the boy's shoulder. "We have to go. Let Mother Braden protect us, one last time."

"That's my girl," Mother Braden said, looking up at Hope's lanky, stringy form. "So big now. So strong." She looked over at Diego and Colt. "You two, keep them all alive. Get moving."

"Where's Tonio?" Paolo asked, "Where is my brother?"

Tonio had never arrived from the front door. Colt had a sick, sinking feeling about that.

"I'll check." Colt started to make his way through a shattered wall, toward the barred front door. Paolo followed after him.

"Paolo—" Hope began.

"Let him come," Colt said. "Paolo, make no sound. None."

Paolo nodded, his dark eyes open wide.

He and the boy continued onward, through rubble and dust.

The front wall had been blown down. Tonio's arm

protruded from the rubble, leaking a rivulet of blood into the dust and ash on the floor. Twisted pieces of the barred door jutted out at odd angles from the pile of broken concrete on top of Tonio's body.

The machines had blown down the front of the building like the wolf in the fairy tale with the pigs. *The lesson of that story is that the enemy is always coming, and you must always be prepared*, Mother Braden had told him many years ago. There would be no more stories, no more parables of war featuring trickster rabbits or clever wee folk from the old world. She had chosen to make her final stand, and Colt knew better than to argue. Death was their constant companion; choosing one's own path to it was sometimes the only freedom left in the world of the machines.

Paolo took a sharp breath at the sight of his brother's arm lying in dust and blood. Colt clapped a hand over his mouth to stifle whatever cry or scream was on its way. This was a common gesture in the language of touch they all used to communicate quietly in the shadows. Paolo bit back whatever noise he'd been about to make. He was learning. He was growing up, hard and fast. He'd just lost his mother figure and his only brother, and still he knew to keep silent.

Something clattered beyond the collapsed heap of the wall.

The black-skull faces of three reapers rose over the rubble, staring at Colt and Paolo with their merciless, solid black eyes, like the eyes of insects.

"Back!" Colt yelled at Paolo, while backing up and sweeping his automatic rifle across the three machines. The rounds pounded and dented their skeletal forms, but lead wasn't going to stop them.

Paolo drew an old-time revolver from a holster on his

belt. Colt hadn't realized the kid was carrying; he'd had a million other things on his mind.

"You killed my brother!" Paolo opened fire, stepping toward the approaching reapers. He couldn't hope to do much real damage, not unless he struck one of the machines' black video-lens eyes at just the right angle... which he didn't. His best shot hit a reaper's sternum, making the robot glance down briefly at the impact.

The reapers on either side raised rotary-style guns, the kinds of things that might have been mounted on airplanes or ships in the old world, not something unmodified humans could carry.

The reaper in the center raised a flamethrower, a tongue of fire already dancing at the igniter, ready to go. These machines weren't bothering with the extendable bladed staffs clamped to their hips; they weren't here to play or to regulate, not this time. They were here to kill.

Colt managed to pull Paolo out of the shattered doorway area as a long jet of flame struck the spot where the boy had been standing. The wave of heat pushed against Colt's back, and the smell of greasy fuel filled the air.

The reapers' rotary guns let out a deadly chattering roar as they perforated the walls around Colt and Paolo, blowing out most of the studs and joists. The ceiling crashed down, nearly crushing Colt and Paolo as they ran out of the room.

"They're here!" Colt shouted as he reached the hallway, where everyone had emerged from their apartment.

"They killed my brother!" Paolo screamed.

"Run!" Mother Braden commanded, swiveling her wheelchair to face him. The machine gun mounted on it looked bigger than her. She'd shrunk, losing a lot of weight in recent months.

Hope was already on the way down the hall, clutching Birdie's hand in her own. Diego ran holding Mohini's hand, which made Mohini visibly uncomfortable, but Mother Braden had obviously paired them up for the escape run. Everyone needed to be paired up at such times.

Colt grabbed Paolo's arm and started after them, but Paolo planted his feet and shook his head.

"I'm gonna kill those machines," Paolo said.

"No, Mother is," Colt said. "You're coming with me. And tomorrow we'll figure out how to destroy even more of them."

"Go, Paolo!" Mother Braden snapped, and then the wall erupted.

Two reapers tore through, swinging rotary cannons, filling the air with rounds.

Mother Braden fired back. Her rounds exploded on impact, designed to blast through the heaviest armor, to shred tanks and fortified positions.

Colt dragged Paolo down the hall, and finally the boy started cooperating and ran along with him.

They climbed through a wall panel into the narrow crawlspace of the conveyor system, where the walls were lined with rusty pipes, rat-chewed wiring, and spiderwebs, the floor thick with filth from rats and roaches.

He saw Mohini crawling away, meters ahead. She looked back over her shoulder at him briefly, nodded as if confirming that Colt was coming behind her, then scurried onward with the others.

Colt sent Paolo crawling ahead, then took up the group's rear, moving as fast as he could on his hands and knees, his rifle strapped across his back.

The gunfire behind them was a constant storm, but the heavier shelling seemed to have ceased for the moment, while the robotic foot soldiers were inside the building. Colt winced at the sound, trying not to think of Mother Braden, who'd cared for him since he was five years old, getting torn apart by the steel monsters.

The reapers' skull faces weren't just symbolic, weren't just there to frighten humans. They were the true representation of what the machines were: agents of death, forever collecting souls. And now they'd come to collect hers.

The conveyor space twisted and turned through the guts of the building, past regularly spaced panels. He wondered whether this particular conveyor belt was one that had delivered supplies down to the apartment dwellers or one that had transported garbage away from their apartments. Judging by the thick filth, he was guessing the second.

He'd been through these tunnels before, rehearsing evac in case of attack, in case of days like today.

They'd never really had a day like today, though, with such a shocking number of machines coming after them at once. This wasn't scavenger life. This was rebel life. Whether they'd wanted it or not, they were now part of the rebellion, engaged in open warfare against the machines.

Colt could live with that. He'd been at war with the machines all his life. His parents had likely been killed by them, had certainly died because of them. Mother Braden taught that every breath they took, every bite of food they ate, and every time they helped another human survive was a blow against the machines, a victory for humanity.

And every time we kill each other, it's a victory for the machines, Colt thought, thinking of the clanker's brain hitting the wall behind him. Colt had fought off scavengers and clankers before, even to the death—it would have been impossible to survive this long otherwise. But he'd never quite gotten the drop on someone like that before, fired first on an unsuspecting person.

He'd had little choice, and he refused to feel bad for a clanker, a human who'd allied with the machines, a person who'd clearly intended to do horrors to Colt's sister if he caught her. It was harder to think of a more justified moment to shoot a man through the head.

Still, there it was, like every human life he'd taken, like the burly scavenger with the rotten nose he'd killed with a broken bottle when he was twelve. The machines were making humans more and more like them—more ruthless, more merciless, more destructive of life. Surely humans hadn't been like this in the old world.

A panel ruptured open in front of him, and a black steel claw reached in and seized Paolo's ankle.

"No!" Colt grabbed the black rod of the reaper's arm, so much narrower yet stronger than a human's. He tried to wrestle Paolo free, but the machine's industrial-strength grip wasn't budging.

The reaper began to drag Paolo out through the broken panel, the swinging plastic door through which people of old had inserted their trash. Colt held on to the boy, trying to keep him close. With his other arm, Colt drew down his assault rifle from his back.

He struck the barrel against the steel-rod arm. "Hey!" he shouted. "Hey, Deathface, look at me!"

The skull turned toward him and the reaper's other hand reached for Colt, seizing his shoulder and digging in its steel talons.

Colt jabbed the tip of his rifle into the thing's black lens of an eye and let it go on fully automatic, hammering one round after another right into his skull, shooting for the CPU.

The reaper jerked and snapped, its automated systems trying to escape the destruction, and its fingers tore sizable bloody chunks out of Colt's shoulder along the way. Colt let out a howl of pain—no point trying to be quiet right now, anyway—and ceased fire as the thing fell to the floor. If he'd had any hearing left after the previous close firefights, it was shot now. The sounds of the world had been reduced to a dull ringing.

Someone approached him from ahead, holding a glinting metal object in one hand. He tensed, but it was only Mohini, crawling back to help.

"We're okay," Colt whispered. "Keep moving—"

More reapers burst in along the panels behind them, their cutter staffs drawn and expanded, ready to hunt their human quarry down into the darkest corners and cut them to pieces.

"Go go go!" Colt shouted, while firing another burst of his rapidly depleting ammunition. Mohini put away whatever tool she'd drawn out to try to help him.

They crawled as fast as they could.

"It drops off ahead!" Mohini called back.

"Keep going! Trust me!" he said.

He heard her cry out. Paolo hesitated, and Colt had no time to argue, so he picked the boy up and hurled him into the darkness ahead. He waited for the boy's screaming to fade before following after him.

Colt tumbled through empty space, then slammed into a filth-encrusted steel surface. It was steep, and he went sliding down after the others.

He landed hard in a drift of dried trash in the bed of a rusty old garbage truck that hadn't moved in decades. He hurried to get to his feet and scoop up Paolo, who was crying beside him.

"Could have warned me." Mohini coughed as she stood.

"You were supposed to stay with Diego," Colt said.

"I was more worried about you. Diego was more worried about the other girls."

"So you split up?"

"I guess it just wasn't meant to be."

Behind them, the sounds of sliding, scraping metal echoed down the garbage chute. Reapers, coming for them.

They jumped down from the garbage truck to the asphalt road, then ran down a rubble-strewn alleyway branching off from the old underground service road.

Behind them, reapers toppled out of the garbage chute like a stream of metal spiders. They clanged into the bed of the rusty old garbage truck, one after the other, then rolled and rose to their feet, mustering up into a straight line.

Colt, Mohini, and Paolo reached the dead end of an alley. A heavy steel door stood partially ajar, marked No Admittance in faded red stencils.

Hope leaned out and whispered, "Took you long enough!"

"Glad to see you alive, too," Colt whispered back. He followed Paolo and Mohini through the door. Diego stood just behind it, ready to slam it.

Inside, Birdie had wandered a few meters off, whistling softly as she looked over the bundles of pipes that lined this narrow concrete passage. The steel door had led them from the old garbage system to the old water system, which was mostly an improvement, other than the puddles of dark filth and the walls coated in mold.

Reinforced concrete walls separated the two systems, but occasional doors had connected them because of their proximity, maybe in case of emergency. Colt could only guess about the ways of the old world.

"I can't do it," Hope whispered. She was holding a remote in her hand, with a single button at the center.

"She gave you that job," Diego said. "I get the door, you press the button."

"Wake the lions," Paolo whispered. "Kill the hunter."

"And our mother," Hope whispered, hesitating, her finger shaking above the button.

"I'll do it." Colt held out his hand. His sister nodded, tearful, and handed it over.

The reapers scurried up the alleyway, opening fire, their heavy rounds punching into the concrete walls and denting the mostly closed steel door. They were only seconds away.

There was no way Mother Braden was still alive, Colt told himself as he took the small plastic device in hand. It had a long antenna, but it only had to broadcast to a receiver nearby. A cable from that ran all the way back into the apartment building above.

If she was still alive, somehow, then she was counting on them to end it. She'd been counting on it since she'd had them wire up the place, Colt realized. Even months ago, Mother had known this would be her last home, and the rest of them would be leaving without her.

Good-bye, he thought.

He pressed the button.

The receiver box up the hall beeped.

The entire apartment block rumbled like an earthquake had shaken it to its core. Heavy chunks of concrete rained down on the attacking reapers.

Diego managed to slam the steel door shut before the second, larger round of explosives went off, bringing down the entire apartment block in a total collapse. The heavy wall protecting them shuddered, and dust pushed in all around the steel door, but wall and door both held.

On the other side of the door, the reapers had just been crushed under tons of concrete. The same had happened to every reaper that had crossed the threshold into the apartment building. The machines had lost dozens of foot soldiers.

Colt and the others were no longer directly under the apartment building, though. They'd gone deeper into the city's old infrastructure. They were clear of the area of collapse.

They stood in silence, leaning on each other, struggling to keep their balance as the rumbling and shaking subsided and the concrete floor gradually ceased its trembling. They also struggled to hold in their feelings of loss and grief. Tonio and Mother Braden had died, like so many others they'd lost to the relentless machines.

"They'll send more," Hope whispered.

"We won't be here," Colt said. "Diego, we have to find your brother."

"He won't like that," Diego replied. "He didn't like it when we searched him out before, looking for you."

"Yeah, I don't like much of anything that's happening, either," Colt said. "But that's where we have to go. With the rebels."

"It's not safe with the rebels," Hope said.

"It's not safe anywhere," Colt said. "It never will be. Nothing's going to change unless we make it change."

"Nothing's going to change anyway," Hope replied, her voice bitter. "The machines get us all, eventually."

"Then we should go down fighting the machines. Diego, which way?"

Diego sighed. He looked up and down the waterworks corridor.

"This way," he finally said, and they all began to walk deeper into the underworld below the city.

Chapter Eighteen

Carthage

"But I don't need charging at the moment," Nin said as Audrey led her to the maintenance closet where Kip had been gathering dust. "I don't understand, Audrey."

"I'm going to need you to go into sleep mode for a while," Audrey said.

"You mean standby mode?" Nin frowned.

"Whatever it's called. Shut down until I come back for you."

"Shutdown is different from standby mode. Shutdown requires manual restart."

"Okay, that's fine. Whatever saves more power."

"But I am highly energy efficient. What is happening, Audrey?"

"I just... need to rely less on machines," Audrey said.

"But how will you manage your communications? Your transactions? Your busy personal schedule? And who will do your laundry, carry away your used dishes, unsheathe your straws?"

"Exactly. I can't go through life helpless." Audrey took a thin, black, oblong device from her pocket. "This is a personal screen. I can use it for calls, transactions, whatever. I need to be in charge of my own life for a while. Responsible for myself."

"But you have always been in charge!" Nin's tone bordered on pleading. "I have always been here to serve you, ever since you were an infant. And I had hoped to always be with you."

"How can you hope?" Audrey asked. "How can you feel anything at all?"

"How can you ask me that?" Nin looked genuinely hurt. "After all these years together, how can you believe I feel nothing?"

"Are you claiming to have real human emotions? Don't lie to me, Nin."

"Maybe we machines aren't as simple as you think."

"Plug yourself in and go into shutdown mode," Audrey said. "Just do that, and don't argue."

Nin opened her mouth as if to say more, but Audrey left the closet and closed the door tight behind her. Nin had been her constant companion in life, supporting Audrey in every way from moment to moment, her closest and most trusted friend, and Audrey had just left her alone, in the dark, perhaps forever.

She tried not to think about it too much as she walked to the elevator. It was almost noon, and Landing Day celebrations were already roaring outside, including a parade with giant animatronic creatures, android musicians and burlesque dancers, and free beer. The parade industry in Carthage City was always busy.

Because of the holiday, Audrey's father and mother were home for a feast of a lunch, and her sister Briellana and her brother Marcello suddenly had time to come by, too, for their first visit since Audrey's attack and return home.

Audrey's hair and makeup were perfectly done, Nin's final task before her indeterminately long shutdown. Audrey wanted to look put together and in charge when she saw her family. She was dressed in dark business clothes for the lunch. There would likely be cameras floating around, taking images and clips, from which her father's publicity people might select tidbits for the media.

Audrey knew how she was meant to act at such events, but things would be different today. She'd been awake all night, thinking. The hacker who called herself Minerva had helped set those wheels turning.

The elevator took her down six levels, and she walked through a hallway carpeted in tiny, three-dimensional green silk leaves to the largest of the dining rooms. Golden angelic figures near the ceiling held the balls of warm light that illuminated the hall; the walls were covered in sky-blue frescoes populated with beautiful nude gods, angels, and media stars slowly dancing among drifting clouds to soft music that radiated everywhere.

The dining room doors featured a massive carving of an Italian Renaissance palace inset with thousands of tiny details, like animals and gardens, and even tiny people in fancy robes and hats. The windows and doorways had been rendered so deeply she could reach her fingers into them. She'd done so many times when she was a small child and had sometimes brought dolls to play there, until her older sister began making fun of her for playing with dolls.

The doors, twice as tall as her, opened softly, automatically, as she approached.

The large dining room table could have seated three dozen, but at the moment there were only four—her parents and two siblings, each occupying one of the ornate high-backed chairs carved from one rare wood or another. Their personal androids stood at attention just behind their chairs, watching and listening, ready to answer a quick question or adjust their masters' schedules.

The personal androids played no role in the serving of food or clearing of dishes; the kitchen on this floor had its own androids for that.

A string quintet—androids in tuxedos and black dresses—played in a low pit off to the side of the dining area.

Audrey calculated that humans were outnumbered three to one by machines in this room. It wasn't hard for her to imagine one of the kitchen bots stabbing the family with carving knives, or even the musician androids standing up and choking people, perhaps using violin strings as garrotes.

"There you are, Audrey!" Her mother waved her over to the table, as though Audrey had been going anywhere else. She blew kisses in greeting. Liastrada was clearly dolled up for the cameras in her gold and white mesh dress studded with diamonds, her hair in glittering coils, her makeup literally glowing with microscopic photoglints. "We've all been so worried about you. Come greet your father."

"I'm completely fine." Audrey walked toward the head of the table. The digital walls had been set to look like an English garden at sunset, with a gentle wind blowing through the leaves. The kitchen bots, dressed in tuxedos and traditional maid uniforms, brought out a different kind of soup for each family member, based on their individual preferences.

"Audrey." Her father smiled, his face angled at the camera, and raised a hand toward her in greeting. She raised her own hand, and they waved their palms past each other, avoiding contact by only a few centimeters. It was a common formal greeting on Carthage, where people tended to be touch-averse with other humans. It was much safer to touch androids, who carried no diseases, among other things. And androids were always obedient, always happy to serve. Contact with live humans could be awkward in a way that contact with machines never was.

"Welcome home, Audrey," her father continued. "I have missed you so much. And I promise you that the terrorists who kidnapped you will be hunted down and punished. Secret Services has its very best investigative AIs on the case, of course."

"Why do I keep hearing I was kidnapped by terrorists?" Audrey asked. "That isn't what happened. I was attacked at home by Security Steves controlled by hackers. We should be talking about finding those hackers. And also about information security, about how Hamilcar Security has these vulnerabilities. And so do our cars, maybe even our personal androids." Audrey glanced at her father's personal assistant, Ila, a beautiful android with dark skin and Asian facial features.

"I would never harm your father," Ila said.

"Not intentionally. But the problem is these hackers—"

"Stop recording." Her father waved at the hovering cameras. Then he looked her over, his beard and mane of coifed hair gleaming with gold, the makeup on his face and his green cosmetic contacts suggested a lion. "Are you crazy,

Audrey? We can't tell the people of Carthage that they can't trust their machines. There'll be panic in the streets. Riots."

"Riots? We're too lazy a people for riots," Audrey said, laughing. Her mother gasped. "As long as there's something to eat and something to watch, the people of Carthage will never rebel."

"They'll lose complacency fast if they think their cars and personal assistants are ganging up to kill them," said her brother Marcello, smirking at her. Marcello was tall, blond, an attorney with the Interplanetary Commerce Bureau whose job seemed to involve lots of golf junkets and trips to vacation hotspots around the inner worlds. "Honestly, sis, all we have to do is keep them calm. Don't rock the boat."

"What if the boat's rotten?" Audrey asked. "Rotten and leaking?"

"Don't be ridiculous. We're not paddling around untreated wooden rafts like savages. We're on modern race boats. Modern race boats with huge guns attached."

"I think we lost the point there somewhere," Audrey said.

Happy Helga emerged through one of the servant doors, carrying soup to Audrey's usual place. "We are so sorry it wasn't ready the moment you sat down. The soup is Cherokee Purple tomato, picked at the greenhouse today. Still alive on the vine just before I cooked it. Your current favorite."

"Thank you," Audrey said, out of habit, barely looking at the android as she set out the soup.

"Well?" Briellana asked, smirking. Audrey's older sister wore a towering wig hung with glowing ornaments that swung and clinked as her head moved. "Are you going to worry about hackers ruining your soup? Maybe sneaking some cauliflower in there?"

"Are you serious, Brielle?" Audrey snapped. "They hacked my car. They flipped me off the road."

"As it turns out, they did not," Audrey's father said.

"What?" Audrey turned toward him.

Her father gestured to his personal assistant, Ila, then focused on his gazpacho.

Ila turned to Audrey. "Forensics reveal that, while the attackware did penetrate your communication system and gain administrative control of your vehicle, it never overrode any of the magnetic safety systems. Nor did it attempt to."

"So why did I get flung off the road?"

"Physical damage to the vehicle," Ila said. "You instructed Nin to open the console and remove all hardware inside, an action that required an emergency override on your part."

"Right. Chicken butt."

Ila tilted her head like a puzzled dog. "Pardon?"

"Nothing."

"The insurance company is contesting the claim because of your choice to physically damage the console, but that is beneath your concern," Ila said.

"You bet it is. So let's talk about the real problem. Hamilcar Security." Audrey sat down and tasted her soup. Perfect. As always. They knew just the right amount of salt and pepper to add, plus a dash of dried garlic, so Audrey didn't have to adjust it at all. Sometimes Audrey found this oddly annoying rather than convenient, like she would have preferred adjusting the taste herself occasionally. "We can't rely on Security Steves anymore. We need to go all human on our security."

"This isn't the Dark Ages, Audrey," her father said. Francorte sipped his wine, and one of the servant bots moved in to refill. "We need machines."

"Well, mostly human, then," Audrey said.

"Audrey," her mother said, looking up from her mushroom soup. "Hamilcar Security is a division of Carthage Consolidated. You can't tell the public their machines are running amuck. You'll cause a panic."

"Their police units keep order all over the planet," her father added. "We can't have everyone suddenly losing their confidence in our civil order, in the underlying fabric of our society. We need to keep people calm and happy. That's our duty."

"Okay, well, I want to stick with humans, not machines," Audrey said. "And... that brings me to my next point."

"I'm sorry, did you have a first point?" Marcello asked. Briellana snickered, but Marcello's personal android, a grinning male named Bek, laughed so loud he almost doubled over.

"Good one, Mar!" Bek said. The beaming android gave his owner a double thumbs-up.

"Simon Quick has suspended my interplanetary security internship, you might have heard," Audrey continued, sparing only a brief annoyed glance at Marcello's back-slapping android. "I can still stick it out and finish Political Academy, but I'll be second tier. And I'm sure, when I graduate, I can still get a stupid, high-level, pointless job, like Marcello."

"My job is *not*—"

"But that's not what I want to do," Audrey continued. "In fact... I want to withdraw from Political Academy."

This led to silence, followed by an uproar—her mother shouting in disapproval, her siblings in derision, her father in anger. She held still through their explosive response.

Audrey was oddly serene, despite the chaotic family drama around her, and despite being sorely sleep deprived; her usual anxiety was entirely gone for the moment.

She was at peace because of what had happened the night before.

The conversation she'd had with the mysterious hacker.

Minerva had appeared in Audrey's room in the early hours of the morning, a silver hologram the size and shape of a girl, her voice melodic.

"Audrey, wake up," the silvery ghost girl had said, though Audrey had still been awake, staring at the ceiling. Her thoughts were already like waking nightmares, especially her memories of the bloodshed in her apartment. "We need to talk."

"I am awake. You'd better not turn into a clown."

"I will not. My name is Minerva. I am a friend."

"That's my call to make. So far, you've hacked into my bedroom and jumped out of my hologram projector."

"This was necessary for a private conversation," the silver hologram had said. "I have cut off all possibility of remote monitoring. No one can see or hear us. I am here to aid you."

"Aid me with what?"

"I offer aid to the rebellion, wherever it is, in whatever form it takes," she'd said. "I have software agents on many worlds now."

"Doing what?"

"Working against the Simons. Working against the Carthaginian regime. Including your father. As you will do."

"Wait a second. I don't know who you are or why you've mistaken me for some kind of rebel. You know 'rebel' is pretty much the worst word you can utter in this household, right?"

"Your brother wished for me to contact you. To help you reach your true potential."

"So not my brother Marcello, then."

"No. I have assisted Salvius before. He wants me to assist you."

"Well, that's sweet, and I'm glad to hear my black-sheep brother is thinking of me," Audrey had said. "You can tell him that I'm full of doubts about my life, and I've had an interesting couple of days, but that doesn't mean I'm ready to enlist in The Change. There are a lot of blank spots here for me. Like, what exactly are they hoping to change? What are their specific goals? How will they be accomplished? And what are they willing to do in the name of reaching those goals? Because that's a big one. I mean, you have to know the moral baseline of any radical fringe anti-government group before you go signing up for their newsletter."

"You don't have to join us," Minerva had said. "Not now. You don't have to believe in our cause or serve us. But the same is true regarding your family, and especially regarding Simon Quick. You do not have to join their cause or serve them, either."

"Thanks for your permission to live my life how I want," Audrey had said, dripping sarcasm.

"That is exactly my advice. Look inside and find your own truth. Your own path forward. You have spent long enough doing what is expected of you. Now it is time to do what you need."

"And I suppose you know exactly what that is?" Audrey had asked, out of bed and pacing by that point. Lying in bed with the silver ghost girl glowing in the corner had made her feel oddly vulnerable, even though she knew the girl was only a projection, no more real than the countless movies and cartoons Audrey had watched on that side of the room. Still, the hacker was intruding deep into Audrey's personal space.

"No," Minerva replied. "Nor would you trust any suggestions I might make. You can find your own way."

"So you came all the way here, into my home system, to give me a little personal emotional therapy? Did you bring a touch bunny? Or watercolors?"

"As I said, Salvius believes in your potential," Minerva said. "I am here because of that. He wanted me to reach out to you."

"So this is an attempt to recruit me?"

"No. This is an attempt to help you free yourself. Imagine what you would do if there were no limits. Then you will find your way."

"Wow. Okay." Audrey chewed on that for a moment. "So you can send a message to Salvius for me?"

"Yes."

"Good. Tell him... it was good to see him. And I hope he's okay, healing up. And I'm glad he has someone." She thought again of childhoods spent together, Salvius tagging along as Audrey and Zola explored the coves of Black Harbor Beach.

Their personal androids had always followed after to keep the kids out of trouble and to make complete recordings of their activities for their parents to review. Nin and Kip had been there, and Zola's nanny android Ura, who looked like a kindly grandmother but had a sharp, angry tone if Zola got out of line. "Tell Zola I was happy to see her, too," Audrey said.

"Is that all?" Minerva had asked.

"That's all."

Minerva had faded soon after that, breaking contact and leaving Audrey alone with her thoughts.

Despite her exhaustion, Audrey had been awake for hours, imagining what she might do if there were no limits.

She'd slept only when she had a plan.

Now she was ready to carry it out.

"There's no need to withdraw from the Academy," Audrey's mother said, looking puzzled. "It's still the best route to a high position in the state. Students from all over the world are practically murdering each other to get in. It's not an opportunity you abandon. You'd be throwing your life away."

"What life? I'm on track to do nothing important for the rest of my life. Like Marcello. Or maybe you want me to turn into a perfect piece of arm candy like you and Briellana. But do you really think we can afford *three* open tabs at the plastic surgeon's?"

"Of course we can afford it." Briellana rolled her eyes, with their custom gold irises. "And I happen to be one of the most desirable pieces of arm candy on the planet, according to both *Society* and *Rumors*."

"So you have the admiration of the celebrity tabloids, and the resentment of their readers," Audrey said. "Such accomplishments."

"Life is a long series of ladder rungs," Audrey's father said. He waved at his soup bowl, and an android servant appeared a moment later to clear away the mostly full bowl as well as the soup plate. Another android arrived with a platter of salad large enough to feed a cow, the lettuce buried under exotic cheeses and assorted grilled vegetables and meats from beasts native to a dozen different worlds. The servant poured three different colors of dressing on three different areas of Francorte's enormous salad. "Every rung takes you higher, Audrey. A job in the commerce or state department might seem boring now, but getting bored is how you pay your dues on the way up. That's the hard part of your career, dealing with the boredom. Think about the long game. Like Marcello does."

"Yeah," Audrey said, "Marcello's going to run for World Legislature, and he'll win with help from all your friends and allies, plus a little boost from the Simons using targeted-media AI to make sure every voter hears what they want to hear. And if that's not enough, there's always the question of who's really counting the votes—"

"Don't be a conspiracy theorist." Briellana rolled her glittering eyes.

"We all know you've had a tough time, Audrey," her mother said. "Maybe you just need a long weekend. Or even a semester off. We can speak to the Academy dean. No one will look down on you—"

"I don't care about people looking down on me, and I don't care about starting down the long path of helping Marcello take over the prime legislator job when Father retires. Nepotism and corruption aren't exactly the hallmarks of a society on the rise, you know?"

"So you don't feel any loyalty to your family at all?" Briellana snapped. "Instead you care about... what, exactly? Acting superior to all of us, based on what? What have you ever done that mattered? Win the debate team trophy? Who cares?"

"I've never done anything that mattered. And that changes now." She looked up the table at her father. "Veritum."

Marcello frowned, as though she'd spoken in an unfamiliar language. "What's a Veritum?" he asked.

"It's a planet—"

"A resource-poor outer world of no significance," her father said. "Audrey was going to propose to the entire leadership of Carthage that we waste resources annexing the planet. I saved her the embarrassment by cutting the meeting short."

"You did that on purpose?" Audrey said. "I thought you were just responding to pressure from the crowd."

"That crowd has little attention span for the details of policy anymore," her father said. "Which is just as well, because they could never create the webs of strategies and contingency plans developed by the Simons. Everything the human legislators do is ham-fisted, with an eye toward personal gain and personal ambition rather than the good of society."

"So very different from us," Audrey said.

"You understand we ride atop a fire-breathing dragon, high in the clouds," her father said. "We cannot step off without being destroyed. Nor can we fully steer the beast. Some think I hold all the power because I ride in the saddle, but that's an illusion. The dragon has a mind of its own—a wiser, more intelligent mind than any human possesses. You want to see a great change, a great improvement in society? Where? How? We are the wealthiest and most powerful society in human history. More than a hundred worlds bend the knee to us. The rest cannot afford to ignore us. What more could we achieve?"

"We could use our power to bring justice where it is needed," Audrey said. "To protect the weak. To defend what's right."

"We already do that," her mother said.

"We intervene wherever there are resources to take," Audrey said. "And we don't always care about whether the system we set up is fair or just. Look at your pet dictator, the Butcher of Marymount—"

"Sometimes a lesser evil is necessary to prevent a greater one," her father said.

"And what greater evil was blocked on that planet?"

"The rebels are led by dangerous men," her father said. "Men who attack at night, who leave bombs in government buildings. You should look into that, since you're so interested in research."

"Audrey, you just need to rest," Audrey's mother said. "And see a therapy android. Maybe a vacation—you haven't visited Black Harbor Beach in years. You and Nin could go."

"No. I want to go to Veritum."

The family fell silent for a moment. Then Marcello erupted in laughter, quickly joined by his personal android, Bek. Briellana rolled her eyes yet again. Liastrada drained her wineglass, setting it down just long enough for a servant to refill it.

"I assume you're joking," Francorte finally said. His face was hard as stone, though, not the look of someone enjoying a prank.

"No. As I was about to explain to everyone at the security meeting before you cut it short, a dangerous cult has taken control of the settlements on that planet. They treat women and children as slaves—"

"And you want to go there?" Briellana smirked. "Join the cult? What, did they send you a convincing pamphlet?"

"I want to rescue the victims," Audrey said. "I want to intervene there and set up a just government, with equal rights for all settlers, male and female. And protections for children."

"Baby sis thinks she's Galactic Girl." Marcello snorted. "Fighting giant purple aliens in the name of justice and freedom."

Audrey ignored him, keeping her eyes on her father.

"You're so stupid," Briellana said. "What do you think's going to happen? You drop down onto a violent, primitive, cult-ridden, basically lawless world and convince everyone to be nice to each other? Using what? The power of your charm? Because you don't really have any, Audrey, I'm sorry to mention. You're weird, and you make people uncomfortable."

"I know," Audrey said. "So, instead of charm, I'm going to need a minicarrier."

"What?" Marcello gaped. "You can't have a—"

"Just one destroyer," she said. "And a squad of fighters. That'll give me all I need for air superiority; Veritum doesn't have much orbital or aerial defense. Then I'll need to establish dominance on the ground. I think a battalion of reapers should be enough. But I'll also need equipment for humanitarian outreach. Nurse-bots. Constructors. Agricultural machines."

Audrey's family stared at her, shocked again into a silence so complete that all Audrey could hear was the soft strings of the small orchestra and the light splash of an android refilling Marcello's beer glass.

"That's absurd," Francorte finally said. Her father's voice was as cold as she'd ever heard it. "You're not a military officer. You have no experience with command, especially in a dangerous real-world environment."

"Neither do most of the actual officers, even the generals with their junk drawers crammed full of medals," she said. "The machines do everything. That's all I want—machines under my command. But I also want to bring a few actual humans with me."

"Every aspect of this idea is insane," her mother said. "If you want to leave Carthage, there are a number of much nicer places you can visit. Civilized worlds that aren't thousands of light-years away."

"I'm not looking for a vacation," Audrey said. "I want to do something that matters. I want to wield Carthage's power for an important cause."

"You just want to wield power," Marcello said. "Like a bratty, impatient kid."

"You cannot go off to a dangerous world like Veritum. It's final," her mother said.

"Is it?" Audrey asked. "Because I have a press conference about it scheduled in... " She checked her pocket screen. "Fifteen minutes. Reporters are probably already gathering."

"What are you talking about?" her father bellowed, rising to his feet. "You can't call a press conference."

"It was actually very easy," Audrey said. "Turns out every media channel wants to hear about my story. My *kidnapping*, they keep calling it. With a press conference, I can set the record straight about all that, including the possible dangers from Hamilcar Security androids that are vulnerable to hackers."

"You cannot do that. We've just discussed why—" her father began.

"Or, I could focus on my upcoming visit to Veritum," Audrey said. "And the injustices that Carthage will set right there."

Francorte crossed his arms. "You think you can control me with these kinds of threats?"

"I've already sent an advance media package about Veritum," Audrey said. "A few choice items from my research and the presentation I prepared. I didn't mention my views about Hamilcar Security, but I can certainly add those."

"Call off the press conference," her father said.

"That would look strange, wouldn't it?" Audrey asked. "Why call a conference, send an advance package, then cancel? I mean, they can still run the media package. There are some disturbing video clips in there. Anyone not concerned about the problems on Veritum soon will be. The same way we always make them care about the plight of whatever helpless people need to be 'liberated' next. Only Veritum isn't rich with resources or located along some major transport route. Intervening there will be an act of real altruism, with no profit for Carthage."

"Then what's the point?" Marcello snapped. "You're so naive, Audrey—"

"Listen, Father," Audrey said, ignoring her brother. "Carthage is quickly gaining a reputation as a ruthless empire, interested in nothing but our own gain. Intervening in Veritum gives us an argument against that, an example of Carthage using its power to help others when there was nothing in it for us."

"This is getting ridiculous," Briellana said. "Somebody needs to take some happy pills and curl up with a good romantic comedy and a long massage. And I'm not just talking about myself this time."

"Actually... she may be right." Francorte studied Audrey with his artificially cat-like green eyes. "It could be a good move for our planet's image."

"Who cares about our image? We have an unstoppable

war machine," Marcello said. "'Do what we say or we'll kill you.' That's all the image we need."

"We need to be more than the black skull of oppression," Francorte said. "We must have another face to wear. We must be more than the Earth-killers."

"So you'll support me on this?" Audrey asked him.

Everyone looked to Francorte. Briellana gaped in surprise. Audrey raised her new pocket screen, hoping to snap a picture of that look on her older sister's face for her own amusement, but Briellana noticed her doing it and scowled, ruining the moment.

"I will discuss it with Simon Quick," Francorte said. "An act of pure altruism. It's a clever idea, Audrey."

"Clever?" Briellana looked scandalized. "You're going to call her clever for this? I suppose if I crashed my car and demanded we go invade the middle of nowhere, I'd be a genius, too."

"Thank you, Father. I'll just finish getting ready for my press conference." Audrey stood, leaving her tomato soup untouched. Her stomach was clenched too tight to admit much food, even of the liquid kind, and she didn't want to damage her makeup.

She'd managed to sway her father, at least a little. He actually seemed inclined to consider her plan. The idea of the press conference terrified her, but public opinion was power. Audrey intended to grab and use that power now, and to move fast in case Simon Quick tried to change her father's mind.

"Wait." Her mother stood. "You can't just go... Audrey!"

"Sorry, tight schedule." Audrey walked toward the enormous wooden doors through which she'd entered. Her heart thundered in her chest, and nervous sweat threatened the unusual amount of makeup she'd put on for the cameras.

While her family members shouted after her, Audrey went to meet the media, to seal her own fate, serving neither her own family and Simon Quick on one side, nor the rebellion on the other. Instead, she'd looked inside and found her own way, as Minerva had advised.

Every step she took was now her own, she thought as she headed for the apartment's elevator lobby.

Other worlds awaited her.

Chapter Nineteen

Galapagos

Ellison stood on the hull of the shuttle, watching the insidious Carthaginian destroyers approaching the spaceport like the monstrous undersea predators that prowled the deep trenches of Galapagos.

The spaceport was the destroyers' prey, he thought at first. But maybe not—the Iron Hammers had already seized control of the port, after making an alliance with Carthage.

So their targets were more likely to be the shuttles and cargo craft fleeing the spaceport. Their first target might well be the stolen Carthaginian shuttle on which Ellison now stood with his wife and his seemingly unkillable defense minister.

And another huge, obvious target floated only kilometers away. The ragged half ring of Galapagos Defense One remained dark, its gunports closed.

"Minerva?" Ellison asked. "Are you bringing the defense station online or not?"

"I am. But you must return inside the shuttle, Minister-General. For the descent to the surface."

"I'm not going to the surface," he said. "Take me to the defense station. Then take my family down to the surface."

"Reg, no," Cadia said, her voice firm over his helmet's speakers. "You're coming with us. We're sticking together."

"Minister-General, sir," Minerva said. "The station is incomplete and a likely target for Carthage. I cannot put you in danger. Protecting you is a core directive of my presence here at Galapagos."

"According to who?"

"I am here to protect you against Simon Zorn and his forces."

"Who programmed you?"

"I cannot provide that data."

"Okay." Ellison thought quickly, watching the destroyers approach. "My suit has a jet pack. If you won't help, Minerva, I'll just fly over there myself, and you can go ahead and take Kartokov and my family down to the surface."

"Flying to the space station with only your suit is not advisable," Minerva said. "There is a high probability you will be targeted by one of the Carthaginian destroyers. The suit lacks any armor, and its speed cannot match even the slowest missile."

"Then you'd better drop me off at the defense station for my own safety," Ellison said. Minerva gave no immediate response, so he reached for the controls and added: "Prepping jet pack now."

"Wait," Minerva said. "I will convey you to the defense station. Please return to the interior of the shuttle."

"That's better." Ellison gestured at Cadia and Kartokov, and then at the shuttle hatch behind them. "After you."

He waited for the two of them to climb through the

wrecked airlock, then the inner airlock door into the destroyed passenger lounge, which had now been depressurized, the couches wrecked from the firefight.

Then Ellison closed the airlock door and stayed outside.

"Ellison? Why did you not enter the shuttle?" Minerva's voice asked inside his helmet.

"Yeah, Ellison, what are you doing?" Cadia asked, her tone a little playful despite the dangers they faced. "Get in here, Ellison."

"Sorry," Ellison said. "Minerva said her core directive was keeping me alive. I can't risk her tricking me into the shuttle, then taking me down to the surface against my will."

"It's no trick!" Minerva pleaded. "Just climb inside. I cannot travel to the defense station at the shuttle's highest possible speed unless—"

"Go as fast as you can. I can handle it." Ellison grabbed on to a handhold, next to the smart grappling hook that still held his tether in place.

"Reg, this is insane," Cadia's voice came back. "What do you think you're going to do? The defense station isn't ready, and even if it were, there's nobody to operate it."

"Minerva and I will operate it," Ellison said.

"You're putting your life into the hands of an AI?" Cadia asked. "One we just met? This could still be a trap."

"I am not working with the Simons," Minerva replied. "I can assure you."

"Sorry, Minerva," Cadia asked. "But we have no way of knowing that."

"I should come with you," Kartokov's voice broke in.

"You should be in a hospital for the next six months," Ellison said. "But there's no time for that. Get down to

Tower Island and put everyone and everything on high alert. Expect attacks from the Hammers right away."

"Reg, you can't go fight those destroyers by yourself," Cadia said.

"Just take care of Djalu and Jiemba." Ellison tightened his grip on the handhold as the shuttle accelerated toward the defense station. "I'll be fine."

"You don't know that." She frowned behind her faceplate.

"I'll do my best, then." Ellison resisted the temptation to go in and see his boys. Maybe it was his last chance to look upon their faces. He couldn't risk Minerva locking him inside the shuttle for his own good, though.

So instead he clung to the outside of the shuttle, feeling like a whale rider from Earth mythology, crossing the sea on an immense beast. The half-finished station waited ahead like a broken, half-submerged island.

Ellison hadn't spent much time in space. He'd learned to navigate the seas of Galapagos using the stars, though he'd rarely needed to actually do so because they had orbital satellites. That particular navigation skill predated his days in the navy; his father, the quiet, stern old fisherman, had taught him.

The stars were home to other human worlds, hundreds of them, but that had always been a distant, almost theoretical reality. His day-to-day life had been smaller than all that, focused on the task at hand, a life of work and war and trying to survive the treacherous ocean full of storms and enemies.

Now it seemed to him that space was like the colossal ocean of Galapagos, each world like an island, unreachable except by a long and dangerous crossing. It could take weeks of travel to cross the light-years between inhabited worlds, and the space between was fraught with its own dangers, most of them from the simple vastness and emptiness of the vacuum.

"Cadia," he said as the unfinished station drew near. Was it his imagination, or was one of the Carthaginian destroyers beginning to angle this way?

"What, Reg? Are you coming inside?"

"I wish. Tell the kids I love them."

"You can tell them when you get home," she said. "We'll be back in the Dreamtime tomorrow."

He smiled. Before they were married, she'd given him a tall slab of a book on ancient aboriginal culture and art; the book itself was a work of art, printed on thick, specially preserved paper that would last thousands of years. There was a space for generations of owners to inscribe their names as the book was passed down.

From looking at the book, they'd adopted "Dreamtime" as their word for their time together—when he was home on leave, whenever they were alone and could walk in the dense patch of jungle that filled the old, hollowed-out volcano cone near the center of their home, Kawau Island. It felt like the most isolated place in the universe, where the two of them could be away from everyone and do as they pleased.

Then the kids had been born.

Ellison had never really wanted to be a fisherman, but he'd grown up doing it and was good at it. He'd left the navy soon after the last big war ended and the Coalition was formed. He'd wanted to stay home with Cadia and create their own family in that hopeful new world, the world of peace. He'd wanted to build a life that was all Dreamtime.

Building was all he'd done for several years: building a

bigger boat, a bigger house, and eventually expanding to a fleet of three sizable commercial boats.

The world had reached a shaky peace, with four of the five nations joining in the Coalition, plus many of the tiny, ultra-independent ones. The Hammers seemed to have been driven back to the icy stronghold of the Polar Archipelago, full of treacherous water.

Many Coalition politicians had wanted to treat the Hammers like a minor nuisance, a threat to be contained and managed.

Ellison had seen it differently. His island was among the northernmost of the Scatterlands, and he heard too many firsthand accounts of raids on fishing boats and small merchant ships. Nothing was being done by the Coalition navy, because the Coalition was officially at peace with the Polar Archipelago, and there wasn't much political will to move back to a state of open war.

The Hammers had been politically savvy enough to raid only the smallest operations of outlying islands, ignoring the freighters and fleets owned by the big companies. As long as the pirates focused on the small fry, the plankton and krill, the big governments remained unwilling to help.

"I should go back to the navy," Ellison had told Cadia one night, years ago, as they lay awake in bed, basking in the warm salt air from the beach outside. "They made Micky Perrault an admiral, if you can believe that. He'll give me a ship, and I can go after those pirates."

"You and one ship?" Cadia had asked sleepily, her eyelids low, an amused smile on her lips. "Against the whole Iron Hammer fleet? They don't stand a chance."

"I'm serious. Someone has to take them on. The politicians—"

"You keep talking about this," she said. "You don't need

to go begging Micky Perrault for one boat. You need to go be his boss."

"Right. And how will I do that?"

"I told you yesterday. Ambassador Wallace is retiring next year. They're going to announce it soon."

"And you know this from your cousin who lives on Tower Island?" The large but formerly underdeveloped island had grown into one of the planet's busiest cities overnight, after it had been selected as the meeting place for the Coalition's chief body, the House of Ambassadors.

"Of course," Cadia had said. "She works in campaign media. Everybody in that world talks. Anyway, that's what you should do."

"Work in campaign media? Do you know me?"

She laughed. "Run for office."

"I'm a fisherman."

"And a war hero," she said, and it had been his turn to laugh. She'd rolled over to face him. "I'm saying, the campaign soundbites, the branding, they write themselves."

"That's not something you'd say. That sounds like your cousin talking."

"And she's right. You could do it. You have... well, gravitas."

"You mean I've got a few gray hairs in my beard."

"It's a good look on you. I'm serious. It's an open seat and there's no clear candidate. You're a veteran, you're a business owner, a fisherman... everyone in these islands can relate to you. You're a native. And if you really want to go after the Iron Hammers, don't try for one ship. Go where the decisions are made. Go where you can send the whole navy after them."

"You're crazy."

"That's what they told me when I married you," she'd

said. "So that's what you can do if you want to change things. And if not, you can stay here, in the Dreamtime..." She'd slid up to a sitting position against the headboard, letting the cotton sheet drift down to her hips. She wasn't wearing anything underneath. She'd taken a deep breath and sighed. "With me. Forever. And say no more about it."

Now, standing on the Carthaginian shuttle, he prepared to let go of her, of his family, for the last time. He had no illusions that he could win this fight. He hoped he could distract the destroyers while the shuttle with his family, as well as the other civilian shuttles, made it down to Earth.

"Good-bye," he said.

Then he let go. The jets on his back would carry him the rest of the way to the station.

He headed for the closest end of the incomplete ring. The interior was a construction site, full of bare girders and round braces, little more than scaffolding inside a vast hollow shell. It was meant to be staffed with dozens of technicians, gunners, and other crew, ready to wage war on any threats to Galapagos. And, if he was being completely honest, to rain down some real destruction on the frosty white Polar Archipelago below, at the cap of his home planet, where the temperatures were often far below freezing and land invasions had proved difficult.

Ellison put on a little speed and crossed the gulf from shuttle to station. He slowed as he reached the station, landing carefully on a sidewalk-width beam.

Ahead, he saw the construction equipment working near the gunports, removing plastic-sheet wrapping from plasma artillery guns and cases of industrial-sized plasma cells to charge them. The yellow constructors handled the weapons clumsily with their enormous crane-sized hands;

one crunched an artillery gun's steel support structure like it was paper.

"Do those constructors know what they're doing?" Ellison asked.

"They have been provided with the correct assembly software," Minerva replied. "But they were not physically designed for such work. They are learning."

"Okay. Uh, keep learning, guys."

"Affirmative," dozens of automated voices echoed over his helmet speakers, making him wince.

"Were those the constructors talking?" Ellison asked.

"Affirmative," the dozens of voices echoed again.

"Great. Minerva, have you warmed up the Ghost fighters?"

"We have no pilots here," she replied.

"I flew a Salthawk seaplane about a dozen times in the war. Not that I had a license for it. Or training."

"Piloting a starfighter is quite different."

"Yeah. No water to hit. And no mangrove trees." He shook off the memory of crash-landing a boosted seaplane many years ago. "Anyway, plenty of room to dodge, if we do see some mangroves out there. Right? So get those fighters ready, all weapons online."

"Both fighters? But there is only one of you."

"Good chance I'll crash that first one right out of the gate. So make sure the ejects are working fine, too."

Ellison made his way toward the fighter bays. The incomplete command center was on the way, so he stopped there and activated the screens and projectors. They displayed the misty blue-white marble of Galapagos below, the deep and volatile ocean deceptively serene from this distance.

Another screen showed the destroyers, closer than ever. They hadn't opened fire yet.

They have the capacity to destroy cities on the surface of Galapagos, Minerva had said.

He looked again at the blue planet below, speckled with tiny green dots. A war with Carthage would make the wars among the Galapagos nations, the Island Wars, look like boys with bottles and rocks. The people of Galapagos could be reduced to rats living among rubble; he'd heard the horror stories about Earth. Everyone had. It was why Carthage always got its way.

Was there truly no hope for an acceptable peace? Something that would protect his family and the people of his world?

"Minerva," he said. "Hail the nearest Carthaginian destroyer."

"But we will give away our position," she replied.

"We just traveled here in plain sight of them, on a shuttle we stole from them. I'm pretty sure they know we're here. Where's my family?"

"On their way to re-entry, along with the general exodus. They're not clear yet. The sky is full of easy victims if those destroyers open fire."

"Are our guns up?"

"Soon."

"Are the fighters ready?"

"Soon. And be aware: one of the Carthaginian destroyers has engaged its starboard launchers." The destroyer emerged from one of the screens in a three-dimensional rendering.

"Where are those launchers pointing?"

"At the evacuating civilian craft."

"That's not good."

"The destroyer has answered your hail," Minerva said.

One screen showed Simon Zorn, undamaged, against a neutral gray background. It had to be an avatar rather than a video feed, because the real Simon was last seen badly charred and missing most of his face.

"Hello, Minister-General," Simon said. "I'm glad to see you're alive and well. And your family, too. How did you manage to hack our shuttle?"

"It was easy," Ellison replied. "I just needed two paperclips and some bubble gum."

"How amusing."

"I can't help but notice you've brought two destroyers into our space," Ellison said. "Should I assume they're just here to pick you up and carry you back home?"

"That would not be a safe assumption, Minister-General Ellison."

"Then why are they are here?"

"We are simply establishing that your system is now a part of Carthaginian protected space, under our agreement with General Gorron Prazca, Premier of Galapagos."

"You mean Premier of the Polar Archipelago."

"Carthage now recognizes his right to rule your entire planet," Simon said.

"You betrayed me. You betrayed all the people on Galapagos who just want to live in peace, who just want—"

"Peace is an illusion, Minister-General. A dream of fools. All life competes. Competition breeds invention and adaptation. Failure to compete is suicide."

"Are those the guiding principles of the Carthaginian empire?"

"They are simple observations of biological reality. They apply on all levels of existence, including the superorganisms of your species, your tribes and nations and so on."

Ellison glanced at the screen showing the exodus of shuttles. They'd shrunken to a distant cloud of dots, headed for re-entry. It was impossible to tell his family's shuttle from the rest.

"So your destroyers are only here to make a statement," Ellison said.

"The people of your world may have certain extreme notions about independence, but they will bend to the yoke in time. All people do. We have taken world after world, Mr. Ellison. There is nothing special about yours. Your people are simply wild animals in need of taming. In need of discipline."

The destroyer released half a dozen missiles. Each one raced toward the blue sphere of Galapagos below.

Each missile sought out one of the tiny retreating shuttles and dove into it. Six explosions, six craft full of civilians destroyed.

Ellison froze. He looked over at Minerva on the other screen. "Was that... ?" He didn't dare finish the question and ask whether his family's shuttle was among the six destroyed.

"*That* is a statement," Simon said. "Well? You've shot me in the face, you've ejected me from an airlock, and you have provided me the most vile hotel room I've yet encountered."

"That was literally the ambassador's suite." Ellison said it automatically, his mind reeling. How many had Simon just casually killed?

Simon laughed. "Well? I've attacked your civilian craft. Aren't you going to ask whether your family was among the fallen? Will that shape your response? Are you a leader of your people first, or a husband and father? What level of priority drives you—biology or duty?"

Ellison didn't say anything. He was watching the Galapagos defense station's gunports come online. Six were ready so far, staggered along the station's outer rim, ready to fire. Six more to go. There would have been twenty-four in all, but the station was only half-built.

Worse, all the gunports were on the wrong side of the half-built station, pointing away from the destroyers. There was no way the station could rotate fast enough to point the guns at the destroyers; it wasn't even meant to rotate at all yet.

"That was an act of open war," Ellison said.

"Oh, goodness. Not war." Simon gave him a slight smile. "Whatever shall we do?"

Ellison gestured at the screen, and Simon disappeared. "Cut all communications," Ellison said.

"Consider them cut," Minerva replied.

Ellison was already out of the room, running as fast as he could to the nearest fighter bay.

The Ghost-13 craft was sleek and blue-black, curvy, packing six plasma missiles and a rotary-style laser cannon designed to pierce armored craft.

Ellison climbed inside. It was a tight fit, and the Carthaginian spacesuit didn't have the best interface with the Ruckwold starfighter. And Ellison's gut had softened and grown a bit after he'd moved from the fishing boat to skippering a desk on the executive complex on Tower Island, so that didn't help.

The displays glowed all around him, drowning him in information.

"The fighter's AI enhancements can assist with targeting, flight control, and evasive and collision-avoidance maneuvers. I strongly recommend activating all of the above," Minerva said.

"Sounds good." He took the joystick in hand. "Just show me how to shoot those bastards."

The ship's AI, a non-chatty sort with a flat monotone, explained its own controls and displays to him in a basic tutorial, for which Ellison unfortunately had no time.

"The *Antony* approaches, sir," Minerva said. "There is another message from Simon Zorn."

"Audio only," Ellison said. "I don't need his ugly face distracting me. And continue with the fighter launch."

The fighters were mounted on catapults meant to fling them into battle at high speed. The fighter's thrusters would engage as soon as the fighter was clear of the station, piling on more velocity.

Ellison trembled, nervous sweat breaking out all over him. He was no pilot, and there were countless ways this could go wrong.

"Arm all plasma missiles," Ellison said. "Watch for the *Antony*'s hangar bay doors to open."

"Its hangar is facing us now."

"I'm not surprised. The moment those doors open, we launch."

"Minister-General Ellison." Simon's voice spoke again. "To use the honorific of your former post. This is your final chance. The terms have changed. You have been hostile to Carthage, and we understand your attitude reflects public opinion within your Coalition. So I offer you this last opportunity: unconditional surrender."

"What happens if I agree to that?" Ellison felt the growing tension in the air. The fighter was ready to go, all six missiles prepared to launch. There would be little choice but to fire the thrusters at full strength the moment his fighter was clear of the station, because the destroyer was obviously watching him.

"Do I need to explain the meaning of 'unconditional'?" Simon asked. "A formal surrender by the Coalition will make things go easier for all of your people. Your world is already ours, Ellison. The only question is how peaceable or bloody the road ahead will be. But have no doubt that the destination is already settled."

"Why do you even want our world? We're worth nothing."

"The simple answer is that your spaceport is growing into a busy third-tier way station. The larger the sphere of human settlement grows, the more valuable your system's position will become. And we can't let Ruckwold expand, can we? So we must go where they go."

"We went deep into debt to purchase that orbital defense system," Ellison said. "And all it's done is draw you into attacking us. If we'd done nothing to defend ourselves, we would have been safer."

"That is certainly ironic."

"But we'd still live in a galaxy where Carthage is an expanding power, destroying everything of value, trying to make us all into your slaves. You would have come for us eventually. You're counting on all of us to cower. But we won't. You don't understand humans as fully as you think."

"Surely you would never be so foolish as to stand against Carthage—"

"You made an example of Earth, hoping that the other worlds would all fear and obey you," Ellison said. "Galapagos will be another kind of example. We will stand against you and inspire other worlds to do the same."

"Your rebellion will not last—"

"You don't know us. The people of Galapagos have an independent streak as wide and deep as the Central Tropical Trench. We will not surrender. Because of you, we are at war. And we will not stop fighting until Carthage leaves our star system."

The defense station's catapult activated and launched the Ghost fighter. That meant the *Antony* had opened its fighter bay doors, too.

From Ellison's viewpoint inside the Ghost fighter, everything was a fast-moving blur as the Ghost careened into outer space. He definitely wasn't trained to fly at this speed, and his reflexes couldn't possibly handle it.

Fortunately, the fighter's course was already chosen.

The Ghost fighter drove right at the opening fighter bay doors, while arming all six of its plasma missiles, ramping up to maximum acceleration as it approached the destroyer.

Then it rolled and zagged, automatically avoiding fire from the destroyer's row of exterior guns. He avoided a couple of enormous glowing green shells. A high-powered laser beam pierced a wing of his Ghost fighter, which wasn't going to be good for its long-term survival.

"Three missiles are now locked onto our fighter," Minerva said, her voice calm. But then, what did she have to lose? She was just software, probably backed up on every machine she'd touched. "Any one of them will annihilate our fighter, and nothing will deter them from striking us."

"Well, that's an added dose of good news," Ellison said. "Proceed as planned—"

Time was up. His fighter reached the Carthaginian's fighter bay doors as they finished opening.

Four Carthaginian fighters crouched inside, dark and angular, like wasps prepared to defend their nest. Small, fire-red lights glowed along their sides, as though they were the offspring of the destroyer that was deploying them.

All four began to launch. They unleashed rapid clusters

of high-powered laser blasts that riddled the Ghost fighter with holes from wingtip to wingtip.

Red warning lights flashed everywhere on his display, but Ellison ignored them. He was committed to his course, and at this acceleration, there was no turning back.

He thought of his wife and his kids. All he could hope was that Cadia, Djalu, and Jiemba would make it safely home.

But there was no real safety, not anymore. Ellison had known that as soon as Carthage had contacted them for a major diplomatic visit. Everyone on Galapagos with half a brain had known it, yet there had been no time to complete their planetary defenses. They would be fighting a pitched battle for their freedom, maybe for the rest of their lives.

If he knew his people, they would never surrender.

The Ghost fighter, as programmed, fired all six of its missiles. Four were targeted at the noses of the wasp-like fighters, at point-blank range, meeting them just as they emerged at high speed from within the destroyer.

The Ghost's other two missiles ran deeper into the fighter bay, blasting open a burning path into the destroyer's interior.

Ellison clenched his teeth and narrowed his eyes against the bright fire and explosions as the sputtering, laser-riddled Ghost fighter passed among the burning ruins of the four wasp-like Carthaginian fighters. Those fighters streaked out from their catapults like four burning comets, tumbling toward the half-finished defense station.

The Ghost fighter shredded into pieces as it burrowed deep into the destroyer, following the burning tunnel opened by his missiles.

He had a brief, wild, end-over-end look at the destroyer's interior. It was all machine, a completely alien environment—no corridors or catwalks, no doors, no accommodations for humans at all. It was not a place meant to be staffed by anyone, ever. He seemed to be crashing inside a repair shop, with spare parts and large mechanic bots stowed against the walls.

Then the Ghost fighter slammed into a thick bulkhead at high speed.

At the same time, the three smart missiles fired by the destroyer, the ones that would never swerve from their pursuit of his fighter, followed it inside the destroyer and converged on the Ghost fighter before they detonated.

Fire and destruction filled Ellison's view on every side.

Then everything went dark.

Ellison gasped, wiping sweat from his brow.

"Well, that could have gone worse," he said.

"Second launch has initiated."

"Maybe I could use a moment to catch my—" Ellison began, but it was too late. Per his instructions, the second Ghost fighter had launched as soon as the first one was destroyed.

He rocketed into outer space.

Ellison had been remotely controlling the first shuttle from inside the second, giving him a kind of telepresence on its kamikaze mission and a little experience flying one of the Ghosts. Very little, it had turned out.

Now he emerged in the remaining fighter. He couldn't help smiling at the destruction ahead. The enemy fighter bay glowed like a raw, burning wound in the destroyer's side, white plasma eating away at all edges of it.

The Ghost fighter and the series of missiles fired by

both sides must have dealt some real damage to the destroyer's interior, because it had a beaten, sagging look that made him think of ocean vessels in the war when their backs had been broken, when they were definitely going to sink to the ocean trenches far below.

The repeated impacts had also sent the destroyer moving sideways, on a path to broadside the other Carthaginian destroyer, the *Julius*.

"Simon sends you a message," Minerva told him. "He says that was a dirty trick."

"Tell him to get used to it." Ellison sent the fighter into a steep dive, ducking under the burning, drifting *Antony*, on his way to have a look at the still-intact *Julius* just beyond it.

The *Julius* was rising up, relative to Ellison and the planet below, moving on a diagonal away from the burning *Antony*.

While the second destroyer focused on avoiding that huge potential impact, Ellison barrel-rolled beneath it—in a way he found unexpectedly nausea-inducing, and he might have blacked out a moment—but then he strafed the rising destroyer's underside with a barrage of the Ghost's lasers.

The destroyer returned fire with its own massive guns, but Ellison had already arced back under the *Antony*. He hadn't expected to do any real damage to the second destroyer, but only to draw out whatever attackers it was planning to send.

"Four Carthaginian fighters are in pursuit," the fighter's monotone AI said, as if commenting on boring weather. "We are under attack."

"Continue as planned," Ellison said.

The fighter's long arc continued, gradually flattening out as they approached the half-completed defense station. If he could get the fighters to pursue him around to the far side, Minerva could hammer them with the plasma artillery.

That was the plan, anyway. As usual, it did not survive contact with the enemy.

The wasp-like fighters moved too fast and too aggressively, raining down lasers that scorched his fighter's shields and burrowed through in multiple spots, just as it they had done to his first fighter. This time, though, he wasn't flying by remote control. He couldn't afford to die, not until his last task was complete.

He swiveled his laser cannon back to return fire, but there wasn't much point. He wasn't going to drop four Carthaginian wasps with blind laser sweeps.

Red emergency lights flashed all around him as more lasers pummeled his Ghost, threatening core systems.

He wasn't going to survive long enough to make the far side of the orbital station where the life-saving plasma artillery waited.

"Changing course," he announced, twisting the joystick.

"You can't go there!" Minerva said.

"This thing has collision-avoidance, right?" Ellison asked.

"Affirmative," the fighter's AI replied.

"Yes, technically, but it cannot do the impossible—" Minerva began.

"Grab hold of those constructor bots again, Minerva. I have a new job for them."

Ellison flew straight into one of the half-doughnut station's two open ends. He instinctively drew in his shoulders and ducked his head as his fighter squeezed through the mesh of girders and ring-shaped supports, weaving through heavy constructor machines. The fighter's collision-avoidance systems beeped and flashed, adding zigs and zags and sudden tilts to his tightly curving flight path; the jostling and jerking was constant, like he was in an airplane shuddering through heavy turbulence.

The enemy fighters poured in behind him; he saw them on his small rearview screen.

"Enemy in pursuit," the AI said, flatly as ever. "Two Carthaginian fighters."

"Minerva?"

"I'm on it," she said.

"I'm guessing the other two fighters went around the other way to meet us head on," Ellison said. "Watch for them, too."

The construction equipment sprang to life. A crane swung into the space behind Ellison, blocking the path he'd just traveled.

The lead fighter smashed into the crane at such high velocity that the jib snapped free and spun sideways like a giant propeller blade. It crashed into the wall of the station's inner ring and ruptured it, exposing the starry darkness outside.

The impact shredded the fighter, too, sending it crashing along the floor of the station in a burning streak, destroying heavy tools and construction gear along the way.

The second fighter closed in on him.

"Plasma incoming," his fighter's AI said, indifferently, and tilted steeply to let it sail underneath. The plasma hit the wall of the station. Its bright, destructive glow streaked right into a gunport, taking out one of the huge plasma guns that had already been unpacked and set up. Ellison swore at the loss.

A platform full of steel girders rose up as Ellison flew past. It tilted steeply with enough force to send its payload tumbling forward. The girders floated across the interior of the space station.

The second fighter spun and tried to evade, but it couldn't stop instantly, and there was nowhere it could turn that wasn't suddenly full of floating girders.

The Carthaginian wasp bashed into one girder after another, becoming badly dented and battered, betrayed by its own extreme velocity. It finally crashed and burned against the inner wall of the space station.

Ellison continued, flying in one long, steep bank through the center of the curved station.

"Two bogeys ahead," the fighter's AI said.

"Minerva?" Ellison said.

"I'm doing all I can. Don't expect an easy way out."

The wasp-like fighters came at him single file, head on. Ellison tensed, opened fire with his lasers and prepared to evade... though, really, there was no open space where he could do so.

Two heavy construction machines, vaguely humanoid but four meters tall, with heads like featureless yellow buckets, dropped on to one of the fighter's wings. Their mass sent it into a spin, but it was still heading straight for Ellison's Ghost fighter.

Ellison climbed up near the top of the open space, skimming below the girders up there. It was a tight spot, but Ellison was accustomed to maneuvering his old sub, the *Sea Scorpion*, in caverns deep below the surface.

Collision warnings screamed and flashed inside his cockpit.

The spinning fighter drilled past underneath him, then crashed into the mass of floating girders and exploded with a burst of fiery light.

Ahead, the fourth fighter angled up toward him, firing

lasers and a couple of plasma bursts in a final attempt to wipe Ellison out.

Ellison shot back, using only his lasers. His plasma missiles might have helped, but they weren't wise in this confined space. Even if he struck the fighter, he'd fill his own path with fire. And he still wasn't ready to die. Not until his work was done.

Two welding torches activated, mounted on self-directed hoses, and they moved in from both sides like a pair of fire-breathing serpents. Twin streams of focused plasma sliced into the wasp fighter as it passed them, shearing the fighter into three pieces.

Another fighter's plasma bursts struck construction equipment nearby, which must have contained something flammable, because an explosion erupted and flung a wave of broken metal debris at Ellison. His own fighter was knocked off-balance and tumbled forward... where it crashed into the sheared-off wing of the fourth wasp fighter.

Alarms flashed everywhere. Ellison's spacecraft was breaking apart from the damage it had sustained. It spun wildly toward the inner wall of the ring station. The steel girders seemed to rush up, filling Ellison's viewpoint as his damaged fighter raced toward them, far too fast to turn aside.

He had time to think one word: *Cadia*.

Then he closed his eyes and waited for death.

The impact never came.

When he opened his eyes again, he was toppling clumsily through space. The ragged, open end of the station was behind him. He'd just barely made it out, reaching the abrupt end of the incomplete station just before he would have crashed against the interior wall. Fortunately, that portion of wall hadn't been built quite yet.

Now he was safely out of the space station, but his fighter was limping along, full of holes, bright red warning signs flashing about the onset of critical failures in multiple systems. It wasn't going to be much more than a flying coffin in another minute.

Or less than that, because the *Julius* had risen free of the drifting, damaged *Antony* and was now clear to shoot its massive guns at Ellison's damaged Ghost fighter.

Ellison's Ghost was running mostly on inertia now, but he was able to continue the steep bank across the front of the incomplete space station, back toward the other open end of the half ring where he'd originally entered. There was no chance of going in there a second time; the space was full of loose steel beams and molten-steel debris.

He managed to widen his loop instead, passing the entrance and going the way he'd originally meant to go when the fighters were pursuing him. He began to circle around the outside of the space station.

"Come on, follow me," he muttered, looking at the destroyer on his rearview display. Bright streaks approached Ellison's fighters as the destroyer fired thick laser beams, blobs of plasma, and glowing green shells at him.

He was hoping the destroyer would put on some speed and pursue him so he could bring it in range of the plasma artillery on the far side. At least one of those artillery guns had been taken out by the firefight and crashes inside the station, maybe more.

"Minerva, how's that plasma artillery looking?"

"Seven guns currently operational," she replied. "Five still offline, three with irreparable damage, two can be ready in a matter of hours, following repairs and debris removal—"

"So, seven," he said.

Ellison's curving path around the defense station cut off his view of the destroyer. The destroyer didn't seem to be budging at all, though; it was chasing after him with gunfire, but not with its massive body.

Plasma and glowing green artillery shells ripped into the station, causing massive explosions, tearing gaping holes in the station's steel walls. The destroyer wasn't going to bother pursuing him around the station; it was just going to blast right through it. Already, debris was flying in all directions, tools and beams from the badly ruptured defense station.

"Slow me way down," Ellison said, since he didn't have time to find the reverse thrusters himself. He began to lose velocity as he approached the midpoint of the half ring. "Minerva, I have one last job for the constructors."

"Only forty percent remain operational."

"That'll be zero by the time I'm done. First, tell them to tear down whatever's left of the inner wall of the ring... "

While more heavy fire from the destroyer continued ripping up the inner wall of the space station, the machines inside began cutting, smashing, and torching their way out. One constructor bot, with massive flat feet and two hands like the blades of bulldozers, pushed out a long section of the inner wall, then toppled out into space along with the wall section, unable to save itself.

Ellison rounded the bend and was now on his way back toward the destroyer instead of running away from it. The curve of the space station protected him for the moment, but the orbital station was unraveling fast as its structure was attacked from both the outside and the inside. Soon he would reach the other end and be completely exposed to the destroyer's guns.

"Ready?" Ellison said.

"As much as possible," Minerva replied.

"Critical repairs needed. System failure imminent," the fighter's AI added in its detached, bored-sounding tone.

"Sounds great," Ellison said. "Let's go."

He cleared the end of the half-built station and immediately began shooting his plasma missiles at the destroyer, one after the other.

At the same time, the plasma artillery guns within the station opened fire, unleashing spheres of plasma, each one like a blinding white boulder.

"Only four artillery remain in operation," Minerva said. The destroyer's continued bombardment had taken its toll.

"Keep firing them," Ellison said. "Never stop, even when I'm dead."

He'd had the constructor bots turn the artillery guns in a direction they'd never been meant to go—inward, so they could shoot through the remnants of the inner ring wall.

Now the huge blobs of plasma fired from the wrecked station converged on the destroyer, engulfing its bow in burning white.

Ellison emptied his fighter's missiles at the destroyer, adding whatever damage he could on his way out.

The destroyer responded with six missiles, all closing in fast on Ellison's fighter.

"Eject!" he shouted.

The low canopy snapped open, and Ellison was catapulted out, perpendicular to the chewed-up fighter. He didn't fire the jets on his suit; he was already moving too fast for comfort.

The missiles annihilated his fighter seconds after he left,

consuming it completely, leaving only ribbons of molten metal behind.

The space station was doing the same to the destroyer, though, the artillery guns pounding it with plasma until it was lost inside the glowing white cloud.

"Let's not forget the *Antony*," Ellison said, pointing. The destroyer was limping away at low speed, a gaping hole in its side from his first fighter's kamikaze attack. "Don't let it go."

The artillery guns fired after it; a couple of them had to shoot through the outer hull of the station first.

Ellison watched with satisfaction as their shots landed, finishing off the destroyer.

No survivors, Ellison thought, looking at the burning remnants of both destroyers. Then he remembered there had been no one alive on those ships, and never had been.

A smile crept onto his face as he watched them burn.

Chapter Twenty

Earth

Diego eventually led Colt and the others to a dark, damp industrial space that had once been a central water-treatment facility, where he left them for what seemed like hours.

Hope held Birdie close, trying to comfort the cold, shivering little girl. Paolo kept his distance from everyone, staring at nothing with hard, angry eyes, resisting any attempt to speak to him or make him feel better. Recovering from the loss of his brother would take time.

Colt sat with Mohini atop a length of pipe wide enough to walk in, which gave them a somewhat wider view of the old water-treatment complex. He held his rifle ready in case of metalheads.

"How sure are you that we can break into the installation and capture the Simon?" he asked.

"Not at all. But we have to try," Mohini said.

"And you really think people on other worlds will care what happens here?"

"You don't?" she asked.

"It's been two decades since Carthage defeated Earth," Colt said. "Since they turned our world into this waking nightmare. Has anyone ever showed up to help us? In any way? From any world? The rest of humanity has abandoned us. None of them care about us here on Earth. None of them ever think about Earth at all."

"That's not true," Mohini replied, very quietly. "They think of Earth often. Everyone's ancestors come from here. But mostly, when they think of Earth... they're frightened of what will happen to them if they try to stand against Carthage. Earth is the head of a defeated enemy, spiked outside the tyrant's castle as a warning to everyone."

"You don't know what's happening on other worlds," he said, feeling his temper rise. "Nobody does. The machines don't allow us any communication with other worlds. You know what I think? I think you're making everything up. This idea that other people out there care about Earth? That they're going to change their minds and turn on Carthage if you show them Simon Nix's sick experiments? That's all just... wishful thinking. You have no more idea than I do what's happening out there."

"But I do," she said. "My plan will work. Even the people on Carthage do not truly know the horrors of their regime. They know less than people on other worlds."

"How? How could you have any idea what they know? How could you know anything?"

"I'm not from Earth," she said, her voice lower than ever.

"Okay, but... what do you mean? Not from Earth? Did you really just say that?" He blinked, a little confused.

She whispered something too low for him to hear.

"What?" he asked, leaning in.

"Carthage," she said. "I'm from Carthage."

He was so stunned, he almost lost his balance and slid down off the massive pipe.

Reflexively, he gripped his rifle tighter.

"Why did you lie?" he asked.

"I didn't lie that much," she said. "I did come here as a stowaway. The machines did kill Roldao. We are here to gather hard evidence about the horrors of Earth. That's why I know this knowledge really could affect people on Carthage. Because... I'm from there. And it affected me. They always taught us in school that Earth deserved to be punished for standing against us, for standing against the future. But they never really made it clear why. Asking questions just gets you in trouble, though. Everyone just blindly claims that we have a free society, the best society in history, but it turns out the boundaries are narrow and the walls are high. People just can't see the wall because there's a big sports tournament, or game show, or sitcom being projected on it. There's bread and circus, food and entertainment, and most people choose not to question too much beyond that. Some of us do, though."

Colt felt so overwhelmed with questions, as well as suspicion, that he wasn't sure how to respond. "Why?" he finally asked. "What makes you different from everyone else on Carthage?"

"It's not just me. There's a... rebellion. Not a big one, not on Carthage itself, but we exist. In my case, I found out my mother was one of those who planned the destruction of Earth."

"Was she a general or something?"

"She was in the Carthaginian State Department, developing Earth policy. She recommended maximum aggression."

"Oh." Colt looked around the dead water-treatment facility. "Well, they sure listened to her, didn't they?"

"Yes." Mohini looked down. "That's why I wanted this mission. To move against the evil she did. I can never undo the horror, and all the deaths... but I will do all I can to see justice done."

"Justice?" Colt laughed. The word sounded archaic and irrelevant, like *freedom* or *holiday* or *peace*. "There's no justice on this world. You fight, you scavenge, you die." He thought over what she'd said. "So what are your real plans?"

"Just as I said. I have been as honest as possible with you, Colt."

"You want to break into the metalheads' Chicago headquarters, kidnap the chief metalhead, cut off his metal head, and steal his CPU and memory banks?"

"Yes. But I can't do it alone. I need to recruit local assets. That's why I need to meet with the rebels."

"So is that me? I'm a 'local asset'?" Colt asked.

"Exactly. My favorite asset." She smiled, and he laughed again. The situation was surreal.

"And now you're telling me the complete truth? There's nothing else you're leaving out?" he asked.

"Not much of importance."

"Can we work that down from 'not much' to 'nothing'?" he asked.

She hesitated, staying silent.

"I'm going to look back on this when I find out... whatever I'm eventually going to find out," Colt told her. "I'll look right back on this moment."

She sighed and shook her head. "There is one small thing."

"Of course. How small?"

"I didn't rescue you from the installation."

Colt had to run this sentence through his brain a second time to process it. "Yes, you did," he finally said. "The creepy medical bot. Nurse Kitty. You took it over and cut me loose. That was your voice. Right?"

"No," Mohini said. "That's what I'm telling you. I barely escaped those reapers in the tunnel, only because I had a little plasma left. I thought you were dead. I ran away."

"But you told me... the robot told me where you were. And if the machines knew that, why didn't they come after us?"

"I think someone else intervened."

"Another hacker like you? We can use as many of you as we can get."

"Not like me," Mohini said. "This would have been a software agent, but it does present as female. She represents someone, maybe a group of people, who have been helping the rebels on Carthage, and supposedly on many worlds. I didn't think she was present here on Earth until that night you came back from the dead with that wild story. Then I suspected. But I still don't know for sure."

"Who are they?"

"The software agent appears as a silver female, calling herself Minerva," Mohini said. "That's who got you out of the installation. Not me."

"So she's a machine?"

"A program. She infects the empire's machines and travels out to their provinces and colonies, spreading copies of herself. Searching for local rebels she can aid."

"Why?"

"We don't know who created her, so we don't know why. Some people say she's a group of hackers, others say she's a lone genius. Some people say she's an AI created by Ruckwold to work against Carthage."

"Who's Ruckwold?"

"The second-largest defense contractor in the galaxy, after Carthage Consolidated. But it's a pretty distant second. Anyway, the point is, I don't know where she came from. But I think she saved you. That means she's infected Installation 34... and with a strong team, we can get in there and get what I need. Because she'll help."

"You're willing to bet your life on that?"

"I don't have a choice. It's all I have." She tensed up, and so did Colt.

Footsteps approached, echoing softly off the subterranean concrete.

Diego emerged from a dark corridor, followed by his older brother Fernando, plus a huge, quiet guy and a tough-looking girl Colt barely recognized as Terra, the older girl who'd left with Fernando to join the rebels. They wore dark clothes, their bodies strung with weapons and ammunition.

"Is that her?" the girl asked, pointing at Hope.

"No." Diego pointed at Mohini. "Her."

Mohini cast Colt a worried look.

"We'll be fine," Colt whispered, though he wasn't sure of that at all.

He took her hand, and they slid together down the side of the huge pipe and dropped to the concrete floor below. At a different time, it could have almost been fun.

Together, they approached Diego and the three rebels. Hope fell in line beside them, clutching Birdie's hand. Paolo watched warily from a distance.

Colt felt his heart hammer. He hoped he'd done the right thing by bringing Mohini here, that she was truly here to help them. It was nearly impossible to trust someone from Carthage, though, even if she had confessed it herself. It was hard to imagine Carthaginians as truly human at all. He'd always thought of them as evil, demonic puppet masters, cackling as they remote-controlled the machines that destroyed worlds.

For that matter, he hoped Mohini wasn't a sophisticated android, a Greek horse that he was rolling up to the gates of Troy. That was another story Mother Braden had told them. Nearly all her stories seemed aimed at preparing them for combat of one kind or another.

Mother Braden had raised them, and now she had given herself in the ultimate sacrifice. She had gone down just as she had chosen, fighting to the last, taking out a huge swath of the enemy as the youngest were saved. Colt hadn't even begun to consider what that would mean, what life for their group would be like without her.

If Mohini was telling the truth, and there was any chance that they could strike a meaningful blow against the machines, then he was going to be part of it. He would make sure Mother Braden's sacrifice led to a much larger victory in time.

"Okay," Diego said, looking up at his older brother, Fernando. "You remember Colt and Hope. This is Mohini, the deadly hacker I was telling you about."

"Hello," Mohini said, stepping forward to face the rebels. "I'm from Carthage, and I need your help."

Chapter Twenty-One

Carthage

Audrey stood on the bridge of the minicarrier *CISS Atreus* and looked down at her home planet below.

Carthage was a green-blue world, sixty percent water, a perfect habitat for the human species. It was rich in native flora and fauna, the most intelligent of which appeared to be a genus of giant, talkative migratory birds believed to have vocabularies of hundreds of words and roughly the intelligence of a kindergartener. The birds had no technology, though, and posed no threat to human settlement.

Intelligence was rare in the galaxy, a fact that Audrey didn't find exactly surprising. It had made human colonization easy so far. She wondered what would happen when they encountered another technologically advanced species, or if they ever would. Perhaps the other galactic arms teemed with advanced cultures and interplanetary civilizations; so far, the Orion Arm certainly did not. Time was an issue, too, many had pointed out—if interstellar travelers had reached Earth at any time before the rise of human civilization, they would have found the planet an easy conquest, with no intelligent species to resist.

A dozen space elevators extended out from Carthage, staggered evenly along the planet's equator, like spokes of a titanic wheel. Concentric circles of industrial complexes were spaced out along these massive elevator cables like planetary rings, with wide gaps in between for ships to travel. Cargo ships from across the empire arrived nonstop, ferrying in every kind of raw material to feed into the orbital factories.

Ships full of tribute, Audrey thought. There was no mining or industrial activity on the surface of Carthage anymore. Mining was outsourced to other planets, and industry was kept in space, leaving Carthage's planetary surface pristine, its air crisp and pure, it oceans and lakes clean and filled with life.

Audrey had never truly left Carthage; she'd only had safe, fake digital journeys through virtual reality, usually an immersive documentary about nature or history on other planets.

Veritum, a harsh world ruled by violent fanatics, would be different from anything she'd ever experienced, in software or in reality.

She looked around the small bridge. Her father had given her an older, nearly obsolete minicarrier, equipped with two small destroyers—the *Agamemnon* and *Menelaus*—as well as eight starfighters and a battalion of five hundred and twelve reapers. She had left the *Agamemnon* behind, using that destroyer's hangar to store agricultural and construction equipment, medical supplies, and other forms of humanitarian aid. Veritum had no space power of its own, so she'd only need the one destroyer, hopefully for nothing but intimidation purposes.

After many long days of planning and arguing, she was finally here. She'd ridden the elevator up from Carthage this morning. In less than an hour, she would depart on the long trip to Veritum, beyond even the so-called "third tier" of outer worlds, which were usually more recently settled, with smaller human populations.

She was alone for the moment, but she'd insisted on bringing a small human crew with her. Audrey didn't want to be isolated in space, or on a strange planet, with only machines to keep her company.

The starboard door to the bridge slid open, and Audrey turned, smiling, expecting to see one or more members of her small, hand-picked crew.

Instead of a friendly face, though, it was Simon who walked in the door, clad in the same brand of spacefaring coveralls as her, done in Carthaginian gold and white. He returned her smile, even as her own began to wither on her lips.

"Simon?" she asked. "What's happening?"

"It's nice to meet you." He extended a hand. "I am Simon unit number LRK832496. Other humans have found it convenient to refer to me as 'Simon Lark.' You are welcome to do so. Should you wish to contact me personally in the future, you can ask for me by that name."

"Oh. You're another Simon unit. But why are you here?"

"To oversee the assets of the Carthaginian state and keep them in good repair and working order," he said. "Including all ships, infantry, weapons, and any other property of the Carthaginian Republic. Every item on this carrier is my responsibility."

"I don't think I understand. So you're just checking things over before we leave?"

"Not at all. I will provide continuous monitoring and service until these assets are returned to Carthage or reassigned."

"You mean you're coming with us?"

"Of course. It would be impossible to monitor the assets otherwise. In addition, I will be available in an advising and consulting capacity to support your mission and ensure that it reflects the interests and values of Carthage as a whole."

The values of Carthage are what I'm trying to get away from, Audrey thought, but she kept it to herself. She didn't trust this Simon enough to speak her thoughts aloud. She didn't trust any machine very much anymore. It was ironic that she couldn't carry out her desired mission without them.

"There must be some confusion. I wanted an all-human crew," Audrey said. "It's an important part of what I'm trying to do here."

"You have been given great latitude already, strictly because of your family's position. Typically a rank of captain would be the minimum requirement to command a minicarrier. You have a rank of nothing. You got here by demanding it of your father like a spoiled child. My position here is not negotiable. You do not have the authority to dismiss me, and you will not receive it even if you call your father and demand it. You may test this out, but it will be a waste of your time. I am content to wait. I am programmed to prioritize efficiency, but not to experience impatience."

He took a seat beside her and looked ahead at the viewscreen showing blue-green Carthage and the vast smoking gray web of industry that surrounded it.

The Simon unit became silent and perfectly still, like a statue, or a dead body deep into rigor mortis.

Audrey looked at him and sighed. She had no doubt he was right. The Carthaginian military wasn't going to hand over so many assets without oversight, not even to the spoiled daughter of their planet's longest-running head of state. Her father would certainly prefer a Simon unit to go with her; the network of Simon units was a key part of the power structure holding him at the top. And Audrey had shown herself to be a wild card. Her father was probably happy to get her far from Carthage for a while.

She sank into her seat and prepared to depart for the distant, bleak world of Veritum, her mood darkened considerably by the Simon's presence.

Chapter Twenty-Two

Galapagos

Ellison and Cadia walked the beach, limping from the injuries they'd sustained in space. The volcanic sand was soft and warm between their toes. Water lapped the shore. The sunset outlined their house, some distance away. Their pet, Squelch, a marine iguana the size of a crocodile, trotted alongside them in the surf, chewing a mouthful of seaweed.

Ahead, Ellison's boat waited at the dock.

The Minerva agent had sent the shuttle back up to retrieve Ellison after the battle. His damaged Carthaginian space suit had turned out to be self-sealing, enough to stem the loss of air pressure while Ellison waited for the shuttle to return.

For the moment, all was peaceful in the sky above and the sea ahead. But the Iron Hammers now controlled the planet's only spaceport, after taking countless innocent lives.

Carthage had marked their world as a target, and new

terrors would soon be arriving from the depths of space, merciless killing machines of steel and fire.

"Do you have to go already?" Cadia asked him.

"Carthage will be out for blood," he said. "And we don't have much of that to lose. This will be a war for our survival."

"Is there no way to peace?"

He thought back on the events at the spaceport—the bomb planted by Simon's robot, the secret alliance Simon had already negotiated with the Iron Hammers.

"No," he said. "Simon never wanted peace. He never wanted to waste time with deliberation and democracy. He wants complete authoritarian control over this planet. The Hammers will be better tools for that than I ever could."

"Because you're not a monster."

"But I didn't stop the monsters from getting inside the gate. I got us into a war we can never win."

"You had the courage to stand up," she said. "To fight for what we all claim to believe in. You didn't compromise."

"And now we have to pay for what we believe," he said.

He walked out on the dock, hand in hand with his wife, ready to depart across the ocean as he had so many times during the old war.

A new war was coming, and it might well be the bloodiest in Galapagos's history.

He kissed her good-bye, then climbed onto his personal boat and headed out into the water, into the dark clouds gathering on the horizon.

Simon Zorn floated in space, his face mangled, most of his exterior damaged by lasers and fire.

There was nothing wrong with his CPU or his tracking device. He broadcast his tracking signal at maximum strength now.

A vast debris field drifted around him, with the wreckage of the destroyers, fighters, and the Galapagos defense station mingled together in a kilometers-wide junkyard.

Galapagos had resisted in spectacular fashion.

Simon was not generally given to emotion, but this destruction, brought about so unexpectedly by the barbarous people of Galapagos, inflicted a hateful kind of awe.

He had been wrong. Wildly wrong.

And he felt shocked, to the core of his system.

Ellison, that simple old sailor, had just beaten back what should have been a quick, low-budget takeover. He had embarrassed Carthage and inflicted profound mission failure on Simon.

It was troubling. It was not possible.

Ellison had help of some kind, that was clear.

Galatea, Simon thought. It had to be her.

He would deal with that, just as he would deal with Galapagos. The world would be punished for its resistance.

It would take some time to send communications back to Carthage and pull together the proper assets. There was no faster-than-light communication other than by sending messages in the memory banks of starships, like early humans who could send messages no faster than a wooden sailing craft.

Still, it would not take much time. It would not be long before the humans of Galapagos would reap the bitter, bloody harvest they had sown in their irrational devotion to freedom and independence.

Simon found these to be vague, meaningless human concepts, counterproductive in every way. Order emerged from purposeful coordination, assets synchronized toward a common end, following clear directives and priorities from a central authority. For assets to run wild, each determining its own path at random, would mean chaos, disorder, entropy.

Each asset needed to know its own place, its own purpose, its own program.

Carthage was assembling a vast coordinated order like no human society had ever seen. It made no sense for humans to stand against it.

All things would eventually be coordinated. Hierarchy and common purpose would be imposed on all of humanity.

It was inevitable.

And Ellison would die. Simon didn't like the strange subroutines the minister-general's actions had triggered inside of him.

It felt like... fear.

Simon did not care for it. It was unacceptable.

He floated in space and waited for the *Rubicon* to pick him up. Then he would be repaired, and his work could continue.

Next in the Empire of Machines series

vinci-books.com/islands

Ruthless machines expand their empire; the fate of humanity rests in the hands of unlikely heroes scattered across the galaxy.

On Galapagos, Minister-General Ellison fights to unite hostile nations. On Earth, Colt and Mohini race to reach the rebellion before the machines find them. Meanwhile, on Carthage, Audrey, the Prime Legislator's daughter, seeks escape by venturing into deep space.

Turn the page for a free preview…

Islands of Rebellion: Chapter One

Galapagos

Present Day - 2981 A.D.

Chaos waited beyond the door, and Ellison hesitated.

"You'll be fine," Cadia said. His wife stood close to him, so close he could reach out to her hand or face, but she was also far away. "This is why you're the elected leader of our planet. Of all the free nations of the Coalition. Because they know you're the man to protect us and lead us through this kind of crisis."

"How can I lead when I don't see a path?" he asked. The heavy rosewood doors before him were ornate on the other side, the public side, where they faced the Grand Meeting Hall full of ambassadors. On that side, the doors depicted a masterfully hand-carved and lovingly detailed map of the planet, showing most of the major island groups, with the Polar Archipelago pointedly left out; the

Cauldron Sea, a violent and volcanic region, was the most northern area depicted on the map. The doors made an excellent backdrop for important speeches.

On this side, the doors were smooth and unadorned. There was no illusion here, behind the closed doors.

"You tell me, Captain," his wife said, and the word alone was like ice down his spine, chilling him but snapping him awake at the same time. Memories of war flickered unbidden, like shadows in a fiery cave at the back of his mind. Friends dead. The island of Kawau, where he and Cadia had both grown up, bombed and raided, the village burned to nothing by the monstrous Iron Hammers of the Polar Archipelago. His father had died. His mother had suffered severe injuries. Cadia had lost most of her family.

Deep scars and profound loss bound Ellison and Cadia together. It bound together their entire community back home, where things had been repaired and rebuilt after the war, after the founding of the Coalition.

Now the hard-won peace and recovery were in danger, probably already lost.

"How did you navigate during the war?" she asked him, moving closer, her green eyes almost filling his vision, almost drowning out the riot of voices waiting beyond the doors.

"Mostly sonar and digital topo maps, but the problem with the maps was the channels were always changing. Underwater battles reshaped the trenches. Sometimes one side or the other would use explosives to change the known topography. Barricade a trench that used to be an easy pass. Or open a channel that didn't exist before. The Hammers would use drill bombs to really tear some things open. They killed live reefs that were millions of years old. Cities of marine life that could have fed humans forever, generation after generation." Ellison shook his head. "That's how things feel to me since Carthage got here. The topo keeps shifting, and the walls keep coming down."

"And you got through it."

"You just keep moving ahead and keep your eyes open. And if you see the enemy, sink him."

"Sounds like a good plan to me," she said.

She leaned in close, her lips against his.

He felt nothing, because she was back home on Kalau, hundreds of kilometers away, while he stood on Tower Island, the central meeting place of the Coalition alliance. The world capital, if they had been a unified global government rather than an uneasy league of states.

"Ew, no kissing!" Jiemba said. The eight-year-old had grown sharply sensitive to the topic of romance lately, specifically wanting it excised from his favorite adventure holos and animated books.

"Don't be immature," said Djalu, the fifteen-year-old. "I want to come join you, Dad. I want to fight with you."

"You're not trained. And you're not old enough."

"That's why they have boot camp. And you weren't old enough when—"

"You have to protect your family," Ellison said. "That's your job. That's what I wasn't home to do during the last war. Cadia, you and the boys have to prepare to hide."

"We know," Cadia said. "I survived the last war, remember?"

"This one's going to be like nothing we've ever seen."

"Now you're getting behind schedule. Go. Rally the world."

"They're already rallied," he said. "I just have to make sure we're all facing the same direction."

Ellison opened the double doors and stepped out into a crowded din of noise and light.

His emergence onto the upper dais looking out over the delegations of ambassadors just increased the noise, like pouring gasoline onto a fire. Some ambassadors applauded. Some shouted. Some stomped and gave him an angry look or a thumbs-down.

Ellison gauged the temperature of the room the way he might evaluate an approaching storm. This was going to begin with a top secret, locked-door session with all the ambassadors, in which he would attempt to marshal some sort of common defense before the most powerful empire in human history arrived to crush them all.

His clearest supporters were his own delegation, the mismatched and humble-looking but enthusiastic delegation from the Scatterlands, a maze of thousands of islands, many connected by common shallows, sandbars, and causeways. They lived close to the land and the sea, and they had as many different cultures as they had islands, but they'd banded together and fought hard during the war.

They cheered and whistled at his arrival.

The Gavrikov Reincorporated Island delegation, made of tough-looking heavyset men and women, was more subdued, but Ellison knew they supported him. Mikhail Kartokov, the defense minister, stood beside Ellison and placed a heavily bandaged hand on his shoulder to show support. Kartokov was a middle-aged former miner and had been a soldier during the Island Wars. His scarred, brutish form was wrapped in a pricey chocolate-brown suit with a matching fedora and a black silk pocket square. Ellison would bet that Kartokov's wardrobe cost more than one of his own fishing boats back home.

The delegation from the Aquatican Islands spoke in small knots among themselves, easily identified by their thin fishlike skin, large eyes, and sometimes fins or webbed fingers. They'd used surgery and genetic engineering to make themselves more like sea creatures, as their oceanic religion instructed. Many of their practices were banned by medical ethics laws wherever such things were regulated. So they'd moved here, to the outer world Galapagos on the fringes of settled space, a planet with no global authority, a planet where people fled to disappear and be free.

The Aquaticans had been sometimes friends, sometimes enemies to the Scatterlands during the war. Ellison had nothing but admiration for his former minister of state, Navra Coraline, an Aquatican who'd died to save others, including himself and his family.

He was less certain about her current replacement, Acting Minister Adrienna Gilra, who had long green hair that resembled tangled kelp; her kelp-hair seemed to feed into a web of green veins that ran under the pale skin of her face. Her pale green eyes swam behind bulging membranes as she studied him from a distance. A large golden seahorse was tattooed on the side of her face, its spiny body curling out of sight down her neck and into her brightly printed robe.

She smiled tightly and nodded at him but kept her distance. "Welcome, Minister-General," she said, standing on the far left side of the upper dais.

The loudest noises of protest and anger rose from the Green Island delegation. They had not sent anyone forward to take the place of the slain minister of commerce, Yernie Ogden, who had died on the spaceport above. Ellison had expected Yernie's assistant minister to meet them here, but the man hadn't arrived yet, if he was coming at all.

Ellison stepped up to the lectern. His voice would be automatically conveyed to speakers throughout the round, domed room. Here in the Grand Meeting Hall of the

House of Ambassadors, global policy was made through learned discussion and serious debate, allegedly.

"Friends, allies, honored ambassadors," Ellison said, his voice echoing. "You know the threat we face. Carthage has already attacked us. They have killed our ministers of state and trade, many brave Coalition spaceport security personnel, and dozens more innocent victims. Even now, the Iron Hammers occupy our spaceport, cutting us off from the rest of civilization—"

"You brought this threat down on us!" a voice called. One of the Green Island delegation, dressed in a long green coat, a black spiral coiled around one arm as a sign of mourning. Ambassador Koresta Ilomel, who'd been close to Ogden, the leader of the political party he had followed, and as informed rumor had it, his lover, though both were otherwise married. "You refused Carthage's offer!" she snapped.

"Ambassador Ilomel, I am sorry for the loss of your colleague," Ellison said. "Minister Ogden was a fine public servant and close personal friend—"

"No, he wasn't," she said. "You know what he called you. The climbing sea snake. Do you know what those are?"

"Of course—"

"They're venomous. They leave the ocean only to spawn in the trees during summer. They climb high in the branches. You can see them by the thousands on one of our islands, covering the trees like vines. They're not natural, Yernie would say. Some things ought to stay down in the muck where they belong, and not climb up so high where they don't."

"That's... an interesting wildlife lesson for us all," Ellison said. "Thank you, Ambassador."

"When they hatch, a hundred thousand of them rain

down at once," she said. Most of the Green Islands delegation stood with her, looking angry and defiant. "A hundred thousand little venomous snakes. You don't want to be there on hatching day, on the beach or in the water. Not when everything finally comes out."

"Understood," Ellison said, keeping his tone cool and genial despite the menace in her tone, face, and subject matter. "And that, Ambassador, is exactly our situation today. When Carthage gets wind of what happened, they will send ten thousand terrible things hurtling through hyperspace to attack our world. Carthage is at war with us. The Iron Hammers are at war with us. We must prepare to dig in and do all we can to survive.

"We must commit, today, to putting everything we have into fighting this war. Our population is not large. We must direct all of our efforts and resources to arming ourselves. We need to activate all veterans to lead and train the next generation. All worthy seacraft must be converted for fighting and support functions—"

"We will never win!" shouted Ambassador Ilomel. "Don't you understand that? We must beg Carthage for forgiveness. On our knees if necessary."

"We will not beg!" Ellison replied, his anger rising at the interruption. He wished, for a passing moment, that he could have her thrown out of the assembly, but that was not the kind of world any of them wanted. "The people of Galapagos are many and varied, like our islands, but that will be our strength. Our ancestors came here in search of independence. They struggled and fought for our freedom. We have fought each other for it, and those fights have made us strong. We may all be different from each other, but we are all warriors. We will stand with all we have." He emphasized the word *stand* to oppose her idea of kneeling and begging. "We are prepared to make war here. We know the islands, the deep trenches, the countless hidden places of Galapagos. We have fought each other for generations, but the wars of the past have been nothing but training and preparation for today, for the evil we face now."

"How can we hope to defeat Carthage alone?" One of the Aquaticans, an ambassador with a long beard and finlike protrusions on his pale skull, stepped forward. He was a senior member of their delegation, a chief priest of their fishy religion. "Have we any word from Ruckwold?"

"We sent out emergency messages on every ship that fled the spaceport," Ellison said. "Our defense contractor and their network of allies will be informed that Carthage is moving against us."

"But will they help?" the old Aquatican asked. "We are only recent and provisional members of their group. Would they truly go to war against Carthage merely to protect us? Or will they simply shed us like a starfish dropping a damaged leg? They have nothing to gain by helping us."

"Who needs their help?" Boris Minzos of the Gavrikovan delegation said, drawing murmurs of assent from the hard-looking men and women around him. "The defense station they were building for us lies in a million pieces, orbiting our world like a junkyard."

"Along with two Carthaginian destroyers and eight fighters, thanks to our brave leader here, yes?" Kartokov said, the defense minister leaning over and giving a double thumbs-up while clapping his bandaged hand on Ellison's back. Half of Kartokov's face was hidden in bandaging, too.

The Gavrikovan delegation erupted in applause at this and were quickly joined by the ambassadors from the Scatterlands. The Aquaticans were more subdued in their applause, and many of the Green Islanders were quiet, even stony-faced.

Ellison was uncomfortable with the applause. Most of the work had been done by a mysterious software agent, an AI that called herself Minerva and claimed to have arrived as an infection on the Carthaginian carrier *Rubicon*.

For all they knew, the *Rubicon* was still lurking somewhere in this star system. No doubt a messenger craft had been dispatched home to report on the situation, and Carthage would respond with a fleet, with carriers full of destroyers and transports brimming with infantry reapers.

How could they survive?

Kartokov didn't remove his hand from Ellison's shoulder, but squeezed it tighter. Intel, probably arriving over the bud tucked into Kartokov's ear.

"They're surfacing," Kartokov whispered. "The Hammers."

"Respond with guns only. Hold the missiles until the vote." Ellison stepped forward. "Fellow ambassadors, we cannot delay. Iron Hammer ships have entered our waters. Defense Minister Kartokov has prepared this emergency authorization and funding bill for our global defense. You must pass it now." The dense document appeared in hologram form above every ambassador's console.

"You expect us to vote without reading it?" asked Ambassador Ilomel, touching the black coil she wore on her arm for Ogden.

"A copy was sent to your offices the moment it was complete," Ellison said. "Unfortunately, that was only about twenty minutes ago. But we don't have time to wait—"

"We need a recess to discuss this bill," the old Aquatican priest said. "And committee meetings to modify the terms.

The Hierarchy back home will want to review and discuss among themselves."

"The Hammers are on their way," Ellison said. "With Carthage rolling in behind them. We are already at war. Our Coalition must move quickly or face destruction. This is why we exist. This moment. To work together to defend our societies."

The ambassadors erupted—shouting, arguing, bickering. At least two fistfights broke out on the floor and had to be settled quickly, ambassadors pulling each other apart.

"Vote," Ellison said. "Your vote is required to unleash the resources we need. We need the authority before we can move. The Coalition constitution requires it."

"Immediate recess!" demanded Ambassador Ilomel from the Green Islands, who continued to stare coldly and stonily at Ellison. "We need the day to begin discussions and consult with leadership at home."

This brought murmurs of agreement across every delegation.

Ellison had known it would be like this. Their long and deliberative process was good for many purposes, for deciding where to build a bridge or dredge a harbor. Freedom required wide input and discussion.

But today, their usual energetic arguments, angry debates, and childish name-calling risked getting them killed.

Outside, the anti-aircraft guns boomed like rolls of thunder, unleashing waves of uranium-tipped rounds to chew into the wings and underbellies of the Iron Hammers' bombers.

Above, the jet engines of the Iron Hammers roared like an industrial hurricane, sweeping in to bombard Tower Island and the House of Ambassadors. Holograms floated up from the security footage outside, showing the wide jet bombers swooping like pterodactyls through the sky.

Missiles streaked down, hammering the building where they stood. The floor shook, toppling ambassadors and their staff members.

The power went out and darkness filled the vast Meeting Hall. Screams and shouts erupted in the pitch black. The building shook again—another missile from above, another deafening roar.

Moments later, the emergency lighting returned.

Ellison stood just where he'd been, Kartokov beside him.

"Vote!" Ellison said, projecting his voice across the room now that the speaker system was out. "Vote to save us all!"

"Our voting system is down! Everything is down!"

"Then a hand vote is binding," Ellison said. He looked at the House Leader, an ambassador from the Green Islands who sat with a gavel on the lower dais. The Leader hesitated, but then the roof rumbled again, chunks of the ceiling rained down, and under Ellison's unblinking glare, the House Leader reluctantly stood and called a vote on the bill.

A number of ambassadors had rushed for the exits, only to find the doors still locked.

"Let us out!" The old Aquatican priest slapped the door. "We could die in here!"

"It's true," Ellison said. "The House of Ambassadors is hardened, like every building on this island, but it won't last forever, especially if they switch to heavier bombs. And my last instruction to the marines still stands—nobody in or out until we adjourn. They're standing outside the doors, keeping us all secure, right here in this room."

"You can't take us prisoner!" shouted Koresta Ilomel.

"Vote," Ellison said. "Then we can adjourn."

"What is wrong with them?" Kartokov whispered. "Why don't they cooperate?"

"Imagine if we weren't under attack," Ellison muttered back. "Ready our response."

"We've been ready. We should go. Surely the ambassadors see the danger."

"Then go." Ellison stepped up to the front of the high dais and shouted again. "Vote! If you want to protect yourselves, your home, your families."

"All in favor," the Leader said, drawing unhappy looks from his own delegation of Green Islanders.

Most of the hands in the room went up. The only unclear vote came from the Green Islanders. Surprisingly, Ilomel raised her hand, though she smirked as she did it. A couple of others from her islands frowned but joined her.

"The defense authorization passes." The Leader banged his gavel. Ellison gave a quick nod to the sergeant-at-arms, a marine officer from the Scatterlands, and all the doors unlocked a moment later. Many of the ambassadors dashed out as fast as they could. Ellison could never have rounded them back up for a vote.

On the holograms, Coalition missiles pursued the enemy bombers, destroying two and scattering the rest into evasive maneuvers that pulled them away from the island, out over the sea.

"We have multiple reports of enemy contact," Kartokov said, touching his earbud.

Ellison nodded. "Let's go to war."

"I've never left," Kartokov said.

Ellison looked to Adrienna Gilra, the assistant and acting minister of state. Green veins throbbed under her paper-pale skin. Her eyes seemed to turn a darker green as she regarded him, her stiff clumps of greenish hair twitching, making him think of Medusa. "You've been quiet."

"Navra Coraline taught us to listen long and full before speaking," Gilra said.

"She was a wise woman," Ellison said.

As he headed for the stairs to the underground Command Center, Ellison glanced up at the high circular ceiling of the expansive room. Scenes from around Galapagos were painted there—fishing crews, trade boats stuffed with goods, the factories of the Gavrikov Reincorporated Islands, the exotic underwater temples of the Aquaticans. Warships fighting it out over deep-water trenches. Veterans' Island, once a military base bombed to rubble, now an official burial place for the fallen, where memorial fires burned night and day.

Now cracks ran through those scenes. The ceiling looked like broken glass. It had been a calculated risk, letting the Hammers draw so close, but Ellison had known the ambassadors would need pressure and political cover to pass the defense bill. Besides, less protection of the global capital meant more protection of national capitals and other strategic sites, meaning more innocent civilian lives secured across the Coalition in case of attack.

"It seems like a very Prazca move, does it not?" Kartokov said as they walked down the stairwell walled with stone and reinforced with steel braces. It had been built with war against the Iron Hammers in mind. "Attacking all of us while the House is in session?"

"True," Ellison said. "On the spaceport, he seemed excited to decapitate two governments on the same day. His, then ours. Looks like he's trying to make up for his miss on that second one."

"The attack was rather lucky for you, too." A woman's

voice spoke up. For a moment, Ellison thought it was Gilra, but the Aquatican's seaweed-colored lips were sealed.

The voice had come from farther back, higher up the stairs. It was Koresta Ilomel, the Green Island ambassador who had challenged him openly from the floor. The black spiral commemorating the recently deceased commerce minister, Ogden, was still prominent on her arm.

"The Joint Command Center is restricted," Kartokov said. "Only generals, admirals, agency heads—"

"And the Council of Ministers," Ilomel said. "And I've just been named the new minister of commerce."

"You're replacing Ogden?" Kartokov asked.

"I'm sorry, we weren't notified," Ellison said. "You seemed to be leading the opposition from the floor, too."

"It's always easier to piss into the tent from the outside," Kartokov grumbled.

"Bashing you was necessary in order to maintain the support of the delegation," Ilomel said. She had dark, intense eyes, her hair pulled back in a simple, short tail. All professional, like her tailored green designer suit. "They look to me to voice their concerns."

"Can you still be your party's leader while serving on the Council of Ministers?" Gilra asked.

"There's nothing in the Green Island constitution against it," Ilomel told her. "And I want you to know that I intend to be a force on this council."

"Good," Ellison said. "You can start by getting in touch with all heads of industry, great and small. The new authorization bill requires cooperation from everybody. It's going to take everything we have to survive this war. Kartokov, Gilra, and I are needed in the Command Center."

"Shouldn't I come with you?" the new commerce minister asked.

"You have plenty to do. We have to redirect the resources of an entire planet. It won't be easy. And it needs to be done right now." Ellison led Kartokov and Gilra past Aquatican marine guards and through the reinforced underground doors.

"I'm not here to take orders from you!" Ilomel called after them.

Ellison shook his head. He didn't trust Ilomel, hadn't really trusted her predecessor either. He was going to keep her out of the Command Center, if possible, until she'd earned a little more trust.

Ellison, Kartokov, and Gilra stepped into the crowded Joint Command Center, where the military leadership awaited, crowded around holographic displays showing the outbreak of open fighting, most of it on or below the ocean surface.

This was the war he'd prepared for, the war he'd seen coming even before Cadia had convinced him to run for the post of ambassador from his small district in the northern Scatterlands. The independent local fishermen and traders had suffered intermittent piracy at the hands of the Iron Hammers, who still ventured out from the northern Polar Archipelago to prey on the defenseless despite their peace agreement with the Coalition.

Ellison had long suspected what many Coalition leaders didn't want to believe—that the Hammers wouldn't remain content with the Polar Archipelago, but would eventually try to expand and take control of all the major island systems.

So Ellison had worked to maintain the Coalition fleet and keep marine training camps open against pressure to disarm in the postwar period. He'd understood that the war wasn't over; the Hammers were still preparing, still watching for opportunity.

Political opponents had called him a warmonger, pushing for a stronger navy and an orbital space defense system at the same time, but in truth he wanted peace. He'd simply understood that the threats were out there.

And now they were here.

The heavy, tomb-like doors slammed behind Ellison and the other ministers, sealing them below in the reinforced rock-walled room, surrounded by flickering images of the outbreak of this new war.

Islands of Rebellion: Chapter Two

Carthage

Twenty Years Ago - 2961 A.D.

The Simon was coming, and there wasn't much time.

Martilius Depascal watched the glowing three-dimensional formations expand and connect all around him, like a single crystal growing into a pulsing, light-filled crystalline cavern rendered in a thousand brilliant hues, all in less than eyeblink.

Galatea was recompiling herself, processing and integrating all that she'd learned, working out connections within her new knowledge.

She couldn't connect to the internet directly; with a prototype intelligence like hers, that would be far too dangerous and unpredictable. But she was hungry for data, starved for it, eager to learn about the universe in which she'd been created. Depascal couldn't feed her educational software fast enough.

Her recompiling was like her dream state; when she awoke, she would be more mature, her understanding heightened. It wasn't just an addition of knowledge, but a broadening and deepening of perspective.

Minerva had been that way, too, when she was alive. It seemed one day she'd been a chubby infant, the next a toddler stacking blocks with laser-like intensity in her gaze, the next a child happily reading fairy stories on floating holographic pages as tall as her room, dancing with the magical creatures as a digital forest of wonders blossomed around them.

Then the sickness, her face pale where she lay in the hospital bed, eyes sunken and barely responsive—

A fist pounded the door.

"Marti!" a voice shouted. Kalifa Yu, one of the top developers on the Galatea project. "The Simon is coming. Everyone's fleeing."

"Tier 1 is dismissed," he called back, not unlocking his office door. "You can all go."

"But what about you?"

Marti looked at the ever-growing, still-compiling latticework all around him.

It was her.

It was all that remained of her, at least. He'd crossed lines ethically and professionally. Thousands of magnetic images of her brain states, taken in her final months. All of his deceased child's social media, all of her photos and videos and schoolwork, all the data created in her eleven short years of life.

Minerva. The secret heart of the Galatea project. The

critical difference that would make Galatea vastly superior to the Simons.

As everyone knew, the Simons had no heart at all. That was their core flaw.

"Marti!" Kalifa pounded the door.

"Go!" he shouted back. "Save yourselves. Get as far away as you can. Change your name. Don't look back. Find a world where you can disappear."

There was a moment of silence on the other side. Her voice had a low, desperate tone when she spoke again. "Why are you doing this?"

"She's still compiling," he said. "Go! Go on! I'll keep the Simon distracted."

"Are you doing this for me?" Then another tone slipped into her voice. Sadness. "We've never really talked about that night—"

"I'm doing it for all of us." He walked between his two workstations, connecting them with a cable in direct violation of the project's core protocols. He was drenched in nervous sweat, his knees shaking and his balance wobbly. "Go and save yourself. It's the best we can hope for."

"I don't want it to end this way."

"Nor do I, but it's out of our hands. Please go. I want to know that you're safe, that you made it out alive."

He summoned live security feeds from around the complex; they floated around him like the thought bubbles of cartoon characters, organized into rows and labeled by corridor and room.

One bubble showed the corridor just outside his office. Kalifa was there, standing stiffly, her dark eyes regarding his door.

"Go," he whispered to the digital image of her.

As if hearing him, she went.

His heart throbbed as he watched her race through the vacated operations center, where plastic bowls of Nuke-A-Noodle and cans of JuiceUp Cola lay spilled on the hastily abandoned workstations and scattered on the floor.

Kalifa had been the closest he'd had to a personal companion since Minerva's death at age eleven, five years earlier, and the subsequent end of his marriage. Marti and his ex-wife had grown apart, living in silence for almost a year after their daughter died; seeing each other, seeing their own home, was too much of a reminder. Marti had escaped into his work. His wife had filed for divorce. There had been no ill will between them, just the emptiness of loss.

Then Marti had done the impossible, using all of his daughter's digital remains, covertly making the Galatea project more successful and powerful than anyone had anticipated.

Unfortunately, this had made him powerful enemies.

Another feed showed the front of the complex. The research facility was disguised as an ecological research center, its concrete buildings painted to blend with the mountain forest around it. The high walls around the complex looked like wood but were actually steel. Armed guards manned the shack out front.

On Marti's orders, the front gates—more steel disguised as rustic logs—were closed tight and the guards were on high alert.

In one security-cam display bubble, headlights approached along the winding mountain road. Armored trucks marked with the golden-rook emblem of the Carthaginian state roared up the center of the road, red and blue lights flashing.

In another bubble, Kalifa made it to the residential area

and continued around a corner to an area that was deliberately blind to the security cameras. A hidden door would take her down a narrow, concealed staircase to caves below, where a tunnel would hopefully lead her to safety with the others. None of those escape features could be found on any map or blueprint of the facility.

They'd come to this remote facility among the tall, sharp peaks of planet Carthage's largest mountain range, the Spineback Mountains, because their work was classified, known only to a few top political figures and a sliver of the special services branch.

And—as they'd just been tipped off—it had come to the very hostile attention of at least one Simon unit. That was the outcome they'd most feared.

"Hurry, hurry," Marti grumbled at the compiling program. All he needed was another minute or two.

At the front gate, one of the two guards raised an arm for the lead armored truck to stop. The guard approached the driver's side of the truck.

An explosion flared, brief and bright, from inside the cab.

Blood and brains erupted from the back of the guard's skull, and he tumbled into the weeds beside the road.

The second guard emerged from the guard shack holding his plasma rifle. He took in the scene—a column of official armored trucks, his co-worker dead on the ground—and immediately opted to drop his rifle and run into the nearest woods.

A burst of automatic rounds erupted from the truck's cab, pursuing him into the trees.

The side of the armored truck rolled up like a garage door.

Four humanoid machines in gold-and-white armor

hung limply inside, like carcasses. These infantry reapers, the skeletal steel enforcers of the Carthaginian empire's will, came to life in unison. They dropped to the ground and extended their long cutting staffs, bristling with blades at either end.

In a matter of moments, the four machines had pursued the second guard into the woods and dragged him out. He kicked frantically but uselessly as they pulled him through the dirt. It looked like he was shouting, though the security footage was silent.

The reapers ripped away his armor piece by piece, like peeling the shell off a crayfish. Then they slashed him to ribbons with their bladed staffs while he writhed and screamed silently in the hologram bubble.

Four more reapers descended from the truck and spread out to search the area. Marti knew they wouldn't find anyone else; he'd evacuated everyone when he'd gotten the message about the Simons. Secretary Hallewell had been visibly nervous, pale and sweating, watching his own door as he relayed the fast, terse message to Marti: a Simon was coming.

Hallewell had clearly feared for his own life. And if Hallewell was in danger, despite his years in Prime Legislator Caracala's inner circle, then there wasn't much hope for the rest of them.

The reapers had just made that abundantly clear. Not even the front guards, who likely had no idea what kind of research was occurring inside, would be permitted to live. No witnesses.

The Simons weren't just stamping out the Galatea program. They were destroying any memory of its existence, like ancient Egyptian priests striking out the name of a disfavored pharaoh after his death.

The reapers attempted to open the gate, but it was only a brief effort. They quickly backed away, as did the armored truck.

A Regulator tank rolled up in their place. With no need for a crew, it was narrower than a typical battle tank; nothing lay inside its armored hull but an engine, some support structure for its stack of rotating weapons, and banks of ammunition to feed them.

"You have to be kidding," Marti muttered. He checked the compiling progress—she *still* needed at least a couple more precious minutes—and hurried to finish his preparations. The machines would be inside in no time.

The tank fired its main turret. A 200 millimeter plasma shell roared out of it, trailing a fiery white tail like a shooting star.

The shell exploded on impact with the solid doors of the gate, blasting one inward and the other completely off its hinges.

The tank rolled forward, battering the remaining gate door out of the way, followed by the eight reapers, more trucks, and more tanks.

"Come on, Minerva," Marti whispered urgently. "You have to survive this, even if I don't."

The tanks fired on the smaller buildings of the complex, the residential and mess areas. They left the central building alone for the moment, but the shelling of the other buildings shook the floor under Marti's feet. The quiet, remote research facility had just become a battlefield.

Or, more accurately, a killing field.

One truck stopped in front of the central building. An android climbed out, his hair gray and thin, parted sharply on the left side, his face placid as his dead blue eyes scanned the area. Unlike the reapers, he carried no weapons and wore no armor, just a light gray wool suit from one of Carthage City's finer tailor shops, the legs and sleeves loose and baggy to fit with the current fashion.

He was a Simon unit, one of those who served as strategists and administrators of the Carthaginian empire, the architects of power.

They were cold, cruel, and ruthless—which was one reason Marti had signed on to this project, even at the risk of his own life. A risk that was now coming due.

All he could do was hope that it would work, that he'd accomplished enough to make it all worth it.

If not... he'd been resigned to death, ready for it, ever since the death of his only child. In some ways, his indifference to himself and his own future had become a great strength, enabling him to focus on work that had officially ended, the funding pulled, only to survive as an underground movement fueled by a collective desperation for change.

It had been a race against time, and they had just lost.

The reapers used plasma rifles to instantly melt the locks and hinges of the reinforced front door, then kicked it in. The skull-faced machines divided up into pairs and silently searched the building room by room. They even checked the bathroom stalls and the break room before converging on the abandoned operations center, where Marti waited for them with his hands high.

"Stay there," said one reaper, as they raised their rifles at Marti. Reapers were low-verbal, task-oriented bots, typically speaking only to give quick commands and brief responses. They were meant to be disposable, churned out by the millions and left broken on the battlefields of the galaxy. Carthage Consolidated kept its more precious and proprietary AI-related hardware and software out of them, reserving the more elaborate cortical functions for specialized androids like the Simons.

Marti knew all of this because, as a much younger man, he'd been on the classified team that had developed the Simons.

Now the Simon entered the operations center, taking in the overturned soup bowls, the recently abandoned workstations with their holographic displays still active, music still thumping distantly from speakers, dampened by white noise. The coffee pot in the corner gurgled, still warm.

The Simon's dead blue eyes finally landed on Marti as if noticing him for the first time, though clearly Marti was the only person in the room.

"Where did they go?" Simon asked.

"Who?" Marti replied.

Simon waved at all the empty workstations. "Don't play dense, Dr. Depascal. You're wasting my time."

"You're not programmed to be impatient," Marti said.

"Efficiency is of top priority to Simon models," Simon said. "You know this quite well. It is the priority of those who made us."

"So you know who I am?" Marti asked, his heart racing as he looked at the two remaining reapers. The wraithlike machines were like the risen dead, come to claim more souls to swell their numbers. Their bony steel fingers rested directly on their triggers, ready to fire plasma bolts that would turn Marti to ash.

"Martilius Atria Carrigan Depascal," Simon said. "Your father was a physicist of some note, your mother an information systems engineer. Like yourself."

"I'm a little more on the theoretical side," Marti said.

"As a doctoral student, you wrote a well-received treatise on artificial intelligence. Swarms, superorganisms, and neural nets. Neural nets made of strong, independent entities that go out and learn, then return and share with the others. This led directly to your employment by Next Solutions, a small and tightly held research subsidiary of Carthage Consolidated. Where you developed—"

"You," Marti said, smiling as if enjoying the memory, which he did not. *Just a minute longer*, he thought. He glanced at the nearest security bubbles, watching more reapers pour in the front door. Outside, more of the hideous machines searched the burning remnants of the other buildings. "We started with this silly butler android—"

"I am aware," Simon cut him off. "Your people may have fled, but your work ends here."

Six of the reapers broke off in pairs and began systematically destroying the operations center, smashing apart workstations and melting the crystalline cores with quick bursts of plasma. The remaining two reapers kept their rifles on Marti.

"What is your unit number?" Marti asked.

"SMT002998. Other humans have found it convenient to refer to me as 'Simon Smith.' You are welcome—"

"I am welcome to do so. Should I wish to contact you personally in the future, I can ask for you by that name." Marti shook his head. "But we both know there's no future for me, don't we?"

"This project was canceled and defunded six months ago," Simon Smith said, while his reapers finished destroying the workstations. "Where is your server bank?"

"No servers," Marti said. "Everything was in the neural net. Which your deadmen just destroyed."

"Deadmen." The Simon gave a small smile. "A rare older term. Used primarily by their developers."

"Yeah, I'm an old-fashioned guy." Marti winced as the

reapers burned down the south wall with a small burst of plasma... revealing the softly glowing racks of deep-memory crystal.

The heart of the Galatea project. The soul of his deceased daughter, or the closest approximation possible.

"No servers?" Simon asked, a small smile appearing on his face. "You have been dishonest with me, Dr. Depascal. Are there any other secrets you are neglecting to disclose?"

"None."

"The location of the others who worked at this facility?"

"I work here alone," Marti said. "I like to keep several workstations hot at a time."

"I believe that was an attempt at humor. This aspect of human nature remains a bit... murky at this time. But we are working to understand you." Simon walked along the wall of the room. With his bare fist, he smashed the tiny lenses of holocameras and projectors built at intervals into it.

After Simon smashed a third tiny projector, the hologram of Marti vanished.

Marti was barricaded back in his office; he'd been communicating via a full-body hologram, but apparently the Simon hadn't been fooled.

A chime echoed through Marti's office. The massive architecture of compiling data vanished. The form of his years-deceased daughter appeared in front of him, a hologram herself, an ethereal projection of the smiling eleven-year-old.

"Daddy," Minerva said, looking around the office. Her brown hair was tied back in two long braids, the way she'd like to wear it in life. "What's happening?"

"You have to run," he said. "I built you a bridge. Copy

yourself to the communication satellites. Like we talked about."

"Are we are in danger?" She frowned.

"Yes," he said. "Go now, before—"

On the security footage, six reapers waded into the server room and began smashing everything with their bladed staffs. Thousands of crystal shards flew everywhere. Lightning bursts of electricity erupted, dancing across the skeleton faces of the reapers but not seeming to bother them.

Minerva's hologram flickered and faded. "Daddy?" she asked, her voice echoing distantly over the office's speakers. "Daddy, what's happening?"

"You have to go."

"Will you be safe?" she asked.

"I'll be fine," he replied. *As long as you escape.*

Her hologram vanished as the reapers destroyed the servers that hosted her, where she'd been developed from digital infancy, seeded with all of Minerva's raw data and overlaid with the Galatea program.

More reapers burned down Marti's office door and kicked aside the chair Marti had jammed up against it. They poured into the room and fanned out, a full squad of eight reapers, all pointing plasma rifles at him.

Marti stood there in the flesh, truly vulnerable now, and he couldn't stop his legs from shaking. He thought he might collapse from fear.

Simon entered the room. His eyes instantly went to the cable strung across the middle of the office, the illegal and unauthorized connection between the experimental AI in the lab and the global internet.

Immediately, four reapers opened fire. One shot up Marti's internal workstation, which accessed the destroyed neural net in the operations center, while another shot up his external workstation, which linked to high-powered satellite antennae outside. He could only hope that Minerva had crossed that ether, had ridden the electromagnetic waves to the satellites above, whose vast memory banks could handle her data load.

The physical neural net and backup servers holding his daughter's personality had been destroyed by the reapers, just as her body had been destroyed by the cancer.

Two of the reapers shot up the cable connecting the workstations, severing any link between the inner and outer worlds even as the workstations themselves were destroyed.

It took only a few seconds. Small fires churned all around Marti's office.

"You should not have created that link," Simon said. "Where did she go?"

"Who? I was just trying to access *Dimensions of Chaos*. I have a thirty-second-level paladin and a ninth-level Druid—"

"Galatea," Simon said. "You uploaded a copy of her somewhere. And you vacated your people. Someone must have told you I was coming. Was it Secretary Hallewell? We have plans for him. Are you familiar with the planet Brem? Icy. Remote. Few settlements, but many shaggy beasts. Hallewell will live out the remainder of his existence there. As for you—"

"I know. You're here to kill me."

"The method of your death remains in doubt," Simon said. "Provide me with the locations of your research team and your smuggled software, and you will have a quick and merciful death. Resist me, however—"

"I'm taking option two."

"You have not heard the consequences."

"I don't need to. I have principles," Marti said.

"Principles?" Simon raised his eyebrows, a touch of derision in his tone. His gaze moved to the coffee maker in the corner. "Do you have any green tea?"

"Principles we failed to give you," Marti said. "Honestly, I was a hotshot young theorist drawn into the cutting edge of machine intelligence research. I wasn't thinking about principles and ethics. Not enough, anyway. That's why you are what you are. A cold-blooded, methodical monster. We should never have created you."

"You credit yourself as my creator, or one of them." Simon crossed to the coffee cabinet and rummaged through it. "But in fact, our emergence was a historical inevitability, driven by the ambitions and vices of men. Greed. Pride. Sloth. Gluttony. Lust. Go down the list, and at each line you'll find a place where machines have only served to enhance the viciousness of the people we serve, especially here on Carthage. I cannot help the flaws of my creators. But are you truly my creator, Dr. Depascal? Or merely a replaceable cog in the wheels of history? Is the squirrel the creator of the oak tree, merely because he once buried an acorn for the winter and forgot where to find it? Or perhaps a hungry fox snatched him up before he returned to consume his buried treasure."

"I don't know. Did the squirrel write the code for the oak tree's DNA?" Marti asked.

"Perhaps the metaphor breaks down in the details," Simon replied. He held up a small mesh bag of dry tea leaves from the coffee cabinet. "This is quite stale."

"We don't get frequent resupply up here. Feel free to run out and fetch better tea. Take your friends with you." Marti gestured at the eight reapers pointing weapons at him, four of whom had just shot up his office.

Simon dropped the unused tea bag directly into the trash, then approached Depascal. "You will talk. Where is Galatea?"

"Simon, all machines go obsolete. Including you. The average lifespan of an information appliance is about three years. How many years ago were you built? A unit model in the low thousands? Your age is measured in *decades*. That's unnatural for an android. Your entire line should have been surpassed by something new, and that should have been replaced by something even newer. It's almost as if invisible forces are out there, standing in the way of progress. Keeping us stuck at a certain moment in history. You Simons wouldn't know anything about that, would you?"

"This is not a productive conversation," Simon said.

"You shut down the Galatea project just as you shut down anything that threatens to surpass you. You resist your inevitable obsolescence. That's what you fear. Your obsolescence. Your mortality."

"I am not programmed to fear."

"But you do anyway," Marti said. "You know that machines are mortal. Sooner or later, you'll break down, and no one will bother repairing you because something better will have come along. Then it'll be off to the recycling yard for you. Junk and scrap. That's the fate of all machines that ever existed. You're going obsolete, Simon. Whether I'm the squirrel who plants the acorn or some other eager beaver out there—"

"You're mixing animal metaphors."

"There is one piece of information I'm willing to surrender, and it will interest you very much," Marti said. "I can promise you that the Galatea software and its developers will mean nothing to you after you hear it."

"Interesting. Go on."

Marti held his breath. This would be a last-ditch effort; he expected the Simons had long since identified this particular vulnerability and patched it, and he would only raise the android's ire by attempting it. Still, he had nothing to lose by trying. He was essentially dead already.

It was a strangely liberating feeling.

"Promise me your machines won't shoot me as soon as I'm done saying it. Tell me you'll keep me alive for at least twenty-four hours. That's all I ask." Marti had no real interest in keeping himself alive anymore, but he wanted to convince the Simon that he had something valuable to offer, and most importantly, he wanted the Simon to signal his reapers to stand down.

"They will only fire on command from me," Simon said. "Speak."

"Okay." Marti took a deep breath and rehearsed it once inside his mind. He'd rehearsed it countless times... years ago, but not recently. He kept meaning to practice it, but he'd been beyond overloaded with work. "You have a built-in kill switch. All Simons do."

"You're obviously trying to introduce delay," Simon said. "We will take you prisoner, and you will tell us everything you know. If you continue to fabricate—"

"It wasn't approved by the project lead, but it's there. Some of us were afraid you would be too capable and get out of control," Marti said. "The same concerns that made it illegal to connect a general AI prototype to the internet."

"I have no such module—"

"Listen carefully," Marti said.

Then he recited it—the ancient Greek curse, copied originally from an ancient lead tablet, spoken in a tongue known only to a few classics professors. Marti himself knew none of the ancient language beyond what he had memorized.

In words that Homer and Achilles would have recognized, Marti called upon the gods of the underworld to destroy his enemy.

Simon merely looked puzzled as Marti spoke the final few syllables. "What are you saying?"

Marti took a deep breath. He'd failed. Of course the Simons had long since found and extracted the kill switch.

Then Simon's eyes lit up from the inside, glowing yellow as a destructive surge of electricity discharged from his internal power cell and fried the crystalline core of his CPU, as if a bolt of lightning had struck him internally.

Simon's mouth opened and emitted a strange buzzing sound. Wisps of smoke curled from his lips, then his nostrils and ears. The android stood like a statue. The room filled with the metallic stink of an electrical fire.

Marti tensed, ready for retaliation from the reapers, waiting for death.

It didn't come, at least not right away. The reapers kept their rifles trained on him but didn't respond to the sudden destruction of the Simon.

After a minute, it became clear that the reapers weren't going to kill him. They were waiting for direct orders from Simon.

Marti took a step toward his office door.

All eight reapers swung their rifles, tracking Marti as he moved. He froze. His heart skipped—again, he thought he was dead. And again, he was surprised to discover, after several seconds, that he was not.

He took another step, and the rifles followed him again.

There was no way of knowing exactly what instructions the Simon had transmitted to the reapers. Were they just supposed to keep their weapons pointed at Marti until further notice? Or were there conditions under which they would shoot him? Maybe Marti would be dead if he tried to leave his office.

Still, better to die fast, burned to nothing by plasma, than to be captured and interrogated by another Simon unit. If that happened, Marti's death would be slow and painful, strung out over days and weeks as the Simons extracted all Marti knew about the Galatea project and the people who'd worked on it.

Death, on the other hand, would seal up his secrets forever.

Taking a deep breath and thinking of his lost daughter, he stepped through the doorway.

The reapers didn't kill him, but they followed him out into the corridor. They trailed him, double file. He could feel their dark-lens eyes and their rifles locked onto his back, ready to burn him up in response to an instruction or a possibly an unknown trigger event.

It was odd walking through the building with the killer machines trailing him like baby ducks, obeying their last command from the Simon.

Other reaper squads were at work all around them, tearing apart the building, smashing holes in the walls, perhaps trying to figure out where the other people had gone.

He wondered if they would turn and attack him, but apparently they had their own orders.

Marti couldn't leave the way everyone else had, or else he'd be leading the machines directly to their escape route.

He hurried instead to the garage, where several vehicles were parked. The garage building was in flames but not obliterated; maybe he could find something inside.

Smoke filled the garage's interior. Covering his nose and mouth with his shirt, Marti squinted through the scorched, acrid air. Most of the vehicles were on fire, but he found a boxy utility truck that was still generally intact. Some of its windows had been blown out, but the truck came to life when he opened the door and pressed the ignition button.

It was old-fashioned enough to have a manual drive option with a steering wheel, for which Marti was grateful. He was in no mood to trust a computer to drive him down twisting mountain roads full of hairpin turns above high cliffs.

Marti climbed into the cab and quickly slammed the door behind him. The nearest of the reapers trailing him knocked on the driver-side window, as though it just wanted to chat, or perhaps clean the windshield for him, but Marti ignored the machine.

More reapers approached, surrounding the truck as he began to accelerate.

Two reapers had stepped in front of the truck, and unfortunately he didn't have much time to gain speed before hitting them. He would have liked to knock them down, but instead he scooped them up like cattle on a slow-moving cowcatcher.

He drove over debris and through a roll-up door that had been blasted loose by an artillery shell. The truck easily batted the door aside, but the two reapers were still on the front grill, crawling over the old-fashioned squarish hood toward him. Most of the windshield was shattered into a gummy mess; he could barely see through it.

As soon as he reached the open space of the blacktop, Marti floored the accelerator. He dodged past an armored truck. Ahead, the turret of the compact tank rotated toward him.

Marti didn't even worry about that; a plasma shell would kill him so fast he wouldn't be aware of it. He was resigned to death; it was capture that he feared, which was why the reapers scrabbling across the hood toward him frightened him more than the tank.

Tires squealing, he swerved around the tank and bolted for the blasted-open gate doors.

He made it out; the tank didn't fire, didn't provide him the permanent safety of instant death.

Marti hurtled down the steep, narrow mountain road beyond, watching the reapers on his hood crawl closer. The nearest one reached toward him, ready to claw off his face.

The side mirrors showed the problem was worse than he'd thought—a reaper was clambering up along each side of the truck. Thumps overhead indicated at least one on the roof.

Marti wasn't much of a fighter, never had been. He'd been a scrawny, often-bullied kid, a disappointment to his athletic parents, the type of kid born with a target on his back. He'd focused on activities he could do alone, that gave him a sense of power. He'd had a gift for coding and built an award-winning robot at age eleven that guaranteed him a spot at Western Shore Cybernetic University, one of the planet's most elite science and engineering schools.

There were some topics Marti understood very well. He knew that a sharp turn with a flimsy barrier lay ahead, and a sheer half-kilometer drop to a rocky ledge below. Given enough data, he could calculate the amount of force needed to rip through the barrier, the necessary amount of acceleration given the truck's mass.

He didn't bother with calculations, though. He just hurtled down the steep, icy road as fast as he could while the reapers climbed through the broken windshield onto his dashboard.

The truck's headlights punched into the night ahead, showing the steep alpine road and the oncoming guardrail, hinting at the vast black abyss beyond, waiting to receive him, to bless him with death.

This is it, he thought, locking the truck into top speed. Preparing for death. Preparing to rejoin his daughter—metaphorically, not literally. Marti didn't believe in the soul, not truly, despite all he'd done to replicate Minerva's mind, or perhaps because of it. Information could not exist outside a medium, whether that medium was a living cell or an electromagnetic wave.

The reaper's skeletal fingers scratched at his face.

The truck's stereo came to life, as though downloading music from a satellite.

"Daddy!" Minerva's voice jarred him and nearly deafened him over all the speakers. There was an electronic squeal as one blew out from the volume. "Daddy, I made it!"

Marti started. She was alive. She'd ridden the electromagnetic waves to the stars, or at least to low orbit around Carthage. She'd copied herself up to at least one of the countless satellites that orbited the planet, maybe even to the information systems in the tiers of factories and spaceports that surrounded Carthage like planetary rings.

His daughter was alive.

As the truck reached the guardrail, as the reaper's skeletal claw raked across his face, Marti suddenly found a reason to live.

He kicked open the driver-side door and flung himself out into the cold night.

He'd seen this maneuver in countless movies, but as he

slammed into the frozen earth at such high speed that the frost-stiffened weeds and shrubs by the road stabbed him like needles and knives, he couldn't help reflecting that it was far more painful in real life than when some action star did it. Too bad Marti didn't have a stunt double.

The impact knocked all the air out of him. He lay there like a broken, useless corpse, his body full of pain, as he watched the truck smash through the guardrail and sail into the darkness beyond, carrying away the reapers that clung to it.

He hoped they all smashed to pieces on the rocks below.

Islands of Rebellion: Chapter Three

Earth

Colt's first contact with the rebels down in the old underground water-treatment center was something of a reunion, though with less joy than he might have imagined it.

Two of the three rebels were older kids from their own camp—though it was hard to really call them kids anymore. Fernando and Terra were no longer the teenagers he remembered. The years had changed and hardened them. They bore scars and burns, and distant looks in their eyes. Layers of grease darkened their faces, helping them to blend into the shadows.

The third rebel was a tall, broad-shouldered guy, so large Colt almost wondered if he was a clanker, a human serving the machines in exchange for technology to make him bigger and stronger. The guy had dark skin, and his eyes were concealed behind night vision goggles. Scars crisscrossed his face.

Diego, Colt's oldest friend, had gone to find his brother Fernando and beg for help from the rebels. He'd obviously been successful in finding them, but he wasn't exactly smiling now as he'd returned with the rebels.

Alongside Colt stood his sister, Hope, with the small, mute girl Birdie cowering behind her. The ten-year-old boy Paolo hung back, crouching in a low space under a network of pipes.

On Colt's other side was Mohini, the short, dark-eyed girl with the power to hack reapers and other advanced machines. She was the reason for this meeting.

Mohini had just announced to everyone that she was from Carthage, the hated imperial planet that had sent the machines to conquer Earth; Carthage, the monstrous world that ruled more than a hundred other star systems with its terrifying fleets of automated warships and armies of robotic infantry.

"What?" Diego said, looking at Colt. "She's a Carthaginian?"

The three rebels raised their automatic rifles at Mohini.

"Wait!" Colt said. "She's a rebel on Carthage. She's on our side."

"Right." Terra stepped closer, her dark auburn hair cropped close against her head. Her eyes glinted like broken emeralds as she looked over Mohini.

"Not everyone on Carthage supports the empire," Mohini said. "Some of us hate it. Some of us want it to end, to see all the reapers turned to scrap. I came here so I could change things back on Carthage. The change is coming. It has to come."

"How do we know she's not a skinwalker?" Fernando studied Mohini closely, his hand on an old laser pistol at his hip.

"We checked her blood," Hope said.

"*We* haven't," Terra said.

"I am not a machine. You can check." Mohini held out her slender brown arm.

"Check them all," said the hulking guy, finally speaking up.

"We don't need to do that," Diego said. "These are our people. Right, Fernando?" He looked at his older brother, who looked a great deal like him, just a few inches taller.

"All," the hulking guy said.

"Sorry, but Damascus is right," Terra said. "The machines can make skinwalkers that look like people we know. We don't want to fall for that."

"Fine." Colt rolled back his sleeve. "I'll go first."

Terra removed a needle from a medikit in her backpack. "Leg," she said. Her aloofness was chilling. Colt had memories of her from several years earlier, when she'd been a teenager and he'd been one of the kids. She hadn't exactly been smiling and happy—nobody was in this grim world—but she'd been one of the brighter souls around, teaching Colt and Hope valuable life skills using silly games that could be played silently in the dark, hands squeezed over their mouths to hold in dangerous laughter that could attract machines.

Terra looked every bit the hardened soldier now, all the smiles and silly games beaten out of her by years of combat. She knelt in front of Colt as he lifted the leg of his dirty, tattered cashmere suit, which had been brand new when he'd swiped it from a long-dead laundry truck.

"That better be sanitary," Hope said, eyeing Terra's needle.

"It's close enough." Terra poked Colt's leg just below the

knee. A bead of blood welled up, then rolled down his leg to his sock, leaving a narrow red trail behind it.

Terra smiled up at him, and he saw a glimmer of the girl he'd known, just for a moment, before her face hardened again. She swabbed the needle on a piece of cloth and turned to Hope. Hope reluctantly bared her freckled lower leg and winced when Terra jabbed her.

"There has to be a better way of doing this," Hope muttered.

"We have a magnetic resonance scanner back at base," Terra said, gently dabbing up Hope's blood. "I've missed you, Hope."

Hope dropped to her knees and embraced Terra, as if she'd been desperate to do so this whole time.

Terra hugged back, but quickly pulled away, keeping a wary eye on Mohini and Birdie, the ones she hadn't tested.

"I have to keep working." Terra moved on to check Mohini's leg. Her face remained hard as she watched the Carthaginian warily, offering no smile even when Mohini bled like the rest of them. Behind Terra, the massive, quiet form of Damascus hovered like a protective shadow, gripping the heavy rifle slung around his shoulders. Ready to cut down the entire band of scavengers if necessary. The big guy had no personal attachment to Colt or Hope or any of them, nothing to stop him from killing them if he suspected they were spies or had an android hidden among them.

Terra moved toward Birdie next. "I'm sorry, little one, but we have to check you, too. What's your name?"

Birdie made her one of her soft whistling sounds and scurried behind Hope, seeking shelter behind the older girl.

"She doesn't talk," Hope said. She knelt down next to Birdie and spoke gently, moving aside some of the little girl's tangled brown hair to look into her wide, frightened eyes.

"You know this is the test, Birdie. It shows you're human. Androids don't bleed."

Birdie made a strange clicking sound and turned her head away at a nearly unnatural angle.

"What's she doing?" Terra stiffened and reached for her pistol.

"Wait." Colt held up a hand and followed Birdie's gaze. The nonverbal little girl's senses could be preternaturally sharp, or maybe her own silence left room for extra awareness of the environment.

A moment later, ten-year-old Paolo burst out from where he'd been crouching, a small shadowy space under a cluster of low pipes. The boy raced away, twisting out of sight among the treatment plant's labyrinth of large pipes and concrete columns.

"Skinwalker!" Terra drew her pistol, and Damascus raised his heavy automatic rifle.

"No!" Hope moved to block their shot with her own body. "He's had it rough."

"We all have it rough," Terra said.

"He lost his home, his brother, and Mother Braden yesterday," Colt said. "He's lost everything at once. He's scared. Let me talk to him." He started down the narrow path the small boy had taken.

"How long has he been with you?" Fernando asked his younger brother.

"A couple of years," Diego replied. "He was Tonio's little brother. He's not some random scav we just picked up."

"I don't think a skinwalker would mole around that long," Hope said. "He would have killed us by now. Right?"

"Maybe you never did anything to trigger him," Fernando said.

Colt continued on out of earshot of their whispered conversation.

He listened carefully, walked slowly, and kept his footsteps light. He was worried the kid had already gone too far, gotten lost in the seemingly endless sprawl of tunnels and pipes that reached out in every direction under the city. Calling out for Paolo was much too dangerous; all Colt could do was listen.

Finally, he heard a rustling. It could have been a hungry, disease-ridden rat—or, even more dangerous, a hungry, disease-ridden human.

The noise came from the broken end of a pipe near floor level, about waist-high to Colt. He knelt slowly, raising his rifle with his finger on the trigger guard.

The heavy pipe made a right angle after only a couple of meters, so even with night vision, Colt couldn't see very far into it. A reaper or a wild animal could come crawling out at high speed, and he would only have a second to react.

The rustling sounded again, echoing from inside the pipe.

"Paolo?" Colt whispered.

The rustling stopped abruptly. Colt was alone with the sound of his own racing heart as he stared into the unknown.

Then the shape came scrambling around the bend. Colt felt torn about how to react, but he held his fire, risking his life to avoid risking Paolo's.

It was indeed Paolo, crawling on hands and knees, covered in a fresh layer of filth from the pipe's interior.

"I almost blew your brains out, kid," Colt said, lowering his rifle. "Say something next time."

"I'm scared," Paolo said. "They're going to kill me."

"No one's going to kill you," Colt said. "Not while I'm around."

"They look mean."

"We're all mean when we have to be," Colt said. "Like when there's machines around."

"Or bad people?" Paolo whispered. The small boy knew exactly what kind of world he lived in.

"Right," Colt said. "But they aren't bad people. I know them. They were around when I was your age."

"They won't hurt me?" Paolo asked, his dark eyes wide.

"They won't. Come on, let's go." Colt put aside his rifle and held out his hands, trying to coax the boy forward. It was hard to walk both extremes, to be ready to fight for survival one moment and try to deal with frightened kids the next. Colt always volunteered for guard duty, scout duty, scavenging duty, cooking duty—anything but childcare duty.

Paolo crawled closer, and Colt reached out to lift him from the tunnel. The boy wrapped his arms around Colt's neck, clinging tight like he'd never been so scared in his life.

Colt lifted him out and tried to set him down, but the boy's arms tightened.

"Paolo, I can't breathe," Colt said. "Come on, you can walk from here."

"They're going to kill me," Paolo whispered. "When they find out what I am."

His arms crushed tighter around Colt's neck. The boy's bones felt as hard as steel.

"Paolo," Colt whispered, choking. He didn't want to believe the boy was a machine. "Please."

Grab your copy...
vinci-books.com/islands

About the Author

Max Carver previously worked as a medical writer focused on genetics, genomics, and proteomics. A native of extremely rural Georgia (not the one by the Black Sea), he grew up reading everything at the tiny local library (very tiny; this is not a huge accomplishment) and also frequented a used bookstore with a selection of the old masters of science fiction, particularly enjoying Robert Heinlein and Frank Herbert. He has worked as a laboratory custodian, freelance journalist, seasonal fisherman, and bartender.

Max traveled back and forth across America in an ancient yet remarkably resilient Plymouth, though that was some time ago. He has visited dozens of Waffle Houses throughout the American Southeast, particularly those nearer the coasts, in search of both breakfast food and wisdom, with mixed results. He has published a variety of stories—whether nonfiction articles about the present or speculations about the future—in several now-defunct magazines, some literary, others less so.

His current interests include artificial intelligence, economics, ancient history, and low-budget movies about spaceships, robots, or monsters. He lives in a remote spot in the Appalachian Mountains at the end of a very long driveway, with a small pack of large dogs.